BEHIND
THE
GREY

UPCOMING TITLES BY BOBBYE L. HUDSPETH

Hot Bubbles and Chocolate
Under the Gun
The Girl in the Mirror
Beneath the Southern Sun

Women of the Civil War: Book One

BEHIND
THE
GREY

By Bobbye L. Hudspeth

SEAHORSE PRESS

Cover photograph © 2013 Bobbye L. Hudspeth

This is a work of fiction. Names, characters, places, and incidents are the product
of the author's imagination or are used fictitiously. Any resemblance to actual
events, locales, or persons living or dead is entirely coincidental.

Cover design by Arliss Paddock

Behind the Grey: A Novel of the Civil War

First print edition

ISBN-13: 978-0-6157-4312-7 (paperback)
ISBN-10: 0-6157-4312-9
ISBN: 978-1-3010-3014-9 (e-book)
BISAC: Fiction / Historical

Library of Congress catalog number: 2013902096

Seahorse Press | Published by arrangement with the author
P.O. Box 312, Lakeville CT 06039 USA
www.seahorsepress.us

To Pete, who always said I could do it

and to Clark, who made me believe it too

Prologue

The young soldier stared blankly, his eyes fixed straight ahead, gazing at something the mortals around him could not see. Someone, stumbling across him in the thick smoke that still hugged the ground trapped by the early morning fog, cursed as their boots tangled in the tattered shirt that still clung to his body in long, bloody strips. But the young soldier paid no mind to either the kick or the curses. Sticks and stones, mortar blasts, and cannonballs could break his bones, but it would only matter to those he left behind. Never again to him.

From behind a tree another young soldier looked out over the broken bodies lying on the blood-soaked soil. A lone tear coursed down a dirty, bloodstained cheek before being brushed hastily away. "Godspeed," a small voice whispered, drowned out by the shouts of the men and the muffled rifle shots of the retreating troops. "May Godspeed you all."

"Hey, you up there? You a soldier, or a damned woman?" a harsh voice yelled. "Quitcher sniveling, and get down here and grab up them guns." The sergeant pointed toward the field that just hours before had been a small cotton field but now was a flat, desolate wasteland, loosely upholstered with scraps of blue and grey material and interwoven with streaks of rusty red.

The young soldier saluted smartly. "Right away, sir. Wasn't crying. Just got a bit of dust in my eye," he explained to the retreating back. "Wish this damned smoke would hurry up and clear out," he mumbled to himself as he scurried to work. He concentrated on putting a veil over his mind to block out the thought of what he was doing as he searched the pockets of the dead men for treasures and pried stiff fingers from still-warm guns. Anyone else would have received a sterner scolding than that for his indiscretion, but the whole company had taken young Alex under their wing. To many he reminded them of young sons they had left back home; to others his innocence was simply a reminder of who and what they themselves had once been.

Later that night the young soldier stretched out by a small campfire on the side of a hill overlooking the camp. The stillness was broken only by an occasional belch, or a groan from one of the injured men lying beside the hundreds of small fires that made the field look as if it were swarming with fireflies in the evening dusk.

Looking over with a hidden smile at the person snoring beside him, a man who had been the best friend a soldier could have had through the hell of the last few months, the young soldier sighed, and on a wrinkled but precious piece of paper, with the stub of a pencil he had pulled from a dead Yankee's pocket, he began to write.

Dear Ones,

I hope all is well with you and that the reports I've received of enemy fire in your area have been exaggerated. Please know my thoughts and prayers are with you always.

I am fine but still cannot share my whereabouts with you. Don't think I am trying to hide from you or from any part of my old life. It is just that to put my location down on paper could bring death to a lot of men whom I have come to respect.

I am surprised, as you most likely are as well, that I can respect or call a man my friend after what has happened to me at the hands of men of my past. But among other things, I am learning that all men cannot be judged by the actions of a few. I am also learning how to sleep while I'm in the saddle, how to cook over an open campfire, and how to dress myself unaided — oftentimes in the dark.

I wonder how many hundreds, nay thousands of the bawdy jokes and gestures of the men around me would have gone undone and unsaid had they guessed that beneath this grey uniform beats a woman's heart. Indeed, I hope they never guess my secret, for their embarrassment would know no bounds.

If I am one of the lucky ones who makes it back to hearth and home when this war is over, oh, what stories I shall have to tell you all around the fire after supper! And what stories of which I will never be able to speak, for the true horrors of war go far beyond what you or I would have guessed from our safe haven.

I still search for information that will lead me to the one blue-coated bastard (I'm learning to curse quite effectively as well) who must not escape this war unscathed. When I find him and kill him, only then will it be possible for me to consider returning to whatever is left of my old life.

Until then I remain yours most truly,

Private A. McKinley, CSA

Table of Contents

Prologue i

Chapter One 7

Chapter Two 22

Chapter Three 31

Chapter Four 43

Chapter Five 48

Chapter Six 66

Chapter Seven 80

Chapter Eight 90

Chapter Nine 106

Chapter Ten 123

Chapter Eleven 146

Chapter Twelve 159

Chapter Thirteen 172

Chapter Fourteen 179

Chapter Fifteen 189

Chapter Sixteen 204

Chapter Seventeen 210

Chapter Eighteen 227

Chapter Nineteen 247

Chapter Twenty 275

Chapter Twenty-One 286

Chapter Twenty-Two 298

Chapter Twenty-Three 307

Author's Note cccxvii

Acknowledgements cccxviii

About the Author cccxx

Chapter One

Alexandria stared ahead, forcing herself to listen to the words of the raggedly dressed minister as he raised his voice to compete with the sound of dirt clods echoing hollowly off a shabby, hastily built wooden coffin. She stood at the open edge of the red clay grave, her hands knotted into fists as she willed herself to ignore the stinging tears that burned behind her eyes. Her sinuses groaned with the pressure of the unshed tears, and her throat felt raw from stifled sobs. She heard a rustle beside her and knew that Aunt Matilda was reaching for her hand.

Knowing that any display of gentleness would bring forth the torrent of tears she was barely able to hold back, Alexandria moved away slightly, wincing at Aunt Matilda's barely audible sob.

Poor Aunt Matilda. And poor, poor Teddy. She closed her eyes and tried hard to remember him as she knew he would want to be remembered. Not as the shell that she had helped lay out in the rough-hewn pine box earlier that morning, but as the handsome, virile young man who was forever flirting with her friends and teasing her about her beaus.

A sad smile twitched at her lips as she remembered last spring's all-day barbecue at the Thompson place. Teddy could never tell the twins apart, so he had talked her into winding a red rose into Lisa Thompson's golden tresses as the girls had helped each other get ready for what had turned out to be the last big social before the threat of war had become a horrible actuality. He had impressed Lisa by being the only one of the young beaus who knew which twin was which. Alexandria had never let Lisa know Teddy's secret, nor her own part in the ruse, but she had used the fact as leverage against Teddy to get her way on more than one occasion since.

Today Alexandria carried a single red rose. Both to remind herself that life had been beautiful before, and as proof of her hope that it might be again.

The parson's droning voice broke through her reverie. "We must never forget that poor Theodore died, in his own way, fighting this oppression that faces us today."

Alexandria could feel the sweat running in rivulets beneath her black dress. In the South, wearing black during the warm months was reserved for the most solemn of events since the dark cloth gathered in the sun's relentless rays and multiplied them tenfold. The hot, humid air hung upon her like a winter shawl that she couldn't take off. A surreptitious glance at the moist faces of the sparse crowd of mourners showed Alexandria that she wasn't the only one sweltering in the summer heat. They had set the hour for the funeral early in the day, before the early summer sun hit its zenith, but they would have had to schedule it before daylight to escape the incessant, muggy heat.

She tried to concentrate on the parson's words instead of his elocution, just in time to hear, "You especially, Miss Alexandria, must never forget how poor Theodore died. As Jesus Christ our Lord died on the cross to save our souls, so did poor Theodore give up his life for yours." He shook his head sadly. "What a wonderful gift, Miss Alexandria. And one that now you can never repay."

Hearing the sympathetic but agreeing murmur that ran through the crowd, Alexandria nodded solemnly, although rage burned through her. Sanctimonious old fool! As if there were any chance that she would ever forget. As if she would not be haunted every day for the rest of her life by the vision of Teddy futilely hurtling himself against the blue-coated man whose body had claimed hers in the darkness. As if she would ever stop praying that it had been she who lay dead at the cursed Yankee's hands instead of dear Teddy.

Her mind escaped the heat and the preacher's voice, and for the moment she was swept back to the evening before, when her life was still normal, or at least as normal as it can be when the world around you is at war.

~ ~ ~

One of the housemaids had wept as she told Alexandria about a friend who was having difficulty birthing her first child. Since Alexandria was well known for her ability to use herbs to heal and soothe, and since Dr. McCory often took his time coming to calls from people of the lower classes, as well as to the Negro quarters, Dessie had asked for Alexandria's help.

Knowing how her Aunt Matilda and her cousin Teddy hated for her go out "a-doctorin'," as they called it, after dark, Alexandria had slipped quietly out the pantry door.

She remembered thinking as she hurried down the pebbled lane through the cool darkness, listening to the serenade of the tree-frogs and crickets and breathing in the fragrances of the flower garden, that she was so lucky to live in such a beautiful world that had, so far, remained untouched by the horrors surrounding it.

All the beauty left abruptly as strange, rough hands grabbed her and pulled her into the dark shadows. "Well, well. What do we have here? A little Rebel princess outside her castle after dark?"

Alexandria struggled against the arms that held her like steel bands and bit the hand that covered her mouth. She heard a muffled curse.

"Damn Rebel bitch is more like it, eh? Let's see how long it takes to screw some of that spunk out of you. I guess I'll find out if all you little Southern gals are put together like the girls in Pennsylvania. I'll bet with all the men-folk from around here gone off to war, you little belles are lonesome for some company. I promise you there's never been a complaint about old Rafe Peterson's ability to please a woman before. I'll show you what it's like to have a real man between your legs."

As one hand left her breast and reached down for the hem of her skirts Alexandria struggled to get away, her hands knotted into fists, striking whatever part of his body she could reach. She tried to use her knee as Teddy had taught her, but the man was too strong and too agile. He kicked her feet out from underneath her, laughing as she hit the ground, the breath knocked from her body.

Suddenly she felt the tip of a sharp object she supposed to be a knife at her throat. "Spread 'em or die," the man growled, his voice ragged with lust. "Don't be playing coy with me now. We've all heard tales about you sweet Southern Jezebels. Don't be pretending you don't want it now."

She began to scream, knowing that the muffled sounds coming from behind his hand were not loud enough to be heard by anyone at the house, and knowing too that even if by some miracle anyone from the house could hear her, it would be too late to save her.

Suddenly she heard the sounds of someone hurtling through the bushes toward them and heard Teddy's panicked voice.

"Alex! Where are you?"

At the sound the man's grip momentarily loosened, allowing her screams to be heard. "Over here, Teddy!"

Too late she added, "Be careful! He has a knife."

Teddy had followed the sound of her scream, not knowing exactly what to expect. He was ill prepared for the battle-worn savage who was intent on taking what he wanted. Gentle-bred, parlor-trained Teddy hadn't stood a chance, and his look of shock was indelibly etched on Alexandria's heart as he looked first at the shadowy form still crouched in battle position in the darkness, then to Alexandria, then finally to the knife in his chest, its barely exposed hilt gleaming brightly in the moonlight.

As he crumpled to the ground he whispered almost inaudibly, "I'm sorry, Alex."

She must have fainted, she decided later. Thankfully the next events were blotted from her memory, although from the way her body screamed in agony when she finally awoke, and from the blood stains on her thighs and skirt, she reckoned that as she had lain there unconscious the Yankee had finished what he started. Her only hope was that Teddy had died quickly and had not been forced to helplessly witness her assault.

As soon as she could lift her head without nausea sweeping through her, she crawled over to Teddy's lifeless body and gently caressed his eyelids down over his staring, unseeing blue eyes.

A sob ripped through her and brought her mind back to the side of Teddy's grave. It didn't seem fair that she and death were such old friends already. Her parents had died in a carriage accident when she was just a baby, leaving her father's brother, James, and his wife Matilda to raise Alexandria along with their own sons Marcus and little Teddy, who was just a few months older than Alexandria.

Ten years later, Aunt Mattie's screams had awakened them all when she had found Uncle James dead in bed beside her, a victim of the heart attack the doctor had warned him about for years.

Marcus had been one of the first to ride in the Confederate cavalry, and after his second battle they had received a letter from his commanding officer telling them that Marcus had fallen in battle, and that they "should not expect his return to Twin Cedars."

Those deaths had been nothing like this, however. She could not remember her parents, so that loss was simply a story she had been told, and although she missed Uncle James's wry humor and unwavering love, she was grateful that he had not suffered and had been able to enjoy life to the end. And Marcus had faced death with a firm resolve that if it came, it would come in a blaze of glory, for it would take him as he fought for what he unerringly believed was a just cause.

Teddy, however, had met death without reason or desire, and she felt his loss stronger already than any of her intense physical pain.

~   ~   ~

Not wanting to face Aunt Matilda alone with the sad news, she had forced herself to walk down the long, well-worn path through the woods to her fiancé's door, where she fell into the arms of his houseman.

"Sammy, tell Del I need him. Please. Now. Hurry!" She had begun to shake as the white-haired Negro led her toward a burgundy velveteen-covered couch facing a roaring fire. She remembered holding her hands out toward the flames, hoping they would bring life back into her shock-chilled body.

They didn't.

"Great God A'mighty, Alexandria!" Del's voice had thundered through the room, shocking the silence. "Whatever are you doing here at this hour? What will the neighbors say?"

Alexandria could almost hear again his sigh of exasperation and his self-centered words. "You know how fast word spreads in these parts, even though God knows there's almost no one left to gossip."

She watched the scene as it replayed again and again in her mind, reliving the horror of the moments that it seemed were going to haunt her forever.

Del frowned as he took in her disheveled appearance. "You look a fright, too. Where have you been? What's all this on your dress?"

"Blood. Mine and Teddy's." Her voice sounded toneless to her own ears. She lifted her head to stare dully into his eyes. "He's dead, Del. Teddy's dead."

For a brief moment she thought she saw a hint of anger flash in Del's china-blue eyes. "Dead? You killed Teddy? What did he say about me?"

"Say—about you? Killed? What did who say . . . the Yankee?" Her mind was too numb to follow his words, and she found herself repeating them like a trained crow.

"Yankee? What Yankee?" Del's voice grew hard as he grabbed her by the arms and shook her. "Listen to me, Alexandria. Great God in heaven! What in blazes have you done?"

She flushed under his intent gaze, and she felt hysteria welling up inside her. Her voice was shrill as she pulled free from his grasp and turned, stumbling toward the door.

"What have I done, Del? I've watched Teddy die before my eyes, and I've been attacked by a Yankee who could have just as well killed me too!"

She tossed her hair back over her shoulder in a gesture of defiance she didn't feel. "I'll go now, Del. Lord knows I wouldn't want to cause you any embarrassment by possibly being seen here unchaperoned—with the exception of the houseful of servants, of course." Her voice grew bitter. "Especially when I'm hurt and covered in my dead cousin's blood," she added witheringly, her lips curling with contempt. "You're right of course to worry about convention before you worry about me. At least your priorities are intact, if not your sensibilities."

Her voice broke with a dry sob as she leaned against the doorframe, wondering where she would find the strength to make the long walk home alone.

Del rushed to her side, his voice and expression softening. "Don't be a silly, Alexandria. You just startled me, that's all. Of course I want to know what happened." He took her in his arms, pulling her head down against his chest. "Now tell me exactly what happened. From the beginning. Where is this Yankee? And who killed Teddy?"

"The Yankee's gone by now, I reckon, and Teddy's still layin' in the bushes at the end of the lane . . ." Her voice broke, and she shuddered at the memory. "With the Yankee's knife in his chest." Her body began to shake as the tears came.

Between sobs, she told Del a brief version of the story, from the time she received the message from Dessie until she showed up on his doorstep, leaving out the more personal details of her attack.

She leaned against his warmth, hoping to feel safe again. "I just couldn't go home and tell Aunt Mattie, and you always told me you'd be here for me no matter what." She closed her eyes for a moment.

Remembering suddenly his earlier words, however, she pulled away and looked up at his face, her brow furrowed. "Why did you ask what Teddy had said about you? And how could you possibly think I would kill him? He was about the only family I had left." She choked on a sob. "And I loved him."

"Sure you did, honey." Del's hand stroked her hair gently. "But you love me, too, don't you?" At her nod he went on. "Well, for some reason Teddy had started to doubt whether my intentions toward you were honorable." The sad tone of his voice didn't match his hard eyes, but she was looking down and didn't notice. "He told me he didn't trust me and that he was watching me. He told me to stay away from you and the rest of his family. The fact that we're engaged to be married didn't mean anything to him, apparently."

Her look was incredulous. "*Stay away?* You can't mean it! Why, we've all known each other since we were children." She paused for a minute, recalling all the practical jokes, some not quite harmless, that Del had played over the years on Teddy, whose good nature had prevented him from ever seeking revenge. Surely Teddy hadn't carried a grudge all these years?

"I'm quite serious, Alexandria. He told me he was going to find proof that I wasn't good enough for you, and then he was going to confront you with it. Perhaps he was hoping to find us together tonight." He shrugged as he pulled her close and hid a cold smile in her chestnut hair, "Whatever he was looking for, I don't think it was exactly what he found."

As she stood at the graveside Alexandria bitterly recalled the tenderness Del had shown as he had carried Teddy's body home to his mother, where he had held Aunt Matilda gently as she began crying as if she would never stop.

Later that night, Alexandria had walked him to the door and thanked him for comforting her.

"You don't have to thank me, Alexandria," he said with a warm smile, gently brushing her cheek with a fingertip. "I love you. What sort of man wouldn't want to take care of the woman he's going to marry?" He turned toward the door and said offhandedly, "You never did mention that blue-coat stole anything from you, or what he said during the attack. Did he give any indication what he was doing in this area, or who or what he was looking for?" Even in the midst of her stress, Alexandria noted the anxiety in his voice as he asked the last question, but she marked it down to his concern for her. "You said you were hurt, yet I don't see any visible trace of damage."

She shuddered as she remembered the rough hands on her skin, hoping that if Del indeed loved her as he claimed, he would understand about the parts of her attack she had left out when she told her story earlier. She followed him out on to the veranda, firmly closing the door behind them. As if reciting a story, she told him the exact intent of the attack, and the extent of her injuries.

His tenderness was replaced quickly by stiffness as her words sunk in, and he left after expressing polite regret at what had happened, with a cursory peck on the cheek instead of the passionate kisses Alexandria had come to expect.

~   ~   ~

This morning as she dressed for Teddy's funeral, the weather being too hot to delay the burial for very long, one of Del's men had delivered a wax-sealed note telling her that under the circumstances he felt that it would be better if they postponed their wedding plans.

As she read the first lines, Alexandria thought he was simply being kind and bowing to the mourning period thought to be socially correct following the death of a family member. But it was with mounting horror that she read and then reread the final lines of the letter, unwilling to believe his words:

> *I feel that it would be unfair to expect you to enter into a marriage so soon after your unfortunate experience. I feel that when you were in my arms, you would remember the other arms that held you. Indeed I know I could never forget.*
>
> *Remember me with fondness, for that is how I will remember you.*

Alexandria opened her eyes and looked down into the open grave at the wooden casket. Her face tightened at the memory, and her hands clutched the piece of paper crumpled now in her dress pocket. So perhaps Teddy's hunch about Del had been correct. If only he had shared his suspicions with her. Alexandria sighed. It probably wouldn't have done any good. She had been so certain that she was in love with Del and he with her that she would most likely not have listened.

Teddy had known her so well. She sighed again. It was too late now anyway. If Teddy hadn't been watching Del so intently, he wouldn't have been close enough that night to hear her screams and wouldn't have tried his futile rescue. In a way, Del was as responsible for Teddy's death as he was for the death of her own dreams.

~   ~   ~

Aunt Mattie's sobs brought Alexandria firmly back to the present. She waited until the preacher had finished his monotonous eulogy, then she walked forward and dropped the red rose, now crushed from being clenched in her sweaty, tense fingers, onto the clods of fresh dirt that barely covered the pine box.

After a brief hesitation and with a venom-filled glance in Del's direction, she also dropped on top of Teddy's casket the crumpled piece of paper from her pocket, hoping that somehow, wherever he was, he would know that she understood and was grateful for his attempt to help.

Teddy already knew that she loved him, Alexandria reasoned. Since she was a little girl she had followed him around with adoration. They had been closer than any siblings could have been, and she knew that his feelings for her were as deep as her own for him.

Her rich alto voice joined the voices of the makeshift choir, faltering only occasionally when emotion and memories overcame her resolve. *Amazing grace, how sweet the sound . . .* She had always hated her throaty voice, thinking it unattractive and too low to be feminine. Now she was grateful that its depth cloaked the hoarseness the tears of the night before had brought. When the last verse was sung, she put a hand gently on Aunt Mattie's shoulder and guided her toward the buggy that waited to take them home.

When they got to the buggy, she stood aside as well-wishers paid their respects to the forlorn mother whose shoulders still shook with sobs. Finally Alexandria climbed into the buggy beside her aunt and said firmly, "I think it's time I got Aunt Matilda home. Thank y'all for everything. We'll look forward to seeing you a little later."

With a deft flick of the whip, she turned the horses toward home.

~   ~   ~

The darkness of the evening found her in front of her bedroom window, the sashes open and the peach satin curtains pulled back to let the cool evening breezes float over her hot skin. The first of the gardenia blossoms on the bushes outside the window filled her room with their cloying fragrance. A tear slid down her cheek as she allowed herself to realize all she had lost in the last twenty-four hours.

She moved away from the window and stood in front of the mirror as she spread aside the front edges of her wrapper and looked at her body, glowing in the golden light from the coal-oil lamp. Bruises showed plainly along her breasts and thighs, but the thing most hurtful by far was something no one could see. She had indeed lost far more than a friend and a fiancé. Thinking of Del stopped her tears and put a fierce look of resolve on her face.

Hearing a knock on the door, she retied her wrapper. "Is that you Verbena? Come in."

"Law, Miz Alexandry, what do you mean standing there half-naked with that window open?" The old black woman scolded as she shuffled across the room, slamming down the window with a loud bang that made Alexandria jump. "You'll catch your death of pneumonia. And it ain't like I ain't got enough to do without taking care of a sick, whiny-assed white woman." She continued to mutter to herself as she began busily tidying the room before turning back the satin coverlet and straightening the eyelet lace-edged sheets.

"Yes, yes, Verbena." Alex smiled at the scolding, then picked up a brush from the dresser and began to brush her hair. Grimacing as it caught in a tangle in the brunette curls, she asked, "Did Aunt Mattie ever settle down enough to eat any supper?" She placed the brush back beside its matching hair-receiver. "I guess I'd better go check on her. Bless her heart."

The expression on the face looking back at herself from the mirror grew sadder still as she thought of the poor, lonely old woman sitting in her room below, now left almost alone in a world that was changing faster than anyone, much less she, could comprehend. Death and fate had indeed been most unkind to Mrs. Matilda Latham. Alexandria's heart was heavy as she turned for the door.

Verbena, who had watched Alexandria grow from a spoiled toddler into the beautiful, strong woman who stood before her now, hesitated before saying, "I don't know as that's such a good idea, Miz Alexandry."

Alexandria turned toward her, startled. "Why ever not, Verbena? Lord love her, I'm all she's got now that Marcus and Teddy are both gone."

Verbena shook her head vigorously. Her hands twisted her apron into a colorful checkered plait. "Chile, I druther tear out my tongue than have to tell you this right now, but Miz Latham done said to tell you she don't want to see you no more. Not tonight. Not tomorrow. She says not never."

Alexandria was stunned. "Verbena, surely you misunderstood." She gave a short, humorless laugh as she reached for a thicker robe. "Heaven knows she can't have meant that. We're the only family we've got left now. We've got to hold onto each other." She added firmly, "I'm going down now and talk to her. Poor old thing. She needs me."

A gentle, dark hand on her arm and a quiet voice held her back. "Miz Alexandry, don't. It'll just make things worse. I knows what I heard, plain as day. She done said she'd take her meals and constitutionals downstairs only when y'all wouldn't be running into each other. She said since you ain't got nowheres else to go you can stay here, but that she can't bear the sight of you." Her gaze was sympathetic when she recognized the pain in the younger woman's deep-green eyes. She spoke softly, regret lacing her words. "Miz Alexandry, she blames you for Massa Teddy's dyin'. Says Massa Teddy done caught you and your Yankee lover lyin' together, and the bluecoat killed him 'cause of it. Says that must be why Mr. Lange didn't stand up with you today at the funeral and why you didn't shed nary a tear during the whole service."

Verbena's voice grew quiet. "I heard you and Mr. Lange talking on the terrace last night." Her words ran together hurriedly as if she were expecting to be chastised for eavesdropping. "I didn't mean to listen, but I heard voices out there when I went to lock up the door, and I couldn't just walk away when I heard the tears in your voice." Her voice dropped with her eyes, "It's a bad thing that done happened to you, Miz Alexandry, but what Mr. Lange done is a whole lot worse." Her voice grew tight with the fierceness of a mother tigress protecting her cub. "But you're better off without his sorry hide. Iffen he really loved you, he would've stood by you no matter what. Man like that ain't worth the bullet it'd take to shoot him."

Alexandria smiled in spite of her aching heart as she nodded in agreement. Her grin faded as she said softly, "Did you know he wrote a note and broke our engagement?" She turned away as her voice cracked, hating herself for showing so much emotion, even to someone she loved as much as she loved the round-faced black woman who had helped raise her almost as much as Aunt Mattie. "He took more from me than that damned Yankee did, Bena. He took away my trust."

She turned and faced Verbena fiercely. "How can I ever trust a man again, Bena? And how will I ever love one?" She felt tears burning the back of her eyes. "And even if I did find someone to love, could he love me back, knowing what happened to me?"

Verbena clucked like a mother hen. "Shucks, chile. For one thing, there ain't no need to tell no man what happened. It ain't likely he'd be able to tell much difference anyhows—and even if he did, what of it? It shore ain't like you're gonna be the first woman for him. What's good for the gander should be just as good for the goose, I allus said."

"That might be true in a perfect world, Bena," Alexandria sighed. "But my world is far from perfect. And I wanted to be chaste for the man I marry. Not for him entirely so much as for me. Now that's not ever going to happen."

"Honey lamb, do you even remember what happened to you that night?"

Alexandria shook her head.

"Did you ask for it to happen?"

Brown curls escaped their pins and tumbled to her shoulder as Alexandria fiercely shook her head. "Of course not!"

"Then no man's ever touched you in your mind or your heart, and they won't be able to touch you there until you let them. Being used ain't the same thing as being loved with. What happened to you is no different than if he'd hit you over the head instead of doin' what he done. He attacked you. You didn't ask him, and you didn't let him. You'll still be chaste for your husband someday, 'cause you're gonna save something for him that no other man has had before."

A dull color flooded Alexandria's cheeks, and she shook her

head in embarrassment. "I can't believe we're even discussing this."

"Lord, honey, don't you be embarrassed with me. I've emptied your slop bucket for fifteen years and explained the monthlies to you when you thought sure you was a dyin'. Who's better'n me to talk to about this? Trust me, Miz Alexandry. When the right man comes along, it won't matter to neither one of you what happened to you last night. All that's gonna matter is what you mean to each other."

Alexandria turned and hugged Verbena, then stood back and put her hands on either side of the older woman's weathered face." You've been more like a mother to me than anyone else in this whole world, Bena. I love you to pieces. And I swear I'm gonna' miss you like pure dee heck."

Verbena looked shocked. "Such talk from a white lady," she clucked. "What would Miz Latham say if she—" She stopped short and looked at the floor.

Alexandria's face grew stony as she finished Verbena's thought. "What would Aunt Matilda say? I guess she'd say that's the kind of talk you'd expect from white trash like me." She walked across the room to the carved oaken chifferobe and pulled down a worn valise, which she laid on the bed.

"Miz Alexandry. What are you gonna' do? Now, don't be doin' nothin' you're gonna regret. Miz Latham'll come around. You know she's just a-grievin' over Massa Teddy right now. She loves you."

"No, I can't stay here. If Aunt Matilda believes these lies, you can imagine what others will believe. I just can't face it all right now. The whispers . . ." She mimicked the hissing whisper of a gossipy neighbor: "*Did y'all hear about what happened to Alexandria Latham. Got what she deserved, I say. The very idea of her takin' a Yankee lover right underneath our noses!*" She shuddered and said in her normal voice, now edged with steel, "Besides, there's something more important I need to take care of."

For a moment she was far away in thought. "You know, Bena, my Uncle Max, on my daddy's side, was a real scoundrel, but he told me something a long time ago that I'm beginning to believe just might be true. He told me the best way to get ahead in this life was not to ever get mad, just be sure you always get even." She smiled a crooked smile that reached no further than her lips. "I can't take back what that damned Yankee took from me, but I sure as the sweet Lord can get even."

Alexandria took off her wrapper as she spoke, then took an old riding habit from its peg in the chifferobe and started to dress. She had a long, probably dusty ride in front of her.

Verbena automatically began helping her mistress as she dressed. "Law, Miz Alexandry, I reckon I know what you're a-thinkin'. But you can't do that." Her black face creased with worry lines. "You ain't got no idea at all where that Yankee is, or even who he is, and . . . well, what would you do if you actually did find him, being a woman and all?"

Alexandria smiled, and this time the smile reached her eyes. "Oh, but I do know who he is, Bena!" She gave a short, humorless laugh. "The dumb jackass actually said his name. And those damned Yankees think we're the stupid ones! He even told where he's from. And I've got a pretty good idea how to find him. I don't know what I'll do when I find him"—her voice grew sarcastic—"'being a woman and all,' but I know I've got to find him before I can put all this behind me and get on with what living I've got left to do."

Verbena followed her across the pine-floored hall and into Teddy's room, where Alexandria began pulling clothes from his dresser and the big chest of drawers beside his bed, tossing them haphazardly into her valise. She waved away Verbena's questions and protests. "Don't worry about me, Verbena. I don't know where I'll be for a while, but I'll write to you. Take the letters to Dessie, and she'll read them to you. If you need me, let me know, and I'll be here for you."

Remembering Del saying those same words to her just days before his betrayal, her voice grew steely. "Aunt Matilda wondered why I haven't cried." She turned toward Verbena, who took an uncertain step back from the raw fury in Alexandria's face. "I won't cry again until it's over." She closed the valise with a snap and reached for her cloak. "And it is one hell of a long way from being over."

She looked around the room, lightly touching Teddy's pillow before walking back into the hall. She walked slowly down the winding staircase, memorizing all the old, familiar objects in the parlor below: the wedding portrait of Uncle James and Aunt Matilda, great-grandmother McKinley's piano, and the glass-front cabinet that housed Aunt Matilda's prized crystal collection.

She smiled, remembering the long hours she and Teddy had spent pounding the keys on that beautiful piano, trying to find combinations of notes that would sound familiar. Teddy had been successful, though she never had. She'd never had the patience for it. She was much more comfortable with riding lessons, and even the forbidden lessons from Teddy and Marcus with Uncle James's squirrel gun and a row of bottles.

For a minute she sat on the forest-green velveteen settee beside the fire, staring into the shadows the dying flames cast on the familiar room. She looked across the room where Verbena stood silently watching her, her hands still twisting her apron into a bundle.

"It's been a wonderful life, Bena," Alexandria said, in a voice strong with newfound resolution.

"Law, Miz Alexandry, don't be a talking like that. You're scarin' me."

"I'm sorry. I don't mean to. It's just that today marks the end of the only life I remember. Tomorrow is a blank page, and it's up to me to write the words on it." She hugged the old woman and wiped away the tears that were falling freely down the beloved black face.

"Don't be worrying about me now, Bena. You just hold things together here, and take care of Aunt Tilly. She needs you and Dessie and all the rest of you to keep things going for a while." She smiled. "And if any of those Yankees show their faces around here, you just get down Uncle James's rifle and run 'em back where they belong."

Verbena nodded silently, "Yes'm. I surely will do that," she said solemnly, "but you take care of yourself, now. I wish you wouldn't do this, but I know I can't change your mind. You've always done just as you pleased. This won't be no different, I suspect. I'll just pray for you and tell the good Lord to keep his eyes on you real good." Her voice broke, and she threw the wrinkled remains of her apron over her head, sobs shaking her shoulders.

Alexandria drew on her cloak, and with a last look around the room, she was gone out the door and into the night.

Chapter Two

The sentry stiffened in his saddle, his hand going automatically to the weapon at his side, his eyes narrowing as he watched the lone rider emerge from the trees, heading north. He had seen enough of war in the last months to make him wary of even the most innocent-looking situations.

For a moment his mind wandered. *What will life be like if—*
He stopped and mentally corrected himself.

What will life be like when this war is over, and I can go back home? Had war changed him so much that Anna and the kids would be strangers to him, and he to them? Could he ever forget the horrors he had seen on the battlefields and forgive himself for the pain he had caused? And after seeing the things one man could do to another in the name of honor, would he ever be able to trust anyone again?

He straightened in the saddle and urged his horse toward the slim youth approaching their camp. He had long ago learned, the hard way, that it was better to face things head-on than leave them to chance.

The young lad on the well-groomed chestnut mare reined in his horse and waited for the uniformed rider to reach him. "Good afternoon, sir," the boy said politely, smiling openly at the man. The boy held both hands plainly in view on the reins of his horse, and the sentry could see that his rifle remained in its scabbard.

The man nodded his head but didn't return the smile. "What are you doin' out this way, boy? Your mama know you're this far from home?"

The boy smiled nervously. "Hell, I ain't seen my mama in a coon's age, but if she did know where I was, she'd be damn proud of me, I reckon."

The man allowed himself a small smile at the boy's bravado. He said dryly, "Who're you looking for way out here, anyhow?" He nodded toward the boy's rifle. "If you're deer hunting, you're in the wrong neck of the woods. All the fighting down south of here's done sent all the game running scared to God knows where."

"No sir, I'm not hunting. At least not game. I'm hoping to run up on Colonel Parker's cavalry unit." He looked at the man hopefully. "You wouldn't happen to be part of it, would you?"

"What makes you think they're anywhere 'round these parts?" the soldier asked nonchalantly, hoping the boy hadn't noticed how his hands had tightened involuntarily on the reins. The location of their camp was supposed to be a well-guarded secret; scuttlebutt should have placed them miles away, almost to Atlanta.

"The men in the camp back aways told me y'all was close by here."

The hairs on the back of the man's neck stood on end as he carefully eased the rifle from its scabbard. "What men was that? What camp?"

The boy's voice was even as he answered, "The two Yankee scouts on their way back to tell their officers where your camp is."

If it was possible, the man's back straightened even further, and his voice was tight as he swore beneath his breath. "How far away is their camp?"

"About a mile down by that creek."

"Take me there now."

The boy shrugged. "I could, but there ain't no need."

"Why not? How long have they been gone?" He groaned, silently picturing the blue-coated men speeding their way back to camp to take news to their commanding officer—news that would mean death for many of his companions, perhaps even himself.

The boy shrugged his shoulders again. "They're still there I reckon, but there ain't no need for me to take you there."

The man urged his horse closer to the boy and in a quiet but steely, dead-serious voice said, "Take me there now, boy. This ain't no game we're playing out here. These rifles carry real bullets. They ain't sticks you point at somebody and kill 'em just by saying 'bang!' And when you kill somebody with them they stay killed. They can't just get up and go home for supper."

The boy looked into the man's eyes and said quietly, "I know what game you're playing, mister. I'm playing in the same game. And my stakes are just as high as yours are now. Maybe higher."

Something in the boy's voice sounded a chord deep in the man's soul, but he couldn't take time to examine the feeling. Lives depended on fast action.

"Take me there. Now."

He followed the boy at a dead gallop across the meadow and into the stand of trees he had watched him emerge from earlier. Minutes later the boy reined in his horse and motioned toward a clump of evergreen bushes that provided a natural screen beside the gurgling creek.

"They're back there," he murmured, dismounting as he nodded toward the bushes, "But if you don't mind, I think I druther stay out here."

The warning hairs on the back of the man's neck stood on end again. Something was wrong, but he couldn't quite figure out what. "No, son, you go in ahead of me. If this is a trap I'd a whole lot rather you get caught in it than me. Ray Turner may be a lot of things, but he ain't no damned fool."

"Pleased to meet you, Mr. Turner." The boy nodded and smiled as he dismounted.

"Dammit boy, this ain't no garden party. Git your tail on in there." He gave the boy an exasperated shove toward the bushes.

The two men in blue made no move toward their guns. They sat there, leaning up against the rocks, looking out over the creek bed with eyes that could see no more. They could have been twins. They wore identical uniforms, and their smiling faces matched down to the tiny hole each now sported in the middle of his forehead.

Ray eased his fingers off the trigger of his gun and said softly, "Who did this? Why?"

The boy turned slowly and looked him in the eye with an expression that made Ray turn his eyes away first.

"I did," the boy said simply. "Why? They're Yankees, ain't they?" His voice was flat. "And I hate Yankees. The only thing I hate worse'n a Yankee"—he picked up a stick that lay in the path and aimed it at one of the dead soldiers—"is two Yankees." He pulled an imaginary trigger and said softly, "Bang, bang, you're dead." He looked at Ray again and smiled a cold smile. "Time for supper, Mr. Turner?"

The cold chill that ran down Ray's spine had nothing to do with the cool mountain breeze drifting across the creek. He followed the boy out of the trees and mounted his horse. "Come on, son," he said tiredly. "I'll take you to Colonel Parker."

~   ~   ~

"There was two of them, sir, ready to high-tail it back to their outfit with a map leading the whole damned patrol right to us." He shook his head. "That kid out there saved our butts all right." He looked through the tent flap and motioned toward the mountain that poked its peak up through the misty clouds. "There ain't no way we coulda got away from 'em in time." He closed his eyes as if in prayer and shuddered. "It woulda been like shootin' fish in a barrel for them." When he opened his eyes again they were flint-hard. "Sounds like a good Yankee sport, don't it?"

For a long minute his commanding officer stared at him, then shook his head. "Lieutenant Turner, one of the worst effects of war is hate." He added sadly, "Sometimes I think you enjoy your job way too much."

Turner shrugged his shoulders, then turned to face the grey-haired man sitting behind the makeshift desk. "No offense, sir, but if I loved these Yankee sons of bitches I couldn't shoot at 'em half as good."

The older man sighed. "I don't love them, Lieutenant, don't get me wrong. I want them off Southern soil just as badly as you do. And I'll do whatever it takes to get them back where they belong, or I'll die trying. But I just can't forget that they're men just like you and me. Two years ago we were countrymen. Brothers. They eat and sleep and breathe and laugh just like we do. And every one of them left someone behind who'll cry real tears if something happens to them. Just don't ever forget that every bullet that leaves your gun carries a whole washtub of tears for somebody back home."

"No offense, sir, but if we all thought about it that way, it wouldn't be much of a war, now would it?"

"And your voice says that would be a pity," the older man said with a wan smile.

"Not a pity exactly. I want to get back to my family just like you do, sir, but I can't rightly say as I care how many of these blue-coated bastards get back to theirs."

"And that, Lieutenant Turner, is the real tragedy of war. Especially a war such as this where the men you're shooting at may have been friends just a few months ago. Or you may even be firing against relatives." He stood up and took a deep breath, facing the flap at the front of the tent. "Whatever my opinion of war, Lieutenant, it doesn't diminish the task set before me, which I plan to do to the best of my ability. And I need good men to get it done. Now, if you will, bring in our young Jack the Yankee-killer."

The young lad who stood before him reminded him greatly of himself years ago. His eyes were not downcast, as were the eyes of most who stood before their commanding officer, but instead met his own coolly and with a sense of self-worth that would stand this boy well in whatever path of life he chose to follow. Although he stood ramrod-straight, he did not seem tense or awed by the colonel's presence.

The colonel smiled. "At ease, son. Where are you from?"

"Just down the road a ways, sir."

"What road? How far a ways?"

"I'm from a little fork in the road just west of Rome, sir."

"Any family left behind at that little fork in the road?"

"Just an aunt, sir, and a couple of house folk."

"What happened to the rest of your folks?"

"They died when I's just a baby, sir. My aunt, she raised me for 'em. I'm the only family she's got left now since the Yankees took her sons."

"Took them? As prisoners? Soldiers?"

"No sir. They're both dead."

The colonel walked around the makeshift desk and put a hand on the young boy's shoulder. "How old are you, son?" He held up a warning hand, "and don't try to lie to me. That peach fuzz on your face'll tell me the truth if you don't."

"I'm seventeen, sir, last February."

The older man looked skeptical, "You're a mighty young-looking seventeen, son. You sure you want to be a soldier? You don't have to join up, you know. Your aunt needs you, maybe more than we do, although God knows we can use any men we can find."

The boy's voice was steely as he answered. "My aunt don't need me no more. And I've got me a hankerin' to do some damage to the Yankee army. A sight more damage than I been doing 'em back on our farm."

"Why do you hate Yankees so much? Do you know anything about the politics that started this war? Do you have slaves you're afraid you'll lose?" He smiled. "Or do you just hate blue?"

"Politics? No, sir, I don't know nothin' about politics. And we didn't have no slaves to speak of, just a couple of house folk. We bought 'em fair and square, but we'd already give them their papers

years ago. They stay 'cause they're sort of like family, you know."
He paused and smiled a tight little smile that never quite reached
his eyes. "I guess it must be I just hate blue."

"It's important enough to make you want to risk your own life
just to kill a Yankee?"

"No sir. I don't want to kill a Yankee." He waited a moment
then answered the question in the colonel's eyes. "I want to kill a
lot of Yankees, sir. And the fact they are Yankees is reason enough I
guess." His voice was cold and his eyes, when they met the
colonel's, were even colder.

The colonel shook his head sadly. "You and Lieutenant
Turner should get along fine, boy." He turned and walked to the
chair sitting along the edge of the tent, easing his tired body onto its
hard seat. "You're dismissed. Tell the lieutenant to find you some
supper and a place to sleep. We start out at daybreak."

"Where are we going?" the boy asked.

"That's not something you need to know," the older man said.
"You're in the Army now. You point your horse in the direction we
tell you to, you go when you're told to go, and you don't stop until
your commanding officer tells you to stop. You'll sleep when we
say sleep, and you'll fight when someone tells you to." His voice
grew softer. "And if you're very, very lucky, son, someday maybe
you'll have one hell of a story to tell your grandkids around a warm
winter fire."

"I'm in the Army now." The boy repeated the colonel's words
proudly.

"Yes. Let's hope you're this happy about it in a few weeks. I'll
get the necessary papers for your signature later. And a checkup by
a doctor, if we ever see another real one. If we were nearer a
headquarters, I'd send you there for assignment, but as it is I
desperately need any extra man I can muster." He looked at the
rifle the boy had leaned against the edge of the tent when he
entered. "Turner tells me you use that weapon pretty well. It seems
we owe you a word of thanks."

"It ain't necessary, sir. I was aimin' to sign up as soon as I
found an outfit that needed me. I just got me a little target practice
early."

The older man shook his head. "Thank you just the same. I'm
very glad, private, very glad indeed that word of our whereabouts
didn't make its way back to the wrong ears." He placed his hands

on either side of his forehead and massaged his temples lightly with his fingertips. As if speaking to himself he went on, "You know, even after all these months, I still can't get used to the fact that we're having to kill our own people to stay alive." His worry-lined face grew sad. "God help us all when this war is over and both sides have to come to terms with ourselves and what we've done."

His dark eyes met the deep green eyes of the boy. "Don't do anything in this war for the wrong reasons, son, and don't do anything you won't be able to live with after it's over." He sighed and shook his head. "If indeed it ever is over."

The boy looked puzzled. "Sir, if you don't mind me saying so, if you hate this so badly, why are you here? Seems to me you should be proud to be helping to write a page in the history books."

The older man smiled sadly. "I'm a soldier, son. I've spent my whole life preparing for this. I worked hard to become an officer, and I'm proud of my accomplishments." He hesitated before adding, "I just always thought I'd enjoy it more." The old man shook his head, and a haze of sadness washed over his tired features. "Somehow writing pages in history doesn't seem quite so grand when you realize they're being written in good men's blood." As if suddenly realizing he was speaking to a rapt audience and not an empty tent, he looked rather embarrassed and said sharply, "Go on now, and get some sleep. Dawn comes early in this man's army."

"Would it be all right if I slept by my horse tonight, sir? She's a little spooked, bein' in a strange place and all. I want to make sure she's okay tonight."

The colonel smiled. "I like a man who cares about his animals. You'll be trusting her with your life very soon, young man. Tell Turner you'll be making your own arrangements tonight, but in the future you'd better stay close to the other men. One man alone in the dark just might get a stray bullet in his brain if the wrong person woke up and saw a stranger in the shadows."

"I understand sir, and I'll be careful." He stopped with his hand on the tent flap. "Thank you for trusting me. I'll make you proud, sir, I promise."

"I don't have a single doubt about that, private." He shook his head, "These last few weeks have taken more of a toll on me than I'd thought. I swear I don't remember Turner telling me your name."

"McKinley, sir. Alex L. McKinley." The boy held out his hand. "Proud to make your acquaintance."

The man's eyes smiled, although his voice was gruff. "You salute your officers, Private McKinley. You don't shake hands. That's for the parlor back home." He looked at the boy for a moment, then reached out and gripped the still-outstretched hand. "Nonetheless, I am just as pleased to make your acquaintance, I'm sure."

As soon as the boy's hand was released it snapped into a picture-perfect salute, bringing the smile from the colonel's eyes to his lips. "At ease, son. Go get some rest."

The boy nodded, "I will sir. And thank you again. You won't regret it."

He turned and exited the tent the way he had entered earlier, not hearing the colonel's whispered words. *I know I won't be sorry, son. I hope to the sweet Lord you won't be.*

The old man wearily made his way to the rickety cot that served as his bedroom. He eased his tired body down on the creaking frame. Deep in thought, he looked at the tent-flap that moved gently in the breeze from the boy's exit. *I hope that the revenge for whatever wrong you're wanting righted is as sweet for you as you expect it to be.* With the wisdom that comes of age and of witnessing far too many battles, he knew that it seldom was.

~   ~   ~

The boy walked toward a flickering fire at the edge of the woods. "Lieutenant Turner?" he asked, hesitantly.

The man sitting by the fire turned and looked at the thin figure standing in the edge of the firelight. "No. Stevens here, Kane Stevens. Turner called it a night early to be ready for first-light watch. Something I can do for you?"

"No sir. I'm going to bed down myself. Just wanted to let him know the colonel said it'd be okay for me to bunk with my horse tonight."

"Well, at least you'll be sleeping with someone," the man said. He waved Alex away. "Better turn in, boy." He reached for a stick to stir the glowing embers, the firelight playing across his face adding black shadows to his finely chiseled features. "Dawn seems to come earlier and earlier around here."

The boy nodded and turned away into the shadows, toward

the string of horses, whose forms were visible in the glow of the campfires that burned near the tents lining the edges of the clearing. Feeling his way toward his horse's bridle, he unfastened it and led her away from the other animals. "Good night, Birdie," he said, caressing her neck. "Tomorrow night you'll have to sleep with the other horses, but tonight I just wanted to sleep beside a friend." He took a lump of sugar from his trouser pocket and held it in the palm of his hand, chuckling as the horse's velvet-soft whiskers tickled his skin. "Do you think you can get used to me riding you astride instead of sidesaddle, girl? It sure is great not having all those skirts getting in the way, isn't it?" He smiled in the darkness. "They may call you a dumb animal, Birdie, but I know one animal even dumber." He looked with scorn toward the row of tents. "Men. *Hmmph!* Cut your hair, put on a pair of pants, let your face get a little dirty, clean out your fingernails while you talk to folks, and talk and swear like an uneducated field hand"—the boy grinned—"and scratch your crotch every once in a while. And no one suspects a thing." He yawned as he finished speaking.

~   ~   ~

It had been three weeks since home was left behind. Three long weeks of hard riding and being regarded with suspicion, a lone woman asking the location of the nearest Confederate unit. Rest was beckoning invitingly. Sleep had not come easily in those weeks, and she had learned the hard lesson that a woman alone was defenseless in a man's world. But no more. That part of life was over. The lad's hand rubbed across his chest, checking the bindings that hid what was beneath.

Alexandria McKinley Latham, belle of three counties, smiled to herself as she went to sleep wrapped in her horse's blanket.

Chapter Three

"No! Get off me! Teddy, help!" Alex kicked and tried to scream as she bit the hand that covered her mouth. She heard a muffled curse, and then her head rattled as she was shaken fully awake. She took a deep breath and opened her eyes to find a man's face inches from her own. She opened her mouth to scream again, and her eyes flashed in terror when the man's hand quickly covered her mouth. She wrestled and tried to escape his grip and was almost successful when her knee connected with the man's crotch.

"Dammit, boy, stop that. You know better than to hit a man below the belt in a fair fight."

With a rush all the events of the last few weeks came rushing back, and Alex relaxed. The man's hand slowly moved away from her face. "You were having a nightmare, son. I didn't mean to make it worse. I'm sorry. Lord, but you've got a set of lungs on you, though there weren't any need to scream like a girl." The voice scolded her, but a teasing tone echoed in the silver-grey eyes.

It was such an honest and familiar scene for Alex, being teased by someone the way Teddy had done for so many years, that for a moment her eyes clouded with tears. The arms holding her tightened, and she allowed herself a moment's luxury and relaxed against the hard chest. Then she pulled herself together abruptly, remembering her disguise, and leaned back against her pallet. When she met the grey eyes again, they were clouded with a confusion she didn't understand.

"I'm sorry. That was a doozy of a nightmare. Thanks for coming over, Mr.—"

"Stevens. Sergeant Kane Stevens. We met last night before you went to sleep. Turner told me what you did yesterday. I guess you're due a nightmare or two after a day like that." His voice grew weary. "I've been fighting for two years now, and every once in a while I wake up with a shout and find myself lying in a puddle of cold sweat." He gave her shoulder a brotherly pat. "Don't worry. No one else heard you, and I won't tell a soul."

"Thanks."

"Don't mention it." The man stood up and held out a strong, callused hand to pull her upright. "You hungry yet? I've got some a coffee and a couple of potatoes we could fry up. It's mighty early for breakfast, but I've been up all night, so it's more like supper to me."

Alex's stomach growled in anticipation. "Thanks. I think I've still got some biscuits and jam left from breakfast yesterday, if you'd like some."

"Real jam? Real biscuits? Share a little of that and you've got a friend for life, McKinley."

"Alex. Please call me Alex, sir."

The man smiled. "Okay, Alex Sir. And you can call me Kane."

A brilliant smile flitted across the peach-fuzzed face as the boy said, "Nice to meet you, Mr. Kane."

The man looked uncomfortable for a moment. "No. My first name is Kane, and there aren't any 'Misters' in the Army, Alex. You can call me Sergeant Stevens, or Kane, but not Mister anything."

Alex nodded her agreement as Kane added, "You'd better look up those biscuits right quick so we can shove 'em down our cake-holes before everybody else wakes up and wants a bite."

She fumbled through her pack and found the biscuits—and a few pieces of fried ham as well—that Sheila, the woman at the boardinghouse where Alex had stayed as she had completed her plans, had thoughtfully included in the traveling bag she had brought to the stable as Alex had saddled Birdie the morning before.

Sheila's eyes had shone with questions about why the genteel young lady who had entered her establishment wished to emerge from it later as a rough young man, but thankfully she had kept her questions to herself. Alex's own thoughts were too scrambled to try to explain them to someone else. Even when Alex had asked for the Confederate-grey jacket Sheila's husband had left behind on his last leave, Sheila had unquestioningly brought it to Alex on the morning of her departure, freshly laundered and pressed. When Alex had pulled it on over Teddy's shirt and pants, then smoothed her newly cropped hair with an oily dressing, Sheila had quietly assured her that no one would guess her true identity. Minutes later she pressed the bagful of food into Alex's hands and wished her Godspeed on a safe journey, in a voice tight with unshed tears. She added a reminder for Alex to please send word to her if she heard any news about her husband.

Alex's thoughts clouded.

Time was moving too fast for her. It seemed a lifetime ago that she had raced hell-bent-for-leather from the only home she had ever known. Had it really been less than a month since she passed, possibly for the last time, between those tall cedars that acted as sentries for the gate to her home?

Kane's heartfelt groan when he spotted the meat brought her back to the present. The look of pleasure that was etched on his face would have made Alex laugh if it hadn't made things so crystal-clear regarding what her life would be like in the days ahead. For a moment she wondered if what she had planned was worth it. Then she remembered the look on Del's face and Aunt Matilda's words, and she knew she had made the right decision. Truly life as she had known it was over. A clean break was best, and the revenge that waited ahead would be sweet. Very sweet indeed. Her jaw tightened.

They sat there in the grey light of early morning, listening to the breeze whispering through the tops of the tall pines as they munched on their cold breakfast.

Finally Kane broke the silence. "It's mighty peaceful, isn't it Alex? I know it sounds funny, but I kind of like pulling the night shift because I get to see the daybreak. And on mornings like this, it makes me sure that peace, real peace, is worth fighting and maybe dying for."

"Yes," Alex answered with a sigh. "I wish my whole life could be as peaceful as this moment."

Kane looked at her thoughtfully, measuring his words before he spoke. "Who's Teddy?" he asked softly.

Alex jumped in surprise and she felt her flesh color.

"I'm sorry," Kane said before she could answer. "That's none of my business. I didn't mean to pry, but it's just that you kept calling out his name in your sleep last night. I couldn't figure out if you were trying to kill him or keep him from being killed."

"He was my cousin," Alex said simply, hoping she could keep her voice even. Crying would be most unmasculine, she knew.

"Did you kill him?" He held up his hand and shook his head. "Forgive me Alex, I'm usually not such a busybody. It's just that you sounded so panicked. If you need to talk, I've got a good shoulder, and I promise I won't tell a soul. I had a brother just a little younger than you back home. I guess you just remind me of him a little. Maybe that's why I feel so protective about you."

Alex shook her head. "I didn't kill Teddy," she said, her eyes flashing with still-unshed tears and anger at the memory her words brought forth. "He was my very best friend and he died trying to save my life." Her voice grew weak as she fought against her emotions.

"There are worse ways to die, you know," Kane's voice was thoughtful. "If I die somewhere besides on a battlefield, which don't seem too likely right now, I'd like to know I died for a good cause. Like saving somebody's life. Especially somebody I cared about." He looked solemnly at Alex. "Don't be ashamed that you're alive and he's not. If he cared about you, he wouldn't want you feeling guilty, I'll bet." He looked down at his boots in embarrassment as he asked quietly, "Did you . . . uh . . . get hurt somehow, before Teddy got there?"

Alex colored quickly, then narrowed her eyes. "How do you mean?"

It was Kane's turn to blush. "Your nightmare seemed pretty violent. Just thought you might need to talk it out. Like I said, nothing'll go any further. If you need a friend, remember that."

Alex shook her head, her mind racing, wondering what she had said in her sleep and hoping she hadn't let her secret slip already.

"Then the subject's dropped. I'm sorry about Teddy, but I'm glad he saved your life." Green eyes met grey, locked in a moment that neither completely understood.

The grey eyes were the first to look away as Kane cleared his throat, his face a deep crimson red. "I'd better go wake Turner. It's time for his watch, and I can grab a couple hours of sleep if I'm lucky." He nodded toward Alex's blanket. "Wouldn't do you any harm either. It'll be a long day in the saddle today, if I don't miss my guess."

"Thanks for the potatoes and coffee, Kane. And the shoulder."

"Thank you for the ham and biscuits. They're the first ones since I left home. Thanks for the talk too. It's the first one in a long time that didn't revolve around battle plans and guns, who didn't make it through yesterday, or how tired I am."

Alex watched as Kane walked toward the nearest tent, which she supposed housed the officers. Although she knew it would be difficult if not impossible to let herself completely trust a man again, she had a gut feeling that he would be one of the rare people she could depend on if things got rough.

She grimaced. "God, please let me have made the right decision." She was certain things were about to get very rough indeed.

~   ~   ~

She went back to sleep and dreamed about the past until she found herself awake and staring into the same grey eyes that had awakened her earlier. "Wake up, sleepyhead," Kane said with a grin. "It's really morning this time. Glad to see no more nightmares bothered you."

Alex shook her head, wishing the thick morning cobwebs would clear from mind, "Nope. Slept like a lamb." She yawned and stretched. "What time is it, anyway?"

"A little after five o'clock. You've got twenty minutes to saddle up and be ready to ride."

"Five o'clock. In the morning?" Alex groaned, remembering the mornings she used to lie in bed until noon and then have a leisurely bath after a delicious breakfast in bed. *Mornings could prove to be the hardest part about 'this man's army,'* she thought wryly.

She stood up and rubbed her aching back. After one long night on the cold, hard ground, she realized with surprise that what she missed the most of her old life wasn't the home-cooked food or the company of her friends—the things she'd expected to miss. What she missed the most so far was her soft, deep mattress.

~   ~   ~

After making certain the boy was awake, Kane left to pack his horse for the day's journey. Walking away, he shook his head sadly. Delicate boys like Alex McKinley were in for a rough life in the army. If they made it through the day's battle, which was hard enough on them physically, many times they had another fight ahead of them to keep lonely, desperate men out of their bedrolls. Kane groaned, remembering the dewy look in Alex's sleepy green eyes when he had awakened him earlier. As if he didn't have enough to keep him busy just trying to stay alive to get himself back home in one piece, now he had a little lost lamb to keep gathered safely into the fold.

~ ~ ~

Alex watched as Kane walked off to pack up his bedroll. He gathered his saddlebags, then moved toward a dappled steel-grey stallion hobbled nearby. Picking up a saddle that lay on the grass beside his bedroll, Kane threw it across the beautiful mount's back with ease. With a furtive glance around, he reached into his pocket and pulled out what Alex recognized as a piece of the treasured breakfast-biscuit, which he offered to the nickering grey. He gently rubbed the horse's forelock, then smoothed down his mane where the morning breeze had ruffled it.

Kane looked toward Alex, who hid a smile at witnessing that hidden moment of tenderness, and motioned impatiently for her to hurry. She nodded and quickly threw her own saddle across Birdie's back, then tightened the girth. She led her across the grassy patch where Kane stood waiting, her eyes bright with anticipation.

Watching the slim young boy walk toward him, Kane prayed a silent prayer to whoever was listening to watch over them through the days ahead. *I know I can take whatever I have to,* he breathed silently, *but I don't know if this little fellow can. Help me keep him safe.*

"You sure you got everything?" he asked Alex. "We won't be anywhere near these parts again for a while, I'd reckon."

"Where are we going?" Alex hoped her voice didn't sound as quavery and unsure to Kane as it did to herself.

"I'm not for certain. We're hoping to join up with another outfit before the Yanks get any closer. We'd have a great surprise party for 'em if we can pull it off. It's a three-day ride to anywhere from here, no matter which way we end up going, and no telling' what we'll run into along the way."

Alex's imaginative mind conjured up all the things they could "run into," and she shuddered.

Kane saw her tremor and said softly, "Don't worry. I'll keep an eye out for you."

She looked at him in surprise. While Alexandria would have wondered what Kane wanted in return for his friendship, Alex was just glad that she had a friend, for whatever reason. Even one wearing pants.

She smiled a grateful smile and pulled her horse closer to Kane's. When the call sounded, she was the first man in the saddle.

They waited patiently until their commanding officer appeared in the opening of his tent. When he called, "Stevens, McKinley—front and center," then turned and reentered his tent, her heart raced. What could he possibly want with her? Could her deception have been discovered so quickly? She gave Kane a quick glance, hoping she hadn't misjudged his seemingly sincere promise to not tell whatever he suspected from her morning nightmare. She was relieved to see that he looked as puzzled as she felt. Together they dismounted and led their horses to the colonel's tent. Handing the reins to the aide, they entered and briskly saluted their commanding officer.

"At ease, men." The older man walked back and forth in front of them. "We need to get a message to General Johnston. The last word we had put him somewhere near Chattanooga." He reached into his pocket and pulled out a waxed-paper-wrapped package, which he handed carefully to Kane. "Lieutenant Stevens, I trust you'll take care that this doesn't fall into the wrong hands."

At Kane's solemn nod the colonel turned to Alex. "Private McKinley. You're to ride along with Lieutenant Stevens. Learn from him. He's one of the best. He's a good man and a good officer. No one could teach you better. When you've delivered this message, bring the answer back to me, wherever you can find us. If you can't come yourselves, send someone you know you can trust. We're headed toward Rome, but Lord knows what detours we'll have to make, thanks to these damned Yanks."

He crisply saluted the men and watched as they walked toward the door. "Sergeant Stevens." Kane turned and looked at him questioningly.

"Yes, sir?"

"Be careful. And . . ." his voice trailed off, then he looked at Kane and smiled thoughtfully. "Keep an eye on that boy, will you?"

Kane nodded. "Yes, sir. I plan to do both, sir." His hand touched the brim of his cap in a final salute, then he quickly exited the tent.

"Ready to move, McKinley?" At Alex's nod, he nudged his horse into a slow canter, with Alex falling in slightly behind.

They rode together all that day in a companionable silence, broken only by an occasional comment about the breathtaking

scenery. Alex had been on shopping trips to New Orleans and
Saint Louis with Aunt Matilda and her cousins, but she had never
been allowed the freedom to explore the country close to home.
The mountains around Twin Cedars were as familiar as the
wallpaper on the bedroom wall, but she found herself staring at the
mountains she was seeing now as if she had never seen such a
landscape before. When she asked Kane about them, he told her
they were following the foothills of Lookout Mountain that would
lead them toward Chattanooga.

She could hear a brook chuckling over rocks, and she ached to
be able to cool her feet in the icy stream, but she knew better than
to ask Kane for a few minutes' rest. He was indeed a man with a
mission. She knew that if he could, he would ride day and night
without rest until the message in his breast-pocket was in the right
hands.

As they rode along she asked nonchalantly, "Where would
Yankee prisoners be taken from around here?"

"Oh, different places," Kane shrugged. "Whatever's closer to
you at the time. Sometimes we'll turn jails into temporary prisons;
sometimes even homes. Then from this area they'll probably get
transferred to Andersonville eventually."

"How does a prisoner get himself captured, anyway?"

"Any man in the enemy's ranks, whether wounded in battle
and left behind or captured in other way, is ours. We sometimes
manage to catch some stragglers who give up when they know
they're outnumbered. Sometimes we can swap them for
Confederate prisoners, but mostly we just keep them. Spies are
usually hung or shot, and the rest are just mouths we have to feed
in prison until the end of the war." He shook his head. "And it's
getting harder and harder to keep our own men fed. Sometimes
prisoners are released after signing oaths that they will not bear
arms in the future."

"Do we keep lists of prisoners? And deaths of the enemy?"

"Well, we try to have a list of prisoners. Not deaths. Lord
knows we can't even keep an accurate list of our own downed men.
Sometimes the prisoner lists aren't completely accurate, but we try
to keep a tally. Why are you asking about all this, anyway?"

"No reason." Alex said, shifting in the saddle, hoping she
would be able to keep up with Kane's pace. Her body screamed
and her thighs ached, but she couldn't risk letting Kane know how

she felt. What he thought of her was very important to her, although she couldn't exactly decide why.

"How would I get a copy of that list?"

Kane looked puzzled. "I don't know, Alex. I'd guess from headquarters, or from the prison."

They rode a while longer in silence, then Alex spoke again. "Kane, how would I find out where a particular Yankee outfit is?"

Kane laughed. "That's the million-dollar question, I'd imagine. If we knew where they all were, it would sure alleviate a lot of problems, wouldn't it?" He looked at her for a moment then said softly, "I take it there's some Yankee you'd like to find—either dead, alive or maybe in a prison somewhere?"

For a moment Alex could feel rough hands and hear a mocking voice: *I'll show you what it's like to have a real man between your legs.* She shook her head, shaking Teddy's scream from her memory. Her lips narrowed and twitched. "Not really. Just curious."

Kane looked at her for a moment, his mouth opened as if to speak, then he shook his head as he thought better of his question. Time would answer more questions than idle talk would, he decided.

On the third day of their ride, as the late-afternoon shadows lengthened and dusk was threatening, they neared the rear lines of one of the many Confederate camps along the base of Lookout Mountain. A dilapidated hospital tent was buzzing with activity, and knowing what gruesome sights would be found there, Kane steered Alex in the opposite direction.

Alex's eyes grew large as she took in a part of life she had never seen before. "Your camp wasn't like this," she said in a shaky voice, watching the walking wounded limping to and from the hospital tents, their bandages dirty with dark stains that she realized must be dried blood.

Kane's voice was gentle. "You haven't been close to the front lines yet, have you?"

She swallowed hard and shook her head. "Will we be staying here long?"

"Not too long. Just for tonight. Tomorrow we'll be back on the road to Chattanooga. We're safer here tonight than we would be in a camp by ourselves again. We're too close to the Yanks now, and there is some safety in numbers. They'll have a sentry who can keep an eye out for us so we can get some sleep."

Hoping she didn't sound like the simpering female that she alone knew was cowering inside her uniform, she said, "Mind if I sleep near you tonight?"

He smiled at her. "Not at all. We're buddies. We have to look out for one another."

Alex smiled back and felt her heart tighten. Kane's warm smile and the light in his quicksilver eyes reminded her of all she had thought missing from her life. *Trust. Hope. Love.* Tears threatened to cloud her vision.

She quickly looked away, but not before Kane had seen first pain and then tears darken her eyes. His hands tightened on the reins. "Just one minute alone with that son-of-a-bitch," he muttered beneath his breath.

Alex flashed her eyes at him. "What?"

"Nothing. A horsefly bit me," Kane answered. "Damned son-of-a-bitch. Brought the blood too," he added, hoping Alex wouldn't ask to see the bite.

"They're pretty vicious, ain't they? Must be the heat." Alex fanned herself with her hat. "It's hotter'n hell today."

"Yep, I'll bet these Yanks are really sweating." Kane chuckled. "They're used to sitting up North keeping cool. But they have my permission to go back whenever they decide it's too hot for 'em down here." Alex's musical laughter joined his deep chuckle in the gathering darkness.

They dismounted beside a campfire that was ringed with men, their clothes dusty and their faces lined with tiredness and the tension that came with facing fear in every waking moment.

One of the men waved at them. "Pull up a log and set a spell. We've got some of what we're calling coffee in the pot, and some beans in the pan. If you've got something to share in them saddlebags, bring it on out, iffen you don't just belly-up."

"Thanks. We've had a hard ride today. On our way to General Johnston's outfit. You hear lately what direction he's holed up in?"

The man looked at him suspiciously. "Why? What're you wanting with Johnston?"

"Got a message for him. From Colonel Parker. Looks like there's going to be some fireworks up ahead, and we want to be sure he's invited to the party."

"Damn. Why won't them blue-bellies go back where they

belong, and leave us the hell alone?" one of the men grumbled.

Another man stood up from the edge of the fire and walked away sadly. "We're trapped here, boys. It ain't never gonna be over. This is a nightmare we ain't ever gonna wake up from—and if we do wake up, the world we're gonna find ain't gonna be the one that was there when we went to sleep," he said in a flat, toneless voice.

Alex watched the man until he blended into the darkness, a lump in her throat. "I've got jam," she blurted out suddenly, realizing as soon as the words left her mouth how trifling they must have sounded after the man's grim rhetoric. But her words worked magic.

"Jam? Real jam with sugar?" one of the men asked hungrily. At her nod he stood up. "Does anybody have any hardtack or flour to rustle up some biscuits?" Within a few minutes, preciously hoarded items had been brought forward, and Alex found herself mixing biscuits and trying to figure out how to bake them over an open fire.

They turned out only slightly softer than the rocks and logs they sat on, but the men declared they were softer than goose down and tastier than any meal they had had before.

When the last crumbs were gone, one of the men spoke up. "I don't quite know how to say thanks, boy. I really didn't think I could get through another night knowing another day was out there waiting for me, but that there jam and biscuits reminded me that there is another world still out there just past the edges of this one. And it's a world worth fighting for."

The men nodded solemnly, and Alex felt the lump returning to her throat. Later as she lay on the ground beside Kane, near the fire he had built, she heard him say quietly, "That was a fine thing you did tonight, Alex. You're a good man."

Alex blushed and surprised herself by saying, "You are too, Kane."

She heard Kane roll over, and soon the sound of his even breathing told her that he was asleep. She put her arms behind her neck, pillowing her head against the hard ground. Time sure changes things, she thought. A month ago she was at home, safe and sound, feeling wicked for allowing Delwood Lange to steal kisses in the rose garden before retiring alone to her freshly beaten feather bed. And look at me now, she mused. Sleeping on the ground a few feet away from a man I've known less than a week but am probably going to have to trust with my life at some point, and in the same camp with more men than I've ever seen in my entire life.

She grinned, wondering what havoc it would wreak if she were to suddenly announce her identity to the men. Her smile faded. She knew without a doubt that any man in the camp would gladly die fighting for her honor. They might be dirty and ragged, but they were still true Southern gentlemen. If her secret were found out, any one of them would throw themselves in front of a bullet for her.

Men, she groaned inwardly. Whyever did God see fit to mess up this perfect world by creating two sexes? Surely an omnipotent being could have figured out a way for a woman alone to have children. And so far as she could cipher, having babies was the only reason she could see to have a man around. Their every thought seemed to center in their crotch.

Suddenly she stiffened. *Babies.* Good God! What if that damned blue-belly's seed had found fertile ground within her? Damn him to hell! She hurriedly counted the days on her fingers. At least she wouldn't have long to wait to find out. She groaned. Monthlies were never easy to hide, and with these damned trousers and hours spent on horseback, things could get impossible. Damn, damn, dammit all to hell and back!

A smile turned up the corner of her mouth. Too bad she hadn't learned sooner how satisfying a good cuss word could be. This being a man might not be all bad after all. No telling what other useful things she'd learn. She was still smiling as she fell asleep.

Chapter Four

Alex jerked awake, her mind foggy, startled to see an
unfamiliar man wearing parts of a tattered, dusty, grey uniform
standing over her pallet and grinning amicably down at her. "Sorry
if I skeered you," the man drawled, as he hooked his thumb behind
a tattered suspender. "Air you the little feller who made the biscuits
last night?" A twig dangled from his mouth as he chewed the words
out around it.

Alex blinked her eyes, trying to adjust them to the pale light of
dawn. "Yes. Who are you?"

"I'm Seth Jones. I was pulling guard duty last night, and some
of the boys brought me a plate of your goodies. I just wanted to
thankee kindly."

"You're welcome. But it really wasn't much," Alex apologized.

Seth pulled the twig from his mouth and smiled a smile that
showed the absence of several teeth. "Shoot, when you get used to
eatin' wormy rations, anything out of the ordinary is really
something. And that strawberry jam sure was way out of our
ordinary lately. My Sarry Beth used to put up jam just like that." His
words were in the present, but Alex could tell his mind was
suddenly far in the past. Not wanting to break into his thoughts, for
God knew these men had little diversion these days, Alex sat
silently as the man described his Sarry to her.

Alex was pretty sure that no man who looked and talked like
Seth would be married to the goddess he described, but she
nodded, knowing that in Seth's mind the woman was indeed a
princess.

After a long narrative detailing Sarry's beauty and prowess in
the kitchen, along with a few smiling reminiscences of her ability in
the bedroom as well, the man finally seemed to become aware of
his surroundings.

"Well, I guess I'd better be getting me some shuteye," he said.
"If I'm lucky I may get in a couple of hours before some smartass
Yankee boys get to feelin' froggy and try to make us jump."

"Are we that close to enemy lines?" Alex hoped he didn't hear the quiver in her voice. Suddenly she was glad she was still sitting on the hard ground, for she wasn't sure her jelly knees would have held her up. It had been one thing to join the army; it would be quite entirely another to actually fight.

"Close to them? Law, if you was to pitch a rock up there in them bushes, I wouldn't be a bit surprised iffen you didn't hear a damn Yankee say ouch."

Hoping he was exaggerating, Alex couldn't help looking over her shoulder.

The man grinned another toothless grin. "You ain't seen no fightin' yet, have you, boy?"

At the shake of Alex's head, the grin left the man's face and he shrugged his shoulders. "Ain't no way on earth I can describe it to you. All's I can say is to keep your head down and don't stop lookin' over your shoulder. Billy Blue may be right there. Don't be a hero neither, boy. Heroes bleed red just like the rest of us. Iffen you get in a tight place, head for cover. The only reason to risk your neck is to save somebody else's." He looked around the camp at the blanket-covered bodies of the still-sleeping men. "You'll make friends pretty soon, and you'll want to know they're there for you, just like they'll want to know they can count on you." He reached over and patted Alex's arm. "You'll be fine, son." He walked away, stopping to hitch his faded suspenders over a grimy undershirt.

Suddenly a series of tremendous explosions rocked on the ground. A loud cry went up through the camp as the sleeping men came awake on their feet, rifles in hand. Grey-clad men began swarming toward the hastily erected gun encampments that ringed the camp. Rifle fire and mortar blasts split the early-morning calm like a watermelon dropped on a hot rock. Alex heard a scream and realized it was coming from her own throat.

"Buck up, McKinley," she heard a gruff voice say. "You're gonna' have to earn your keep this morning. It seems somebody invited Yankees for breakfast." Through a fog combined of morning mist and the smoke of a hundred rifles, Alex saw Kane's worried face. He tossed her rifle to her. "Find something solid, and get behind it. Shoot anything in blue that moves toward you. And shoot to kill. Now git!"

She watched in terror as he darted from tree to tree, aiming his rifle with dead precision before pulling the trigger. Screams, shouts, curses, and death cries combined with the gunfire created a cacophony of sound that Alex knew she would remember for the rest of her life. She absentmindedly lifted her hand to swat away a bee that buzzed by her ear, then realized with horror that a bullet, not an insect, had come dangerously close to ending her army career—and her life.

She dove for cover behind the cedar log that had served as a makeshift bench for their impromptu dinner party the night before. She shuddered, knowing that most likely some of the screams and cries of horror and pain came from the mouths of the same men she had shared a meal with hours earlier. "Dear God, be with them all," she prayed fervently.

Suddenly a flash of blue caught her eye. A tall, swarthy man dressed in Yankee blues was creeping around to the back of the camp. Alex knelt behind the log, took careful aim and watched the man fall back, almost in slow motion, clutching his chest, where a bright red stain crept through the rough blue wool. "Martha," he screamed as he fell. Alex felt a moment's pang of regret, and then steeled herself against the emotion.

"That's for you, Ted," she said, ignoring the single tear that coursed its way down her grimy, smoke-stained cheek.

A shell whined overhead, and Alex again found her face in the dirt. *Thank goodness I learn pretty fast,* she thought. The air was thick with the acrid smell of burnt powder and the sound of heartrending screams and moans. Another shell whined its way past her, finding its target among the men in grey. Torn bodies leaped crazily in the air with the force of the hit, reminding Alex of a puppet show she and Teddy had watched together years ago. The men, or what was left of them, fell in a heap beside the crater left by the shell. With rising horror, Alex recognized the stained undershirt and suspenders of Seth Jones. She realized with a wrench of sadness that in that moment, on the side of a pine-treed Georgia foothill, Mrs. Sarah Beth Jones, goddess extraordinaire, had suddenly become a widow.

Kane found her there an eternity later, her rifle gripped in hands frozen into the shape of her weapon. He gently eased the gun from her fingers and shook her gently. "Alex, it's all over. The ones that could still move ran like rats back to their den." He pointed toward the heap of blue material that had been a soldier that morning. "You did a good job. He could have taken a lot of us out from back here. You saved a lot of lives with that shot. You're going to be a good soldier."

Alex looked up at him. "I couldn't move, Kane. I tried to make myself get up and join you. I knew you might need me. But I couldn't move."

Kane smiled in understanding. "Alex, you did okay. Hell, the first time I went into battle, I hid behind a tree praying I wouldn't soil my pants. I didn't. But I wasn't sure it wasn't going to happen. Don't be ashamed of being afraid. It's when you stop being afraid that you get yourself or somebody else killed."

Alex stood up. "What happened? How did they sneak up on us like that? Where was our sentry?"

"Bushwhacked. He never saw them coming. It happens, Alex. You have to be aware that at every moment there might be a Yankee behind every tree or every rock. And that they've got their sights on you."

The hair on the back of Alex's neck stood on end. "This is all so pointless, Kane. We shoot at them, they shoot at us. When will it all be over—when we're all dead? What then?" She stumbled away from him, wanting desperately to get away from it all, at the same time knowing that for the time being, she had left herself nowhere to run. She had chosen her path, and right or wrong she had to stay on it until it got here where she had to go. Wherever that was.

She stumbled over a log, and then stifled a scream when the "log" groaned. She gently reached down and rolled the man over so the early rays of sunshine could shine on his face.

"Mother?"

Before Alex could answer she saw a trickle of blood edging through the right side of the young man's mouth, his eyes suddenly opening in wide amazement. For a moment he laid there, looking at something that Alex could not see, then his eyes slowly closed and his body went limp.

Alex whimpered. Where was the glory in this? She had listened with stars in her eyes as Marcus had described how he would ride into battle with sword and rifle held high, smiting the Yankee beast who dared to trample Southern soil. She looked at the boy dressed in blue whose last word had been a plea for his mother. Where was the glory in taking his life? What damage had he done Southern soil, except to moisten it with his blood? Lying there with a forelock of blonde hair, now stained brilliant red, he looked very little like a Yankee beast and very much like a frightened boy, far from home.

In that instant, hate drained from her body, leaving her feeling empty and alone. She knew, after watching life drain from the boy dressed in blue, that she would no longer see Rafe Peterson's face above every blue uniform. Revenge would still be sweet, when it came, but it would have to be Rafe Peterson himself who suffered. Bullets she sent flying toward the enemy would be for her homeland and what it had lost, not for her own personal vengeance.

"Alex, I guess maybe you want to be by yourself right now, but it's really not safe out here. Come on back to camp." Kane's eyes followed her gaze. "Poor devil." He reached down and took the gun from the boy's hand. "What size boots do you wear, McKinley? I know they're too small for me."

Alex looked at him in horror. "You'd steal from a dead body?"

Kane's grey eyes turned steely. "Look, Private, I know this is tough for you to have to take in all at once, but you're in the middle of a war. This is the way you exist. I'm not stealing. Stealing is taking something that someone might miss, need, or want again." He knelt down and began unlacing the boy's boots. "I promise you that wherever this boy is right now, he don't need his boots or his gun."

Chapter Five

The rest of the day was spent helping to bandage the wounded and bury the dead. Alex's thoughts kept going to her saddlebag, where the dead Yankee's uniform was balled up into a tight wad. Kane had explained with tight lips, in a manner that brooked no argument, that good clothes and boots that fit were worth their weight in gold. Both sides wore some of the same pieces of clothing, so everything except the blue jacket would come in handy in time. Alex had learned long ago to never say never, but she knew the circumstances would have to be grim indeed to force her into the now-bloody material.

She helped an old man who looked as if he would have been more at home in a rocking chair on a porch somewhere than in a uniform. Doing anything for himself was almost impossible because of splints and bandages on his arms. He had informed her proudly that although a Yankee bayonet had "pert near clean cut my arm off," he had managed to take down a half dozen of the "blue bastards" before he had been hit with a minie ball in his other arm and lost consciousness. Alex prayed that the surgeons he'd be seeing as soon as the transport train could get him there would be kind and not amputate both arms. She had heard horror stories all day of men who were lying in hospitals in Atlanta and Rome, praying for death because overworked, understaffed, and undersupplied surgeons had amputated limbs that had been injured in battle, limbs with wounds that might have healed in normal situations.

"They tell me you're doing a great job here." Kane's quiet voice and his arm on her shoulder scattered her frazzled nerves, and she jumped. "Sorry, son, I thought you saw me walk up."

"No. I was busy." She smiled at him and offered him a dipper of water, hoping he'd recognize it as a peace offering. It seemed he did, for he returned her smile and patted her shoulder.

She had snapped at him earlier, calling him a grave robber and asking if he spent his nights digging through graves looking for something he might have missed in the light of day. Her words rang in her ears now, mocking her for her foolishness. She had seen many men near death, lying in bloodstained beds, hands tightly gripping some trophy of war—shoes, a gun, a knife, playing cards, or some other object of interest—that had been plucked from the dead hands of the enemy, or of a friend who needed it no longer in this world.

Kane had had every right to knock her into next weekend, but he had simply dropped the boots at her feet and stalked off into the woods. Later he had found her to tell her that the uniform had been placed in her saddlebag, and why. He had walked away then, and Alex had known a moment's fear that she wouldn't see him again. Her heart lifted to know he forgave her harsh words.

"We need to be going, Alex. It's going to be dark in a couple of hours, and I'm hoping we can make it to Rossville by just after dark if we can ride out now and not have to stop for anything."

Alex nodded. She poured the rest of the dipperful of water over her bloody hands and wiped them dry on the seat of her pants. Good hygiene practices are a thing of the past apparently, she thought after she realized what she had done. She said goodbye to the old man and wished him well on the journey that she hoped would quickly take him home, hoping he had a passel of family to coddle him through the rest of his days.

She followed Kane across the camp to where their horses waited, already saddled and packed. "Thanks," she said, nodding at Birdie.

"You were doing a good job back there," he said. "I didn't want to take you away until I just had to." He swung his lanky frame onto the stallion's back. "The aides said you were as good as a woman at making those men feel more comfortable.

Alex hid a smile. "High praise indeed, I guess."

Afraid he had hurt her feelings, and guessing that because of her slight stature she had received many hurtful taunts, Kane added sincerely, "The aides did consider it high praise. Not many men are good around a sick bed. You gave those wounded men a few minutes of comfort, and that's something I couldn't have done, nor could most of the other men back there."

Alex smiled at him. "It's okay, Kane. I didn't take offense to what you said. I'm glad I could help in some way. Lord knows I sure didn't do much while the shooting was going on."

"It's a hard thing to get used to, Alex. Not that you ever really get used to having somebody shooting at you. But you did all right. I was proud of you. Colonel Parker would be, too."

"Where were we, anyway? What do you think they'll call this battle?"

Kane shook his head. "That won't get a name in the history books or on the map. That was just a little skirmish between two small outfits that just more or less happened up on each other in some deep Georgia woods and fought their way out of it."

" 'Little'? 'Skirmish'?" Alex shuddered, remembering the chaos of gunfire, broken bodies, screams, and the smell of death. "God help anyone who sees anything any worse than that."

"Well, it does get worse, Alex. I've been in battles where you just had to turn off your mind, because if it registered on the horror around you, you'd lose it. I've seen men literally torn apart by cannon blasts. Good friends who had to be identified by a birthmark or a ring or the holes in their socks because that's the only part of their body that was left."

Alex shuddered. "I know we won today. And seeing the backside of them damned Yankee blues was a wonderful sight. But I didn't see any glory, Kane. What's wrong with me?" *Maybe I'm just seeing this through a woman's eyes,* she thought. *Maybe there's some vital part missing in me that a man would have.*

"There's not much glory like you mean. War's been glorified by people who've never been shot at. Or had to shoot at someone else. For most of us, there's no glory in killing another human being. The glory comes later from the feeling you get when you limp off the battlefield and realize you've got all your parts intact and you've lost a minimum amount of blood. The glory's there when you've been fighting as hard as you can go all day, and you're just about ready to throw up your hands and surrender, and then you look through the smoke and the dust and you catch a glimpse of our stars and bars flying free. There's your glory. To know without doubt that whatever they can throw at us, we can pitch right back at them and give better than we got. Being certain that we're superior to them in all the ways that matter. And knowing that we offered our life for something we believed in, and being grateful that for today at least, we weren't asked to give it all. I guess that's glory enough for any man."

Alex nodded solemnly. "I'll do better next time, Kane."

He nodded. "I know you will."

Looking up at the darkening horizon, he urged his horse into a canter. "Better get going if we don't want to spend the night on the ground again."

They rode for about an hour, stopping only once to get a drink of water from a spring-fed stream that ran beside the path.

"Do you think we'll be coming close to any prisons, Kane?" Alex asked, as she wet her handkerchief in the stream and applied the cool cloth to the back of her neck. For once she thanked the Lord that she didn't have her usual mane of thick hair blanketing her neck and shoulder.

"I don't think so. You still thinking about looking up some Yankee?"

"Maybe. Or talking to some of the men there to see if they've ever heard of him."

"You want to tell me yet why you're looking for him?"

She shook her head, unable to speak, her mind echoing again with the man's voice.

He didn't question her further but looked at her carefully, noting the red splotches on her cheeks and the white knuckles that gripped Birdie's reins.

As he looked at her, his eyes narrowed, a knowing expression suddenly darkening his face. Certain he was coming close to the answer to a question that had been bothering him since hearing Alex's screams that morning, he found himself gripping his own reins a little tighter, hoping he could be there when Alex found the man he sought. *So the son of a bitch was a Yankee,* he thought. The hand resting in his lap tightened. *One more reason to put a few holes in some blue uniforms. Kill 'em all, and let the angels sort out the chaff from the wheat.*

After a couple more hours of companionable silence broken only by the creaks of the leather saddle and the snorting of the horses, Alex could see flickering lights just past a thicket of trees.

"Is that Rossville?"

"Yep. I was beginning to get a little worried we weren't going to make it. I've heard some rumors that there's some Union troops hunkered down in these parts, and I'd just as soon not meet up with them unawares. Much as I hate fighting, it beats sitting out the rest of the war in some rat-infested prison somewhere up North. We're both pretty good shots, but I don't think we could take out a whole outfit before they got us."

Alex shivered. "Where are we going to stay? Is there a hotel?"

Kane looked at her and in the dusky light she could see the play of a grin on his face.

"Well, it's sort of a hotel, I guess, although most people don't spend the whole night there. But I think I can get us a couple of rooms for the night." His grin got bigger. "And the best part is we won't have to sleep alone tonight."

"We didn't sleep alone last night either, you were just a couple of feet away," Alex said, a puzzled expression putting a frown on her face.

Kane looked at her quickly then raised an eyebrow. "Alex," he said hesitantly, "have you ever had a woman?"

Glad he couldn't see her blush in the deepening dusk, Alex swallowed hard. "How do you mean?" she asked, feeling fairly certain she knew the answer to her question.

"Have you ever slept with a woman—screwed her, made love to her, known her Biblically? You know . . . *had* her?"

Alex's blush deepened, and suddenly her ears roared with shock as she realized with sudden clarity what kind of "hotel" Kane meant. She had heard Teddy and Marcus joking about Miss Lydia's bawdy house in town and what went on there, and she had a sinking suspicion that such a place just might be Kane's destination. Her mind raced.

"There's this girl back home . . ."

"Have you ever slept with her?"

"Well, not yet, but I'm going to when I get back."

"Hell fire. You're smack in the middle of a war in case you haven't noticed, Alex. You may not get home. I think the nicest thing you could do for that girl back there is to get rid of some of that stress you're carrying around. And the best way to do that is under one of Pearl's sheets."

"No, really . . . I . . . I really don't think that would help at all. I'll wait outside for you, though, if you . . . need to."

"Do you like spinach?"

Thinking she must have missed something in Teddy and Marcus's conversations and in Verbena's motherly lectures, she questioned cautiously, "What does spinach have to do with it?"

Kane's laugh burst the silence. "Nothing! But I'll bet you didn't like spinach until you tried it, did you?"

"Well, no. But it's not the same thing at all. It's not that I don't like women. I do." *In fact some of my best friends have been women*, Alex thought with a hidden smile. "But really, tonight I'm just sort of tired, and I'd rather just get a bed somewhere and go to sleep."

"You'll be in bed before you know it, and you'll sleep like a baby after Pearl or one of her girls gets through with you," Kane promised.

"Pearl?"

"Pearl McVane. Red-haired Irish lass with velvet hands . . . and other parts to match. Folks come from all over for a night with one of Pearl's girls, and since I've known Pearl for a long time, I'm pretty sure I can talk her into spending the night with you herself."

He looked so proud of himself that Alex couldn't find the words to tell him how unnecessary, indeed how utterly impossible, his suggestion was.

"Really, Kane. I just don't think I'm up to it."

"Hell, Pearl's been known to get men 'up to it' who haven't been able to in years."

"That's not what I meant, Kane." Alex bristled, her mouth set in annoyance. "I didn't say I *couldn't*. I could if I wanted to—I just said I didn't want to." Lord, she thought. Here I am defending my nonexistent male sexual prowess. This being a man was getting more and more complicated, mentally as well as physically. Little-boy brains must be shaped differently from the start, she thought, for her girl brain reeled with the information she had acquired in the weeks since she'd shed her former life.

"Okay, we'll just let Pearl fix us some supper and we'll get cleaned up, then we'll see what happens."

Being quite certain that nothing would "happen" tonight, Alex agreed, her mouth watering in anticipation of some real food.

They hitched their horses in front of the neat, white-clapboard house that, except for its size, looked more like the home of an old-maid schoolmarm than what Kane said it was. Late-summer roses climbed up a trellis beside the porch, tingeing the cool evening darkness with their perfume. Lights shone behind most of the windows, bathing the yard in amber light.

"This is it. Bring in your saddlebags. You got a fresh shirt, or do you need to borrow one?" Knowing that Alex was doing a mental inventory of her saddlebag, he said defensively, "Besides what I put in there this morning."

Alex shivered, remembering the young boy in blue, and she offered another quick prayer for his soul. "Yes, I've got a fresh one."

"Good. We'll let a couple of the girls give us a bath, and then we'll relax while we eat. It'll be good to eat real food again, and even better to be able to smell the food instead of myself."

Alex had grown up being bathed by Verbena, so the thought of a woman giving her a bath didn't shock her, but she was suddenly overcome by giggles at the image that flashed through her mind of the poor soiled dove's shock at finding more—or rather less—than she had bargained for underneath this particular grey uniform.

Kane flashed her a quick look. "Are you okay?"

She sobered instantly. "Yes. But Kane, I want you to understand. I'll go in, and I'll eat with you, and I do want to take a bath, but I don't want any strange woman putting her hands on me. Okay?"

Before Kane could answer, the door of the little house opened and a woman dressed in the most garish costume Alex had ever seen came out onto the porch.

Shading her eyes from the lamplight, the woman stared at the two of them. "Are you boys in grey or blue?" she asked.

"Grey," Kane answered.

"Thank goodness," the woman breathed. "I've got me a couple of other boys in grey upstairs," she grinned, "or at least they was wearin' grey when they came in, and I sure don't want no trouble for them." As they walked into the lamplight, the woman took a closer look at the two new arrivals. "Praise the Lord, is that you, Kane?"

"It's me in the flesh, Pearl."

"And that's the best way to be," she said with a suggestive chuckle. "I swear you're a sight for sore eyes. I heard tell how bad it was up there, and I was afraid you wouldn't come back in one piece. A lot didn't."

"I'm lucky, Pearl. I was there for most of the worst of it, and so far, knock on wood, I've come through without a scratch." He shrugged and added, "Course it ain't over yet, and there may be a bullet out there with my name on it yet."

Pearl shuddered. "You hush that right now. The angels are a-lookin' out for you. I know. I asked 'em to myself."

She held the door open wide. "Y'all come on in and make yourselves right to home. We've got a big pot of stew on the stove and some cornbread, unless you'd rather head right upstairs." She waved toward the staircase that led up to a balcony that ringed the room. Muffled thumps, bumps, and giggles came from behind the dozens of doors that opened onto the balcony.

Alex felt her face flush. She looked down at the floor, hoping her blush wouldn't be too obvious in the flickering lamplight. She moved closer to Kane as he said, "Matter of fact, Pearl, we'd rather have a bath first, stew second, and a couple of your girls thirdly."

Alex cleared her throat. "Actually, Miss Pearl, I just want a bath and some stew. I won't be needing the company of one of your . . . uh . . . girls tonight." She cleared her throat again, and looked at the floor, missing the pointed look Kane gave the other woman, as he motioned for her to meet him on the porch for a private conversation afterward.

Pearl nodded over Alex's head as she said, "Let me help you take care of your horses, Kane, and then I'll take care of you two." She patted Alex on the shoulder. "Honey, you just go right on up them stairs and take the first room you come to. I'll send Silas up with some hot water for your bath." At Alex's panicked look she added gently, "There's a lock on the door. Nobody's gonna' bother you unless you want to be"—she looked sideways at Kane and grinned—"bothered."

Alex looked at her gratefully. "Thank you kindly, ma'am."

She picked up her saddlebags and started up the stairs. "Do you mind unsaddling Birdie for me, Kane?"

"Nah, you just go on up, and I'll take care of everything. You've had a tough few days."

Pearl and Kane watched until the upstairs door closed behind Alex, then Pearl whispered, "I've already had Silas and Lije take care of your horses."

Kane took her by the hand and led her out onto the porch. When they were alone, she hugged his neck and said quietly, "All right, Kane. What's the story with the little fellow? You looked like a proud daddy in there, taking his son on his first trip to the whorehouse. Where'd you pick that one up?"

"He come riding into camp a few days ago, and he just sort of attached himself to me. I don't think there's been too many people in his life who've been good to him. Colonel Parker sent him along with me to take a message up north a ways. That's where we're headed now. I feel sort of sorry for him, Pearl. Being such a wisp of a boy and all, I think he's had to take a lot of teasing. And Pearl"— his eyes fell to the porch floor, and he blushed, for the first time he could remember—"I think some Yankee bastard forced himself on him. I think maybe that's why he thinks he don't want no woman tonight. He had some nightmares the first night he came into our camp, and he was begging somebody not to touch him. From the screams I reckoned whoever it was didn't listen. He's pretty scrappy, but hell, if the other feller was a whole lot bigger than him, there ain't much he could've done. I'm figuring that's the only reason he's signed up, to find the son of a bitch who hurt him."

His eyes met Pearl's again as he shook his head. "It's right pitiful, Pearl. Makes me sick to think of some bastard hurting him." He shook his head sadly. "And he's got some girl waiting on him back home, too."

Pearl smiled. "I'll take care of him, Kane. Take care of him real good. Don't worry about him tonight. You just go on up to Jenny's room. She'll give you a good bath, some stew, and anything else you want."

She laughed and pointed at the bulge that was suddenly apparent in Kane's trousers. "Something tells me you won't make it all the way through that bath alone, Kane Stevens." She swatted his rear end playfully. "Don't y'all be gettin' the floor all wet now. My room's directly below Jenny's, and I don't want your old dirty bathwater drippin' on my things."

She opened the door and they walked back inside. She watched until he disappeared behind Jenny's door. "Lucky Jen," she said softly.

She smiled and looked up at the room Alex had gone into earlier. She took a deep breath, hitched up her skirt, and started up the stairs. "I think we need to have a talk, young man," she said beneath her breath.

Alex was sitting on the edge of the bed waiting for someone to bring her bathwater when the knock on the door came. She unlatched the latch and stepped back, panic freezing her motions as she watched Pearl saunter into the room. *Dammit all, she thought. How the hell am I going to get out of this one?* It seemed that the whores might be as hard, if not harder, to dodge than the bullets.

"Miss Pearl," she said, her voice cracking under the stress, "I don't want to hurt your feelings none, but right now I don't want nothing but a bath and something to eat. I'm tired, and I just don't think I could . . . do anything tonight." She looked at Pearl hopefully and said, "Maybe tomorrow," knowing that Kane had said they would have to be gone at first light.

Pearl sashayed seductively across the room, pushing Alex toward the bed. "Come on and take your clothes off for Pearl, sweetheart."

"Really, Miss Pearl. I don't want to be rude, but I don't want anything but a bath and a clean bed right now."

"What about something to eat? A minute ago you wanted something to eat." Pearl put her hands firmly on Alex shoulders and pushed her down onto the edge of the bed. She put one foot on the bed beside her, pulling her gown seductively up over one black web-stockinged knee. "I don't think you know exactly what you want, young man." She grinned leeringly. "But I do. And I'm going to make sure you get exactly what you really want tonight."

Alex's mind raced as she cursed inwardly. "Miss Pearl. Please don't do this," she pleaded. An idea dawned suddenly. "I've got a battle injury, Miss Pearl. And I can't perform yet. It'd be plumb embarrassing to me to try and not be able to." She gingerly pushed Pearl's foot off her bed and said hopefully, "But I sure could use that bath."

Unfortunately Pearl was determined. "Why, you poor thing. What you need is a good rubdown. Sugar, you just lay back here, and let's have some layin' on of the hands. I've been told I've got magic fingers, you know. I've been known to get men in the mood who haven't had a hard-on since God was a teenager."

"So I've heard," Alex said, her voice rising with frustration.

"You just lay right back here and let me make you feel good." She rubbed her hands over Alex's chest and trailed her fingers down toward her crotch. Alex jumped up as if she had been branded.

"Miss Pearl! I really mean it. I don't want to hurt your feelings, but you're beating a dead horse here, and there ain't no sense in it for neither of us. Don't you have someone else you could be . . . pleasuring?"

"Nobody who needs me as much as you do, darlin'."

"But that's just it, Miss Pearl," Alex almost wailed she was so frustrated. "I don't need you. And I don't want you. I just want to be left alone." She added wistfully, "And I do want a bath and something to eat."

Pearl looked at her for a minute, seemingly giving in. "All right, honey. Let's see if you feel better after you've washed some of that trail dust off'n yourself." She opened the door and motioned for the old black man who stood at the end of the balcony. "We're ready for that water now, Silas."

She held the door open as the old man brought several buckets of steaming water and poured them into the tin tub that sat in front of the window. "There you go," she said after the last bucket was emptied. "You can set there in the tub and look at the stars. Won't that be nice?"

Imagining how wonderful the warm water was going to feel to her saddle-weary body, Alex almost purred. "Yes, ma'am. It surely will be. And I thank you kindly."

She stood up, waiting for Pearl to leave the room. Instead she watched in horror as the woman walked over to the cane-bottomed chair sitting by the oak dry sink and sat down, arranging her skirts around her legs.

"Go ahead, honey, strip down."

"Huh?" Alex sat back down on the bed. *Oh shit, oh shit, oh shit,* she thought. *What now?* "I thought you were leaving me alone," she said, trying to hide her panic.

"Lord no, honey. What kind of a woman would I be to go off downstairs and leave an old wounded veteran like you up here to try to bathe yourself?" She picked up a bar of soap and a towel. "Come on, hon, take off them old, dirty clothes and get in here. Let's see what we've got under all that dust and grime."

Certainly nothing you're expecting, Alex thought dryly.

Pearl laid the soap and towel back down and walked purposefully toward the bed. "Don't you think you'd be more comfortable with that old uniform off?"

Alex began to sweat.

Pearl unbuttoned the top button of Alex's jacket, and Alex was sure her heart would burst out of the gap she had opened, it was pounding so hard. Her mind raced as she tried to think of a reason, any reason that Pearl shouldn't do what she was doing. She almost fainted when Pearl caressed her cheek lovingly, then couldn't believe her ears when Pearl leaned in closer and whispered softly,

"You'd sure be more good to me tonight if you had as much between your legs as you've got bound back on your chest, honey."

Alex sat there speechless as Pearl suddenly threw herself down on the bed beside Alex, and put a pillow over her face to hide her laughter. She's lost her mind, Alex thought.

It took a minute for her words to register in Alex's befuddled mind, then she realized with horror what Pearl had meant. "Wh—what?" she stuttered, as the bed shook with Pearl's giggles.

"Oh, come on honey, you didn't fool me for a minute! Hell, I knew you were a girl when you walked in the room tonight." She leaned back against the pillows, wiping the tears from her eyes. "Oh, if you could have seen the look on your face! 'Oh, please, Pearl, not tonight . . . I've got an old injury.'" She sat up and breathed a deep breath, giggles still shaking her body as she patted Alex on the knee. "It's okay, honey, you're safe for tonight. No big, bad whore's gonna' force herself on you. Now, get out of those clothes and get in that tub. You can tell me your story while you get cleaned up."

"But how did you know?" Alex wailed, crestfallen at how quickly her disguise had been seen through. She was sick at the thought that now Kane was going to know how badly he'd been fooled. He had been such a friend to her, and she knew she could trust him. It would break her heart for him to find out that he couldn't trust her the same. "You won't tell Kane, will you? Please. Promise me."

"Good Lord, honey. I've seen women in all kinds of uniforms and disguises. You'd be surprised what some men ask for. As it happens, I've got a couple of sister-boys who come in here, and the only way they can get it up for a woman is if she's dressed like a man, especially if she's dressed like an army man. I usually tousle up one of my girls' hair and put some dirt on her face, and she'll look just like you. Only difference is that you cut your hair." She reached out and touched the thick, dark curls. "Shame, too. I'll bet it's a glory when it's long."

"Are you going to tell him?" Alex asked again.

"Tell who—Kane? Why should I? Maybe what this war needs is a few more women fighting in it." At Alex's look of gratitude she went on, "You're not the first, you know. I've lost a couple of girls to the army. One to the cavalry, and one to the infantry. Maybe you'll happen up on them."

She took the soap and began to wash Alex's neck and back. It had been weeks since the last time Verbena had helped Alex bathe, and since it had quickly become evident to Alex that baths and army life didn't mix, she had sorely missed the luxury. "Mmmm," she breathed. "You have no idea how I've missed this."

"Girl like you who's used to having somebody wait on her, why'd she want to cut off her hair and join the army?"

"Cavalry, actually. I ride better than I walk, and I can shoot better than I do either."

Pearl shrugged. "Whatever. But what happened to make you want to leave a safe home?"

"If it had been safe, I wouldn't have ever wanted to leave," Alex said with a catch in her throat.

She told Pearl the entire story, from the Yankee's attack, to Del, and finishing with Aunt Matilda's abandonment. "So you see, I don't have anything left except the chance to get revenge. To get revenge, I have to find Rafe Peterson from Pennsylvania. And what better chance would I have to find him than to sign up with an army that's lookin' for him . . . and a few thousand other men just like him, too. "

Pearl shook her head. "Revenge is a curious thing. And it ain't always as sweet as you think it'll be, Alexandria. Better be sure it's worth running the risk of getting your own head blown off, to find this one man out of the thousands. What are you going to do if you find him, anyway? Yell at him? Tell everyone what he did?" She shook her head, curls tossing wildly. "You can't shame a man like him. Shoot him? Castrate him? What can you possibly take from him that will be enough to make up for what he took from you?"

Alex frowned. "I don't know. I guess I may not know until I actually find him." Her eyes flashed. "But I *will* find him, Pearl. And I'm pretty creative. I'll come up with something when the time comes."

Her voice grew soft and her expression penitent as she added, "I have learned one thing, though, Pearl. You're right. Revenge is a dangerous thing. And it can't be bought with somebody else's blood." Her eyes dropped to the floor. "I did something I'm right ashamed of, Pearl. When I first left home and started looking for an outfit to join up with, I came up on two Union soldiers taking a rest. Brothers. I know they were, because they looked just alike. I looked at them, and I'll swear they both had Rafe Peterson's leering face on their blue-clad shoulders. So I talked to them long enough to get some information out of them, and then I shot them both. Right between the eyes." She grimaced. "You know what's funny? I'd do the same thing again today, but for different reasons. Today I'd know that they could be carrying maps or messages that could mean ruin for a cause I believe in and men I've come to care for. But some mother lost her sons because I took out my anger on them for something someone else did. I can't help but think I did a wrong that I won't ever be able to right, because I took their lives for the wrong reason . . . if there ever is a 'right reason' to kill somebody. But at least if I did it today, I'd be able to live with it easier."

Pearl patted her shoulder. "Come on, honey. Let's get you dried off and in bed." She looked at Alex standing there in the lamplight. "I'll bring you a tray up from the kitchen," she said, knowing that even the most addlebrained of men would recognize Alex's sex in a minute, no matter how she was dressed, if they saw her sleepy eyed and fresh-smelling from her bath. "In the morning, I'll help you get strapped back into that getup," she said, motioning to the pile of bindings on the floor. She grimaced, and rubbed her chest. "Thank the good Lord I can let my girls run free. I don't think I could stand having them all bandaged up."

Alex grinned at her description. "I don't think I've ever heard breasts called that exactly," she chuckled.

Pearl shrugged, and then joined her chuckles. "All right," she said affecting a drawing room voice, "I do not believe I could bear it were my mammaries bound in such a tight fashion against my body.'" The two women giggled together.

"You know, you can sound like a—"

"—like a regular woman? A true lady of the South?" Pearl finished Alex's sentence, one eyebrow raised questioningly. "You're not the only one with a story," she said enigmatically as she opened the door. "I'll be back in a minute with a bowl of hot stew for you."

She left Alex alone with her thoughts for several minutes, then Alex heard footsteps outside her door. A voice whispered, "Alex, are you all right?"

Her heart raced. "Yes, Kane. I'm fine. Uh, are you okay?"

"Never better. How's it goin' with Pearl? I saw her coming back down the stairs."

"It's . . . uh . . . going real well, Kane. Thanks. She's coming back in a minute. We're not . . . um . . . done yet."

"Good!" Kane silently clenched his fist in a sign of victory. *Bless her heart, Pearl's done it again,* he thought. Aloud he said, "Well, that's great. I'm in the last room down the hall, if you need me tonight." He grinned at the closed door. "Lord knows, with Pearl, you just may need some help." He walked away chuckling, leaving Alex fuming on the other side of the door.

"'Need his help' indeed," she said huffily, then dissolved into giggles at catching herself defending her male prowess once again. "Nope, Mr. Stevens, I don't think I'll be 'needin' your help' at all with the lovely Miss Pearl tonight," she said as she strutted around the room.

After she ate the delicious stew that Pearl brought to her room, Alex snuggled into the downy quilts and was almost instantly asleep. She never knew when Pearl crawled in beside her and was surprised the next morning to wake up and find Pearl's arm sprawled across her body.

"Good morning," she said quietly.

"Mmmm? Is it morning already?" Pearl yawned and stretched. "How'd you sleep?"

"Like a babe. I sure wish I could fit this mattress in my saddlebag. I hate sleeping on the ground like the very dickens," Alex said, with a languorous stretch. "Gosh a'mighty, it's nearly daylight. I'd better be dressed when Kane comes to get me."

Pearl giggled. "You know, I can believe that some stupid colonel would sign you up for the army, and I can believe that a lot of tired old men wouldn't look at you twice, but I have to say I'm disappointed in Kane. That boy's a real connoisseur of women. I can't believe he hasn't caught on."

"I don't know, Pearl. I catch him looking at me funny sometimes. I don't know what he's thinking, but it makes me nervous."

"Honey, I promise you he don't suspect a thing. In fact, he's looking at you funny because he's worried about you. The dumb rascal did figure out that you were raped, but he imagines that some sister boy grabbed you. He has no idea that you're a woman. Trust me. And after I tell him what an absolutely wonderful lover you are, there won't be a doubt in his mind."

The two women were still giggling conspiratorially when

Kane knocked on the door. They had bound Alex's chest again, and she was once more dressed in Confederate grey. When she had complained about her ragged uniform, Pearl had brought out a fresh, clean uniform that she said had been left by a former customer.

"Alex, are you up yet?"

"Honey, if he gets up again I'll die, I swear," Pearl called to the door, stuffing a lacy handkerchief in her mouth to muffle her giggles. She began rumpling the bed and threw the pillows on the floor. She pulled one arm of her gown down off her shoulder and tousled her hair before she nodded for Alex to let him in.

Kane sounded embarrassed. "Uh, yeah. Well, good—Alex, are you ready to go?"

Alex opened the door. "Yep. I'm ready. Do you want me to saddle the horses for you?"

"Yeah, if you don't mind." Kane's gaze took in the rumpled bed, not missing Pearl's disheveled hair and gown. "Looks like you two got along just fine," he said, a twinge of jealousy in his voice.

"Like a house afire," Pearl said, reaching out and patting Alex's butt as she walked past her to the door.

They watched her walk down the stairs and out into the dark morning. "I'll tell you Kane. You may be right about him being attacked and all, but it ain't hurt his performance a bit. That little feller packs quite a wallop"—she winked at him—"if you know what I mean."

"Are you sure about that, Pearl?"

"I'm sure three times over." Pearl nodded.

"Three times?"

Pearl nodded again.

"Hell, I was just able to twice, and I ain't had a woman in near two months."

Pearl shrugged her shoulders, her gown slipping even further down her arm. "All I can say is that still waters run deep." She leaned over and put a hand on Kane's arm. "You look after him for me, will you Kane?"

He gave her a quick peck on the cheek and nodded. "I surely do miss you, Pearl."

"Honey, you know we've been better friends than we ever would've been lovers."

"I don't know about that. I think maybe we coulda set the

sheets on fire."

"Yeah, but you have to admit it's nice to just sit and talk, and that's something we've always been able to do."

"Are you sure you're doing what you want to do here, Pearl?"

"Of course I am, or I wouldn't be doing it."

"I hate to think of you—"

"—whoring? Go ahead and say it, Kane. It's what I am now. A whore. But I'm proud to say that I'm the best there's ever been in these parts. Nobody made me what I am, I did it myself."

"Do you need anything, Pearl? I can send you money if you need it."

"Aw, you dear, sweet man. But I'm doing okay. I've got five girls working pretty much full time. Four who think they're ladies, and one who truly is. Four with white skin, one with black. We can fill pretty much any request any man that drops in might have. Men will pay for the company of a lady when their bellies are groaning for food and they have to make a choice between the two. The fact that I always offer them a good supper afterward keeps them coming back here. So far at least, we haven't wanted for anything, anymore than everyone else around is wanting."

She giggled. "Do you know that Earl himself has paid us a visit here?"

Kane was astonished. "Good God! Your ex-husband, here? How'd he find you? What happened?"

"About what you'd expect. He didn't have any idea I was here. He sauntered in, expecting every girl in the place to fall all over themselves for a chance at him, and then when he saw me he went as limp as a dishrag. Even Lisbeth couldn't get him up, and she's the best I've got—besides me, of course, and I sure as Hades wasn't going to lie with him. Not ever again. I made sure he understood that if he laid a rough hand on one of my girls I'd kill him." Her voice was grim. "And I would have too. I've learned a lot since I left the Honorable Mr. Bartlett."

Alex returned to the door.

"Kane, the horses are ready. Are you coming?" She looked at the two of them hesitantly, sensing that she'd come in the middle of a very private conversation.

"Yeah. We'd better get on the road. We've still got about a ten-hours' ride to Chattanooga, and then who knows how long it'll take us to find Johnston's men."

Pearl reached out and gently touched Kane's face. "You take care of yourself, now, you hear?"

"I hear. And you do the same. If the Yankees get too close, you take your girls and head out for Atlanta. You'll be safe there."

"I know. I will." Pearl kissed Alex on the cheek. "You two watch out for each other. You're two of my favorite men-folk. I'd hate for anything to happen to either one of you."

Alex hung behind as Kane walked down the stairs. She returned Pearl's kiss on her cheek. "Thank you so much for everything, Pearl. When all this is over, I hope we can stay in touch."

Pearl smiled warmly. "Honey, you don't have to say that. I know a woman like you don't have much in common with a woman like me. When all this is behind you, you just get on with your life, and don't worry none about me."

Alex shook her head. "For one thing, I'm not a 'woman like me' anymore. And secondly, we have more in common than you realize, Pearl. And I'd be honored to call you my friend."

Pearl reached out and touched Alex's cheek tenderly. "You're one hell of a woman, Alexandria Latham. I envy your tenacity in going after what you believe in. Don't you worry about wrongs you think you've done. You're a good person, and you'll make the right decisions."

Kane happened to look up at that moment, as the two figures at the top of the stairs hugged each other. "Dammit, Pearl don't overdo it," he grumbled.

He saw Pearl reach out and gently touch Alex's chest and wondered what they found so richly amusing.

"Take good care of the girls for me" were the words he couldn't hear, but he could hear their laughter all the way downstairs and out onto the porch.

Chapter Six

They rode in silence for most of the day, both of them thinking of the events of the night before. Finally Kane smiled at Alex and said nonchalantly, "So you ended up having a good time after all, did you?"

The lines in Alex's face softened, thinking what a good friend she had found in Pearl. "One of the best nights of my life," she said honestly.

Kane smile grew wider. "Good. I don't like to say I told you so. But I did, you know."

He was spared her bantering reply as suddenly the air was split with rifle fire.

"Stay low!" Kane yelled, as he spurred his horse into a gallop.

Fast on his heels, Alex leaned over Birdie's mane, praying she could stay in the saddle. She could hear hooves behind her, and she knew that whoever had fired on them was gaining on them fast.

Suddenly Birdie seemed to rise in the air, and before she could straighten up out of the way, the saddle horn hit Alex squarely in the chest. She lost her breath and saw stars for a moment, then realized she had lost her grip along with her breath. Her world tilted and then turned black.

~ ~ ~

"He's coming around," she heard someone say, and then she was aware of a groan and a curse. With surprise she realized the sounds had come from her. *When I get back home it's going to be really hard to keep from cussing,* she thought with a smile. *It's a wonder I haven't spent more time speechless in my life, since it sure seems like now there are sometimes that a cuss word is just the only thing that'll do.*

She opened her eyes, and the smile faded from her lips. Everything was quite fuzzy, but she could see well enough to realize that the man standing over her was dressed in blue.

"Who are you?" the man demanded. Alex blinked and could

make out an officer's badge of some sort on his shoulder.

"Who are *you?*" she asked, with what little breath she could muster.

"Silence. You are now a prisoner of the United States Army. I will ask the questions, and you will provide the answers."

Alex shook her head, trying to clear the webs from her consciousness.

Thinking her motions were meant to convey a refusal to cooperate, the man in blue took her firmly by the arm. "You apparently did not understand me, you damned Reb. That wasn't a suggestion, that was an order. What is your name? And who is your commanding officer?"

Alex rubbed the back of her head, wincing as the movement of her arm brought a sharp ache to her chest. "Alex McKinley, sir."

"Is that your name, or your officer's?

"Mine."

Your rank?"

"Private."

"What were you two men doing out here by yourselves? Looking for anyone or anything in particular?"

Alex felt a momentary panic. Kane. Had he gotten away? Where was he? Her mind raced as she searched for a story to cover their mission.

"We were visiting a whorehouse," Alex said, her voice wavering.

The man's lips twitched. "I see. Was this with your superior's blessing? Or were you AWOL?"

"No sir, I mean yes, sir," Alex shook her head again. "Oh, my head hurts."

"Your head's gonna' be the least of your problems," the man said, "if you don't decide pretty soon to cooperate." His hand tightened painfully on her arm.

"We were headed to Atlanta to scout out some horses." Alex's mind quickly patched together a story she hoped sounded plausible.

"Horses? In Atlanta? Somehow I never pictured Atlanta as the horse capital of the South," the man said sarcastically.

"Well, not usually." Alex warmed to her story. "But we were meeting a man from Arkansas who was bringing a string of horses to replace the ones that keep getting themselves killed." She shook her head. "I surely do wish y'all could shoot a little better. I've done had two horses shot out from under me already." She shrugged, hoping she sounded as dumb and uneducated as the Yankees seemed to expect from Southern folk. "Of course, I guess if y'all shot better, I wouldn't be here on my way to Atlanta now, would I?" She grinned a dim-witted grin and winked at the officer.

"You should be aware that we realize you weren't headed toward Atlanta," the man said quietly, in a voice edged with steel.

Alex looked down at the ground for a moment as her mind ran through a number of possible excuses. "No, sir. Actually, we'd done been to Atlanta. On the way back we took a little detour. See, Michael's got a girl down this a ways, and he had a hankerin' to see her, so we figured the captain wouldn't know no different if we took a couple of days longer to get back with them horses. We figgered we could tell him as how the horses broke loose and we'd been hunting 'em for a couple of days. Michael felt sorry for me not gettin' none while he was with his girl, so he took me to a whorehouse he knew about in these parts on our way back to where we had hid the horses." She looked up hopefully. "And that's the God honest truth." It rankled her that she had to make an insincere oath in the Lord's name, but she rationalized that since it was made to a Yankee, God would surely understand.

The man looked at her skeptically, loosening his grip on her arm. "Who were you meeting to get those horses?"

"I ain't rightly sure of the name," Alex said, frowning. "It was McPeters, or McPherson." She shrugged. "You know, one of them Mick kinda names."

The man looked over Alex's shoulder. "You ever heard of somebody with a 'Mick kinda name' with horses in Arkansas?"

Alex jumped when a deep voice behind her said, "Well, sir, there is a David McAlbert, but I thought he was selling all his stock to the Union."

She suddenly realized there were two other Union officers standing behind her, both with guns trained on her. Her mouth went dry.

"Apparently he's buttering his bread on both sides."

"Sir, should I send word to Captain Butler that we've got a prisoner who may have some information we need?"

Alex's eyes widened, imagining what means of torture they might have at their disposal to make her talk. Seeing the panic that flashed in her green eyes, the officer's eyes narrowed. "You don't have anything to worry about, son, unless you're carrying some information that you're not sharing with us."

"I've told you everything I know," Alex said. *And then some,* she added to herself. "I didn't even have the directions. Michael knew where we were going, since he was from around here, and he had met this man once before to get some horses, so I was just more or less along to help keep the horses in line. I don't even know where we're supposed to meet up with our outfit. Michael's the one who knew the way." *Dear Lord,* she prayed, *please let Kane have gotten clean away,* knowing that if he were caught he'd have some serious explaining to do, and almost impossibly, since he wouldn't have any idea how to collaborate on her fabrication.

As if reading her mind the officer said, "Well, whoever this 'Michael' is, it seems that you men nabbed the wrong part of this particular duo."

"Hell, they wouldn't have caught me if my horse hadn't stumbled," Alex boasted with sudden bravado.

The man laughed. "You may be right, son. I do hate to admit it, but I've never seen horsemen like you Johnny Rebs." He looked at her closely. "How old are you anyway, boy?"

"Seventeen."

He looked at her for a moment longer and then shook his head. "This has become a war of babies. I swear when this started I felt like a spring chicken, and now I'm feeling more and more like an old rooster as the men filling these uniforms just keep getting younger and younger."

"And a lot of 'em won't get a chance to get any older," she said sadly.

"That is a sad fact, young man," the man patted Alex on the shoulder. "But maybe you'll be one of the lucky ones. At least you won't be seeing any more battles. If you can live through prison, you'll get a chance to dandle some children on those knees someday."

Alex's heart sank. She had maintained a hope that when they realized she knew nothing and was unimportant in any master plan they would let her go. Those hopes were dashed by his words.

"Excuse me. I don't know exactly what protocol you follow when taking someone prisoner, but I'm sort of at a disadvantage here." She looked around. "Y'all know who I am and where I'm

from, and you even know where I'm goin' now, but I don't know
y'all from Adam's housecat."

One of the men snickered. "You know, no matter how much I
hear you people talk, it still makes me laugh."

Alex shot him a venomous look. "And I guess y'all think you
don't sound funny to us?"

The man shrugged. "Hell, it doesn't matter anyway. This is all
going to be over soon. When Rosecrans gets his men to
Chattanooga and joins up with Grant, there'll be hell to pay for all
you damned Johnny Rebs. There won't be enough of you left
talking to keep us entertained anyway."

"Shut up, Travis," the man with the officer's stripes said. "Keep
flapping those gums and I'll shut them for good. You never know
what ears are hiding in these bushes. This young fellow won't be
able to do much damage, but surely you realize you're gabbing
about information that is crucial to our effort."

The man looked abashed. "Sorry, sir."

"Well, what are we going to do about you?" The officer turned
his attention to Alex once more. "Since it appears you'll be with us
for a while at least, I see no reason we should not introduce
ourselves, maintaining some semblance of civility. I am Captain
Jacob Sullivan, and this is Lieutenant Josef Peterson, and the big
fellow over there is Lieutenant Travis Tyler."

Alex's legs went weak. "Did you say Peterson?" she asked, her
voice quivering with emotion.

"Yes, why? Do you know some Petersons?"

"I have indeed heard the name Peterson." Alex chose her
words carefully. "But the name didn't go with that face," she said,
realizing that the slight build of the man in question did not fit the
shadowy image she carried in her mind. "Do you know a Rafe
Peterson?"

"Rafe Peterson . . ." Sullivan paused and narrowed his eyes
momentarily. "Do you know where's he from?"

"All I know is somewhere in Pennsylvania. And he's a big
fellow, too. Real dark complected, rough voice." *And rough hands
and a big knife,* she thought sadly, her mind flashing again on the
horror that he had brought into her life.

"I've heard the name, but I don't know him. He's not a relation
as far as I know. I'm from Kentucky," the man introduced as
Peterson said.

"That's the man that General Craig brought into his outfit, isn't it?" said the slim man standing slightly away from the other two. He moved closer. "He's been doing some special, uh, work a little south of here. I hear he has some . . . friends who live there that he visits quite frequently."

Alex realized the men were speaking in some sort of code, but she couldn't decipher it. Whatever they meant, it was enough to hear that they knew the man she looked for.

The captain nodded. "Yes, I do believe you're right." He turned to Alex and said softly, "How did you meet Lieutenant Peterson? Were you a contact, or did you meet him by accident?"

"Very much by accident," she said coldly. At the questioning look the men gave her, she said evenly, "Your Captain Peterson raped my sister. I plan to find him and kill him. If indeed you know him and have any contact with him, you might share that piece of information with him."

One of the men laughed. "You may have sort of a problem doing that, son," he said. "For one thing nobody finds Peterson unless he wants to be found, that's why he's so good at what he does. And in the second place, you talk mighty big for a fellow who's standing in an enemy camp without a firearm and with a one-way ticket to Monroeville."

Alex said firmly, "I didn't say I had set a date to do it. I just said I plan to do it. He will pay."

The captain looked at her with sympathy darkening his hazel eyes. "I understand how you must feel, private. And I will pass along your grievance about Peterson to the general. But surely you realize that in wartime things are done that would never be accepted in peaceful times."

Alex's eyes met his unblinkingly. "I know that some men, in blue as well as grey, use the excuse of war to do a lot of despicable things to other men . . . and women," she said. "But that doesn't make it right. And it shouldn't make it acceptable. I admit I've fired my gun in the direction of a few blue-coats, but not before they aimed theirs first at me. And I've felt nothing but pity every time I watched the last breath of any man, no matter what color of cloth covered his heart."

She turned and walked to the edge of camp. Hearing three rifles ease off their safety, she turned around and said sarcastically, "You don't have to shoot me in the back. I know when I'm outnumbered. I'm not stupid, no matter what you may think of us Johnny Rebs."

"At ease, men," she heard the captain say. He walked toward Alex. "Until we decide what to do with you," he said, "you may move around at will within this camp. One of the men will stand watch. If you don't make any overtures toward escape, I see no reason to tie you up. However," he added, his voice hardening, "if you even give the impression that it is crossing your mind to attempt to escape, I will give the order to fire, and despite your opinion of Federal marksmanship, I assure you my men won't miss."

"I understand," Alex said simply.

Her mind was already running through every possible scenario of escape, with each idea abruptly hitting a dead end. She spent the rest of the day pacing back and forth in the middle of the clearing the Union officers were temporarily calling home, until finally the men told her to sit down before they shot her simply because she was driving them crazy. She found a mossy spot beneath a pin oak tree and sat there, idly digging a small hole in the dirt with the sharp end of a broken twig. She cringed every time she heard a rustle in the forest behind her, fearing that Kane either had been discovered and was being dragged into camp or was planning to do something stupid, risking his own safety to try to save her.

By the time the sun went down behind the hill to their left, her nerves were frazzled to the point that she almost jumped out of her skin when she heard the captain's voice.

"I thought you might be hungry. Heaven knows you've walked enough around here today that you should be ravenous." He smiled as he held out toward her a tin plate filled with beans and small piece of jerky.

Alex entertained the thought of tossing the food back in his face but realized the stupidity of the idea almost immediately. Not only had the officers treated her so far with kindness and dignity, but if escape became possible, she would need all the energy she could muster to stay ahead of the boys in blue.

"Thank you," she said.

"Wait until after you've tasted it before you thank me," the man said dryly. "It's little more than pig slop, but it's the same thing we're eating, if that makes it more palatable."

"It can't be worse than what I've had the last few weeks," Alex said, her stomach grumbling at the sight of the full plate. She took the plate from him and began nibbling at the edges of the piece of jerky.

"Why just the last few weeks?"

"That's when I joined up."

"Where were you before that?"

"At home. With my aunt."

"What made you decide to join the Confederates?"

Alex looked at him and said honestly, "I want my life back. The one I had before this damned war started. You people came down here and you've turned the lovely lady our land used to be into an old, worn and torn woman. I want it to be over. And I'm willing to give whatever they ask me to give to make it be over faster. At the same time I intend to avenge my . . . uh, my sister's attack."

The captain nodded. "In the first respect, we share the same feelings, Private McKinley. I too just want to go home. To the home I used to know. If it's still there."

"Where are you from?"

"Indiana." A longing note in his voice told Alex that he loved and missed his home as much as she loved and missed her own.

"This is hell, isn't it?" she muttered. "It certainly does make you wonder. If you and I can sit like this and share a meal and a conversation without trying to blow each other to Kingdom Come, then it certainly seems as if our leaders could have sat down together and come to some sort of compromise."

The captain shrugged. "They tried. It just wasn't possible. They couldn't come to terms that both sides could live with."

Alex snorted. "Couldn't, or wouldn't? And how many thousands of men have already died because of their pigheadedness? I wonder how fast they'd have called for war if they'd thought that they themselves were going to be facing down the business end of somebody's rifle."

They sat there in companionable silence, listening to the crickets and the night birds. Somewhere in the distance a coyote howled, and Alex shivered.

"It's a lonely world you've got down here, McKinley."

"It doesn't seem lonely to me. It seems peaceful." Her mind went back to the conversation she had had with Kane on their first morning. He had said he thought the peace he felt sitting alone in the dawn made it worth fighting for. She knew how he felt. She was filled with a fierce resolve to find a way to escape.

Sullivan cleared his throat and started to speak several times before finally saying, "You said you had visited a brothel near the place you were captured. I wondered if perhaps it was an establishment run by"—his voice hesitated and broke for a second—"Miss Pearl McVane?"

Startled at hearing her new friend's name, Alex nodded.

The man smiled, and his handsome face lost its lines and furrows and became gentle. "Ah. How is sweet Pearl?"

"She's fine," Alex said. "And how do you know Pearl?" Instantly her face reddened as she surmised exactly how the man "knew" Pearl.

"Not the way you're thinking," he smiled at her. "I knew Pearl and her husband in what she probably calls her 'former life.' He was the judge in the town I grew up in." His voice was kind, and Alex knew the smile he wore was not for her but for a memory he cherished. "Pearl used to bake the best shortbread in the county, and as a young law student I used to find every excuse I could to visit Earl and ask questions about my law classes, just so I could sample her cooking."

Alex's mind fixed on one portion of his statement and she said with a muffled laugh, "Earl? Her husband's name was Earl? Earl and Pearl McVane?"

He laughed with her. "Yes. Unfortunate, wasn't it? But it wasn't McVane. When Pearl left him she took her mother's name. Earl's last name was Bartlett."

"What happened to him?"

"Far as I know, he's still a judge somewhere, but he was pretty much run out of our town after what he did to Pearl." His voice became granite hard. "And he knew that he was a dead man if he ever returned."

"What did he do?"

Sullivan turned to face her in the late-evening dusk. "How well do you know Pearl?"

"I thought I knew her pretty well, but she's only hinted that she had a 'past,'" Alex admitted. She added truthfully, "I consider her a very good friend. One of my best."

"Funny you would say that. Most men don't think they can have women as friends, only as sexual conquests. Paid for either with money or their name."

Alex tried to think like a man, a task made even harder by her throbbing headache that hadn't eased much during the day. "Pearl is a good woman," she said slowly. "Maybe if more women were like Pearl and more men were like you and me, none of us would have to play the games we have to play to be accepted in our society. Pearl just says it like she sees it. I heard her tell . . . Katy, one of her girls"—she began to sweat, knowing how close she had come to calling Kane by name—"that she might be a whore, but she wasn't ashamed. That she was good at what she did and she did the best she could. And that was good enough. I think she's right. We talk a lot, Pearl and me. Any man could learn a lot from spending time with Pearl. If he'd just really listen to what she said."

"Then she's not just a whore you paid for time with," the man mused. "That doesn't quite fit the story you told earlier, does it?"

"Well, it was all true, except that I didn't know it was Pearl's place we was goin' to. I was pretty surprised when she opened the door, let me tell you," Alex improvised quickly. "I had no idea where we were."

"Is she doing a brisk business?"

Alex grinned. "I counted six doors, and there was action behind every single one of them."

"Including Pearl's?"

Knowing that somehow her answer was important to him, Alex lied. "I don't think Pearl handles any business personally. She just has girls working for her."

He looked relieved. "You know, she was one of the best and kindest women I ever knew."

"She still is," Alex said softly. She looked at him for a moment, her eyes narrowed. "You loved her, didn't you?"

"I still do."

"Then why are you telling me, and not her?"

"I did tell her. And she told me she was a married woman and I should never say such things again."

"And you didn't?"

"I never got the chance again. When it might have mattered …" His voice trailed off for a moment.

"I found out that Earl had come home drunk one night," he said, his voice empty as he recounted a memory that Alex knew must run over and over in his mind, much as her own was filled with the evening her own nightmare began. "And Pearl mentioned to him that I had been there earlier and he had just missed me. Even though he knew I was really there to see him and it had been he himself, never Pearl, who was unfaithful to their marriage, he went mad. He started hitting her. He almost killed her. And when I found out, I could have killed him." Alex saw his hands tighten into fists. "I called him out, but he was too much a coward to face me. Pearl lost a baby that night, and Earl tried to make everyone believe it was mine."

The lines in his face grew deeper as his voice dropped to almost a whisper. "God, I wish it could have been." He shrugged, "Of course, if it had been I would have killed him with my bare hands, and no man's law would have stopped me."

"What happened then?"

"Pearl just disappeared. I was gone for days looking for Earl, and when I went back to her home, she was gone. Just like that. One day she was there, and a friend of the family was visiting her. The next day she had vanished. Nobody knew where she'd gone, or what had happened to her. Then months later I heard from a friend in Atlanta who had been traveling near Rossville that he had encountered there the most charming madam I could imagine. From his description I could only guess that it was the Pearl I had known. I guess she figured that if Earl had thought her capable of such things, she would see how well the shoe fit. I don't know how she ended up down here, but I like to think that she finally found a home."

Remembering Pearl's warmth and her open smile, Alex said, "I think she has found the shoe fits her very well indeed. She seems very happy with the life she's chosen."

"Do you see her often?" His voice was thick with wishful yearning.

"Not often enough. This was a rush visit, just one night, so we didn't have a chance to really catch up. I hope to see her again soon for a lengthier visit."

Sullivan narrowed his eyes and looked at her for a moment. "By the bye, where are these horses you supposedly were on a mission to obtain?"

Alex plastered a regretful expression on her face, hoping she was a better actress than she was soldier. "On their way east to General Bragg, I would imagine," she said sadly. "With Michael

and my horse. Lordy, I'll miss her. I've had her since she was a
filly." She'd added a bit of truth, hoping it would make her sound
more convincing.

"Damn. We could have used some fresh mounts," Sullivan
said. "How much are you people paying for good horseflesh these
days?"

Although Alex had handled the transactions to sell much of
Uncle James's stock of horses to the Confederacy, and in fact knew
as much about the business as either Marcus or Teddy had, she
decided to continue her act of ignorance. "I don't know. Michael
handled all the money. I just know he kept saying that with the
amount of money we carried on the way over, we could have
jumped the lines and gone to Californey to sit out the war." She
added pensively, "I kinda wish we had done it now."

"And be shot for a deserter?"

"Dead's dead. At this point I don't figure I got much chance of
making it out of this war alive. If bullets don't get me, the dysentery
will. You know as well as I do that no prisoner is going to get food
that the government wants to send to their fighting men. We don't
do it, and I'm sure you don't either. It's another of those facts of war
you keep tossing at me."

Sullivan sat for a moment, looking up at the sky, then down at
his feet. He drew a deep breath and said quietly, "Private
McKinley. I am considering doing something very stupid. I'm not
sure I have the heart to send you into what I know awaits you at
Monroeville. Shooting at nameless faces dressed in grey, capturing
prisoners, and all the other parts of war I can do in good
conscience, knowing it is all for a good cause. Sending the young
friend of another very dear friend to a slow but nonetheless sure
death, however, is not something I'm so sure I can deal with. I'm
going to trust that you're telling me the truth. That you will forget
any information you may have inadvertently been privy to. And
that my letting you go won't jeopardize my cause."

Alex listened patiently, although she felt as if her heart was
going to jump through her throat.

Sullivan went on. "I'm in the middle of a mission that I simply
cannot foul up. Having you along would not only slow us down
but could bring attention to our party that I can ill afford." He drew
lines in the dirt with the toe of his boot as he contemplated his
decision.

When he spoke again, Alex let out a breath she hadn't known she was holding. "Tonight, when I tie you to assure my men that you will not escape, I will assume that if you found the ropes to be loose, you could escape into the darkness without arousing the guard on post. I would suggest that you run very quickly and very quietly toward the southeast. We have come some distance from where you were captured." He half-smiled. "That was some tumble you took. You were unconscious for quite some time. So don't waste time looking for landmarks. What happens from that point on will be entirely up to you."

He stood up briskly, as if having made the decision he had no further use of discussion, and held out his hand. "It was a pleasure to meet you, Private McKinley. Perhaps after all this madness is behind us, we can meet again and perhaps visit our old friend together."

He started to walk away but suddenly turned back toward her. "I wish you Godspeed on your escape, but if you are clumsy and my men catch you, do not expect my help again. And I will deny any accusations you might make toward me." The lines were back in his face, and for one brief, crazy moment Alex had to curtail the impulse to try to smooth them away.

Instead she nodded her acceptance of his terms. "I understand. Thank you, sir," she said simply. Without thinking about what she was doing, she gave him a snappy salute that he acknowledged with a nod and a smile.

"Do not make me regret my actions, young man."

Alex followed him back into the middle of camp and sat with the other men beside the glowing fire. She held her hands toward the yellow flames. *You can almost feel fall in the air,* she mused.

As if reading her thoughts, Peterson asked her, "How the hell do you people stand this weather? Today I sweated down to my drawers, and tonight I feel like I'm going freeze. It's a wonder you don't all die with influenza."

"We're just tough, I guess," Alex grinned. Remember Kane's earlier remark, she said with a laugh, "If you boys can't take it, you have my personal invitation to gather up your play-pretties and go home."

After another hour of shared conversation, Sullivan stood and stretched. "I think it's time we all tried to get a good night's sleep. I don't think there'll be a need to have a watch tonight. With just the three of us, it isn't likely that anyone will stumble on us in the dark. Put out the fire, though. There's no need to send a beacon to the enemy."

"But what about the prisoner?"

"I plan to tie Private McKinley's hands and feet," Sullivan said. "He won't be a problem."

Alex watched as he untied a length of rope from his saddle and walked toward her. The firelight captured the clear-cut lines of his face; the day's growth of beard gave him a devil-may-care look that the Alexandria of yesterday would have found quite attractive. Alex didn't spend much time on that thought, however, as she was intent at the moment on keeping her ankles and wrists as far apart as possible without being obvious.

When the ropes were tied to Sullivan's satisfaction, he patted her on the back. "Sleep tight, McKinley," he said loudly, and under his breath he added, "and good luck. And, boy, if you see Pearl before I do, tell her I said hello."

Alex smiled and nodded, then leaned back against the tree roots that would be her pillow.

She sat there awake, every muscle tense, until the steady breathing and occasional snores made her certain that everyone was asleep. She gently eased her hands from their restraints and sat up, working her feet loose from the ropes as well. She flexed them for a moment and then began crawling toward the edge of the clearing.

One of the men talked in his sleep and she froze in place, certain that he had awakened and spotted her shadow. When she reached the edge of the woods, she scrambled to her feet and began running, cursing the leaves that seemed as loud as cannon shots as they crunched beneath her feet. She ran until her sides felt as if they had hot arrows piercing them, then she braced herself against a tree to catch her breath. Suddenly strong arms spun her around, and she stifled a scream.

Chapter Seven

"Great God A'mighty, Alex!" Kane exclaimed in a muffled whisper as he leaned against the tree beside her for a moment, his breath coming in ragged gasps. "You run like a damned deer. I was just about to come in and get you with guns blazing, and then I see you just hop up and run out of there like the devil was after you. I took off on your heels, but I couldn't do more than just keep you in my sight. I swear, if you hadn't gotten winded, you'd've ended up in Chattanooga without me."

Alex was so thrilled to see Kane's familiar face in the moonlight that she almost hugged him. Remembering suddenly who she was, she simply laid a hand on his arm and said with a silly grin spread ear to ear said, "Good to see you Kane. I've been in somethin' of a mess, ain't I?"

Kane shook his head, returning her grin with a wry shake of his head. "That's putting it mildly, McKinley. I just about busted a gut when I looked back and found Birdie following me with an empty saddle. I started backtracking, and I saw them three blue-bellies with you. Sure had to whet my tracking skills though to follow you all day without them seeing me. Whew, you were sure lucky you were able to get away."

"Luck had very little to do with it," Alex admitted. "They let me go. Or at least the captain did. He tied me too loose on purpose."

"Stupid bastards." Kane grinned.

"No, he wasn't being stupid. He was being kind."

Kane looked disbelieving. "*Kind* ain't a word that you can use to describe them blue-coated sons of bitches, McKinley."

"It is for this one," Alex said stubbornly, remembering how gentle Sullivan's voice had been as he spoke of Pearl.

Kane shook his head. "Whatever you want to think," he said grudgingly. "Let's get our horses and get the hell out of here. Whether they meant to let you go or not, I don't want to be around when daylight comes and you're not there."

"Me either," Alex admitted, remembering Sullivan's warning. A Yankee prison had almost been her fate, and she didn't want to tempt destiny.

They walked back through the quiet night to where Kane had tethered their horses. They mounted and started their journey through the night toward Chattanooga.

"Thanks for holding on to Birdie for me," Alex said, burrowing her head in the mare's mane and breathing in the familiar scent. "I don't think I could stand being separated from her."

"She's an awful pretty mare," he agreed. "And she sure is attached to you."

"I raised her on a bottle," she explained. "I think she still thinks I'm her mother."

Kane laughed. "I don't think Patch ever mistook me for his mother, but I'd like to think he's pretty attached to me. I know I'd sure hate to lose him. When all this killin's over, he's going to help me make my dream come true."

"What dream?"

"When I was a little boy I visited a big horse farm with my daddy. There was some of the finest horseflesh in all of Kentucky, right there on one place. I watched some young colts frisking around some old-timers that had been put out to pasture, and I thought that was about the prettiest sight I'd ever seen. I swore then that someday I'd have my own farm, and everybody around would know that if a horse carried my stable name, it was the best money could buy." He fell silent for a moment, one hand caressing his big stallion's shoulder. "I sold my mama's place just before the war and took the money and bought old Patch. I guess I should have bought a cheaper stallion and a couple of mares, but when I saw him, I just knew I had to have him."

He ruffled the horse's mane. "The old son of a gun oughta thank me, too. The man who had him didn't care a flip about him. Said he was meaner than 'Old Patch'—meaning the devil, you know." At Alex's nod he went on. "That's why I named him that. His registered name is Silver Satin, or something like that. Real sissy-like. But he wasn't a sissy. He wouldn't let nobody curry him, and he'd put his business end toward you if you went in the stable with him. All the man's stable hands were scared of him. So they kept him in this little old stable so they could grab hold of his halter without having to actually go in with him. They'd get a couple of longe lines on him, take him to the mare that had to be serviced, and then when he was done, drag him back to his stable."

He shook his head. "Weren't no kind of life a'tall. Plumb broke my heart." He shrugged. "The man thought I was crazy when I offered to buy him, but that didn't mean he cut me no deal either. He had imported him from New York state, and I reckon I paid him for everything old Patch had cost him from the beginning."

He looked at Alex and grinned. "He wrote me a letter and offered me double my money for him back when his colts started dropping, said they was some of the best he'd ever had. Yep, when all this is over, me and ol' Patch are gonna' find us a little farm somewhere in a pretty little valley with lots of creeks and pastures with flowers in them, and we're just going to sit back and watch his kids grow up."

"It sounds lovely," Alex said with a catch in her voice. "That's what I've always wanted to do. My uncle had horses, some of the best, before he got in such bad health he couldn't take care of them. He sold most of them, and my aunt gave the rest to the army when the call came." She patted Birdie absentmindedly. "Birdie's the only thing left from his bloodline. And I think she's the best thing he ever bred."

"She's a beautiful mare," Kane agreed. "Maybe we can work out a deal to breed her to Patch when the time's right."

They rode in silence for a couple of hours, each deep in their own dreams. When dawn began covering the mountain with a pink and gold glow, Kane reined in his horse. "I think we can stop for a few minutes and get some rest," he said. "I don't think they'll bother chasing you this far—and besides, we're too far out of Yankee territory for them to feel comfortable."

"I don't know . . ." Alex squinted her eyes as she tried to remember what had been said in the camp last night that had so upset Sullivan. Suddenly it all came back to her. "Rosecrans and Grant are going to converge on Chattanooga and ambush Bragg. That's what those men were doing here, checking to see exactly where the Confederate forces were hunkered down in these parts."

Kane looked at her for a long minute, his brow wrinkling into a frown. "And just exactly how did you come to that conclusion?" he asked. "Did you forget to tell me about your Gypsy background?"

"No," Alex said exasperatedly. "I overheard the men talking last night, and Sullivan reprimanded them for talking about it out loud."

"Sullivan?"

"Their captain. He's the one who let me go."

"Look, McKinley, do me a favor," Kane said in exasperated tones. "Don't be tellin' nobody else that you got yourself captured by the Yankees and they just 'let you go.' Ain't nobody goin' to believe you. I sure as the red devil don't."

"I don't give a rat's ass whether you or anybody else believes me or not. They were not animals, Kane. They were good to me. They fed me, they fixed me a bed, and the one who tied me did a shoddy job . . . just like he'd said he would."

Kane shook his head. "If you want to believe that, go ahead. But I just say you got lucky."

Alex rolled her eyes in exasperation and decided to change the subject.

"It's hot today. It sure don't feel like fall, does it?"

Kane nodded. "It's Indian summer for sure. I don't know when I've seen this hot a weather in September. And the sun ain't even all the way up." He mopped his brow.

They dismounted and made camp, both of them falling asleep almost as soon as their bodies hit their bedrolls. When they woke up, the sun showed high noon, and Alex could hear Kane's stomach growling almost as loudly as her own.

"Do you know where we are?" she asked. "I got lost riding in the dark. We could be in Texas, for all I know."

"Didn't your daddy ever teach you how to ride by the stars?"

"My daddy died when I was little," she said, sadness creeping into her voice. "He wasn't around to teach me anything."

The sadness almost turned into tears when she thought of Teddy. "My cousin tried to teach me, but I'm hopeless. The Big Dipper always just looks like a flower to me, and I can't even find the North Star."

"Well, you'd better stick close to me at night then," Kane said. "We don't want you riding into enemy camp again."

"I didn't ride into that one. If you remember, I was following you when they started shooting at us."

"I was real worried about you back there, McKinley. I was afraid you'd be eatin' breakfast with George Washington this morning instead of with me."

Alex smiled. "You know, I never thanked you for coming back after me, Kane. It was a real decent thing to do, and I appreciate it. I owe you one."

"Shoot, you don't owe me squat. You'd have done the same thing for me, although I hope to the sweet Lord you don't ever have to." He shuddered. "I'd rather be shot down on some unknown field somewhere and let the buzzards pick my bones than to just fade away, forgotten in a prison somewhere."

Alex nodded. "That was what I kept thinking. I had been so worried about going into a real battle, and there I was wishing I was there instead of where I'd ended up. Life's funny, ain't it? My Aunt Matilda always said, 'You'd better be careful what you wish for, it might come true.' I guess she was right."

"Tell me about her, Alex."

Alex looked pensive. "There's not really a lot to tell. I was as close to her as her own sons. She and Uncle James had a horse farm down on the Alabama-Tennessee line. Like I said, they raised some of the best horseflesh in the South. Then Uncle James died, and we sold off most of them, keeping just a few of the best ones. He had given me Birdie's mother, and I kept her after breeding her to the best of the stallions before we sold him. Birdie's the product of six generations of Twin Cedar horses. Now I guess she's the last of the line. Just before I left, the cavalry had confiscated most of what was left that was of any account. Of course Aunt Tilly was glad to give them to serve the cause. I was surprised she let me keep Birdie, but I guess she knew how much she meant to me."

"Does she know where you are?"

"No, she just knows where I'm not."

"Don't you think she's worried about you?"

"No," Alex said sharply. "She's just glad I'm not there." She stood up and reached for Birdie's saddle and blanket. "I don't know about you, but I've got to have something to eat. My stomach's so empty it thinks my throat's been cut. Let's get out of here and go rustle something up."

Kane started to question Alex further, then decided to wait. He figured that Alex would tell him what he wanted him to know, when he wanted him to know it.

They rode for most of the day before reaching the Tennessee River, which wound its way around Chattanooga. They meandered along its bank for a few minutes, letting the horses drink small amounts at a time so they wouldn't colic. They had munched on some hardtack Kane had in his saddlebag, but they were both hankering for a real meal. They spotted a stooped old woman sitting on a porch and asked her for directions to any place that could provide them with food.

The woman rose and opened the screen on one of the two front doors. "Y'all come right on in and stay a spell. M' name's Elmirah Greene. I ain't got much, but what little I've got I'd be proud to share with boys wearing Confederate grey. My two boys rode off nigh onto a year ago wearing grey, and I ain't heard nary a word from neither of 'em since. I keep hoping every time I see a spot of grey coming around that bend that it's one of them. It ain't been yet, but I figger both of y'all's got a momma somewhere that'd be right tickled to know that somebody was fillin' up their boys' bellies. So, like I said, 'taint much, but you're welcome to what there is of it."

They followed her in the house and on into the bright kitchen. Whitewashed wood glistened in the sunlight coming through the cheerful yellow curtains. Watching the old woman bustling around her kitchen, whistling merrily, reminded Alex of Verbena. For a moment she allowed herself the luxury of thinking of home and remembering the good times.

"Do you live here alone?" Kane asked.

"Depends on whether you consider living with a cat and a dog 'alone.'" The woman scrunched her wrinkle-lined face into what Alex supposed was a grin.

Kane must have supposed the same thing, for he grinned back at her. "How long did you say your sons have been gone?"

"They left right after they heard what a bad time our boys had in Bridgeport. They was just fifteen and sixteen years old, but I couldn't make 'em understand what they'd stand to lose by joining up so young." She sighed and shook her head sadly, "I just hope the Lord's lookin' out for 'em." Her eyes got a bit misty, but her voice never wavered as she said, " I reckon there's a right good chance they're with him already, bein' as I ain't heard from 'em."

"Maybe they've written and the letters got lost," Alex said hopefully. "Lord knows our mail service is surely lacking."

Kane nodded in agreement. "I got a letter from back home last week that had been written two months ago. I wouldn't worry just yet. I'll tell you, it's true that no news is the best news."

The old woman smiled at them. "I swan, you do this old woman's heart good. I surely am proud that you picked my house to ride up to this morning."

Kane inhaled the smell of fresh bread cooking and said with an open smile at Alex, "I think we're the lucky ones, ma'am. I ain't had any fresh-baked bread since . . . well, I can't remember the last piece I had."

The woman patted his shoulder. "Honey, I wish I had some of old Piggy Sue left for you. That was our old sow," she explained, in answer to the question in Kane's and Alex's eyes, "but I fixed the last of her a couple of weeks ago to send over to the Widder Perkins. She got word that all three of her boys and her daddy had fell in the same battle. We don't know yet if any of 'em pulled through or not. Lord love her, I cleaned out my smokehouse for her and her babies, she's got them two little girls still at home, but iffen I'd had some idee that you boys would be a-comin' through, I'd have kept a little back."

She bustled around, opening up door after door in the cabinets and pie safes along the wall of the kitchen. "I surely do apologize for the stingy table I'm gonna have to set." Under her breath she began talking to herself. "Now, I know I put a jar of huckleberry jelly in here. I was planning to take some of it to Brother Jack and his wife next Sunday."

She gave a small whoop of delight and came out of one of the cavernous cabinets clutching a small jar. "Well, this ought to make dry bread go down a little better. I'll fix y'all some bread and jam to carry with you when you go. For now I've got some turnips that I cooked yesterday, and there's a couple of Irish potatoes, if you boys don't mind eatin' 'em cold. Or I could het 'em up if you want to take the time."

Kane looked longingly at the bread the woman was gingerly taking out of the old cookstove. "Ma'am, that there sounds better than any meal ever set before the president. You don't need to apologize a bit. I'd plumb forgot how good it felt to sit at a clean table in a bright kitchen and listen to somebody whistling as they fixed my dinner."

The woman grinned. "And it does me good to be able to set a table again for two handsome boys." Her face clouded. "I just hope and pray I get the chance to do it again for my own boys in this lifetime."

Alex patted her hand gently. "Miss Greene, you just keep on imagining those boys of yours rounding the corner, and I've got a feeling it'll happen."

The old woman's chin trembled. "I keep telling' myself that iffen they don't come back, it was the Lord's will—but God help me, I can't help wonderin' what I'll do without 'em." She cleared her throat and shook her head. "Oh well, what's done is done, and you can't change the past. You boys enjoy your dinner, and I'll go out back and see if I can rustle up some apples for dessert."

Alex picked up one of the sandwiches from the plate in the center of the table. "What do you reckon it is?" she whispered to Kane, who was also peeking at the grey mush oozing from the edges of the bread.

"I don't know. But I reckon I've eaten a sight worse in the last two years. And right now I'm so hungry I could eat just about anything." He gingerly took one bite and then quickly another. "Whatever it is, it tastes mighty good," he said between bites.

Alex bit into hers, realizing that Kane was right. No telling what it was—and she was quite sure she didn't want to know—but it tasted good, and there was enough of it to keep them both fueled up for the rest of the day. She was learning that in this new life, that was about all you could ask for.

Minutes later they both leaned back in their chairs, their appetites completely sated for the first time in weeks. "If I'd had a meal like that before Shiloh," Kane said, "I might have been able to send a few more blue-bellies home to their maker."

"You were at Shiloh?" Alex had heard and read the accounts of the bloody battle, and after seeing the hell a brief skirmish could bring, she could not imagine a battle that went on for hours and hours on end.

"Yes." Kane's voice was solemn. "And I hope that someday God grants me total amnesia where that day's concerned. I saw things that day that no man should live to tell about."

They both were silent for a moment, then Alex quietly spoke. "It sounds terrible." Before she could catch herself, she reached out and touched her hand lightly to his.

Kane jerked his hand back as if it had been burned. He looked at Alex strangely for a moment, and when he spoke again his voice was huskier than usual. "Some things are just best left in a deep

dark closet in your mind. Going in there can bring out beasts that
could devour the world if they were turned loose again."

She looked at him sympathetically. "I can't imagine it, Kane.
You know I can't help but wonder when it's all over if we'll all look
at each other and realize that we've given up way more than we
would have lost had we not gone to war."

Kane nodded. "I know. But don't ever say those words out
loud to anyone but me, Alex. They've hung men for treason who
uttered far less truths."

Her face turned white. "Treason? But I love this land. I'm
proving that by offering my life for her, ain't I?"

"I don't know. I'm not sure of anything anymore. I believe that
you're a good boy, Alex. But saying things like that won't go far
making some quartermaster believe it. It's best to just keep
thoughts like that to yourself."

She nodded sadly. "What kind of world are we helping to
make?"

He was spared having to reply by the reappearance of Mrs.
Greene. "Look here what I found you boys!" She proudly offered a
pie of some sort. "I was telling Mary Beth Steward about you boys
bein' here for dinner, and she wanted to give you this. It's an apple
pie, baked with the very last bit of sugar in Chattanooga."

Alex looked at the pie hungrily. "You know, about two
seconds ago I would have swore I couldn't eat a thing. But that
looks mighty delicious."

Kane grinned. "My mouth started watering when you walked
up the doorsteps. My mama always said I could smell an apple pie
a mile away. She used to tell Pa that if I ever run away, she wouldn't
have to do nothing but bake a pie to bring me back. Said that'd set
my heels to pushing my toes toward home."

They all laughed. As the chef from next door, Mrs. Steward,
joined them, they sat around the table, talking companionably as
they ate. Alex looked around the table and thought to herself that
they could be any family in any place. Instead they were strangers
brought together by a strange fate. Her throat grew tight as she
thought of the factors that had brought her to this moment. She
looked at Kane, strong and handsome, gentle and trustworthy; and
at the ladies, willing to go about their daily chores gallantly, with
smiles intact as if they weren't aware their small worlds were
crumbling around them.

In that instant she knew that whatever was asked of her to help maintain a way of life that would produce men and women like these, she would do without fail. No price could be too high. Her pie tasted slightly salty from the tears she could not shed.

Chapter Eight

After they had finished their feast, Kane and Alex walked out onto the porch and stood looking at the mountain that towered above the small cabin. The top was shrouded in a white mist, and for a moment Alex imagined what it would be like to be on the mountain looking down below through the gauzy film.

"Is that Lookout Mountain?" she asked Kane.

"Yeah. Pretty, ain't it? Me and my brother rode up to the top once, a long time ago when we came to visit my Aunt Prudie who lived in Chatty. You could see for miles and miles. A horse and buggy looked like a couple of ants crawling along a road made out of string. For a few minutes you could imagine you were a bird, you were up so high. If you ever get the chance to go up there, you ought to. It's quite a sight. Nearly always smoky, like somebody's campfire got smothered out, but on a clear day you can see pert near into forever."

"Mmmm." Alex pictured the view Kane described. "Does anybody live up there?"

"There's a couple of farmhouses and a little bit of farmland right on the top, but there ain't much you can do to homestead on the side of the damned thing but pray that your toehold holds out."

"I hope we've got some scouts up there watching for Yankees," Alex mused.

"Hell, they won't get nowhere near here this time. We learned our lesson the last time they came through Chatty. I heard tell there's a batch of them headed to Murfreesboro, but they won't last long. They'll be headed back up north fast as they go, with their tails tucked between their legs. When they run into our boys that are holed up at Stone's River, they'll know quick enough that they've met their match," Kane boasted.

Alex looked skeptical. "I don't know, Kane. Ain't nothing in this damned war gone like whoever's supposed to know said it would. First they said we'd whup 'em in one battle, then they said it might take a month, and now three years have gone by. Three long years, and it ain't over yet."

Kane shook his head. "Don't nothing happen without a reason, Alex. Don't forget that. It'll be over when it's over, and until then you and me'll just keep doing what we're told and hoping that every battle will be last one. And someday it will be, one way or t'other."

He stretched and yawned. "I swan I sure could use with a good nap right about now, but I guess we'd best be on our way. We're not gettin' any closer to General Johnston a-settin' here on Miss Greene's front porch."

After saying their goodbyes to the old lady, they pulled themselves into the saddle and rode to the north. Finding Johnston's men took longer than it should have, thanks to the diligence of the civilians in the area who sent them on one wild goose chase after another, fearing they were Yankee spies.

Suddenly, Kane reined in his horse and waved his rifle in the air. "Take your rifle out of its scabbard and hold it high," he said softly.

Alex did as he said, and a few moments later a lone Confederate walked from his hiding place beside the trail. The early-evening mist covered the ground in most places, making it appear for a moment as if the man were a ghost hovering above the ground. Alex shivered.

She was glad when the apparition spoke. "Who goes there?"

"Sergeant Stevens and Private McKinley, CSA. Requesting a meeting with General Johnston."

"You boys have any proof you are who you say you are?"

"I know that the red cow loves clover."

Alex's eyes grew wide with shock at Kane's words. Her mind flashed first on stories she had heard of men gone mad with the horrors of war, then her fear grew that this sentry would shoot them both, thinking them either crazed lunatics, or . . .

Her mind stalled in amazement as the strange man smiled and said, "Right this way, sir. The General will be glad you made it through all right. We were beginning to worry, sir."

Alex reined her horse in behind Kane's, and they went single-file down a worn path. Less than a mile later, the path ended at the edge of a clearing. As far as she could see there were cloth tents and a few hastily assembled wooden cabins.

"General Johnston is waiting for you there, sir," their guide said with a wave toward the largest of the cabins. They dismounted and Kane handed his reins to Alex. "I'll be right back, Private McKinley. Just wait here for me." Alex frowned for a moment, realizing how Kane's mannerisms had changed with their advent to the camp and wondering what was the reason.

The sentry nodded at Alex. "If you're needin' some water or something to eat, the mess tent's back behind the second row of tents. Just follow the smell." He grimaced, and Alex smiled. The food seemed to be a common complaint no matter where you were these days.

"What'd you boys have for dinner?"

"One of the men happened up on a wild turkey back a ways, and we roasted it. Wasn't nothing like Thanksgiving, though," he said wistfully. "One turkey spread over two hundred men don't go too far." He grinned suddenly. "I can't imagine the bird it'd take to satisfy that many men, though—can you?"

Alex returned his grin. "My cousin caught a thousand-legged worm once. I reckon a turkey'd have to have legs like that to give everybody a drumstick, wouldn't it?"

They shared a chuckle, and then the man's smile faded. "We've been a-waitin' on Sergeant Stevens for a couple of days now. Do you know what the message is that he's bringing?"

"No. It was sealed when Colonel Parker gave it to him. I don't know if he even knows what it says."

The man shook his head. "Whatever it is, I don't reckon I'm gonna' like it none. I doubt if it's news any of us want to hear. We've got plumb settled in here." He waved his hand toward the crude cabins. "Some of the boys even sprung up some sheds. It'll be a shame to just march off an' leave them." His voice dropped. "From what I've heard, though, it may be that they're gonna be needin' us at Stone's River."

Alex nodded. "I'm afraid so. I heard some scuttlebutt that the Yankees was headed there."

She dismounted and walked Birdie to a cedar-railed paddock. As she slapped her on the rump and watched her trot off toward the other horses, she smiled.

"It's been a long time since she's been out to pasture," she said.

"Yeah, she's a pretty mare. Where'd you get her?"

"I raised her. She's special to me. It's good to see her get to enjoy herself for a while. She's been through a lot lately."

The other solider turned to her and said with a wry half-smile, "Yeah, so have we all. Wish a good roll in the dirt and a few mouthfuls of green grass would make all my troubles go away."

The watched the horses in silence for a while before the soldier stood up and stretched and gestured toward the General's cabin. "There comes your buddy out. Let's see if he'd like to grab a bite to eat with us."

Alex tried to read Kane's face as they neared, but it was inscrutable.

As they stood in line waiting for their food she whispered, "Well, what did the note say? Where are we going next? Back to Colonel Parker, or somewhere else?"

He gave a curt reply. "When you need to know, I'll tell you, Private McKinley." He sighed when he saw the look of surprise mingled with sadness on her face.

"I'm sorry," he said, putting a hand on her shoulder. "You just can't ask me those kinds of things. Especially not when we're in camp around other men. When it's just us, it's different. We can talk. And we can be friends. But right now, it's business. And I am your ranking officer. I'm sorry."

"That's okay," Alex said. "I do know that. I just can't get used to not being able to ask questions and know where I'm gonna be headed tomorrow."

"Yeah," Kane said dryly. "That's something we'd all like to know right now."

Alex looked at him from the corner of her eye. "So, there's some big news brewing?"

Kane laughed. "You are incorrigible, ain't you? Come here." He took her arm and led her out on the porch. After looking around carefully to make certain no one could hear, he said quietly, "You're not going anywhere right away. Neither am I. We're waiting on word from another outfit before we finalize our plans. So, for probably the rest of the week, we stay put, sit tight, and wait for orders. If I knew where we were going I'd tell you. But I don't. I do promise that if I have anything to do with it, wherever we go, we'll go there together."

Alex felt a warm glow and lowered her eyes so he wouldn't see them welling with tears. "Thanks, Kane. I know you're not supposed to tell me that. But it does make things a lot easier."

Kane sighed. "I know, Alex. You kind of got thrown in the

deep end of the crick. You've learned how to swim pretty quickly, but don't forget you could still sink. All I can tell you is that if I could make you go home, that's what I'd do. But I reckon you've got another agenda, and I can't stop you. All I can do is be a friend and make sure you know I'm here if you need me."

Alex laid a hand on his arm. "Thank you. That means more than you'll ever know," she said simply.

A man lurched around the corner of the cabin, holding a half-empty bottle in the air, "Well, well, well, ain't that the purty sight, though? We've been a-needin' some entertainment around here. Pretty kind of Colonel Parker to send it along with you, Captain Stevens."

Kane cursed under his breath. "Get back to your tent, Jackson. If the General finds you drinking out here, he'll have you drawn and quartered."

"Hell, right about now, I'm so bored, I'd nearly be glad of it, if it'd give me something to do." He took another swig from the dirty bottle and handed it toward Kane and Alex. "Here, don't make me drink alone. Have yourself a drop—and then on second thought, let's go back to my tent. My friend's in the hospital with the runs right now, and we'll have the whole place to ourselves. You can have the first time around with the little fellow, and then I'll take what's left over." He belched loudly and grabbed at his crotch. "That is, unless you got your fill on the way here. In which case, I'm ready to ride right now."

He never saw Kane's fist aiming at his nose, and he whined softly as he slid into darkness.

Alex's grip on the porch railing turned her knuckles white. She turned toward Kane and her voice wavered as she said, "What the hell was he talking about? 'Turns' with what?" Her stomach churned. "He didn't mean . . . with me? Did he?" She ran to the end of the porch and emptied her stomach contents off the edge. She jumped at Kane's touch.

"Are you all right?" he asked, gently.

"No. Yes. I will be."

Kane felt a shudder run through the slight body. "Don't worry about him. He's trash. I'll tell the General what happened, and he'll . . ."

"No!" Alex wheeled toward Kane, panic in her eyes. "Don't tell anyone anything. I couldn't bear to have everyone looking at me . . . knowing he wanted to—" Her eyes cast downward to the porch floor. "I don't want to give anyone else any ideas that might not have occurred to them yet, Kane." She lifted her eyes to his, pleading with him to understand. Over and over in her mind played the rough voice, *Show you what it's like to have a real man . . . show you what it's like . . .*"

She shook her head, erasing the voice.

Kane patted her shoulder and said softly, "I do understand, Alex. All right, I won't say anything to anyone. Unless you want me to." He looked with disgust at the mound of dirty uniform at the bottom of the steps. "But what do we do about him?"

"Him?" Her mind raced. "Why should we do anything? He was obviously drunk—he tripped and fell going up the steps?" Her voice tapered off as she watched Kane's face, looking for signs of agreement. When she saw them, she relaxed.

"What the hell's going on out here?"

Kane and Alex wheeled around toward the man who had stepped out onto the porch.

"Nothing, sir," Kane replied. "It appears that Lieutenant Daniel here," he curled his lip in disgust, "tipped his bottle a little too high and had an accident."

"Really?" the man looked at them both for a long moment. "One of the men said he saw you punch Lieutenant Daniels."

Kane laughed. "I tried to help the poor bastard. Obviously he is way too far gone to be helped. He slipped and hit his face on the railing."

The soldier leaned forward and looked at the man's face. "Looks like he's going to have a headache in the morning when he wakes up. In the hoosegow." He walked back to the door and motioned to two men sitting beside the doorway. "Take Sergeant Daniels here and lock him up. Full security."

One of the men said, "You mean Lieutenant Daniels?"

"Not any more," the older man said firmly. "I've told you men that I won't have any scenes caused from an overdose of liquor. If you want to drink in the privacy of your own tents, when you are off duty, you have my full permission. I imbibe from time to time my own self. I will not, however, have a drunken man reeling around my outfit, besmirching the Confederate uniform he should be wearing proudly."

He stood in silence beside Kane and Alex for a moment,

watching the two men drag the slobbering man toward a cabin that Alex supposed served as their "hoosegow."

The older man turned to Kane. "I don't know what really happened here, Captain, and I suspect it's best that I continue to stay in the dark. Don't let it happen again, however. And if there are any more"—he turned and gave Alex a searching look—"problems, I assume you'll come to me, instead of taking matters in your own hands?"

Kane saluted sharply. "Yes, sir."

Alex followed suit. They both watched the older man go back inside and pick up a tray of food that he carried back toward the General's cabin.

"Was that the General?" Alex asked.

"In the flesh," Kane replied. "A very good man. I feel honored to work under him. He is a true hero."

"But he's not very sharp, is he?" Alex chuckled.

"What do you mean?"

"Well, he kept calling you Captain. And that other man did too." Suddenly she looked at Kane suspiciously. "Kane, you told me you were a sergeant. Aren't you?"

"If that's what I told you, then that's what I must have meant. Right?"

Kane turned sharply and went back inside the cabin, headed again toward the chow line. Alex followed him, chewing her lower lip, wondering why he hadn't actually answered her question.

~ ~ ~

The next few days spread into weeks as they waited for their next instructions. Kane and Alex spent the time helping the other officers clean their guns and tack, and she held a few of the horses while they were shod. Alex discovered Birdie was about to throw a shoe on a hind foot, so with Kane's help she replaced both rear shoes.

"You're pretty good at that," Kane said, admiringly. "Is that what you did before you joined up?"

"Huh?" Alex shook her head. "No, I didn't do much of anything. I helped out a little around the farm, but by the time the war got started there wasn't enough money around for anyone to start any kind of business. I learned how to do it because I didn't want anybody else messin' up Birdie's feet."

For a moment her lips curved into a smile as she pictured prissy Miss Alexandria Latham slaving over a white hot fire and anvil all day making a living as a farrier, her dewy skin dry and blackened from the heat and sweat. "I used to help my cousin when he shod my uncle's horses. He taught me how."

"Teddy?"

The name flew to Alex's heart, causing a pain as sharp as the knife that had ended Teddy's life. "Yes," she murmured.

She quickly gathered up the tools and old shoes and headed for the makeshift barn before Kane could see the glistening of unshed tears. *Damn!* She clenched her hands into fists and dug her fingernails into the once-soft tissue of her palms, and wondered, *What keeps men from dropping tears with no notice?* She took a deep breath and wiped her eyes.

She looked behind her to make sure no one was watching and then suddenly slipped into an empty stall. Lying back against the fragrant, just-cut hay, she looked at the ceiling. She watched the shadows shift as the sun began to crawl toward high noon. Things were just too hard, she decided. It was getting far too difficult to maintain her disguise, and she didn't think she could bear to see the scorn in Kane's eyes if he discovered her lie.

Maybe it's time to go home, she thought sadly. Then Rafe Peterson's voice danced through her thoughts again—*show you what it's like . . . show you what it's like*—and her fists clenched again.

"Hell, no, it ain't time," she said aloud, standing up and brushing hay off her trousers.

"Well, actually, yes, sir, it is," Kane said, a note of concern in his voice. "Didn't you hear the General?"

"Hear what?"

"It's time to ride, Alex. We got our orders."

"Where are we —" Alex hesitated.

"We're headed to Murfreesboro. The command at Stone River is just barely holding on. They need our help." He hesitated for a moment. "Things could get really rough there, Alex. Nobody would think less of you if you stayed behind to keep watch over camp."

For a millisecond Alex considered the idea. "No," she said. "I'm getting too damned bored here. I'm ready to ride."

They saddled their horses and swung astride. Joining the band

of whooping soldiers, they fell into line near the rear, riding side by
side.

Alex looked at Kane for a moment. "Thanks again for what
you did back there when we first arrived," she said.

For a moment Kane looked puzzled. "Oh, you mean
Lieutenant—er, *Sergeant* Daniels?" He grinned. "No problem.
You'd do the same for me, wouldn't you?"

Urging his horse into a canter, following the lead of the other
men, he drew ahead of Alex for a moment. Before she urged Birdie
forward to match Patch's rhythm, Alex watched Kane's broad back
for a moment. "Yeah, that's real likely to happen," she said under
her breath, wondering what fool would consider taking advantage
of Kane in such a way. Her heels nudged Birdie's side, and they
cantered easily to take their place beside the strong-shouldered
man and his muscular grey stallion.

~ ~ ~

Alex lay still for a moment, her eyes tightly closed, moving
each finger and toe one by one and counting. She let her breath out
when she came to the number 10. She slowly opened her eyes, and
then closed them quickly when the large pine trees overhead began
dancing and swaying. Little by little, she pulled herself into a sitting
position, leaning back against one of the trees that had finally
decided to stand still and stop crazily dancing around.

She looked around the thicket. Closed her eyes, then opened
them and looked again. The scene stayed the same. Blue- and grey-
clad bodies sprawled in undignified and unnatural positions,
almost completely covering the thicket floor. Flies walked across
unseeing eyeballs before gathering to drink from pools of
congealing blood. Alex's stomach lurched, and she made her own
contribution to the fluids seeping into the ground.

"You alive, or just a ghost? Must be alive, I ain't never seen no
ghost puking up his guts."

The voice burst the silence of the death-filled thicket. Alex
spun around looking for its owner, the action causing her to lose
what little balance she had left. She shrieked as strange hands
caught her before she fell into the middle of a tangle of bloody
limbs, some separated permanently from their owners.

She opened her eyes slowly and breathed a sigh of relief to
find the arm supporting her was clothed in grey. "Thank you."

"Aw, sometimes we all need a shoulder to lean on. How'd they miss you when the wagon came through?"

"I don't know. I don't remember anything past coming up on this thicket and hearing Kane tell me to get off my horse and get behind a tree." She looked around suddenly, her mind flooding with distress. "Kane. Birdie. Where are they?"

"Kane? That your horse?"

"Birdie is my horse. Kane is my friend. I've been riding with him since I joined up." Her heart sank as she looked across the thicket again, realizing with despair that if Kane were within calling distance, he certainly would not be able to hear her.

She took a step toward a fallen log, easing her aching body down. "Were you here? Did you see what happened?"

"I was here, but I come upon it too late to do anything. I'd been out scouting for horses for Cap'n Black. I've got a little place not far from here, and I took a detour to check on my old woman. I heard shots and thought I'd see if somebody needed some help. By the time I got here it was mostly over." He shook his head. "You're one lucky son of a bitch, boy. I reckon the Yankees must have left you for dead." He reached down and touched Alex's forehead gently. "I reckon you was just creased, though. You'll have a fearful headache for a day or two, but you'll be back in the saddle before you know it."

Alex gingerly touched her forehead and felt the ragged skin before the pain from being touched reached her. She winced and looked at her bloody fingers. "Not if I can't find my horse," she said, the thought of losing Birdie distressing her almost as much as being separated from Kane.

"I caught up with about a half a dozen horses that scattered when their masters fell. You want to check and see if one of them's yours?"

"Oh, please! I think a lot of that horse. And I'd like to see if my friend's horse is there, too. If I can't find Kane, I can at least see to it that Patch is taken care of." She squinted and cursed. "Damn, I think I've started bleeding again."

The stranger pulled a handkerchief from his pocket and quickly tied it around her forehead. "You just set a minute. I'll go bring the whole string of 'em closer. Or if you feel like it, you could wander around and see if you can find your friend." Alex watched the man saunter out of view before she forced herself to go toward the piles and piles of dead soldiers.

She could hear the scream of birds overhead and knew that before long they would swoop down on the uncovered bodies. That knowledge caused her to walk faster, looking at sights that would have caused her to faint not long ago.

Turning to look past one clump of trees where more men had fallen, amidst a tangle of limbs she spotted a jacket that looked just like Kane's. At the sight of it a hollowness hit her as though she'd been punched in the chest. Swallowing hard, she carefully turned over the body, but the face had been mutilated beyond recognition by a mortar blast. Her heart finally settled back into place when she looked at the man's feet and saw that they were covered by heavy black boots, instead of the familiar brown ones that Kane wore. Although the rest of his uniform was always impeccable, he insisted on wearing his own boots and so far had gotten away with the indiscretion.

For almost an hour she walked among the bodies, becoming more and more used to the horrors until she could turn over one that lay face down without wanting to vomit at the sight she uncovered. She walked back to the man who had helped her earlier with a lighter step, knowing that wherever Kane was, he had not joined this particular group of men on their final journey to heaven or hell.

When she finally got back to the edge of the woods, she found the stranger sitting on a rock, smoke from his cracked pipe curling upward.

"Didn't find your buddy?"

"Thank God, no. But I'm right puzzled as to where he could be. He ain't the kind to turn tail and run. And I know he wouldn't have left me anyway. He's already saved my skin a bunch of times. He wouldn't have left me now."

"Maybe not if he could help it."

Alex's heart sank suddenly. "What do you mean?"

The man looked down at his boots. "Well, the Yankees could have took him with them. They brought their wagons in and picked up all the wounded, and the few men that couldn't run away fast enough. That's what I said earlier. They must have thought you's dead, or they'd'a took you too."

Alex remembered Kane's worry about becoming a prisoner. "Oh, dear Lord, no. Which direction did they go in?"

"I think I recollect hearing somebody say that the Yanks had set up a prison in the old jailhouse in Monroeville. That's probably where the poor bastard is." The man shook his head. "I'd ruther be one of them," he motioned with his head toward the scattered bodies, "than to be locked away like a mad dog." He shook his head. "Poor bastard."

"How do I get to Monroeville?"

The man shook his head again. With a snort he said, "Ah, wouldn't do you no good, even if you could make your way through Yankee lines. Once a man's in a Yankee prison, the only thing left to do is pray for his soul, and hope the prayer gets to the good Lord pretty quick-like."

Alex stamped the ground. "Dammit, if you know the way to Monroeville, tell me!"

"Keep your britches on, boy. Ain't no sense in gittin' in no all-fired hurry. Yore friend ain't going nowhere fast, except mebbe to hell. If you're bound and determined to join him there, just keep on going East. You'll find what you're lookin' for afore you know it."

"Thanks, mister. Now, where's those horses? If I can't find my own, I'll take whatever you'll give me."

She scanned the string of horses he led before her, her heart sinking. She shook her head. "She's not there." She felt tears stinging her eyes. Suddenly the man looked down at the ground and kicked the dusty brown dirt.

"Well, there was one more mare I found back a ways. I'd thought about taking her back home with me and breeding her with my stud horse. Reckon that might be your Purdy?"

"Birdie? A mare? Dark chestnut with a flax mane and tail?"

The man nodded slowly. "Sounds like her, sure enough."

Alex followed the man back through the patch of woods to a small cabin in a clearing. She heard Birdie's familiar nicker before she could see her. "That's her," she yelled back over her shoulder at the man.

"Well, good," he said, shaking his head at his loss. He smiled as he watched the reunion between the two of them. "I ain't never had a horse care about me that much," he finally said. "I'm glad you two found each other. She wouldn't of been worth two twigs to me if she'd'a allus been grieving for you."

Alex beamed at him. "I can't thank you enough for catching

her for me. She still ain't used to gunfire, and I have a hard time controlling her when things get loud. I guess when I fell off her she just took off. Good thing you were there." She reached into her pocket. "Here, let me at least give you something for your help. She means a lot more to me than this, but it's all I got."

The man refused her offer. "Hold on to it, son. You never know when you'll need it to get out of a tight spot."

Alex's throat suddenly felt dry. "I reckon I'm right likely to get in a tight spot if I do go to Monroeville, then?"

"If you're fool enough to head straight into trouble, you can expect a few tight spots before you get out," the man agreed solemnly. "Are you sure that's what you want to do?" He again dragged a toe in the dust. "Boy, you think careful-like before you trot off to get yourself killed trying to save somebody else's neck. It ain't likely that whoever you're heading out to save would do the same thing for you."

"Yes, he would," Alex said firmly. "He's already saved my skin more than once. I owe him." She knew Kane would risk life and limb again to save her neck, although she hadn't quite figured out why, or why she felt the same bond with him.

"He's a right lucky man to have a friend like you. I hope he knows it."

"I'm the lucky one. Like I say, he's already got me through a couple of pretty bad scrapes. 'Turnabout's fair play,' my Aunt Tilly allus said." Alex smiled at the memory of Aunt Matilda sternly scolding Teddy for failing to play fair with Alex, not knowing that poor Teddy was often enough punished at Alex's own hands. The memory brought a tear to Alex's eye that she quickly brushed away.

"Kid, you sure you don't want me to ride along with you a ways?" the man asked hesitantly, as if dreading an affirmative answer.

"Thanks for offering, but I think I can maybe slip in unnoticed better by myself," Alex said.

"Sure do wish there was some way you could let me know how you get on. I'll be thinking about you."

"I'll try to get some word to you," Alex promised. "My name's Alex McKinley, and the man I'm going after is Kane Stevens."

The man held his hand out. "Peterson, Billy Ray Peterson. Pleased to meet you."

Alex's heart skipped a beat. "Peterson? Got any relatives in Pennsylvania?"

The man looked uneasy. "Mebbe. Why?"

"I knew a man from Pennsylvania a while back. Name of Peterson, Rafe Peterson."

The man looked over his shoulder before answering quietly. "How did you meet Rafe? Where are you from?"

"Down below Rome a piece."

"Below Rome? Your name Lange?"

Alex hoped her shock didn't show on her face. "Lange? No it's McKinley."

Peterson shook his head. "You must . . . um . . . work for Lange, though, you know, if you met old Rafe."

Alex's mind spun as she nodded and lied. "Uh, yeah . . . right. Me and Lange worked together for a few months." *If nothing else, I can go on the stage when all this is over,* she thought to herself.

At Peterson's knowing nod she added, "Are you and Peterson related?"

"He's my granddaddy's brother's boy. We growed up together, but he went off up North, and we didn't see each other until all this shit started and he needed me to . . . um . . . help him out some."

"Yeah," Alex nodded, grasping at straws to keep the conversation going. "I guess he has a hard time getting men to help him who are good at . . . what he does."

"Too damn many hotheads down that way that can't or won't listen to reason," the man agreed. "There ain't but one way this thing can end, and I reckon it's up to folks like us to hurry it along."

"Folks like us?"

"Yeah, men like you and me and Lange who are smart enough to know which side our bread is buttered on. And knowing how to keep the butter side up if the bread gets dropped."

Suddenly the man's words came together like pieces of a puzzle. "Spies," she almost shouted.

"That's a dirty name. And one you can get hung for." The man looked over his shoulder uneasily. "I'd be a little bit more careful about bandying that word around, son. You never know who may be listening. I ain't paddin' my pockets now to weigh myself down while I'm swingin' from a rope."

Alex swallowed down the bile that was rising in her throat, "Yeah, I guess I'd better be more careful. Lange always said I'd have to learn to watch my mouth before he could trust me with the important stuff."

"What kind of jobs y'all do together?"

"Little stuff. A few notes back and forth. Getting information for Peterson. You know."

The man nodded. "Ole Rafe's a hell of a guy. He could wring information out of day-old bread."

Alex's throat suddenly burned, remembering the harsh voice and rough hands. "Do you know where ole Rafe is these days?" she asked nonchalantly.

"I dunno. I heard tell he was going to Monroeville to swap out some prisoners. Poor bastards. Bad off as Monroeville is, it's a sight better than what old Rafe has in mind. Son of a bitch gets hisself off I reckon hearing men scream. I can't stomach some of the things I've seen him do. But I guess it works for him. Lord knows they say he's the best at what he does."

"Swap out prisoners? But he's a Yankee. And the prisoners are all our boys—you know, Rebs."

The man chuckled. "That's good. You play dumb real well. Hope you don't ever have to use it in no Rebel court, but iffen you do you just might get away. You're pretty good."

Alex swayed for a minute and sat down on the rock Billy Ray had recently vacated. She put her head in her hands and choked back the tears and the vomit that suddenly rose in her throat.

The man's voice was surprisingly gentle as he said, "Don't worry none, all you'll have to do is tell Rafe you don't want your buddy hurt, and he'll leave him there. Not that Monroeville's much better than what Rafe'll have planned, but he'll probably live a while longer." He put a hand on Alex's shoulder. "This is the toughest part, I guess, getting attached to men you know are going to have to either die or be locked up." He drew a deep breath. "But when you know your way is the only one, I guess we can do anything." He gave Alex's back a quick slap. "Ain't that right, boy?"

Alex stood up, fighting back the urge to knock the complacent grin off the dirty, unshaven face. "Yeah." She hoped the man would assume the roughness in her voice was caused by pain, and not the loathing she felt. "Guess a body can do just about anything iffen he has to." She took Birdie's rein from Billy Ray's hand and taking hold of the horn pulled herself into the saddle, ignoring the white flashes of pain and the nausea that gripped her. Gritting her teeth she said, "Just one thing, Billy Ray. If you see old Rafe before I do, you might want to mention to him that he better make peace with whatever God he worships."

Almost blinded by the steel glint in her eye, Billy Ray took a startled step backward. "What the hell?"

"Tell him the woman he raped near Adairsville was not only Lange's fiancée, but she was"—Alex's voice faltered before she added strongly—"my sister. And I plan to kill him for it."

She wheeled Birdie away and took off at a gallop, leaving a stunned and bewildered Billy Ray Peterson behind. "Well, I'll be damned," he finally stammered. One eyebrow raised slightly. "Hmmph. The old coot may have met his match after all this time."

Chapter Nine

It took Alex almost a week to find her way to Monroeville. She finally knew she was on the right road when she began finding an occasional grey-clad body slumped in the ditch or even in the middle of the road. She wondered whether the Yankees were disappointed each time to have one less prisoner on the way, or glad to have one less responsibility. She carefully checked each body to make certain they were truly beyond her help, and also to make sure it wasn't Kane. She contemplated burying the men but decided that Kane should be her first priority. She prayed a brief prayer over each man and then left him in God's care.

When she neared the town, she slipped into the woods and made her way silently, until she came to a clearing on the hillside above the small town. Carefully peeking from behind a leafy sumac, she gasped when she saw the hundreds of bright blue uniforms walking the streets. She silently backtracked a mile or so from town, and after unsaddling and hobbling Birdie and tying her with a long line so she could graze and drink her fill at a secluded grassy spring, Alex sat down to finalize her plan.

Although her first thought had been to simply ride into town with guns blazing and set Kane free, the sight of the many Yankees walking the streets made that idea obviously more suicide than bravery. She groaned. At the first sight of her grey uniform, she would either be shot or thrown into the same prison as Kane. That wouldn't help anybody, least of all herself.

Suddenly she sat upright, her eyes drawn to the saddlebag that hung from a low branch. "God bless you, Kane," she breathed, hoping he had forgiven her for her harsh words earlier.

An hour later, a shabbily dressed young Yankee private rode into town, covered in dust and sporting a bloody bandage above his brow.

"Halt. Who goes there?"

The soldier's hand went to his brow and he swayed, pulling himself back upright at the last minute. He swayed again, and suddenly strong arms were helping him from the saddle.

"Looks like you've had a hard time of it, soldier."

The soldier nodded.

"From enemy fire?" the voice was clipped but kind.

Another nod.

"Anything we need to be aware of for our safety here?"

A slight shake of the head.

"Good man. I know you don't feel like talking now. I'll take you to get that wound cleaned up, and when you're feeling a little better someone will be by to talk to you. Can you walk?"

Alex nodded weakly, then she swayed again. She hoped she wasn't overplaying things, but she wasn't ready to talk to anyone yet, and perhaps she'd end up in a hospital where Kane was being cared for.

She suddenly found herself belly-down over the man's shoulder. She tried to look around through squinted eyes as the man carried her down the street, hoping to catch sight of a building that looked like a jail or a hospital, but everything was moving too fast, and being upside down made it hard to for her to comprehend what she was seeing. Having the headache from hell didn't help matters any, either.

"Is Miss Ellen at home?" she heard the man ask politely.

"Good Lord, not another one. I'm running out of bedrooms, young man," a gruff voice answered.

"But this one's just a boy, ma'am," the soldier replied. "And he's not hurt too bad. I expect he'll be up and out of there in just a day or two."

"That's what you told me the last time, and that blue-coated devil was under my roof for nigh onto a month."

Alex felt the shoulders beneath her tremble as the man chuckled, "Yeah, but if your doctor had checked him a little closer, he might have found out sooner that Trey's symptoms just got worse when it came time for him to leave Miss Ellen's company." His voice grew serious. "And Miss Graham, you be careful what you're calling our men. You know what the captain said. I'd hate to see you get in trouble after all you've done for us."

"Just remember, I didn't do anything for you Yankees because you're Yankees. I just did what I could to make another human being's suffering easier. I pray to God that there are some Yankee women up there with sense enough to do the same for some of our boys. Just because I let you bring some of your men here to be nursed back to health don't make me no Yankee lover. Just a good Christian woman who hates to see any of the Lord's sheep suffering. I keep praying y'all'll come to your senses some day soon and go back where you came from."

The woman's last words were less audible as Alex heard her turn and walk out of the room. "Bring him on in here," she called gruffly over her shoulder.

The man followed the woman, and a few seconds later Alex felt the man's muscles tighten as he bent over to deposit his load. Suddenly she was enveloped in a cloud of fragrant linen as the soft feather mattress beneath her gave under her slight weight.

She looked up and smiled at the man. "Thanks," she said, and then closed her eyes.

"Poor little lamb. Just looks all tuckered out," the woman clucked over her, before gently removing the stained bandage from her forehead. "Poor thing. I'll be back in a flash with a poultice for that, and then we'll get you out of those clothes and into something decent."

"Just so long as it isn't grey," the man warned her, with a glint of mischief in his blue eyes. "We wouldn't want the 'poor lamb' to be shot again, by his own men this time, would we?"

The woman slapped at the man with the tea towel she carried slung across one shoulder, "You git on outta here, Jones. And don't be bringing me no more men to take care of, now, you hear?"

"I hear you, Mrs. Graham," the man said, with an obedience that wasn't reflected in his eyes. He tipped his blue hat and walked out of the room whistling.

"Danged old fool. Bringing me folks to patch back together like there weren't no doctor in town." The woman fussed as she paddled out of the room. "I'll be right back, honey. You just lie there a while and relax, and I'll be back with some bathwater and fresh bandages."

Bathwater! Alex sat upright. She hadn't counted on someone wanting her to take a bath again. Damn! She had hoped her wound would get her into town, and maybe into a Yankee hospital where she could get more information, but she hadn't planned on this. Her fist pounded the down comforter.

Hearing the woman's heavy tread coming down the hall, she lay back against the snowy pillows and closed her eyes. For a moment she imagined she was back in her own bed at Twin Cedars and the padding feet were Verbena's bringing her breakfast in bed.

"Do you think you can sit up?" the woman asked.

"I think so."

"As soon as we get your wound cleaned up, I'll have Joshua bring up a tub of water, and we'll leave you alone so's you can take a bath. I don't know about you Yankees, but around here we believe that cleanliness is next to godliness."

Alex breathed a deep sigh of relief at her words and relaxed. She grinned as she said, "Where I've been lately, ma'am, it's more likely next to impossible than godliness."

"Don't you be pokin' fun at the Lord now, boy," the woman said brusquely, her words belying the twitch at the corner of her mouth.

"Yes, ma'am. Ouch, dammit all to hell and back!" Alex hollered as the woman pulled the handkerchief from the wound.

"Don't be cussin' in my house, boy," the woman scolded. "Mmm. It's a little deeper than I thought. And this rag was stuck down in it. But this poultice will stop it from bleeding, and we'll get some clean bandages on it. It's a wonder all you boys don't die from the gangrene, the way you don't take care of yourselves when you get hurt."

"Ma'am, begging your pardon," Alex said, wiping the edges of her eyes where tears had gathered. "We don't usually have much choice. I was lucky to have a fairly clean handkerchief to wrap up with. Most men don't have that." She fell silent for a moment, remembering the rough hospital units she had helped with in the last months, the dirt and grime and blood mixed together in festering wounds.

"There ain't no excuse. Iffen old Abe had give more thought to this dad-blasted war before letting everything get out of hand, he'd have knowed he'd have to supply good medical care to you boys."

"I don't think old Abe gives a damn about us boys, ma'am."

"I said don't cuss in my house. And he cares a sight more for your boys than he does for ours."

Alex nodded. "Yes, ma'am."

"How'd this happen?"

"I got shot."

The woman slapped Alex' shoulder. "I know that, fool, I mean where. In a battle? Running from some jealous husband? Or some irate livestock owner you was stealin' from?"

"No, ma'am. I mean yes, ma'am." Alex leaned back against a downy pillow, gingerly touching the fresh bandage the woman had somehow managed to affix during the conversation. Her voice shook as she said, "I'm so tired I don't know what I mean, ma'am. I don't remember much. I was riding along. Somebody said lay low, and I guess I didn't lay low enough."

The woman patted her shoulder kindly. "I'm sorry, boy. I didn't mean to give you a hard time. I know it's as rough on you men as it is on our boys. I can't say I'm not glad every time I hear that our boys won some fight or t'other, but I can't help but be sorry for every mother that's gonna get a letter full of misery, or even worse for the one who won't never find out for sure that her boy won't be coming home. Lord have mercy on us all."

Alex felt tears burn in her eyes. "Thank you very much, ma'am. It's nice to hear kind words again and lay in a soft bed. You couldn't begin to imagine how much this means to me."

The woman stood up abruptly and straightened her apron. "Well, just hurry up and get yourself healed and outta my house. I told the captain I'd cooperate if he needed me, but I've got better things to do than wait hand and foot on damn Yankees."

"I'll try not to be any trouble," Alex said softly. "Could I maybe carry in my own bathwater?"

"Don't be silly. Joshua will bring it right in. Just lock the door behind him. I don't want Ellen happening in on you in here in your skivvies."

"Ellen?"

"My stepdaughter. She's the one who offered our house to the Yankees in return for some food and safety. Our neighbors'll probably never forgive us, but that's their loss. We can sleep at night knowing we're safe, and that's more than they can do. I ain't giving the damn Yankees nothing that they ain't gonna' pay for one way or t'other, and that way it's just business. I ain't helping them no more than they're helpin' me."

She stood up and bellowed down the hall, obviously forgetting her self-imposed ban on cursing. "Goldang it, Joshua, where's that dang-blessed water?"

In a few minutes, an elderly black man came banging into the room, carrying a large copper tub. Soon it was filled with steaming water, making Alex almost swoon in anticipation.

Minutes later she was sitting in the tub, knees drawn up to her chest, her back to the securely locked door. For the first time since the night at Pearl's she relaxed in warm, soapy water, even getting a chance to wash her hair. *It's getting a little long,* she mused. *Better find some scissors tomorrow and whack it again.* She had lost even more weight, and soon it was going to be harder to keep her disguise. Impossible if her hair gave her away. She rubbed her breasts, tender from being bound for so many weeks. Occasionally she could loosen the strips at night, allowing them some freedom, but most of the time Kane slept so close by, it wasn't possible.

Kane! She closed her eyes for a moment, opening them as tears began to squeeze through, dripping into the lukewarm water. "I'll do whatever it takes to get you outta there, Kane," she whispered, in a voice hard with resolve.

She sat in the tub reveling in the almost-forgotten comfort of being clean until she heard footsteps coming down the hall. They weren't the pounding footsteps of Mrs. Graham, and they startled her into a quick dry-off and rapid rebinding of her breasts before putting on the clothes Mrs. Graham had sent in with Joshua earlier.

She turned the key in the lock as Mrs. Graham had instructed and was almost back to her bed when she felt soft arms go around her. "Need some help, soldier?" a feminine voice spoke quietly in her ear.

Alex jumped. "Yes, ma'am—I mean, no ma'am. I'm feeling much better after my bath, ma'am."

She sat on the edge of the bed and looked up into the deepest violet-blue eyes she had ever seen, ringed by lashes of deep bronze. Her own eyes widened, and she leaned back against the pillows. "I thought you were Mrs. Graham."

"Really?" The voice had a wry edge. "Most people can tell us apart."

Alex smirked. "Yeah, I reckon so. What I meant was that you startled me, 'cause I was expecting Mrs. Graham."

"She had to go run some errands. She told me to look in on you and make sure your wound wasn't bleeding again." Her fingertips gently brushed across the still-white bandage on Alex's forehead.

Her smile was so open and friendly that Alex couldn't help but respond. If things were different—very different indeed—this was someone whom she instinctively knew could have been a fast friend from the start.

"You just lie back now and relax, and I'll bring your supper. If you're hungry."

"I can't remember the last time I ate, ma'am."

"Ellen. Please call me Ellen."

"Yes, ma'am—um, Ellen. I'd be much obliged for something to eat."

The girl looked at her strangely for a moment. "You sure don't sound much like a Yankee," she said slowly.

Alex gulped. "My mother was from Alabama," she said. "Everyone says I sound more like her than I do my father. He's from Ohio," she added.

The girl nodded, a sad look passing over her delicate features. "I've heard my father talk about the war he fought in, and the ones my grandfather told about. And in all of them the two sides were so different it was easy to tell your enemy. This horrible war, between kin . . . the color of the uniform is the only thing that really tells you men apart." Her voice broke and caught in a sob.

Suddenly straightening, the girl pulled her shoulders back, and Alex could see the struggle within her as she composed herself. "I'll be back with your supper in a minute," she said, her voice calm and controlled again.

"Miss Ellen?"

The girl smiled. "I'm sorry, I don't usually break down like that in front of strangers. I declare I don't know what's wrong with me." Her composure cracked a little. "Actually, I do know what's wrong, but I can't fix it."

"Is there anything I can do?" Alex asked.

A small smile flitted across the girl's face again. "You know, when I first talked to the captain about our allowing some of his men to be nursed back to health here in our home, I did so thinking that I might be able to get some information from some of the men . . . about . . ."

"About what?" Alex prompted.

"My fiancé." Ellen turned suddenly, and her face almost glowed. "His name is George. George Davis. He's a corporal in the Confederate Army." Her tone turned defensive. "And I'm very proud of him." Her voice drooped. "But I miss him so terribly bad, and I haven't heard from him in over a month. My heart keeps telling me he's all right, but my mind argues that if he were, he'd have found some way to get in touch with me."

"Ma'am, if it's any consolation, I've been out there. And sometimes we'd stay holed up for weeks in one place, with orders not to have any contact with the outside world, for fear of letting on to our whereabouts." She reached out her hand and touched Ellen's gently, marveling at the difference in her own scarred, reddened, and callused hand against the white softness of the other. Remembering that not so long ago her own hands looked as well-kept and pampered as Ellen's brought a lump to her throat that she quickly swallowed. "Just keep on listening to your heart, Miss Ellen, and keep asking questions. Remember, it's a good thing if these Yankees—I mean, if we—don't have information about your George."

Ellen's face lit up. "That's right, isn't it?" She patted Alex's hand. "You're a good man, even if you are a damned Yankee . . . goodness, I don't even know your name."

"Alex Mc—" Suddenly cautious, she improvised quickly. "McDaniel. Alex McDaniel."

Ellen gave a mock curtsy and smiled. "Pleased to make your acquaintance, Mr. McDaniel. And now, if you'll excuse me, I've spent so long in here I'm way behind on my chores. I'll send Joshua up with some vittles for you. I've got to go to the church and help the ladies wrap bandages."

"For the Yankees?"

Her look of scorn took Alex aback. "Of course not. You have my sympathy, Mr. McDaniel, for your wound, but my heart and soul belong to the South and her cause. I would never bring bodily harm to a Yankee, myself, and I will soothe any suffering I can, sir. But when you meet our sons of the South on the battlefield, my cheers will be for them, sir, for every drop of blood they cause you Yankee devils to spill brings us one minute closer to having our lives back."

"Ma'am," Alex said sadly. "I've been there. If every drop of blood that has been spilt so far stands for a moment of time on this earth, neither you nor I nor our grandchildren, nor theirs, will live long enough to spend those minutes." She lay back against the pillows.

Ellen stood there for a moment looking at the boy in blue. Then picking up her skirts haughtily, she swept from the room.

After eating the best meal she had been offered in months, Alex fell into the first real, deep sleep she had known since the night she left Twin Cedars. She awoke the next morning when the first rays of sunshine entered the room and she heard the faint murmurings of the house coming alive around her. She stretched and yawned, enjoying the luxury of awakening to a warm feather bed beneath her instead of the cold, damp ground and seeing a pristine white ceiling above her instead of a dripping tent or tree branches. She looked across the room, wishing she could see Kane's face as she had every morning for months. Her resolve grew deeper as she lay there, her mind running over the plan she had carefully plotted before she slept.

She feigned sleep when she heard Ellen come into the room, keeping her eyes closed until she heard the footsteps growing fainter and fainter and finally heard the door slamming behind her. She tiptoed to the window and watched as Ellen crossed the street, carrying a basket of eggs.

Suddenly she saw Ellen's body jerk sideways and saw her hands fly into the air, the basket filled with the eggs sailing through the air before falling to the gravel in the street, a mess of cracked eggs and broken wicker.

Thinking Ellen had simply tripped on the uneven sidewalk, Alex started to turn away from the window, until something made her look a moment longer, and she saw blood trickling from the side of Ellen's brow. Another jerk of her body, and a second trickle started down her arm. Ellen looked up to the window where Alex stood and their eyes met, Ellen's lips forming the word *help*.

Without thought, Alex ran through the house and out onto the street. Ellen lay crumpled in a heap on the ground beside the sidewalk, her hands to her head.

Alex rushed to kneel beside her. "Miss Ellen! What happened? Are you all right?"

Hearing shouts from behind her, Alex turned and saw a man dressed in blue wrestling with an old woman who was screaming curses at him. Alex started to go toward them when she felt Ellen's hand clutch her shirt. "Don't let 'em hurt her," she whispered, pain tightening her words.

Alex looked at Ellen for a moment, her puzzlement apparent on her face until she noticed the two stones lying near Ellen, their shape and size different from all the other stones in the roadbed.

Her face relaxed, then tightened again in anger. "Ellen, why?"

"Just don't let them hurt her," Ellen pleaded again, her eyes wide, reminding Alex of a young fawn she had once had in her rifle's eyesight. She had not pulled the trigger then, and she quickly squeezed Ellen's hand in assurance that she'd show that same mercy now.

"Are you all right, Miss Ellen?" the man in blue demanded as he pulled the old woman closer. "One of my men said he saw this woman throwing stones at you." He gave the old woman a stern look. "You know, of course, that the Grahams are protected by the same orders the captain gave regarding our own men. Any show of disrespect or attempts to harm them means imprisonment or death."

"Damn Yankee lover," the woman hissed, then she screamed in pain as the man's grip on her arms tightened.

"Shut up," the soldier said, a wicked smile creasing his face. "Remember, I can break your arm like a stick, you old Rebel witch."

Alex stood up and faced the soldier and the old woman. "Sir, that will be enough. Unhand this woman immediately until we get to the bottom of this situation."

The soldier looked at Alex without tightening his grip on the old woman, who was now beginning to whimper in pain and fear. "Who the hell are you?"

"Lieutenant Alex McPherson," she replied, drawing herself up to full height, and giving herself several promotions to ensure the other soldier's respect. "I am temporarily staying in the Graham home while my battle wound heals." She turned and offered her hand to Ellen, who pulled herself up and stood beside Alex, swaying a little before Alex's firm hands steadied her.

"I never heard of you. You're not from our company." The soldier gave Alex a suspicious look, his hold on the old woman tightening.

"No, soldier, I'm not. And if you can tell me what gives you the right to ask, Private"—Alex hoped she read the soldier's insignia correct, and that the Union army carried the same ranks as the Confederate—"I'll be happy to take the time to explain my reasons for being here. Perhaps your commanding officer would like to be part of that conversation?" Her tone became deadly. "Now, unhand that woman."

"Sorry, sir." The private's eyes were downcast, and his hold on the old woman's arms relaxed. He stepped back as the old woman stepped free of his grasp, rubbing her arms and shooting looks of hatred toward Ellen.

"Now, Miss Graham, why don't you tell us what happened here," Alex said.

"I—I was carrying some eggs to the store to sell—" Ellen's voice faltered.

"Go on," Alex prodded.

"—and I tripped on some stones and fell." She lifted her eyes and looked at Alex with a smile. "The next thing I knew, Lieutenant Mc—" Her eyes widened in shock as she realized Alex's faux pas the very second Alex herself realized it. Without taking her eyes from Alex's, Ellen covered smoothly. "—McPherson was beside me. I feel so stupid." The long, bronze lashes batted furiously at the young private. "You must think me so clumsy."

The private looked distressed. "Oh, no, ma'am, Miss Ellen. I think you're the—why, no ma'am, you're not clumsy at all."

Alex hid a smile. "Then what's this fuss about this woman throwing stones?"

"Begging your pardon, sir. One of the other boys said they saw her throwing stones, and then we saw Miss Ellen on the ground sir, and we just . . . well, sir, we just assumed."

"Don't ever assume anything, soldier." Turning to the old woman whose eyes were now filled with puzzlement instead of fear. "I trust you'll forgive our overzealous soldier for his assumption, ma'am."

The old woman nodded, never taking her eyes from Ellen. "I was just tossing some stones at the neighbor's chickens scratchin' in my garden," she added helpfully. "We just planted some summer squash, a-hopin' to get a few picked before frost."

Hoping no one would bring up the fact that any chickens to be found anywhere nearby were now floating in soup, Alex quickly added, "And I'm sure you'd be happy to help Miss Ellen into her home, wouldn't you?"

"That's not necessary," Ellen protested.

"Yes, it is," Alex corrected sternly. "We want to make sure there's no doubt in anyone's mind that Mrs.—"

"Torrents," the old woman stammered.

Alex picked up the offending rocks and tossed them into a

nearby ditch. "—that Mrs. Torrents truly meant no harm to you, and indeed you simply slipped on these stones and fell." She touched Ellen's brow. "You're going to need a patch put on that. I'm sure Mrs. Torrents will be happy to oblige. Won't you?"

The old lady nodded obediently.

Following the two of them back into the house, Alex grinned. *When all this is over, I'm definitely going on tour,* she thought. *I'm a better actress than even I imagined.*

Once inside the house, the docile Mrs. Torrents once again became a she-devil. "None of this would have happened if you'd not got yourself involved with that Yankee scallywag," she hissed.

Alex started to interfere, but a sharp look from Ellen silenced her.

"Mrs. Torrents. I like to think of myself as a good Christian. Do you?"

"That's not the point."

"That's exactly the point, Mrs. Torrents," Ellen snapped. "I seem to remember a Bible verse that says that any good done to the least of the Lord's servants is the same as doing it to him personally. I can't think of anyone lesser than one of these damned Yankees—" This last was said with an apologetic look toward Alex, which was acknowledged with a smile. "—and I just hope that wherever my George is, if he's wounded, that there's a Christian Yankee woman, if indeed there is such a thing, somewhere who'll feel the same way and give him a chance to come home to me. My putting a few bandages on Yankee men doesn't mean diddly, except that *I*"—she accented the "I" with a toss of her copper curls—"accept that these men have confiscated our homes and our lives for the time being, and *I'm* doing the best I can to make a bad situation just a little bit easier." She reached out and touched the old woman's hand.

In a softer tone she added, "Carolanne, I don't blame you a bit for feeling toward me like you do. If I thought you were doing anything that would make this war last longer, or that you were switching sides on us, I'd hate you too. Please understand, I love my George and I love this country. But if patchin' up a few Yankees keeps 'em from burning this house and harmin' my mother, I'll bandage the whole goddamned army."

At the old woman's look of shock Ellen's eyes widened. "Oh, goodness!" she said, one hand going to her mouth.

The old woman's lips grew tight then began to twitch at the

corners. "I'd say that lump on your head put a few words in your mouth, wouldn't you agree, young lady?"

"Oh, Carolanne, I'm sorry," Ellen's face looked like a sunset, with the purple bruise mingling with the red of her blush.

"No, darlin', I'm the one who should say I'm sorry. I'd just been down to Widow Jenkins's, and she was going on about how she didn't see how you and your sweet mama could just open up your home to these damned Yankees, and then I saw you sashaying down the street, and I just didn't think." She gingerly touched the welt on Ellen's face. "I'm so very sorry, Ellen. Thank the Good Lord my aim's not better."

Alex watched as the old lady puttered around, bandaging Ellen's bruises and making them all a cup of weak tea. When the door finally closed behind her, Ellen turned to Alex and with a hand on her hip said primly, "And now, Mr. Alex McDaniel/McPherson/ Mc-whoever the heck you are, I think you've got a bit of explainin' to do?"

Alex's mind raced. To tell Ellen the truth could put not only herself but Kane in danger. However, to make up yet another story could mean being found out and put in even greater danger. She looked at Ellen. Hoping she wasn't being taken in by sweet words and big, violet-blue eyes, she said quietly and honestly, "To tell you the truth puts my life and that of a Confederate officer in your hands, Ellen. Can I trust you?"

"You're not a Yankee, are you?"

At Alex's surprised nod, wondering what had given her away, Ellen went on. "I didn't think you sounded like you'd ever even been up North, much less lived there. And you came to Carolanne's defense much too rapidly, and took my and her word too easily against that of a Union soldier. Which I might add I thank you very much for. She's a sweet old thing but gets way too carried away." She grinned. "Once some of the women were talking about their men-folks' transgressions at one of our quilting bees, and she went home and hit poor Harry, her husband, over the head with a broom. He hadn't done anything, she just got carried away with everyone else's stories, I guess." She and Alex chuckled for a moment, then Ellen grew more serious. "But if you're not a Union officer, where'd you get the uniform? And why? What are you doing here, and how'd you injure yourself?"

Alex took a deep breath and let it out slowly as she carefully chose her words. "You're right. I am not a Union officer. I'm a Confederate soldier." She groaned as she eased herself onto a tattered but comfortable over-padded chair. "I was wounded in our last skirmish and left for dead by the Union troops. My best friend in the whole world, who's saved my skin more times than I can count, wasn't among the dead, so I have to believe he's a prisoner here in Monroeville." She shook her head sadly. "If he's not, I don't where to start looking for him."

Ellen looked puzzled. "But what can you do? You know, even posing as a Union officer, they won't release him to you without the proper paperwork. Do you have that?" Alex shook her head, and Ellen went on. "Then what do we do now?"

"We?"

"Well, whether either of us likes it or not, I'm part of it now. What's the plan?"

"You'll think I'm crazy."

"I already do. Go on."

"Have you ever been inside the prison?"

"Every Tuesday and Friday evening, I take the Confederate men a special meal and watch to make sure they get it and not their guards. It's a special arrangement provided by the captain." She added defensively, "He's basically a good man, even if he is a Yankee."

Alex's heart soared. "That's perfect. This is Monday, right?" Ellen nodded. "Then tomorrow night when you go you'll be accompanied by your cousin."

"They'll never buy that," Ellen shook her head. "Why would I have a cousin in the Union army who came all the way to Monroeville just to take supper to Confederate prisoners?"

"Get me a dress and bonnet and you may change your mind."

Ellen looked skeptical. "A dress. Now I know you're out of your mind."

"Just go. Bring it to my room"

A few minutes later, Ellen knocked on Alex's door and entered, carrying a blue- and white-checked gingham dress and matching blue bonnet.

"What about drawers and petticoat?"

Ellen blushed. "You're getting a little pertinent, Lieutenant Mc—whatever your name is."

"Just get them. I'll explain later."

"It better be a very good story," Ellen grumbled.

"It will be," Alex promised.

Thirty minutes later, an amazed Ellen was staring at Miss Alexandria McKinley Latham and searching the room for traces of Lieutenant McDaniel. "How in the world? Where did you . . . where'd you get . . . *a bosom?*" Her cheeks reddened with her last words. "I mean—"

"I know what you mean. And I can't begin to tell you how good it feels to be back in a dress again after all these months in pants and having my chest bound."

Ellen looked stunned.

Alex held out her hand to her. "My name's Alexandria Latham."

It took Ellen a few moments for it all to sink in. "This is getting a little hard to believe, you know. In the space less than twenty-four hours I've been introduced to a young, injured Union officer, a Confederate spy, and now a woman—and the funny thing is, you're all the same person."

Alex smiled ruefully. "I'm sorry to have to involve you at all, Ellen. If I could think of any other way, you know I'd do it. I don't want to get you in any trouble. And I promise you if it comes down to it, I'll tell them this was all my idea and I forced you at gunpoint to help me."

"Like the devil," Ellen snorted. "For one thing, we won't get caught. Nobody who's as good as you are at disguises is going to get caught, no matter what crazy scheme you have in mind."

"Hold that thought until you've heard it," Alex said with a grin. "But the first thing to do is determine whether or not Kane is really inside."

"What are you going to do until tomorrow night?" Ellen asked. "Won't somebody notice if that nice young Lieutenant just disappears into thin air?"

"Maybe," Alex mused. "I guess he'd better get some orders pretty fast to hightail it outta here, huh?"

With a conspiratorial wink, Ellen walked out of the room and came back with a piece of paper she pressed into Alex's hand. "I thought this might come in handy, but I had no idea how handy."

Alex read the paper, then looked at Ellen in amazement. "This is perfect. Listen to this." She read aloud. "To Lieutenant Alexander McGraw: Report immediately to company headquarters in Delworth, Kentucky for inquest proceedings. Signed, General Robert Stagg." She giggled. "This is marvelous!" Her mood suddenly sobered. "But won't someone recognize that name?"

"No, it really is perfect," Ellen said. "Nobody really knew McGraw. He was a real bad egg. He showed up with a broken jaw and some busted ribs, had been in a fist fight somewhere apparently, and the captain brought him here to recuperate since he was trying to pick a fight with some of the other men in the hospital tent. He couldn't talk well, so nobody asked him many questions, waiting 'til his jaw healed. I don't know that anyone even knew his name—they just called him Mick. Anyway, one of his broken ribs must have done more damage than the doctor thought, 'cause mother found him dead in his bed the next morning. I found this in his jacket pocket and decided to keep it."

"Good thing."

"Indeed," Ellen agreed. "Anyway, if anyone should question the papers, I'll tell them that McGraw is the name you told me. They'd have no reason to not believe me, and if that private remembers you gave him a different name, I'll just have to convince him he misunderstood. Why would a Union officer show up, then disappear . . ." Her mouth trembled. "Sweet Jesus, I hope they don't think we killed him and dumped the body."

"I guess someone needs to see him ride out of town, don't they?"

"Are you sure that's the only way?"

"The only one I can see. And I can leave behind that slip of paper. You can even take it to the captain tonight and tell him you found it in my room. When you get back home, you'll get a surprise visit from your cousin from Atlanta."

Ellen's eyebrow's raised. "What about your horse? I've got her in the stable out back. If you leave on her, won't someone recognize her?"

Alex thought for a minute. "We'll whitewash a star on her forehead. By the time it wears off, I'll be long gone."

"You've thought of everything, haven't you?" Ellen said admiringly.

"I hope so," Alex replied, hoping Ellen couldn't hear the fear in her voice. Things were coming too fast, and her plan was having to take too many side trips. One false step and it would all be over.

Her hands smoothed the folds of her dress. "Maybe they'll go easier on a woman than they would on a man," she mused, wondering if even the Yankees would shoot a woman.

Chapter Ten

At her regular hour on Tuesday evening, Miss Ellen Graham opened the door of the Monroeville County Jail, now the home of hundreds of Confederate prisoners. No one would guess from looking at her serene face and gentle smile that she was nervous as a canary in a cat cage, or that she had any mission other than bringing comfort to her countrymen. She made her usual rounds, emptying the heavy box of linen-wrapped sandwiches and fried pies. She made her way to the rear of the building and sat down on a straight chair in the corner underneath a small, dirty window, waiting for the men to finish eating. Often she'd be there for hours after the men had eaten, writing letters home for them, reading letters, and providing basic medical aid where needed. Her routine had become such a usual occurrence that the young private at the desk barely looked up when she entered.

The young man in the blue uniform also didn't look up from his paperwork when the door creaked open again a few minutes later. When his eyes finally lifted from his work, they opened wide as they took in the pink apparition that floated toward him. Alex tried to remember to walk like a girl, or rather sway as she had noticed Pearl doing, and from the wild jumping the boy's Adam's-apple was doing she assumed she had learned well. His eyes moved up from her skirts but reached no further than the cleavage that peeked above the pink silk and Cluny lace, rising up and down with each breath. His discomfiture was obvious, and she silently thanked Ellen for changing her mind about the blue gingham and loaning her this dress that was causing the poor boy before her to all but drool down the front of his spotless uniform.

She set the small box she carried on the edge of the desk, and in a voice that dripped honey and added syllables to her ordinary accent she said, "Excuse me, suh, are you the may-un in charge here?" She let a tone of awe slip into her voice as she batted her eyelashes until she was sure she was going to grow dizzy.

She had never perfected her flirting skills, and she was amazed to find that they worked as well as Ellen had promised. She could almost see the boy's chest swell before her eyes. His eyes finally raised to meet hers as he stood up and walked around the desk. "Yes, ma'am."

Honesty forced him to add, "At least for the next six hours I am, ma'am. The captain took most of the men to pick up some supplies. He took the men along in case some of these damned-stupid Johnny Rebs tried to jump them again. They've been gettin' rather brave about picking our men off as they ride into town, but maybe this time they'll get a surprise." The pride dropped from his voice as he remembered to whom he was speaking, and he added embarrassedly, "Begging your pardon of course, ma'am."

Alexandria smiled a bland smile, making certain her dimples were in place, hoping the boy would think her too stupid to realize it was her countrymen he was slandering and threatening.

"Ooh, I just can't believe this silly old wah's still goin' on," she cooed. "I just can't imagine what they're thinking of, to let it just drag on and on and on. And I'll swear it's taking the best men from us. Why, before long there won't be an able-bodied man in three counties." She looked the boy up and down, her gaze lingering on his crotch. In a seductive tone, with a wink and a shrug—a move she'd practiced in front of Ellen's mirror so that it loosened her shawl and revealed even more cleavage—she said, "At least it's takin' most of the ones I knew. Maybe I've just been lookin' in the wrong places for my men, huh, sugah?"

The boy swallowed hard.

She leaned closer, giving the young sergeant a view of her quite-ample-when-unbound breasts. "How long did you say you were here alone for, honey?"

"About six hours, ma'am. Why?" His voice croaked, and he shifted uncomfortably as if his trousers were suddenly too tight.

"Well, I desperately need a favor, and I'd just be so grateful that I'd"—she dropped her eyes modestly—"well, you just can't imagine how very grateful I'd be to anyone who could help me."

The bulge in the boy's trousers that he tried in vain to hide behind a sheaf of papers told her quickly that his imagination was as vivid as she had hoped. This would make her job much easier.

"What exactly can I do for you, ma'am?" he croaked.

"Well, I wondered if I might be allowed to look around inside and see if my very dear friend is being . . . incarcerated here. He's been missing for some time, and I thought while I was here visiting

Cousin Ellen, I'd be a fool not to check and see." She looked at the boy and smiled, winking slightly. "And like I said, I'd be ever so grateful to you. You can't imagine how grateful." She turned, allowing her dress to slip further from one creamy white shoulder.

The boy swallowed hard but straightened his shoulders and said firmly, remembering his duty for a moment instead of his aching crotch, "Absolutely not, ma'am. Them's the captain's orders. Nobody gets in to see the prisoners. Too much chance of escape."

"Escape? How could I possibly get one of the prisoners by you, silly? In my reticule?" She opened her silk purse slightly, allowing a whiff of the perfume inside to waft out into the stale air of the corridor. "Or perhaps under my skirts?" She daintily lifted her skirts, giving the boy a glimpse of perfect ankles and the bottom of her eyelet-trimmed petticoat.

He swallowed hard again. "No, ma'am. I don't think you'd try nothing at all. But them's the orders, and I have to go by them."

Alex smiled at him again. "But you let my Cousin Ellen in, honey. Forget orders. That's for when you've got commanding officers here looking over your shoulder. Then I think the best thing you could do is to obey your little rules. But today, today there's nobody here but just you and li'l ole me—and Cousin Ellen, of course. And if you were to find it in your heart to give me just a few minutes to find my friend, I can promise you that I can find a way to fill the next six hours that you won't ever forget." Her eyes held promises that his young brain almost overloaded trying to comprehend.

He bit his lower lip for an instant, his principles and his lust raging for control. Lust won.

"Well, if you really are Miss Ellen's cousin, I don't reckon the Cap'n would mind. What would be the name of your friend?"

Alex smiled. "Stevens. Kane Stevens."

The boy rifled through a ledger on the desk. "Stevens? We don't have a Stevens here."

Alex's heart sank.

The boy spread other sheets around the table. "We do have an unnamed prisoner back there, though. Maybe he's the man you're looking for."

"Why don't you know his name?"

"He's been unconscious ever since we brought him in. He got

busted up pretty good when his horse fell on him. Damned shame, too."

For a moment Alex thought she detected a glimmer of compassion. Those thoughts were proved wrong by his next words, however. "Damn fine animal. I saw him get up and run, and I chased after him and caught him, but it took me nigh onto an hour. Son of a bitch ran like the wind. Beggin' your pardon, ma'am." Alex smiled forgiveness, and he went on. "I'd like to ride him into a battle or two myself," the boy bragged.

"Have you been in many battles?" Alex hoped her voice sounded as if she gave a tinker's damn, which she certainly didn't.

"That was my first one. And I wasn't even supposed to be there. I was marching with a unit headed this way, on my way to my post here. We got waylaid. It was close for a while, but we finally whipped some Rebel butt. We lost a couple of fine men, but we sent more to hell than they sent to heaven."

Again he remembered too late to whom he was speaking. "Begging your pardon of course, ma'am."

Alex smiled her forgiveness, although her fists were knotted tightly at his words. "I'm sure you were very brave," she said adoringly. "But if you don't mind, I'd really like to visit with Mr. Stevens, if indeed it is him, for a while." She dropped her head and looked at him through her eyelashes. "The quicker I get in to see him, the faster I can get back here and hear all about your brave exploits."

"Through this door, down the corridor, fourth cell on your right—here's the key." The boy almost dropped the key in his hurry to hand it over. For a moment Alex was reminded of Uncle Max's prized coonhound stud, drooling over one of the many bitches that were sent to him for service.

"Why, thank you, suh. And I had been led to believe that there were no gentlemen in the ranks of the Yankee army."

The boy smiled openly. "I'll let you go on alone so you can say your goodbyes in private. Then you come right back here, and I'll be waiting on you. I'll try to rustle up some coffee, if you'd care for some."

Alex stopped short. "Goodbyes?"

"Yes ma'am, I'm sorry. He can't last much longer. He ain't eat nothing since we brought him in here. The doc set his leg and his ribs, but he must be broke up inside. He hasn't known anything since he hit the ground." He shook his head. "And poor devil'd be better off if it happens that way. If he lives, it'll just be for long enough for him to be hanged."

Alex's heart sank, but the boy's words deepened her conviction that the wild plan she and Ellen had concocted would indeed be Kane's last and only chance. Its dangers did not weigh nearly as heavy against the alternative.

"I can only hope you're wrong, suh. I brought some soup I'd like to take to Mr. Stevens—if it is him, I mean. Would you happen to have a spoon, since it appears he won't be able to drink it from a bowl?"

The boy fished around in the desk drawer, pulling out a grimy Army-issue spoon. "Here you go, ma'am."

Alex thanked him then gingerly made her way down the corridor, hoping not only to find Kane but to find him in better condition than the boy had intimated.

The latter wasn't the case.

He lay there on a dirty cot, one leg unnaturally straight, the other hanging from the cot as if he had tried to stand and hadn't made it. His face, or what she could see of it through streaks of rusty stain, was ashen, and his hair was matted with clotted blood.

"Oh, Kane," she breathed. She bit her lip to hold back the sob that threatened, then reached into her reticule and brought out the small packet of powder that she and Ellen had mixed the night before.

She closed her eyes for a moment, her face tilted upward. *Dear Lord, let this work,* she prayed. As she mixed the potion into the bowl of lukewarm liquid, she added, *and if it doesn't, please tell him I'm sorry.*

~ ~ ~

A few minutes later her screams shook the prison walls. "Oh, sweet mother of Jesus," she sobbed, "don't let it be so! Sweet Jesus, don't take him from me!" She collapsed against the wall, watching the hallway carefully for the entrance of the young Yankee. He was there in moments. She hurtled herself into his arms, her sobs shaking her body.

"Ma'am, ma'am. What's wrong? Did that man hurt you?"

"He's dead—dead, I tell you!" Tears rushed down her cheeks and fell on the front of his spotless uniform. Her burnished curls tumbled across the young man's chest as she sobbed on his shoulder.

"Well, ma'am, I'm rightly sorry, but I did tell you he was in pretty bad shape." Alex tried not to notice that his hands that rubbed her back soothingly sometimes dipped below the line of modest convention.

"He just opened his eyes for a minute and said my name, and then the angels took him," Alex said dramatically.

"Ma'am. Just you come with me, and I'll take care of you. When the men get back I'll see to it that someone buries Mr. Stevens, and for you I'll even see to it that a parson says a good word over him."

Alex pulled away from the boy in blue and threw herself on Kane's prostrate body. "You don't understand," she sobbed. "He can't be dead. He just can't be. He was supposed to marry me this Christmas. He was going to get to come home, and we was going to get married."

The boy's eyes dropped to the floor. "I'm rightly sorry, ma'am. But this is war, you know. There's a lot of men won't be coming home for Christmas—or their weddings or anything else."

Alex's eyes grew hard and glittery. "Yes, suh, and who's to blame for that? For all I know, it might be your bullet that took my Kane's life." She threw herself onto a bench alongside the wall, watching below lowered lashes for some sign of Ellen, who appeared in moments.

"Cousin, whatever's wrong?"

"Oh, cousin Ellen, the worst thing in the whole world has happened."

Ellen's show of concern was perfect, Alex thought. The two of them had their act so down pat, it was hard to imagine that scarcely forty-eight hours earlier they had not even known each other.

"What is it, cousin?" Ellen's hand flew to her mouth. "Oh, it's not Mr. Stevens, is it? You found him here?"

"I found him, and then I—" Alex's sobs began again, her shoulders heaving, pulling the shawl completely from her shoulders and leaving the tops of her breasts straining out of the pink bodice. "—and then I lost him," she wailed.

The young soldier's eyes were plastered on the vision of the luscious bosom that heaved with each of Alex's sobs.

Suddenly a voice boomed into the stillness. "What the bloody hell is going on here, Masterson?"

The young soldier wheeled around and saluted sharply. "Captain, sir. I didn't hear you come in, sir."

The man stood in the shadows, but for a moment Alex thought she recognized his voice. *Impossible,* she thought. *Well, so this is the mighty captain. Guess our performance had better be good.*

"I don't suppose you could, Masterson, what with all this caterwauling. Anyone want to tell me what's going on? Miss Ellen? Or perhaps the other Southern magnolia can explain?" His voice was curt and angry, his eyes taking in Alex's dress, her provocatively exposed bosom, and the lust apparent on the young soldier's face—as well as in his pants.

Ellen spoke first. "I'm sorry, captain. I didn't dream anything like this would happen. This 'Southern magnolia' is my cousin. On my father's side. She's from Atlanta and decided to come for a visit, not knowing that we already had, shall we say, company visiting. She had been engaged to a young sergeant in the Confederate army." Ellen moved closer to Alex, her voice quieter. "When his letters stopped coming she fell into a deep depression, and her mother thought it best if she get away for a while. When she arrived and found out there was a Confederate prison here, she wanted to come see if anyone knew anything of Mr. Stevens." Her voice broke with emotion as she reached over to touch Alex's hair. "Poor dear, I gather she got more than she expected."

"He . . . he died in my arms," Alex wailed.

The captain frowned and took a step backward. "Died? How the hell—?" He addressed the young private. "Would you like to explain, Masterson? Or would you rather just stand there drooling?"

"I don't know, sir. Truly, I don't. She went back to see the man in Cell Four, the one who was so bad off, and in just a few minutes she come back out here wailing like a baby, saying he was dead. I swear, sir, he was still alive when I checked everybody a half-hour ago."

The captain's brow furrowed, and he pushed the boy out of his way. "I'd better go see for myself." He waved at the women. "You women stay put. I'll be back in a moment."

Seconds later he walked back down the hall, his footsteps heavy. "I'm sorry, but apparently your cousin is correct, Miss

Ellen. The man is indeed dead."

Alex's wail grew shrill, and the captain spoke with exasperation. "For the Lord's sake, get that woman out of here before she puts every man in here in a fever fit," he demanded, for the first time stepping fully into the front room and out of the dark hall.

When the sunlight hit his face, Miss Alexandria Latham did something she had never done before in her life. She fainted.

~ ~ ~

Her next conscious thought found her lying on a padded couch in a dimly lit office. Judging by the framed pictures, certificates, and wanted-man posters on the walls, she supposed it had been the sheriff's or deputy's office in a former life. Probably now the captain's. Her eyes closed again, and she groaned quietly. *The captain.* She had met only one Union captain, Jacob Sullivan, a while earlier, when he had allowed her to escape. What were the odds, she wondered, of finding that same Union captain, counties away from where they'd met, in this prison?

She felt Ellen patting her hand, then heard her whisper quietly, "Good job, Alexandria. For a minute there I thought you really had fainted."

Alex gritted her teeth and said under her breath, "Whatever you do, don't call me by my name. And I *did* really faint, dammit!"

She leaned back against the cushions as she heard footsteps nearing the door. "Is she all right, Miss Ellen?" the captain's voice asked.

Ellen's voice held a faint trace of puzzlement as she looked down at Alex. "I guess so, Captain Sullivan. I really don't know what's wrong with her," she added truthfully.

Alex fluttered her eyelashes and tried to sit up. "Tell me it's a bad dream, Ellen. Tell me Kane's all right."

"I'm sorry, honey. But you've got to get a hold of yourself. You can't do him any good anymore. You have to think about yourself."

The captain spoke gruffly. "I'm very sorry, miss. Indeed, I don't think I can begin to tell you how very sorry I am. Until now I've been spared having to watch this kind of histrionics."

He looked closer at Alex, his eyes narrowing. "Is it possible we have met before, miss? You do seem most familiar."

Alex's eyes met his squarely. "I can't imagine any social

situation we might have had in common, sir—can you? In fact, I
see no reason at all that you could even consider that I had ever
have come in contact, by choice, with a damned Yankee."

"No, miss," the captain said tiredly. "I don't suppose you
would."

Alex's hands tightened into fists. "And how dare you call my
grief simply histrionics, sir."

The captain touched the brim of his cap. "My apologies, I'm
sure, miss. I've had a long, tiring day and this, this"—his waving
arms encompassed the entire scene as words failed him, his voice
rising—"this is just too much!" He took a deep breath as he fought
for control. "You have my abject apologies, Miss—" He looked
questioningly at Ellen. "I don't believe anyone has told me her
name," he said, with an apologetic shrug.

Alex stood up suddenly. "Don't talk about me as if I weren't
here, Captain Sullivan."

He turned toward her slowly. "As I said, I don't believe we've
been introduced. You seem to have the advantage," he said, his
eyes hooded.

"I heard you call me a Southern magnolia, captain," she
quickly improvised, before Ellen could speak. "How perceptive of
you. My name indeed is Magnolia. Magnolia McVane."

Sullivan moved his hand to touch her creamy shoulder then
removed it almost instantly, as if he'd been burned. For a moment
he stood there looking at her, with an unfathomable expression
making his dark eyes even darker. "I'm sorry we had to meet in
such grievous circumstances, Miss Magnolia," he said quietly. He
turned to the young soldier, who had followed him down the hall
and into the room. "We'll bury Mr. Stevens in the morning. Please
make the arrangements with the parson from the church down the
street."

Alex's voice was firm. "No . . . I want to take him home. And if
not home, at least to my aunt's home. She lives near Rossville. That
can't be more than a day's ride from here. Y'all can loan me a
wagon, and Cousin Ellen and I will take him back where he
belongs. I won't have him spend eternity in the town that killed
him."

Captain Sullivan shook his head. "No, miss. I'm sorry, but
that's just not possible. If we sent every single body—Union or
Confederate—home for burial, we'd be so busy packing coffins

and escorting grieving women that there'd be no troops left to carry on."

Alex's upper lip curled in scorn. "And I suppose you think that would be a bad thing? Maybe if you had to get a little more personally involved with the horror your bullets carry, you wouldn't be so free about shooting them."

The captain moved closer to Alex, and she could see a vein in his forehead bulging. His jaw tensed as he spit out the carefully measured words between tight lips. "Don't ever make the mistake again, Miss Magnolia, of assuming that I am not personally *involved* with this war, or thinking that I'm somehow *above* all the killing."

His eyes looked far past hers for a moment, and then his voice grew soft and sad. "I've watched good men, good friends, die horrible deaths, and I've sent men home with arms and legs missing, to lives that most of them don't want to live anymore. How many of those men do you think went to heaven, or the hell they'll call their life until God finally graces them with death, with Confederate bullet holes in their hide? You think I don't understand the horror that comes with every rifle shot and cannon blast?" His eyes met and held Alex's, and hers were the first to look away. He spun on his heel and strode from the room, speaking back over his shoulder, "I understand far better than even you ever will, Miss Magnolia."

As she watched his broad shoulders disappear through the door, Alex's heart suddenly dropped. She turned her face toward Ellen. "Now I've gone and made him mad at me, and Kane's going to die. Oh, Lord, why can't I learn to keep my mouth shut?"

She stood up and paced around the room. *What am I going to do?* she wondered, looking up at the ceiling as if divine guidance might provide her the answer.

"I'll just have to go talk to him," she finally said quietly. "He's a good man, he'll accept my apology. And if he doesn't, we'll just have to think of something else. We've got about thirty-six hours before Kane will start coming around. I had hoped to be at Pearl's place before then, but I guess we can slip him another dose and keep him out for another day or so if we have to. We just have to make damned sure nobody buries him or leaves here with the body without our knowing it." She touched Ellen's shoulder. "You'd better get home and get us some things packed. Be sure my saddlebag is on Birdie."

A thought hit her and she smiled. "And be sure there is an extra tie-line on the wagon. I'll be bringing another horse along."

Ellen looked at her, puzzlement widening her violet eyes, but she quietly nodded and left the room.

Alex sat there for a few minutes and then followed her. She walked quietly toward the young soldier, who was once again ensconced at his desk, elbow-deep in paperwork.

She cleared her throat politely, and when he looked up she asked, "Could you please tell me where I can find the captain?"

"No, miss, I'm sorry. I can't. He's gone for the evening. He told me to escort you home, and offer his apologies." His eyes lowered. "He told me to leave your . . . friend . . . in his cell tonight, and he would take care of things in the morning." His eyes met Alex's again. "I'm truly sorry, miss. I wouldn't have let you go back there if I'd had any idea things would end like this."

Alex smiled at the boy. "It's not your fault, I know. But it seems to me that the captain and I got off to a wrong foot, and the only thing that can make things right would be for me and him to have a sit-down talk."

The boy blushed. "Miss, he ain't going to be doing no sittin' down or no talkin' for the next couple of hours, but I'll tell him you were looking for him, and he might look you up later tonight."

As Alex turned to go, he said, "Miss, beggin' your pardon, but if you'd like to have Mr. Stevens cleaned up a bit before the funeral tomorrow, I'll be happy to oblige."

Alex hoped her voice didn't reflect the panic she felt at the thought of anyone moving Kane and possibly doing more internal damage than he had already suffered.

"Please don't, sir. And please promise me on your mother's Bible—if she has one—that you won't let anyone else touch him except me. This is very important to me," she pleaded.

"I promise," the soldier said solemnly. "I'll be on duty all night tonight, and I swear nobody will bother him." He looked embarrassed. "I doubt that he's got anything left in his pockets that might be of any value to you, miss, even for sentimental reasons, but I could check if you'd like."

Alex shook her head. "No, that's all right. I'll be back first thing, and I want a few minutes alone with him. I'll look then, although I know that in battle 'to the victor go the spoils,' and I understand."

She walked back to the Graham house, her thoughts rioting. "If only I could find the captain," she said in a low voice to herself. Teddy had always accused her of being obsessive when she got a thought in her mind and worried it like a dog with a bone until she was satisfied. She sighed. "Guess you were right, Ted," she admitted. "But this is just too important to let it go till morning."

The soldier's words kept running through her mind. Suddenly remembering his embarrassed blush, she almost gave a whoop of delight. She ran up the front steps and into the house, throwing open the door and startling Ellen—who dropped the china vase of flowers she was holding, breaking it into a thousand shards. Stepping gingerly through the soggy mess, Alex grabbed Ellen's shoulders.

"The whorehouse," she said breathlessly. "Where is the town's whorehouse?"

Ellen stepped backward. "Whatever—? Why, Alex, I don't know. How would I know?"

"Think, Ellen. This is important. What house in town has lots and lots of company, mostly men, mostly at night, lots of loud music, every light in the house on?"

Ellen looked puzzled. "That would be Mrs. Radley's house, down by the blacksmith's, but I'm sure that's just a rumor that Carolanne and the other women started. She and her nieces seems like such nice ladies. And they wear such pretty, colorful clothes."

Alex grinned and kissed Ellen on the cheek. "You're wonderful!" she shouted over her shoulder as she ran through the door. "Be ready to go at daylight."

She left Ellen standing there dumbfounded, holding a broken stem of daisies and a piece of blue china.

~ ~ ~

She crossed town, staying mostly in the shadows to avoid being seen by anyone, until she heard piano playing and lots of laughter coming from a house that shone like a beacon in the evening dusk.

She walked up to the front steps and knocked on the door. A woman answered, dressed in a costume that looked like a cheap imitation of the dress Pearl had been wearing the night they'd met. "Honey, I don't know who you're looking for, but I promise he ain't here. You just go along home now, and I'm sure he'll be there before you know it."

Alex pushed past her and walked into the parlor. "I think he is here," she said to the woman who was following her and protesting loudly. "But if you'll just give me a minute, I'll make sure, then I'll be out of here quicker'n you can kiss a cat."

"Lady, you can't just walk in here off the street, and—"

"Sure I can—I just did. And unless you want all the neighbors to know for sure what goes on in this house with you and your nice, 'colorfully dressed' nieces, you might think twice about throwin' me out!" She stood defiantly at the foot of an ornate stairway, her hands on her hips. "Now, is the captain in there"— she motioned with a toss of her head toward the closed door of the parlor—"or is he upstairs?"

The woman closed her eyes tightly. "The captain?" She groaned. "You're puttin' me 'tween a rock and a hard place, honey," she said finally. "You know I can't have the women of this town on my ass. They'll run me and the girls out on a rail. But if I tell you where the captain is, he'll keep his men away, and quite frankly they're the only ones in town with any money." She grimaced toward the parlor. "If one more smelly old fart comes in here carrying a chicken or a dozen eggs instead of money—"

"He'll never know you told me. I'll swear I busted in here and found him myself," Alex promised. "And I don't see any reason the women in town need to know about this place. Seems to me if they was giving their men what they needed in their own houses, they wouldn't want to visit yours so often."

The woman stood there looking at her for a moment, her mouth slightly open. She closed it slowly and said admiringly, "If you ever need a job, you just let me know. I can spot quality further than a coon can spit, and you're it, darlin'. Real quality." She walked around her slowly, looking her up and down. "Nice butt. And good, high breasts too. Waist is a little thick, but we can hide that."

"Thanks," Alex chuckled. "I'm sure I never had higher praise."

The woman pointed up the stairs and whispered, "Fourth door on the right, keep to the right of the hall, the middle floorboard squeaks. It's kind of a built-in alarm," she explained.

Alex nodded and began to climb the stairs. She passed three doors, trying to ignore the sounds emanating from each. When she heard what sounded like a pig squealing, she began to hurry toward the fourth door. She stood outside for a moment, her mind spinning with pictures of what she might find behind the door.

Inside the room, things weren't going the way Jacob Sullivan had planned. He had left the prison in a troubled mood and decided to work off his emotions in the bed of the lusty Monique. He had mused about her obviously fake name as he walked up the familiar stairs. Her French accent sounded a little too Southern to be real, and the extent of her knowledge of the language seemed limited to *Parley voo, my amoray?* He grinned as he opened the door, knowing that what she said and sounded like wouldn't matter once they got between the sheets. Miss Monique was a businesswoman, and she knew her business very well. Very well indeed.

But once inside the room, something went wrong. Terribly wrong. Every time Monique opened her mouth, he heard another voice. Another's words. And instead of seeing Monique's lily-white face and pale blue eyes, he kept seeing freckles and green eyes dark with tears. And over and over he heard Miss Magnolia's tear-strained voice begging for his help.

"Damned minx. Get out of my head," he mumbled, turning to his side on the lumpy mattress.

"What ees the matter?" Monique asked, pouting beautifully. "Just lie back and let Monique take care of everything."

But he was already on his feet, pulling on his trousers and buttoning his jacket front. Suddenly the door burst open.

~   ~   ~

"Captain Sullivan, I need to talk to you," Alex said, as she swung the door open and strode boldly into the room. Just as quickly, she cast her eyes downward as she realized, perhaps too late, what she might be interrupting. When she cautiously raised her eyes, what she saw was certainly far from what she had feared. In front of her was the captain, fully dressed, standing next to the bed. A voluptuous brunette wearing a red-silk teddy and garter belt attached to torn and badly mended black-net stockings, who had been so intent on her seduction that she hadn't registered the intrusion, pulled on one of his arms.

Alex froze in place as the woman spoke. "Come back, Sullee. *My amoray,* let me try once again." Ignoring, or perhaps still not seeing the other woman in the room, the scantily clad woman clutched at the back of Sullivan's jacket, and she said in a voice that lost most of its accent with the realization that a pocketful of some of the last hard currency to be had in the state was about to walk out her door, "I learned something new last week that'll melt your toes, I promise, sugah."

Finally recognizing that there was someone else in the room, she reached for her robe, and in her normal backwoods Southern voice said, "I didn't know you had a lady friend, Cap'n. That's okay, then. Sometimes men can't get it off when they're thinking about someone else." She looked relieved to have decided that his lack of amorousness had nothing to do with her. She tipped her head to one side and said provocatively, casting one last throw for a few Yankee dollars, "Maybe you'd like to try a threesome? Or do you wanna just let her watch?" At Sullivan's shocked gasp she said, "Or are you one of those who'd rather do the watching yourself?"

Alex didn't quite catch what the woman was talking about but was suddenly aware of herself still standing there just staring at the captain's chest, which seemed to double in size with his intake of breath at the whore's words. She looked up and began backing away quickly when she recognized the cold fury in his eyes. "I— I'm sorry," she stammered.

Iron hands grabbed her arm and pulled her into the hall and toward the staircase. He guided her toward the front door after tossing a wad of bills toward the woman Alex had talked to earlier. "Y'all come back," the woman called after him.

Once they were on the street, Alex tried to pull her arm from his grasp. "Captain," she protested, "Let me go."

"Miss Maggie," he said, his voice quiet and controlled, belied by an occasional tremor of tension that ran through his body, "that was an outrageous thing to do, what you just did."

"Look, I said I was sorry. I tend to rush into a plan before it's completely formed," she admitted.

"*Plan?* You call that a plan? What the hell were you thinking, lady? Coming into a private dwelling and bursting into somebody's room?"

"Captain, are you just embarrassed 'cause I found you at a whorehouse? You don't need to be. Those women haven't got anything I've never seen before—and besides, I won't tell anyone where you were. I just had to talk to you tonight, and I didn't know where else to look."

"Didn't know where else to look? My stars, woman! You insult me earlier by telling me you can't imagine a social situation where we could have met before, and then you're not embarrassed to follow me into a whorehouse—which is the first place you thought to look for me when you wanted to talk? What kind of social situations are you accustomed to, miss?"

He looked at her for a moment, and a dawning awareness lit his face. "Oh," he said simply, his hand loosening its grip on her arm.

"What?" she demanded. Then as she realized what conclusion he had drawn, she burst free from his grasp. "How dare you think that about me!" She stomped her foot and swung her hand, barely missing his face.

He ducked his head to the side and responded with a sound she couldn't identify at first, and then she realized it was a deep chuckle. The stern, stiff captain was laughing. At her. She saw red as she swung her hand again, to find it encased in his.

"It's all right, Miss Magnolia," he said softly, touching her hair. As he moved his hand away, his fingers lightly brushed the creamy mound of her breast that peeked over the too-tight bodice of Ellen's dress. Earlier that day her décolletage had seemed perfect, but now she felt vulnerable.

He moved closer, saying nothing more, his breaths deep and even. As his mouth slowly neared hers, Alex closed her eyes. His lips were feather-light against hers, and for a moment she leaned against his chest, lost in the feelings that raced through her body. Her legs felt weak and she thought she would fall, but suddenly his arms were around her, giving her support as his mouth lingered on hers.

Suddenly Alex heard another voice and felt rough hands. *I'll show you what it's like to have a real man between your legs.* With a quick shudder she pushed away from the captain and backed away from him, her eyes open wide in horror.

He stepped toward her hesitantly, concern showing in his face. "Miss Magnolia . . . Maggie. Are you all right?"

She sank to the brick sidewalk as her legs folded beneath her.

"I'm all right," she said.

"No, you're not—you're crying."

"No, I'm not," she protested, although when she felt her

cheeks they were wet. "Oh, Captain. I've made such a mess of things, haven't I? I made you mad at me today. And then I just wanted to talk to you, and I thought if I—if you were there—I could talk to you, and you'd listen to me, and I could apologize and then we could be friends, and—"

The captain laid a finger on Alex's lips. "Shhh. It's okay. I don't think I totally understand, but I guess I don't have to. You've had a bad day, and I helped make it even worse for you because I'd had such a bad one myself. I apologize for my actions. I should never have kissed you."

Alex looked up at him in amazement. "Oh, I didn't mind you kissing me." She blushed and looked down at her feet. "I mean, I should have minded, but—"

Sullivan found himself smiling at the forlorn little creature who had faced him earlier that day with such defiance. "Let's just forget it happened. I didn't mean to scare you. I assure you I meant you no harm, and nothing would have gone further than a kiss. I promise."

"I never held much with Yankee promises," Alex said, then regretted it and hurriedly added as she felt him stiffen, "I mean, before tonight. But I know you're a good man, Captain. And I know you wouldn't have hurt me. It's just that I don't like being touched."

He smiled gently at her. "Let's walk back to the Graham house, shall we? We can talk along the way." He looked up and down the street. "I don't know how safe we are out here alone after dark. Personally, I don't want to get myself shot by some honest but stupid Rebel who looks out a window and thinks I'm Yankee scum accosting a Southern belle." Before she could reply, he added, "And as much as I like to think my men maintain themselves in a decorous fashion when not on duty, I'm sadly afraid your virtue might be at risk were someone to see you here in the darkness alone, so I'll walk you back home."

Alex shuddered. "I do thank you, sir. And I do apologize for . . . for bursting in on you earlier. My family always says I'm way too quick to go off on a tangent without thinking about what I'm doing. And I guess they're right," she admitted. She stopped suddenly and faced him. "But I just couldn't stand waiting till morning to talk to you about Kane. Please, Captain. Please. My aunt would skin me alive if I didn't bring Kane's body back.

Besides, I don't want to leave him here, where no one will even know or care whose grave it is, and they won't plant grass on it, nor bring flowers on Decoration Day. He is a good man." Her voice broke as she corrected herself. "He *was* a good man. And he deserves better." She started walking again, following the captain, who had kept walking slowly ahead.

"I know there'll be hundreds, thousands, of men whose families won't even know where they fell, much less even have a body to bury. But I know where Kane is. And I can't just leave him here. Alone."

"Be at the back prison gate at six o'clock in the morning," Sullivan said softly.

"I'll just die if—" Alex stopped suddenly, her head turning sharply toward him. "What did you say, sir?"

"Be at the back prison gate at six o'clock," Sullivan repeated. "A wagon will be waiting for you there. One of my men will help you put Mr.—er, Kane's—body in the back and will escort you to—where did you say you were from?"

"I'm from Rome, but my aunt lives near Rossville. That's where I'd like to take him." Alex suddenly couldn't believe her ears.

"Rossville? And your last name was what?"

Alex thought quickly, trying to remember her latest alias. "McVane," she said.

Sullivan threw back his head and laughed, the sound booming in the night's stillness. Somewhere a dog barked, setting off a chain reaction as dog after dog followed suit.

Alex stood looking at him for a moment. "Did I say something funny, sir?"

"I'm pleased to make you acquaintance, Miss Magnolia McVane, from Rossville, Georgia."

Alex looked at him suspiciously. "And you as well, Captain Sullivan," she said slowly.

The captain began to laugh again. "No wonder you didn't mind marching into a whorehouse!" He stopped to wipe the tears from his eyes. "Good Lord. Only Pearl would have a niece like you. Who would have ever imagined it? What a small world it is indeed."

Alex's mind whirled. It had been part of her original plan to use Pearl as an ace up her sleeve to get the captain's help, but she hadn't thought about what he might think of her. She groaned inwardly. And this escapade in the whorehouse couldn't have helped. She frowned suddenly, troubled over why this Yankee's opinion meant so much to her, then tossed her head, deciding that might be a question she didn't want to dwell on too deeply.

"A small world maybe, sir, but you're in a corner of it now where it's considered a breach of good manners to laugh at a lady."

Sullivan grinned, showing a glimpse of sparkling white teeth. "Begging your pardon, miss. I certainly wasn't laughing at you. Just at life in general."

"And you'll forgive me for not being able to find much to laugh about at the moment."

His eyes darkened quickly. "I am sorry, Miss Magnolia. It's just that my life has been so devoid of humor recently that I tend to gather my rosebuds where I may, if you will."

Alex nodded her head slightly. "I do indeed understand that, sir, but I fail to understand the reason behind your jocularity."

Sullivan stopped walking and turned toward her. "You surprise me, Miss Magnolia."

"And how is that, sir?"

"You seem very well educated—"

"For a dumb rebel, you mean? We're not all uneducated row-croppers." Her voice broke as a sudden memory of Uncle James rapping her knuckles when she daydreamed during her lessons.

Sullivan blushed. "You didn't let me finish. I was about to say, you seem very well educated for such a beautiful young woman. Unfortunately, I have found that many parents don't see the need to educate a marriageable daughter much beyond the social graces."

"Perhaps," Alex conceded thoughtfully, remembering the days she had sat with Uncle James poring over Shakespeare and math tables while her friends were visiting the dressmaker and taking trips to New Orleans to purchase new finery to tempt eligible bachelors. Uncle James had laughed at her complaints then, telling her that men who couldn't see through expensive jewels, feathers, ribbons, and velvet deserved to find nothing of real interest there when they finally got the girls out of them. "On the other hand," his voice would boom, "when a man gets to really know my girl, he'll find some substance." Alex had grimaced at his words at the time, envying her friends their excursions and exquisite clothing.

Not that she had dressed shabbily—quite the contrary. Her closet boasted gowns from French designers and hats straight from England, but she had never been able to devote as much time to enjoying them as she had been required to devote to her studies.

Sullivan's voice brought her back to the present. "Have you seen your aunt recently?"

"My aunt?" For a moment Alex was still back at Twin Cedars in her uncle's schoolroom, and the only aunt she could remember was Aunt Matilda.

"Not for several months," she said quickly, remembering who she was supposed to be, conjuring up a mental picture of Pearl. "I declare I do miss her. And she'll absolutely curl up and die when I have to tell her about Kane. She loved him almost as much as I did."

Sullivan looked down at the ground. "I am sorry about your . . . friend. If it's any consolation, I did have a doctor look at him when he first arrived."

At Alex's look of skepticism he defended himself. "Yes, I did. I'll admit it's not customary, but one of my men had a bad case of food poisoning, and I wanted to make sure it wasn't something all the men were going to catch. While Dr. Gates was looking at Williams, I had him look in on your friend. He said there was really nothing he could do. But I assure you, your friend never suffered. From what I understand he truly never knew what hit him, and never knew another thing after."

Alex shuddered, remembering Kane's limp body sprawled on the uncushioned cot. Her body screamed to be doing something for him, instead of whiling away the hours with a Yankee captain.

"Will you please see that he isn't disturbed at all before we leave with him tomorrow morning?"

"I promise, I'll see to it," he said solemnly. "Are you sure you don't want someone to wrap him up for you, though? I hate to think of you riding all the way to Rossville with an open corpse in the wagon with you."

Alex shivered, and Sullivan removed his jacket. "Are you cold? I'm sorry I should have noticed that your dress wasn't—er—wasn't good protection against this night air."

But you did notice, Alex thought with a hidden smile. The first time their eyes had met, his had been on the up-rise from a quick glance at her bosom, and he'd certainly noticed her exposed cleavage just moments ago when he thought she was a soiled dove. The thought brought more pleasure than any she had felt recently, and she relaxed in the warm glow without trying too hard to examine the feeling.

"I'm plenty warm, thanks. I just still can't stand to think of Kane being gone." The vivid memory of her last view of Kane put a catch in her voice.

Sullivan's voice was soft. "Miss Magnolia, you accused me of not realizing or caring what is going on around me, but I promise you by all that's holy that I have never for one moment ignored the fact that our bullets are causing just as much sorrow as those from Southern guns." His eyes hooded, and he looked past Alex into the dark night. "These woods are going to be alive with a lot of restless souls for generations to come," he said sadly, "if there's any truth at all to the belief that a life taken too early or for the wrong reasons causes the soul to refuse to go to the Beyond."

Alex turned to look at him, her eyes wide. "I've had that same thought," she breathed, remembering soft rustles that had awakened her in the night. While one part of her mind had reasoned that it was just a scared rabbit or mouse searching a safe haven, the other had countered with the thought Jacob Sullivan had just voiced.

He shook his head. "There's no time for fanciful notions," he said firmly. "I'll watch until you get safely inside, and then I'll go make the necessary arrangements for your ride. I'm expecting a visitor from headquarters late tonight, so I'll be in my office anyway."

As they reached the lane to the Graham house he gallantly opened the gate for her, closing it with a firm click behind her. "I'll see you in the morning, Miss Magnolia." He grinned suddenly, with a flash of white teeth so like Teddy's smile that Alex felt quick tears burn behind her eyelids. "Thanks for a most interesting evening."

Alex turned with a quick flounce of skirts at his teasing and made her way along the gravel path. "Six o'clock, Captain Sullivan. Don't be late."

Long after she disappeared behind the curtained door, Sullivan stood beside the gate. Finally, with a sigh of something he couldn't quite name, he turned quickly on his heel and made his way back to the office, a small smile teasing his lips. He had hoped for a quick dalliance that would put him in a better mood for this dreaded visit from headquarters, but he doubted that Monique's energetic if not particularly talented lovemaking could have given him a better afterglow than the first good belly laugh in months had. He smiled in the darkness again, remembering Alex's blushing bravado in Monique's room.

"You must have been one hell of a man, Kane Stevens," he said quietly. "If it harelips hell, I'll do what I can to see to it that you get a proper send-off."

~ ~ ~

He might not have felt so charitable if he'd seen the young boy in a blue uniform climbing the paddock fence and whistling a short whistle just a few short hours later. When one horse walked away from the herd, he quickly put a halter on it and led it through the gate. The sleeping sentry never heard a thing. "Good thing he likes coffee," Alex muttered to the darkness, "and didn't notice the addition of a little extra potion. Now, if he just wakes up before morning, and nobody knows to look for anybody missing, we're home free, old Patch." She patted the satiny-smooth nose that was nuzzling her pockets, looking for treats. "Good think I learned to copy Kane's whistle, huh, boy? You'd'a been headed into the front lines carrying some blue-coated bastard before long, wouldn't you?" The horse snorted and tossed his head. "No," Alex laughed, "you're right. I'll bet they don't have a man in the whole army who's man enough to ride you." Her thoughts suddenly turned to Sullivan. "Well, not many, at least," she whispered.

Shaking her head free of her thoughts, she led the horse into the night. Minutes later, the door to the Graham stable creaked open, and Alex stepped into the warm glow of Ellen's lantern. "I've got all the things you asked for," Ellen said. "I waited until mother was asleep; she can't answer any questions later if she truly doesn't know the answers."

Her worried eyes watched as Alex turned the beautiful grey stallion into a scruffy bay. "How long will it take that to wear off?" she asked.

Alex shrugged. "I dunno. I know when I get walnut stain on my hands it takes a while. At least we don't have to worry about the rain washing it off."

"You didn't get any on your hands tonight, did you?" Ellen's voice was tense and worried.

Realizing all that Ellen was putting at stake with her duplicity, Alex smiled at her and patted her hand. "It'll be okay, Ellen. I'm not really stealing him, you know. He belongs to Kane. And he should be going with him."

Ellen relaxed a bit, but her face still held its worry lines. "I know," she sighed. "I'll just be glad to get on the road tomorrow, and get this over with."

Alex nodded her agreement.

They stabled the new bay horse beside his old friend. When they left, he and Birdie were whispering what Alex assumed were sweet nothings over the stall divider, glad to be together again.

Chapter Eleven

Captain Jacob Sullivan was a man with a job. A job he was finding more and more dissatisfying every day that he awoke to find his country still at war. One of his more distasteful tasks awaited him when he returned to his office. When he entered the room, he nodded at the man who sat partly hidden in the shadows cast by the oil lantern.

"Lieutenant Peterson," he said, swallowing again the bile that always rose in his throat when he faced this man.

"Sullivan," the man nodded back, insolently disregarding the captain's superior rank. "Got word you had a bunch of men here that might be able to share some information that'd help us out over in Tennessee."

After a long pause, Captain Sullivan shook his head slowly but firmly. "No, Sergeant Peterson," he finally said, choosing his words with care. "Consider this a formal order from a ranking officer. You've interrogated the last man from behind these walls so long as I remain in charge here."

Peterson grinned, showing his teeth, many blackened by decay and the rest showing deep tobacco stains. "That might be the key words then, Sullivan." His eyes narrowed. "You know, I've always wanted to be in charge of one of these outfits. Nice little town, lots of folks sworn by the law to do as I say or die, whorehouse close by full of willing women, and maybe more'n a few women around that ain't so willing. But hell, they're still close. You're a lucky man, Sullivan. Sure you want to risk it for a few Rebel hides?"

His eyes met Sullivan's and locked, a flush rising slowly up Sullivan's neck as he felt the man's hatred as plainly as he felt the heat from the lantern behind him. "I do still outrank you, Peterson," he said barely containing his rage, wishing he could be allowed the luxury of saving a dentist the chore of removing the other man's teeth. For a moment he imagined the release he would feel seeing his fist smash the leer completely off Peterson's face, watching his teeth, blood, and bone mix.

He shook his head. Thoughts such as that scared him into believing perhaps he was no better than the animal that now stood before him.

He forced himself to breathe slowly, sorting his thoughts before he spoke again. He took a deep breath and said evenly, "Sergeant Peterson, I have watched you torture men in the name of our country. I have watched what were probably very good men die at your hands, and I have watched you smile as you carried out what you call your sworn duty. I have heard men scream in agony for hours as you asked them questions, the answers of which you knew they had no way of knowing. I have done all of those things, Sergeant, and I have hated myself for not stopping you."

Peterson stood up angrily and started to make a reply, but one look at the captain's face stopped him.

"But I am stopping you now," the captain said, his voice quiet but deadly in the stillness of the empty room.

"You will no longer be able to use any poor, unfortunate man who finds himself incarcerated in this facility as your personal punching bag, your way of working out your frustrations with what passes as your own sorry life. You can tell them whatever you please at headquarters, for I assure you, I plan to make a report of my own, and I feel certain that although I'm sure you have supporters there, even they will be unable to publicly support what boils down to pure, unadulterated brutality."

He turned toward his desk, feeling the man's eyes boring a hole in the back of his neck. He methodically turned his chair to face the desk, sat down on it, and restacked a sheaf of papers carefully. He looked up to see Peterson walking slowly toward him. Every muscle tensed as he awaited the attack. Instead Peterson smiled.

"Have you ever heard that old saying, Sullivan, 'It ain't over 'til it's over'?" His gravelly laugh sent a shiver up Sullivan's spine. "I'll let you know when it's over," he said. The smile faded from his lips as he spoke quietly in a voice of pure venom that made Sullivan's stomach clench. "You may outrank me at the moment, *Captain* Sullivan, but someday you're going to take that uniform off, and when you do, you better start looking over your shoulder, 'cause you can bet your sweet ass I'm gonna be there."

"And you can bet yours I'll be waiting for you," Sullivan said evenly, his eyes never wavering from Peterson's. He sat and

watched the man swagger from the room, slamming the door
behind him. He listened as the heavy boot-steps faded away down
the hall, then released the breath he hadn't been aware he had been
holding. "You dirty son of a bitch," he said between clenched
teeth.

The sharp thud of his fist hitting the oaken planks of the office
walls reverberated throughout the building.

He sat there lost in his thoughts until he realized the wick was
burning low in the lantern. He stood, stretched, and yawned, then
walked to the window. *I must have dozed off,* he thought with
surprise. The sun was beginning to peep from over the tip of the
mountain. He shook his head. The first thing he was going to do
when all this was over was to find a room somewhere with a soft,
downy bed and a lock on the door, and he was going to use both.
Sleep until he dreamed away the horrors he'd seen, sleep until he
felt rested enough to face whatever life he'd still be able to pull
together from the wreckage left behind by the war.

A soft knock startled him, and he spun around as he said
automatically, "Come in," half-expecting to see Peterson framed in
the door that opened slowly.

His lips relaxed into a smile when he saw Magnolia McVane's
freckled face peering through the crack in the semi-open door.

"Am I bothering you?" she asked cautiously.

"No, not at all," he replied. "Just trying to decide what will be
the best way to accomplish your plan."

"I really do appreciate all you're doing, captain. I know it's
very unorthodox, and I know how few men in your position would
do this for me."

Sullivan wondered to himself if she had any idea how
appealing she looked in the well-worn blue gingham dress. A
faded blue bonnet hid her hair except for a few wisps of dark-
brunette curls that escaped its edges. He frowned. Hair that
beautiful shouldn't be covered up.

Misconstruing his frown, Alex said hastily, "I didn't mean
your position as a Yankee, sir, I meant in your position as a
commanding officer. I meant no offense."

"No offense taken," he said, nodding slightly. "I am at your
service, Miss. Perhaps I should have told you last night, but as soon
as I knew you were Pearl McVane's niece, you could have asked
me for the moon and I would have started looking for a long

ladder."

Alex cast her eyes downward, remembering his earlier confession to a scared young Rebel captive he had thought to never see again.

"How do you know . . . Aunt Pearl?"

He grinned again, feeling ridiculously young for a rare moment. "I don't 'know' her the way you think, young lady." He reached out a hand and tilted up her chin until green eyes met with hazel. Not really sure why he felt the need to explain to this young firebrand, he found himself saying, "Your aunt Pearl was a very dear friend to me, nothing more. I will always think kindly of her. My time with her was a very special memory for a young boy teetering on the edge of manhood."

Alex smiled at him, her dimples deepening. "She is a very special lady, isn't she?"

"Yes . . . a lady," he said firmly, his voice soft. He suddenly cleared his throat and turned toward his desk. "I'll need to clear up some paperwork here, and then we'll look for a wagon for you to take to . . . where did you say Pearl lived now?"

"Rossville, just a piece below Chattanooga."

For a moment Sullivan's hand was stilled as it shuffled through a stack of papers. "Chattanooga," he repeated softly. He drew a deep breath that he let out in a soft hiss through his teeth. "Miss Magnolia, I want you to promise me that at the very first hint of any action in that area, you and Pearl pick up immediately and head south. Don't stop for anything. And don't head for Atlanta. Don't ask questions. If anyone comes to you and tells you they were sent by me, and gives you a letter with my signature underlined twice, don't stop to pack. Walk straight to the barn, harness the horses, and don't wait for anything or anyone." He turned to face her, his face solemn and tired. "Do you understand?"

"No," Alex said honestly. "I don't. But I believe you, and I have to trust you. So I'll do as you say. And I'll make sure Aunt Pearl knows."

Sullivan swallowed the lump that suddenly swelled his throat.

"If you were to leave Rossville," he said, his voice rough, "which direction would you go?"

Thinking this was some sort of test, Alex recited, "South. I won't stop for anything or anyone. I won't ask questions, if the instructions come from you. Underlined twice."

Sullivan smiled and shook his head. "Good girl. But no—I mean, where would you go? Do you have a place to aim for when all this over? If I—er, I mean anyone—needed to find you later, where should they go?"

Alex thought for a moment. "Twin Cedars," she said, without hesitation.

"And where is that?"

"A day's ride from Rome, south, just past Creeksville. It's my . . . well it's my mother's family's place. I have other family there." For a minute, a picture of her room at Twin Cedars, Teddy's laughing face, and Aunt Matilda's sorrow-lined face swam before her eyes, and a huge tear gathered in one eye, trickling down her face.

Sullivan reached out and wiped it away gently. "Don't be scared," he said softly, misinterpreting the tear as a sign of fright. "Maybe you won't need to leave Pearl's place. I don't know anything for sure, just a rumor." He exhaled slowly, shaking his head. "And Lord knows this war's been filled with rumors. Unfortunately, way too many of them were true."

He sighed. "Let's get that wagon loaded up and get you on your way before I change my mind and send you straight to your Twin Cedars." Seeing Alex's stricken expression, he smiled weakly. "Don't worry. I gave you my word. As a gentleman, not a Yankee." His smile strengthened as he noticed the embarrassed blush that spread across Alex's cheeks. "I gave you my word that I'll see to it that your young man reaches his final resting place at your aunt's."

He stood up and pushed his chair back against the wall. "Now, let's see who's on duty that would like a nice ride through the country today."

It wasn't hard to find men willing to leave their duty for a ride through the countryside with two beautiful young women. Ellen had insisted on traveling with Alex, assuring her mother and Sullivan that to leave Alex alone in such a situation would not only be cruel, but un-Christian. Alex didn't know how much of the truth of the situation Ellen had shared with her mother, but whatever she had told her had gained her full support.

Sullivan chose from among the men carefully, finding reasons to leave some of the more crude and perhaps untrustworthy men behind.

As the wagon finally rolled away from the prison he stood

there watching, his hands clasped loosely behind his back. Long
after they had disappeared in a cloud of dust he stood there,
wishing he could follow them. Just to make certain that women in
his promised care arrived safe from harm, he assured himself.
Nothing more. He sighed deeply and turned to face his duty.

~   ~   ~

The wagon creaked and shook as it rolled across ruts and
potholes left behind by the autumn rains. Several times they had to
make detours around piles of bodies left to decompose in the
deceivingly cheerful sunshine. Ellen had to ask their drivers to stop
while she ran to woods to retch the first time they passed one of the
macabre piles, but she seemed to harden herself to the sight after
her initial concession to the horror. Alex often heard her
whispering simple prayers for the officers' souls. She leaned closer
to Ellen and whispered, "While you're talking to Him, mention that
it'd sure be nice if he kept an eye on Kane, too." Ellen smiled.
    "He already is," she said simply. "He sent you to be his
guardian angel, didn't He?"
    Alex smiled, and smoothing Kane's hair, she said, "More like
he was sent to me, I think. I owe him so much."
    The sun mercifully stayed behind the fluffy, high clouds
during the hottest part of the day. As the shadows began to
lengthen, the wagon passed a clearing in the woods dotted with
rectangles of fresh soil and marked with rough-hewn crosses.
Suddenly a spot in the clouds allowed a ray of sunlight to escape its
boundaries and bathe the rows of crosses in a golden glow.
    Alex had often questioned how the world could keep on
behaving in such a normal manner with such a terrible turmoil in
its midst. How could the birds sing and the butterflies flit through
fields of flowers so unaware of the horrors that lay below them?
    "There should not be any sunshine," she said aloud suddenly,
surprising herself as much as Ellen at the sound of her own voice.
    "What?"
    "Sunshine. There shouldn't be any bright sunshine.
Everything looks so peaceful and . . . normal," she said with a catch
in her voice. "The skies should be black, and there should be a chill
in the breeze. So much death. So much heartache. And it's like the
world doesn't care."
    Ellen reached across the pile of straw that lay between them,

patting her hand. "I know, darling," she said. "But isn't it wonderful that in the midst of such a maelstrom of grief, we have blue skies and white clouds and breezes through tall pines to remind us that life does go on? And it will be better soon."

One of the soldiers Sullivan had finally chosen to drive the wagon turned around and said quietly, "That's a beautiful thought, Miss Ellen." He sighed. "Sometimes even with all the sunshine, it don't seem like there's much promise for tomorrow. Especially when there's so many men like him," he cocked his head toward Kane, whose body was stretched out with his head between the two women, "who don't have any more tomorrows."

Seeing Alex's eyes welling with tears, he swore under his breath and quickly turned around to face the road.

Suddenly, Alex saw Kane's hand twitch and heard a feeble groan.

"Oh, my God, Ellen, he's coming around," she whispered frantically. "What am I going to do?"

Ellen's eyes opened wide as she whispered back. "Oh, my! Do you have any of the potion with you?" She nodded at the reticule that lay at their feet.

"Yes, but how in the world am I going to explain to these men why I'm giving a dead man medicine?"

Kane suddenly twitched his whole body and groaned, bringing one knee up toward his stomach in a gesture of intense pain.

Ellen took a deep breath, stood upright, and without a word, pitched herself off the wagon backward, rolling into a ditch filled with honeysuckle vines.

~   ~   ~

Alex's first thought was that Ellen had suddenly gone mad. Then when the wagon lurched to a stop as the men discovered they had lost a passenger, she realized Ellen's plan.

As the men raced back to Ellen's side, Alex scrambled to her feet, quickly found the little brown bottle in her reticule, and without taking time to measure the portion, dropped a few drops in Kane's mouth.

He opened his eyes for a moment. "Forgive me, Kane," she whispered, caressing his cheeks gently between her palms. "It's the only way, I swear." His eyes looked puzzled for a moment, and she

could see the pain and confusion in their depths, then his eyes
rolled back into his head, and again he slept the sleep of the dead.

When she was certain he was completely relaxed, she turned
to see the men helping Ellen to her feet, questioning whether she
was all right to walk and arguing about what had caused her to fall.
Ellen, who was apparently pretending to be in a swoon, looked
over the men's heads toward Alex as they bent to pick her up. Alex
gave her a nod, and Ellen straightened and stood up on her own.

"Oh, my," she said. "How very, very clumsy of me. I do
declare, I could have killed myself!"

"You be careful now, Miss Ellen," the older of the two men
said with a worried look on his face. "Captain Sullivan would have
my neck if I let anything happen to either of you. He told me he was
holding me and Jake personally responsible for the two of you, and
if so much as a hair got ruffled on either head he was going to see to
it that we dug latrines for the rest of our normal lives."

His brow wrinkled, and he looked at Ellen accusingly. "How
on earth did you do a fool thing like that, anyway? Iffen' you
wanted to stop, all you had to do was ask."

Ellen laughed, her voice breaking through the tense moment
like the tinkling of chandelier crystals in the wind. "Sergeant
Decker, I do declare, you worry like an old settin' hen." She patted
his cheek. "You're very sweet to worry, but I promise I'll be fine.
Just a few scrapes and bruises. It was my own fault."

The younger man stuttered, "B–b–but what happened, Miss
Ellen? You was sitting there quiet and calm and then just pitched
yourself off the side."

Ellen blushed. "Private, or Lieutenant—I'm sorry, what was
your name?"

"Donahoo, Miss. Lieutenant Donahoo. But you can call me
just Jake."

"Well, Just Jake," she smiled, "I'm sure I must have looked like
I lost my mind, but I reckon I must have been daydreaming, and I
forgot where I was. For a moment there, I was back on Mama's
veranda, and I had decided I wanted to go in and get myself some
of her lemonade. You know, I did bring some along. Would either
of you gentlemen care to share some with Al—er, Maggie—and I?
I'm sure the horses would appreciate the rest." She looked at the
two docile horses tied to the rear of the wagon. "Even our horses
that aren't really having to work.

The men looked at each other for a moment, questions obvious on both their faces, then they shrugged. "Sure," they said in unison.

Alex breathed a sigh of relief and sat back down on the straw with a silent prayer of thanks to Ellen for her quick thinking. After taking a short break for lukewarm lemonade and gingersnap cookies, they hitched the horses back to the rear of the wagon and resumed their ride in silence. After a few minutes, when the men up front had begun what appeared to be a lengthy argument about the pros and cons of some newfangled rifle that was being shipped from the North to some of the Federal troops, she leaned across Kane's head and whispered to Ellen, "You were wonderful. How on earth did you think of that?"

Ellen's grin was wry. "I didn't." She shrugged. "I was going to stand up and go up front to talk to the men using my body as a shield for you to work on Kane. I stood up just as we hit a bump, and I went flying." She grimaced, "Lord knows if I'd been plannin' it, I'd have chosen a softer place to land." She hiked up her petticoats and showed Alex the scrapes and bruises on her legs. "When all this over, Mr. Stevens owes me a lot."

"When all this is over," Alex repeated with a sigh. She closed her eyes and whispered what sounded like a prayer to Ellen's ears. "Lord, I just want to be at Pearl's and let Kane wake up, and get him a doctor." Her voice trailed and her eyes widened. "Oh, Ellen, what if he's hurt too bad? What if—?"

Ellen put a finger to Alex's lips. "Shhhh," she warned. "Not so loud."

Alex's eyes flew to the front of the wagon where the men still argued, their arms gesturing wildly.

"Sorry," she said with an abashed look. "I just don't know how much longer I can keep Kane asleep. This can't be good for him." She looked again toward the men. "Oh, why can't they drive faster?"

"They're going as fast as they can on this road," Ellen said, her voice sounding like a teacher Alex remembered from her childhood.

She closed her eyes for a moment, remembering sunshine on her face as she sat in the garden with Miss Templeton, learning her alphabet. She smiled. Miss Templeton had probably not been any older than she was now herself, but she had seemed ancient to the fidgeting six-year-old. When Alex was seven, Miss Templeton had been found in a "compromising position" (as Aunt Matilda explained behind her fan to the pastor) with the husband of one of their neighbor's. Alex could remember hearing that phrase and wondering what position Miss Templeton had been in. She had told Alex she didn't like to ride horses because she said she was too stiff.

Alex remembered the pictures her seven-year-old mind had drawn and she giggled. The best she could come up with then was she must have been trying to stand on her head. And nothing in her mind could figure out how Mr. Culbert could have been involved with that. Aunt Matilda had been horrified when Alex had asked her outright if when they got caught in their compromising position, had Mr. Culbert been holding her feet up for her.

Alex's giggle grew into a belly laugh. She had been in close contact with men long enough in recent months to learn exactly in what "positions" men and women could find themselves.

She opened her eyes to find Ellen looking at her with a worried expression in her violet eyes. She turned and was embarrassed to see both men turned around in their seat staring at her as if she had grown a second head.

"Oh, for heaven's sake," she snorted. "A body can laugh sometimes without it meaning they've lost their mind." She flounced, trying to adjust the straw to a more comfortable position.

Sergeant Decker's voice drawled as he quietly said, "Yes'm, that's for sure, but usually not when they're sittin' beside a dead man."

Alex quickly sobered as she looked at Kane's white face.

"I'm sorry," she said. "I just tried to forget for a minute, and I guess I did a pretty good job of it."

Sergeant Decker smiled a gentle smile. "Good for you then, Miss Maggie. There's been a lot of times here lately I've wished I could do the same thing."

Alex leaned back against the side of the wagon, wriggling until she found a comfortable spot. The sun continued to beat down with the intensity that only a Southern sun can muster in November. She could feel rivulets of sweat forming into puddles between her breasts. She tried to find a place to sit where her shadow would cover Kane's face but still shield him from view of the two men driving the wagon.

When she shifted uncomfortably in the scratchy straw, one of the men turned toward her and said, "Miss Maggie, you and Miss Ellen are welcome to come sit up here in the front with me and Mac."

Alex smiled a faded smile at the young soldier. "Thank you very much, sir, but I have so little time left with my Kane, I don't want to waste a moment away from him."

She pretended not to hear the snort from the older soldier handling the reins. "Pretty soon we're gonna' all want to get as far away from him as possible, this heat wave holds out."

Under the cover of their voices, Alex leaned closer to Ellen. "I'm getting worried that Kane's going to start coming around. I'm going to give him a little more tonic. Come sit beside me so they can't see."

"Aren't you afraid you'll give him too much?"

Alex looked at her for a long moment, unshed tears making her eyes glisten. "Of course I am. And I'm afraid I won't give him enough. And I'm afraid someone's going to figure out what I'm doing. And I'm afraid Pearl will give us away somehow before she figures out what's going on. And I'm . . . I'm just afraid. Just plain afraid." Her voice shook. "But I don't have a choice. I'm all he's got. And he's all I've got. And I know he'd rather die out here in this wagon under a hot sun than laying on some filthy cot in a damn Yankee prison."

Ellen nodded sympathetically. "You're right, Alex—er, Maggie." She took Alex's hand in her own and rubbed it gently. "You're doing the right thing." She smiled wanly. "I hope wherever my George is that someone brave like you is taking care of him if he—" Her voice broke. "If he can't take care of himself," she sobbed.

The men's voices grew louder, trying to drown out the sounds of the sniffling woman behind them. Suddenly, Kane shifted position and groaned loudly. Alex turned panic-stricken eyes toward Ellen, who quickly moved nearer to Alex, and under the pretext of putting her arms around her friend shielded the view of Kane's face from the men.

Alex quickly reached into her reticule and pulled the cork from the small brown bottle. As she touched Kane's lips to open his mouth, his eyes opened as well. For a moment they sat there, each mesmerized by the other's eyes, each looking deep into the other's soul. Alex moved closer, picking up Kane's head and cradling it in her lap. She smoothed back the hair from his forehead.

"My angel," Kane breathed, then groaned loudly as the wagon hit a deep rut. Alex's arm jumped, and she dumped the entire contents of the bottle into his open mouth. He swallowed loudly, his throat tightening for a moment before his body relaxed and went slack again.

"What was that?" One of the men asked, putting one leg over the seat as if to come into the back of the wagon.

"*Ooooh,* my back hurts," Ellen groaned. "And that last rut back there just about drove my backbone all the way up through my neck." She smiled openly at the man. "I'm sorry, I didn't mean to bother you."

"No bother, miss." He sat back down and reached for the reins. To his partner he said under his breath, "Let's hurry up and get this cargo to Rossville. I'm starting to hear things. I coulda' swore that was a man's voice back there."

The other man snickered. "Yeah, if you start hearing that one talking, I'm gonna worry about you, Jake."

The day stretched out unbearably long for Alex and Ellen. The road seemed to get worse and worse, and by the time the sun had hit its midday zenith the path had dwindled down to barely more than a pig trail crisscrossed with ruts and deep mud puddles.

The wagon creaked and groaned as the women were tossed and jerked, their bodies aching from the bumps and bruises on almost every part of their anatomy, as they were tossed into each other, the sides of the wagon, and even the floor as the straw shifted beneath them. Alex's anxiety grew with each moment as she tried to keep Kane's hand near hers, checking his almost nonexistent heartbeat frequently and hoping she hadn't inadvertently undone all her hard work to save his life by overdosing him accidentally.

She tried to steady Kane's body over the worst of the bumps, bringing another look of disgust from the men. "Miss Maggie, you need to take care of yourself, miss," the younger man said. "Trust me, he ain't hurtin' none. But you're gonna' be black and blue tomorrow if you don't be careful."

The fuse on Alex's temper sizzled, and she gave him a withering look. "While I do appreciate your concern, Lieutenant, I assure you I can indeed take of myself. And I intend to get take care of my Kane so long as I can. Soon enough, I won't be able to touch him, to feel him, to shield him from any pain." Her voice broke. She had no problem summoning up tears. And the young man had no way of knowing that they were tears of frustration, anxiety, and physical discomfort rather than of simple grief.

"And soon enough you won't want to," the younger man said under his breath. "Good Lord, is she still gonna be cuddlin' that body when it starts rotting?"

"Ummph!" the older man pulled his elbow out of Jake's ribs.

"Don't say that where she can hear you," he warned. "No need to upset her." He frowned. "You know, I think you're just jealous. You know no woman wants to be that close to you now, and you're not even dead." He looked over his shoulder and saw Alex tenderly running her fingers through Kane's hair. "It sure has been a long time since any woman got that close to me," he said sorrowfully.

Chapter Twelve

A shout and the sound of horse's hooves brought Alex out of her slumber. She looked at Ellen and saw that she was looking in the direction of the sound, her eyes widening in horror at the sight of the three blue-uniformed men thundering toward them in a cloud of dust.

"Whoa, there!" Jake pulled the horses to a stop and waited for the men.

"What are you doing?" Ellen demanded, her face flushed and her eyes bright with fear.

"Miss, don't worry. Me and Lance will take care of you." He looked at Sergeant Decker, who patted his rifle and nodded affirmatively.

"But—"

"Miss, they probably just happen to be going in the same direction as us. I doubt they're even going to much notice we're here," Jake assured her. "Besides, they're wearing blue, miss. They're not a threat to us anyway."

Jake was wrong.

The leader reined his horse in with a flurry of hooves, and a spray of spittle and sweat from the massive horse flew over the two women. Alex was wiping her eyes with her sleeve when the man spoke. His voice sent shivers of fear and rage down her spine, and her eyes opened wide in recognition.

"Well, hell. What've we got here?"

The two soldiers driving the wagon saluted, and the older one said crisply, "Sergeant Lance Decker and Private Jake Donahoo on an errand of mercy at the orders of Captain Jacob Sullivan, sir."

"Captain Sullivan, eh?" The man's rough voice grated on Alex's nerves as well as her memory, and her grip on the side of the wagon tightened until her knuckles were white. He returned the men's salute. "Lieutenant Rafe Peterson. I'll ask you men to step down now, and I believe I'll just take over this 'errand of mercy,' as you call it." He leered at Ellen and Alex. "I believe I can show these 'ladies' the kind of mercy they probably won't even admit they're needing."

He snorted. "It sure looks like that fellow there won't be able to give them anything they're needing in this lifetime." He laughed at his own joke and prodded Kane's side sharply with the barrel of his rifle.

He raised his eyes, narrowing them slightly, to meet those of the two drivers. "I said step down."

Alex saw Jake's grip tighten on the rifle-butt leaning against his seat. Decker spoke first. "I'm sorry, sir, but we are under direct orders of Captain Sullivan to stay with the wagon and to protect its . . . cargo . . . until our duty is completed."

"Perhaps you didn't understand me, soldier." Peterson's voice was ragged with fury at the soldier's disobedience. "Perhaps if I speak slower this time." His voice was dangerously soft. "Step. Down. From. That. Wagon."

Decker's hands shook slightly, but his eyes never wavered from Peterson's as he replied firmly, "And my reply remains the same, sir. Begging your pardon, but I have received orders from my superior officer. One who, begging your pardon again, sir, outranks both of us. I'll remain with the wagon until my duty is completed."

Alex swore she could hear Peterson's teeth gritting. "If you don't get your skinny ass out of that wagon and on the ground in ten seconds, soldier, you can stay with it laid out in the back like that Confederate bastard you're hauling." His lips curled. "Sullivan is such a Nancy-boy. I heard he was taking men from their duties to deliver a dead man home to be buried. Not even a U.S. hero—a traitor." He hawked and spit. "I don't know what this army's coming to when they turn a command over to an oatmeal-mouthed half-man who . . ." His voice trailed off, and he shook his head and sighed loudly. "It's a crying shame, is what it is. If they'd give me a command post, I'd bring these damned bunch of yokels to their knees in no time." He snorted. "And bring the women to their backs at the same time." He leered at Alex and Ellen, exposing his yellowed teeth set in bright-red gums.

Alex's stomach tumbled at the thought of that mouth on her own and she shuddered, tearing her eyes away. Peterson's eyes caught the movement, and he watched her for a moment. He took his rifle and hooked the barrel under her chin, bringing her head around toward him. His eyes met hers. For a moment he was startled by what he saw there. Not fear, which he could usually instill in a woman with no problem, but hatred. He smiled again. *Hmmm.* Hate might be sort of nice for a chance. Wonder if hate put more fight in a woman than fear? He decided to find out. Either way, anything was better than indifference.

"Come on down outta there, sweetheart," he said, his leer widening, changing his face into something that reminded Alex of the jack-o-lantern Teddy had carved her when they were kids. Uncle James had complained about the pumpkin slime all over his best hunting knife, but he had helped them put a tallow candle inside it, and he'd hidden in the bushes with them to listen to the screams of the unsuspecting folks who happened on it in the twilight.

Her mind raced, and her heart beat so hard she was sure its vibration was visible outside her dress. If she defied Peterson he might kill them all. If she went with him it still might not make a difference. She had a feeling Peterson seldom let emotions get in the way of any decision. A fleeting tumble in the bushes most likely wouldn't change his mind about letting them ride away in peace.

Her eyes went down to Kane, his face still hidden behind the linen cloth. Whatever decision she made could mean death to him. If Peterson commandeered their wagon, she was certain they'd never reach Pearl's and a safe haven for Kane. If she fought him and they were all killed, Kane would die silently beside them.

She stood up slowly and faced him. "I will come with you, Lieutenant Peterson, if you will allow the wagon to leave safely and continue its journey."

She waved down Ellen's protests. With a humorless smile she added, "Do I have your word, Mr. Peterson? If not that of a gentleman, at least that of a Pennsylvania Yankee?"

Before Peterson could answer, Decker stood up slowly, bringing his rifle up to his shoulder, with Peterson's forehead obviously in the sights.

"Sit down, Miss Magnolia," he said quietly but firmly. "You're not going anywhere with this man. And this wagon *will* complete its mission."

Peterson straightened his back and sighed. "Oh, my, I do wish you hadn't done that, Decker. I'll swear, where does Sullivan find you men? You bunch of panty-waisted little boys playing at being a soldier." He nodded toward his men. "There are three of us, and

even though there are five of you," he chuckled, "two of you are
women, and one of you is a"—pleased by his own humor, he
chortled loudly—"a dead man." He cocked his head to one side
and said with mock sympathy, "Now, Decker. You want to rethink
aimin' that rifle at me before I tell my boys to open fire?"

Alex saw the young soldier's Adam's-apple bob quickly, but
his voice was firm and unwavering when he answered. "No sir,
Lieutenant Peterson. I just want to remind you that my rifle is
already trained on the spot right between your eyes. Your men may
be good, but they can't draw and fire quick enough to stop me from
pulling the trigger and dropping you right where you stand. Now
maybe you want to rethink *your* position?"

Peterson stepped backward, watching Decker's rifle follow
him. Alex could see his mind turning the problem over and could
almost see his brain scurrying for a solution as fury, fear, and
confusion narrowed his eyes.

Suddenly Ellen stood up and said calmly, "And Mr. Peterson,
just in case you're still concerned about the sides not being even . . ."
Alex's eyes widened as Ellen brought her hands from beneath her
skirts, exposing the small but very deadly pistol she had hidden
there. "Now I'd say the odds are a little more even-numbered,
wouldn't you say, sir? Three guns against three?" She smiled a cold
smile. "Of course, since two of our guns are now pointed at you,
and your men don't seem to be too inclined to draw their own
pistols, I'd saw the odds just leaned in our favor." She nodded
toward the road they had just traveled. "Now, I think the very best
way to solve this situation would be for you to haul your own fat
ass back down that road, taking these two fine soldiers with you so
we can all forget this happened."

Peterson's lips curled. "I won't forget anything, little lady.
Count on it. As it happens I'm on a rather important mission, and
quite frankly, I don't have time to play these party games with you
four ladies." He tipped his hat toward Decker and Donahoo, now
both standing with rifles drawn. He nodded to his men, who
turned their horses around and began cantering away.

Peterson pulled his horse up short suddenly and came
galloping back toward them. Alex heard the two rifles cock before
Peterson stopped short of the end of the wagon. His voice was cold
and hard as he said simply, "Decker, you tell your captain for me
that the threat of his name didn't change a thing here today. I'm not

afraid of him. And I meant what I said before. When the time is right, I plan on killing him." Before the other soldier could reply, Peterson kicked his horse in the flank and disappeared in a cloud of dust.

"Oh, my God." Ellen's knees suddenly gave way beneath her and she crumpled into the straw. Her face was white, and her lips bright red where she had bitten them.

"Are you okay, miss?" one of the soldiers asked hesitantly.

"Yes . . . no. I will be," Ellen stammered.

The two men watched her for a moment before slowly sitting back down, then Sergeant Decker picked up the reins. "Ladies, I hate to do this, but if we're going to make Rossville tonight, we've got some hard riding to do. If you're sure you're okay, we'll be on our way." He and Donahoo shared a glance, and Decker added quietly, "It also won't hurt any to put some miles between us and Peterson. I'd hate for the son of a bitch to change his mind." He blushed and looked at the women. "Begging your pardon, ladies, for my language."

Ellen and Alex both nodded in agreement, and Alex smiled. "Actually, Sergeant Decker, I quite agree with your description of officer Peterson's mother. And I also ask that you excuse my language as well. I'm afraid"—she blushed becomingly—"I got a little carried away in the heat of the moment."

The wagon pitched forward with a creak, and the two women rocked back into the straw. Alex reached across and patted Ellen's hand. "Are you sure you're going to be okay?"

"For the love of God, Maggie, did you see what I did? I pulled a gun on a man. Another human being. And I would have shot him, too. Without even blinking an eye." Her voice shook. "Dear God, what an awful man." She looked at Alex and shook her head. "I didn't really know there were men in the world like that." A tear coursed down her cheek. "I was so scared, Maggie. I knew if you went with him he'd either kill you, or he'd—" Her cheeks flushed. "Well, he'd hurt you."

"I know exactly what he's capable of," Alex said softly. She waited until their drivers began arguing about what they would have done if Peterson if had pushed any harder, then she leaned closer to Ellen and whispered, "Ellen, I want you to know that if you had a bullet through Rafe Peterson, you would have been doing the world a favor. It wouldn't have made you a bad person, or damned you to hell. The Lord would probably have added a few stars to your crown for saving him the trouble of finding a more horrid death to end Peterson's life."

Ellen frowned. "How do you know his first name, Maggie? Nobody called him anything but Sergeant." Her eyes widened in realization. "And you called him a Pennsylvania Yankee. Now, I know nobody mentioned where he was from."

Alex nodded. "Yes. We've met before." Her voice grew very hard as she quietly described her first meeting with Peterson. When she was finished, Ellen bit her lip for a moment, obviously searching for the right words. When she spoke, her voice was ragged with emotion.

"Now I wish I had shot the son of a bitch," she said.

Alex laughed. "Oh, my. I'm afraid there's one more discreet Southern lady who has learned the advantages of adding curse words to her vocabulary."

Ellen gave Alex a swift hug. "How did you stand it? I'd have just died. Curled up and died."

Alex shook her head. "No, you wouldn't. You proved that a few minutes ago. When the chips are down, you do what you have to do. No matter how unpleasant. No matter how hard. You know something I've never given much thought to?" Ellen shook her head. "They call us 'Southern belles,' and they take that to mean that we're all fluff. Just lace and ribbons and pretty dresses and bows in our hair. But think about it, Ellen. Did your mama have a dinner bell?" At Ellen's affirmative nod she added, "And what was it made of?"

Ellen smiled. "Iron. Cast iron."

"Exactly. So maybe these Southern belles are made of a little tougher stuff than we're given credit for."

"I'll second that, miss."

Alex jumped as Decker spoke again to apologize. "Sorry miss, begging your pardon, but I just couldn't help overhearing what you said. And I'd have to agree with you, miss. And I wanted you to know I was proud of both of you ladies back there. You, Miss Maggie, you was ready to go off with that son of Satan back there just 'cause you thought he wouldn't cause us no more trouble. And you, miss"—this last with a nod at Ellen—"I have to tell you I about had a coronary seizure when you stood up and flashed that little pistol at old Peterson." He chuckled. "I'll bet it gave him quite a start too, whatcha bet?"

He and Donahoo laughed and chortled and slapped each other on the back. Alex quietly asked, "And how much more of my story did you hear?"

The men grew quiet, and she saw the back of Donahoo's neck grow red. Decker turned around and said, "More than you meant us to, I reckon, miss. And enough to know that if I ever have Peterson in my sights again, I won't let him go without pullin' the trigger. You're a brave woman, Miss Maggie." He turned around and slapped the reins on the horses' backs, saying in a husky voice, "Git up, now."

The rest of the ride passed in silence except for general conversation and a few remarks about the scenery. Luckily they had passed through the major line of skirmish, and the only signs of battle along the roadside were a few unmarked mounds of clay and an occasional scrap of shrapnel lodged in a tree trunk.

Alex dozed for a bit, always alert even in sleep for the slightest movement from Kane. She wavered between relief that he had not regained consciousness since the overdose, and fear that the overdose would indeed prove (or had proven) fatal.

When she noticed a familiar barn beside the road, she straightened and nudged Ellen. "We're almost there," she whispered. She gestured for Ellen to take her place beside Kane, and she crawled toward the drivers.

"Please let me off here," she said. "I want to go on ahead and kind of prepare Aunt Pearl."

The drivers brought the wagon to a halt. "How much further is it?" one of them asked.

"I think about a half a mile. I'm not sure. But you won't have to wait but a minute, I promise. I'll take my horse and let her stretch her legs a bit too." As she spoke Alex was scrambling down from the wagon and tossing the reins over Birdie's neck. Before the men could respond she was almost out of sight beyond the next curve, lying low over the mare's neck as the flying hooves stirred up a fog of dusty red.

She raced into Pearl's yard, dismounted, and quickly looped the reins over the rickety gatepost. She almost fell into Pearl's arms as the door opened. "Kane. Shot. They think he's dead—he's not. You've got to help us." Her words came out short and breathless.

Pearl put her hands on Alex's shoulders to calm her. "Slow

down, darlin'! What's happened?"

Pearl's face paled as Alex repeated her words.

"Kane's been shot. The Yankees are bringing him here to bury him. But he's not dead."

Alex leaned against the doorframe, her breath coming in short gasps. "It's really bad, Pearl. I didn't know what else to do. I mixed up a potion to slow his heartbeat and put him in a deep sleep so they'd think he was dead. Then they wanted to bury him. I talked the captain into letting me bring him here to bury him."

"Bury him? But he's not dead? I'm confused, hon."

Alex's frustration flared. "The wagon will be here any minute. Trust me, Pearl. He's not dead, he's just in a deep sleep. Unless I've overdosed him. But anything was better than the hellhole where I found him. The men with us haven't got any idea they're not bringing a dead man home to be buried."

Pearl suddenly sprang to life. She snapped orders to the black man standing behind her. "Lije, get some hot water and bandages, and take them to Becca's room."

"Yes'm" came the reply. "But ma'am, Miz Becca's got somebody in there with her right now."

"Then get them out. Offer them a free visit for the interruption, then take them up to Cille's room, it's empty."

She glanced at Alex. "Becca has a room with an outside entrance that may come in handy." Alex could almost see the wheels turning in her mind as she laid out a quick plan. "Let's see. We'll tell the men—" She turned to her. "How many men came with you?"

"Two. Very nice men. For Yankees. They kept us from getting killed or worse by—oh, Pearl, I found him. Rafe Peterson. But I couldn't do a thing, 'cause I was afraid it'd keep me from getting Kane here."

Pearl patted her on the shoulder distractedly. "You can tell me all about it later, hon. Right now we've got work to do."

She turned and walked to the elderly Negro man who had returned and now stood silently behind her. "Is Becca out of her room?" she asked. The old man nodded, and Pearl began to talk quietly to him. Within minutes he nodded again and scurried through the door.

In seconds they could hear the wagon wheels squeaking as they turned into the path from the road.

"Looks like we've got company," Pearl said grimly.

She screwed up her face, and in a minute a tear rolled down her cheeks. She began to cry softly, her wails getting louder by the minute.

"Pearl, what's wrong?" Alex asked, her heart sinking, certain she had based Kane's last chance on a mad woman.

"Get out there," she heard Pearl hiss, "and help me down the steps." Alex looked at Pearl in bewilderment and was amazed to see a small wink appearing behind the lace handkerchief Pearl had pulled from her pocket and with which she was dabbing her eyes.

"Oh, my Gawd!" she wailed loudly. "Not Kane—oh, no! What will we do?"

She stumbled across the weedy yard and reached inside the wagon, taking one of Kane's hands in her own. "Oh, my sweet Jesus, it just can't be!"

Slowly realizing what Pearl was doing, Alex followed her and put her arms around her shoulders. "Let's just get him inside, Aunt Pearl."

When the men jumped down from the seat, Pearl sobbed, "Please, let my man carry him in. We'll put him downstairs, where I can lay him out proper-like." She bowed her head. "Be gentle with him now, y'hear?"

The men shrugged and looked at each other. Alex hid a smile when she heard one of them whisper, "Do you reckon all Southern women carry on like this, or are we just in a nest of 'em?"

They stood back and watched as Elijah and the soldiers carried Kane carefully into the house.

Pearl stood back and seemingly struggled to regain her composure. She followed the men into the house, drew a deep breath, wiped her eyes, and said in a voice that was rough with tears, "Sirs, please do forgive my manners. I'm afraid I have not been very hospitable. Please allow me to fix you a bit of refreshment to thank you for your time in bringing our Kane back home to be buried." Her voice caught, and she wiped an errant tear from her cheek.

"No, thank you very much, ma'am. We'll be off, we want to get an early start tomorrow, so we plan to make camp a couple miles down the road."

Alex heard the door open behind her and a female voice said, "Oooh, Pearl, you didn't tell us we had comp'ny. Now boys, what'll be your pleasure tonight? A bath, a back rub, or just a quick tickle? We're running a special this week, I guess Pearl told you. Anybody in blue gets a free shave and haircut."

Pearl turned and looked daggers at the young whore who was hanging on the edge of the door, allowing the men a long gaze at her bare legs peeking out beneath the fringes of a pink wrapper. The girl ignored her look. "Come on in, fellows, I think Lila's free tonight, and together we'll see if we can't get you out of that blue and into some skin." She licked her lips seductively as she crooked her finger, beckoning the soldiers inside.

The men almost fell over themselves heading for the door, then slowly stopped and turned, looking at Pearl. "Go ahead, fellows," she said with a small, wan smile and a wave. "I guess that'll be a bit more refreshin' than the pie and iced tea I was goin' to offer you."

"Hot damn!" one of the men whispered to the other. "Reckon Sullivan knew we were coming to a whorehouse?"

As the men disappeared inside, Pearl turned to Alex and said between gritted teeth, "Damn that Mona. I've warned her about coming out and propositioning men I haven't cleared for the girls. She's going to get us all killed or worse one of these days." She let out a deep sigh and shook her head. "I've told her wait until they've come inside, met me, and I've determined that they're okay to send on upstairs. I swear that for a dollar she'd take on anything wearing pants."

Alex shrugged and said in a whispered panic, "Now what do we do? We can't take care of Kane with them in the house. I think they'd lock us up for crazies if we start bandaging a dead man. It's been hard enough to make them understand why I didn't want him buried or wrapped."

As they started up the steps to the porch, Alex suddenly remembered Ellen, who was still outside with the wagon. She had helped the men put Kane's body gently on the board they'd used to take him inside and then stood there uncertainly, waiting to be invited in. Alex motioned for Ellen to join them, and Ellen reached into the wagon bed to get the pillowcase she and Alex had quickly packed before they left Monroeville.

"This is Ellen," Alex said when Ellen had reached the porch. "First she helped me find Kane, and then she helped me get him here. I couldn't have done any of it without her."

Pearl started to hold her hand out to Ellen, then stopped. Alex, realizing Pearl's reticence in forcing Ellen to return the gesture, said quickly, "I already told Ellen what kind of business you run here. She's not going to judge you, Pearl."

Ellen nodded, and she suddenly surprised Alex and Pearl by putting her arm around Pearl's waist and pulling her close. "Anyone who Alex trusts has to be special," she said with an open smile. "Although I don't imagine my mother would have been too eager to let me come if she'd known I'd be staying in a . . . a . . ."

"Whorehouse?" Pearl inserted dryly.

Ellen smiled politely. "Well, ma'am, you know that word isn't in the vocabulary of most women, but yes, ma'am, that is indeed what I meant—although I was going to call it a house of pleasure. That makes it sound much nicer, don't you think? And I wouldn't care if you were Satan's handmaiden yourself if you can help us with Kane."

Their smiles faded as they remembered the duty that lay ahead for them inside.

"How bad is he?" Pearl asked, pleasantries forgotten as they turned and started together into the house.

"I don't know. The doctor at the prison said his leg was broke and he was all busted up inside. I know he wasn't even conscious before I gave him the draught. Then after taking it he's just come out long enough to look at me." Her words broke off as she recalled the look of pain and bewilderment Kane had given her during the few seconds of brief lucidity. "Anyway, he isn't conscious now, so if you're going to have someone check him out, now would be a good time." She grinned wryly. "I don't suppose either of the two soldiers are going to be noticing what we're doing for a little while."

Pearl returned the smile. "If I know Lila and Mona, it'll be a good long while. They think they're getting paid by the hour. They don't know yet that this one's on the house."

The women walked through the cool parlor and down the dark hallway to the rear of the house. They found Kane lying on a makeshift table in the middle of the room. He was lying flat, covered only by a sheet. Someone had taken off his clothes, which were lying in a puddle of dirty grey beside the door. Pearl picked them up and laid them outside in the hallway. "We'll get these washed up for him."

Alex's breath caught. "Then you think he'll be okay—okay enough to be needing those clothes again, Pearl? I've been so worried."

"Well, I don't know for sure yet. I haven't even laid eyes on him, for heaven's sake, much less my hands, but if there's any way me and Jesus can pull him through this, we will. He's a good man, and we can't afford to lose any more than we already have." The expression on her face was serious and determined, and Alex relaxed for a second, relieved to finally put the burden on someone else's shoulders.

Pearl walked to the side of the table and gently caressed Kane's brow. "Got a hell of a bruise there," she said softly. She turned to the women. "We're going to need a lot of things out of the herb garden. Alex, since you seem to know a little about that." She gave Alex a list of herbs to gather and sent her and Ellen out the door with a gathering basket and a knife.

Alone in the room, Pearl leaned over and kissed Kane's cheek. "Trust me, Kane. You're safe now. You're here at Pearl's." A tear slid from the corner of her eye and dropped to Kane's bare shoulder. Seeing it, she took the corner of the sheet and dried it, then dried her own cheek. Setting her shoulders squarely, she peeled back the sheet and began to gingerly prod the bruised and broken body, deciding what needed work first.

Alex and Ellen brought in the basket, now filled with greenery and blossoms. "Couldn't find any comfrey," Alex said. "And you didn't have boneset on the list, but I figured you'd need it so I found some."

"Good girl," Pearl said. "Now, go into the kitchen and tell Lije to get Becca and bring her here. She's going to have to help me with Kane. We've worked together before, and she knows what she's doing," she said, when she saw Alex's mouth open and knowing an argument was coming. "You and Miss Ellen go on out and wait for me. We'll be out in a bit. If the men come back down, send them on their way. You'll be more useful out there than in here for a while."

"Aren't you going to call for a doctor?" Alex asked.

"Doctor?" Pearl's snort seemed to rattle the windows. "Girl, there ain't anybody left in Rossville except us and whatever soldiers are passing through on their way to somewhere else. Old Doc Wiley was in the first wagonload outa' here. I imagine he's somewhere in Atlanta spending the day in some"—she nodded at Ellen, and the edges of her mouth curled in a slight smile—"house of pleasure, being fanned by some Oriental gal in red underwear."

She snorted again. "He never was much of a doctor, anyway. I've cured more folks than he has, and I've seen more bodies, too." She winked at Ellen, who blushed bright red clear to the roots of her hair.

Pearl gathered her apron and shook it at them, shooing the girls from the room. "Go on, now. And send Becca on in here, we've got work to do."

Chapter Thirteen

Alex and Maggie walked up and down the length of the hallway, softly talking and worrying aloud, wondering about what was going on behind Kane's closed door. There was no doubt what was going on behind the closed doors upstairs. Occasionally a particularly loud thump, and a groan or shout would automatically pull their eyes upward, causing them to share an embarrassed grin when they met each other's eye again.

Ellen smirked. "I can't imagine doing—*that*—for money. Can you, Alex?"

Alex shook her head. "No. But not too long ago I wouldn't have imagined I could wear a man's uniform and shoot a rifle aimed at another human being, either. Time and circumstances change everybody, I guess."

Ellen nodded her agreement, and added with a blush, "Sometimes I can't imagine doing—that—at all. Even with George."

Alex smiled. "Oh, I imagine you'll change your mind the next time you're alone together."

Suddenly the door to Kane's room cracked open a bit, and Pearl stuck her head out.

"All's clear," Alex said softly. "The men are still upstairs."

Pearl opened the door and walked into the hall, her apron now blood-spattered and her face wan and pale. She looked at Alex and shook her head. "I don't know, Alex. We've done the best we could. The rest is up to the Lord now."

Alex's heart fell. "What all's wrong with him, Pearl?"

"Well, the doctor that checked him was right, his leg was busted up pretty bad. He's going to have a limp—if he can ever walk again at all. That's the least of his problems, though. He's pretty busted up inside. A bunch of ribs busted, for sure. I taped 'em up best I could. And I hear some air hissing through his lungs that I don't like the sound of. I mixed up a poultice and taped it to his chest. It could just be pneumony trying to set in, but could be a rib's busted into a lung. We'll hope not." She pulled a chair closer and sat down tiredly.

"That long ride here in the wagon sure didn't do him no good." She held her hand up to ward off Alex's protestations. "Yes, I know, you didn't have a choice, but whether or no, it didn't do him any good."

Ellen reached for Alex's hand and squeezed it tightly. "We'll just have to keep praying, Alex—er—Maggie." She looked at Pearl, and then at Alex questioningly. "What do we call you now?"

"I guess I'll just stay Maggie for a while," Alex said thoughtfully. "You can introduce me to the girls that way, and then nobody'll have a chance to get suspicious. Although I can't imagine anyone confusing me with the raggedy-ass greyback who came here with Kane a month ago. Good Lord, Pearl. Has it just been a month?"

Pearl smiled at her. "You've seen a lot of miles since then, I'll bet. When you get rested, I wanna' hear all about 'em. Glad to see you in a dress now. Right now, I hear Mona's door opening, and that means we better get back to grievin' for our dead soldier boy."

She stood up and walked into the parlor, where she watched Sergeant Decker walking down the stairs, adjusting his belt self-consciously. "Uh, Miz Pearl? Er . . . Mona said I was supposed to . . . er . . . take care of . . ." He fumbled in his pocket, obviously looking for money.

Pearl smiled at him. "There's no charge. For either of you. I hope Mona treated you right. It's the least we can do to repay you for bringing our beloved Kane back home."

"Yes ma'am, my buddy and sure do thank you for your generosity." He looked upstairs. "I reckon I'll just go wait in the wagon for Jake." His face stretched into a grin that faded when Alex walked into the room.

"Uh, Miss Maggie, I don't rightly know if Captain Sullivan knew for sure where we were headed. We'd be happy to give you a ride back to town with us if you don't think you'll be . . . uh . . . comfortable here."

"Thank you," Alex said with a smile. "But I'm sure I'll be quite comfortable here at Aunt Pearl's. Do please be sure to tell the captain we thank him for his kindness."

Sergeant Decker continued to twist his hat in his hands. "Well, what about you Miss Ellen?" He turned to look at her.

Ellen smiled and handed him a folded piece of paper. "There's

a note for my mother. Please see that she gets it, and tell her I'm
fine. I'm going to stay with Maggie for a while. I think she'll need
me to, well, get over all this. Tell Mother I'll write, and I'll plan on
meeting her in Charleston next month, as we planned." The man
turned and walked toward the door.

"Oh, and sergeant," Ellen's words stopped him. He turned and
saw the corner of Ellen's lips turning up into a mischievous grin. "I
don't think there's any need to describe Alex's aunt or her
occupation in great detail to my mother."

"Oh, no, ma'am," the soldier agreed with an embarrassed
blush. "No need at all!"

A few minutes later they heard a door slam upstairs and heavy
footsteps coming down the stairs. The tousled hair of the young
soldier brought a wan smile to Pearl's face. "Your friend is waiting
for you in the wagon," she said, holding out her hand to the man.
"Thanks again for bringing my niece and her friend home"—her
voice caught on a slight sob—"and for delivering my dear Kane
home to be buried."

The soldier looked down at his boots for a moment. "Ma'am,"
he said suddenly, "Decker and I would be honored if you'd let us
take care of burying Sergeant Stevens for you."

Pearl's surprise and consternation was no act. "Oh, no, sir. We
couldn't let you do that. We really couldn't. Elijah will take care of
digging the grave, while the girls and I will lay him out proper. You
get along now, you've got a long ride ahead of you."

"Well, ma'am, see that's part of the problem," the soldier said,
scratching his hair, then trying in vain to smooth the unruly strands
back into place. "We met some rather unsavory characters on the
road earlier today, and I don't much relish running into them again
after dark. Or having them run into our camp, either. We'd be very
grateful if you'd allow us to camp out here tonight, maybe even
sleep in your barn, and then we'll be out of here at first light. We'd
have before dark to get the grave dug and get your friend taken care
of."

Pearl stuttered. "Oh, that's most kind of you, sir, but as I said,
we just couldn't let you do that." Her look of panic was mirrored
on Alex's and Ellen's faces.

The man insisted. "Ma'am, it's really the least we can do in
return for your"—he cast an embarrassed glance toward Alex and
Ellen—"your hospitality."

Pearl looked at him for a moment, then shrugged and said with a serene smile, "Well, if you're certain it won't be any trouble for you, we'd be most obliged. I'll have Lije show you where the shovels are, and if you'll come with me now, I'll show you the spot I've got picked out for Kane."

Ellen and Alex turned pasty-white, slack-jawed faces toward Pearl.

"But Pearl—"

"What are you—?"

Pearl held up a hand. "I know where Kane wanted to be buried, girls. It'll be all right. You've both had quite a day. You go along now and unpack. Maggie, you and Ellen can share the room you had when you were here last." She nodded her dismissal of them as they slowly picked up their bags and walked upstairs.

"What in the world can she be thinking?" Alex hissed when they were out of earshot. Her fists were clenched, and her stomach felt no larger than an acorn.

"I can't imagine," Ellen said, shaking her head. "Good heavens. They're going to want to bury a body, I'm thinking. In a casket." She sat down on the chair beside the window and let out a long breath. "I just can't see any way out of this one, Maggie."

Alex shook her head. "I do trust Pearl, because Kane told me he did. I just can't believe she'd sell Kane out to the soldiers." She slowly shook her head again. "I sure hope she comes up with something pretty quickly, though." She nodded out the open window, where the soldiers had removed their jackets and could be seen digging at the hard, red clay beneath a huge cedar tree. "I think those boys are going to be mighty unhappy if they don't get to put a wooden box with somebody in it down in that hole when they get through digging."

A tap on the door hushed their voices for a moment. "Come in, it's open," Alex said.

Pearl opened the door and came inside. "Girls, it appears we're in a bit of a jam."

"That's rather an understatement, isn't it?" Alex said wryly. "How do you plan to get out of it? Why on God's green earth would you agree to let those men stay here?"

Pearl replied with a grim smile. "I've done the best I could for Kane." She reached out a hand and gently laid it on Alex's arm. "I want you to know that we all did the absolute best we could. Kane will know that, too. Whatever happens." A tear trickled down her cheek, and she sniffed loudly.

She took a deep breath. "Now I gotta get back downstairs and see to things." She opened the door and stepped into the hallway. "You both stay here until I call for you, understand?"

"Yes, Pearl, but I sure wish you'd let us know what's going on."

"No. I don't think you'd like it. And I don't have time to argue with you." A moment later the hallway was empty except for the echo of her light footsteps on the stairs.

Alex and Ellen spent the next half-hour combing the brambles from Ellen's hair after her tumble into the ditch. Alex found a silver comb and artfully arranged Ellen's silky tresses into a lovely style, with a few tendrils allowed to escape and curl around her face. "I can't wait until my own hair grows back out," she complained. "I used to be able to sit on it, and now it barely reaches my shoulders."

"But it's lovely," Ellen exclaimed, reaching for the brush. "It's such a rich, deep shade. Here, let me see if we can't do something with it."

Pearl's voice boomed up the stairs. "Girls, you need to come on down now."

The tone in her voice sent a shiver down Alex's spine. She looked at Ellen and reached for her hand. Together they slowly descended the staircase into the parlor.

There in front of the fireplace was a freshly made coffin, its pine lumber tingeing the air with its scent. Alex looked at Pearl with fear and confusion in her eyes. "Pearl?" She said in a tiny voice.

"I'm so sorry, Maggie," Pearl said, tears flowing down her cheeks. "I am so very, very sorry."

She came and put her arm around Alex's shoulders as Alex swayed and reached for one of the velvet-covered chairs that flanked the coffin on each end.

Pearl leaned closer and said, "Kane is in God's hands now."

Alex's eyes widened in protest. "Oh, no, Pearl!" She shook her head. Before Pearl or Ellen could reach her she fell across the coffin, scratching at the lid, trying to raise the lid. "He can't breathe in there, Pearl. Get him out!"

The soldiers, standing in the corner of the room, shuffled their feet and exchanged embarrassed glances.

"Honey, you've got to let go," Pearl scolded. "What's done is done. And now there's nothing more we can do but leave him in God's hands. I told you that before. Remember?"

Alex nodded. "Is Kane really in there?" she asked quietly, her eyes lowered toward the floor.

Pearl put her finger beneath Alex's chin and gently lifted her tearstained face. Alex met her eyes squarely and asked the question again. Pearl nodded, then sighed and walked over to the coffin and raised the lid. Kane was dressed in a starched white shirt and black leather tie, his tanned face looking darker still against the crisp white-linen pillow that cradled his head. His callused hands were clasped, and his face had a serene half-smile, as if he were privy to a joke no one else could hear.

Ellen gave a gasp and a short cry as she reached for Alex's hand.

Pearl took a deep breath, obviously fighting back her own tears. She looked at the soldiers and said, "If y'all don't mind, I'd like a moment alone with Kane. This all happened so suddenly, I haven't had a chance to really say goodbye to him. I want to cut a lock of his hair for my locket too. Then Lije can nail the lid shut, and if y'all would be so kind, then you can carry him out to the gravesite for us."

The soldiers nodded and somberly escorted a stunned Ellen and Alex out onto the front porch.

After a few minutes of hearing muted mumbles and an occasional sob, they heard a few staccato taps with a hammer, and then Pearl opened the door for them, her face streaked with tears.

"I think we're ready now," she said, her voice breaking.

Alex's sobs shortened into hiccups. She stood aside as the soldiers and the old Negro men carried the coffin through the parlor, down the hall, and out the door into the backyard. She followed slowly, her thoughts going back to another hillside, another red clay grave, and the days that had started her downhill tumble to the present.

She listened as one of the soldiers read a verse from the Bible, and her voice joined with the others in the old, familiar words of "Amazing Grace," but her voice was toneless to her own ears. Suddenly it all seemed too much to comprehend at one time. Too much death. Too many funerals. Too many men who would never be given the dignity of a funeral or being laid to rest in familiar soil.

She had risked so much. And gained so little.

The edges of her vision grew dark, then her vision faded completely. Alex welcomed the darkness, and for the second time in her life, sank into it gratefully.

Chapter Fourteen

"Alex? Maggie? Wake up, child."

Alex felt a sting on her cheek, and she opened her eyes slowly. She blinked a few times and then tried to sit up. Her nose burned, and her sinuses groaned in agony. "What on earth?" She reached up and rubbed her nose and gasped a deep breath through her mouth.

"Smelling salts. I'm sorry, but we've got a lot of work to do. We need you."

"Smelling salts? Why? What? And did you just slap me?" she said angrily. Memories flooded into Alex's mind, and she closed her eyes against them. She leaned back against the embroidered pillows.

"The funeral. Kane. Did I faint?"

"Yes. Somehow you don't strike me as the fainting type, but Ellen says you did the same thing at the prison." A light blush spread up her neck and tinged her cheeks, as her eyes narrowed. "You're not with child, are you, Alex?"

Alex was stunned. "Of course not," she snapped. Then her voice grew husky with memories. "Sometimes I think my mind can only hold so many horrors, Pearl. After a while, I guess it just has to shut down to give me time to absorb things." She gave a short, humorless laugh. "In my defense, though, I've only fainted twice in my whole life, and both times I think it was very much warranted."

She stood up, her legs shaky beneath her.

"Have the men gone?"

"They left about an hour ago."

"An hour?

"They brought you back inside. Then they finished filling in the grave while Ellen and I made you comfortable. And then they left to set up camp in the barn. They'll leave at daylight. Soon as they were gone, I decided you'd rested enough and I brought you around."

"Where's Ellen?"

"She's upstairs. And she needs you. Go on up. Second door on the left."

Alex walked up the stairs slowly, her feet feeling as wooden as her heart. To have gone through so much to save Kane's life, only to have him die just as they'd reached safety. She closed her eyes and leaned against the wall. "What if I killed him?" she whispered. "Maybe he'd have been better off taking his chances in the prison."

Ellen answered her knock with a soft "Come in."

Alex opened the door and walked inside, closing it behind her. "Pearl said you needed help," she said, her voice ragged with tears both shed and unshed.

"Yes," Ellen said. "Please light the lantern on the dresser if you don't mind. It's getting hard to see."

In the dim light, Alex could see Ellen leaning over the bed, adjusting the pillow underneath the head of a shadowy form. "What are you doing?" Alex asked dully, knowing that Ellen's answer didn't really matter. As the light from the lantern grew brighter, her eyes widened in disbelief. Her legs felt like rubber, and she reached for the footboard of the white iron bedspread.

"Kane?" she asked disbelievingly.

Ellen's smile would have brightened the room without the lantern's help. "Yes. Isn't Pearl wonderful?"

"But how? He was in the coffin. We both saw him. We all saw him." Alex walked over and gently touched Kane's brow. "His fever isn't as hot as it has been, is it?" She pinched her arm and watched as the red mark grew. "I'm not dreaming, am I?"

"No, you're not dreaming," said Ellen. "Although you have been out for quite a while. Please don't make a habit of this fainting. I swear, it scares the bejeebies outta me." She laid her hand against Kane's cheek. "Becca's been keeping a cool poultice on him since we got him upstairs, and his fever broke about an hour ago."

She made a motion toward the dark-skinned woman standing at the end of the bed, who smiled at Alex and said, "Iffen you listen close, his breathing doesn't sound all whistly like it did when he first started really breathing again."

Alex shook her head. "I don't believe it."

"Neither did I," said Ellen. "But he's here. And if he makes it through tonight, I'd say we've got a good chance of keeping him with us for a while longer." Her smile lit the room. "I have to say, I'm looking forward to getting to know your Kane, Maggie. He must be a wonderful man to have generated such affection from you and Pearl."

Alex walked to the window and looked at the bare red-clay rectangle that spread beneath the big cedar, its dark red in brilliant contrast with the lush green lawn. "If he's not in there, who is?" She sat down suddenly as her legs started to give away. "I just don't understand."

"I haven't had a chance to get the whole story from Pearl either."

Ellen's sentence was cut short by Pearl's appearance in the doorway. "Well, girls, I think we pulled it off." Her sigh of relief was heartfelt. She walked over and put her hand on Kane's forehead. "Feels better already."

"Pearl, I don't understand. How did you get Kane up here? We were right there. I saw him in the box. I heard you nail it shut. And I saw the men start covering the coffin with dirt."

"Right on all counts," Pearl said with a self-satisfied smile. "We did indeed put Kane in the box. And we nailed the box shut. And the men put it in a hole, and they filled it in. But in between all that, there was the time when I had my moment alone with him. Lije and his buddy Silas lifted Kane out of the box and carried him upstairs, still laid out on the board that was in the bottom of the coffin. It was the same board Kane was laid on in the back room there. We don't dare move him around too much till some of them bones get themselves mended. The wooden box was one Lije had just finished making to bury some of my grandmother's china and silver before the Yankees get a chance to get a hold of it. We just put it to a different use first and then got the Yankees to bury it for us. And now I've got a nice tilled-up spot to plant me a little herb garden close by to the house."

Her smile grew broader at Alex and Ellen's amazed expression. "It really wasn't all that hard girls, just a little bit chancy. Soon as Kane was out of the box, the girls brought in all the china and silver wrapped up in pillowcases so it wouldn't rattle and give us away. I nailed the lid shut, called you all back inside, and you know the rest."

"Weren't you afraid he'd wake up while we all were looking at him?" Ellen asked.

"No more so than you must have been on the long ride here."

Alex shook her head. "How can we ever repay you, Pearl?"

"You already have. You saved Kane's life, Maggie. And Ellen, well, I doubt you could have done it without her help. So that's payment enough for a lifetime. Now if you'll just help me nurse him back to health, we'll be even."

Alex walked over and laid her head on Kane's chest. "It's so good to be able to hear his heartbeat again," she said softly. "I was so afraid I'd killed him with that last dose."

"More than likely that was what saved his life," Pearl said. "My granddaddy was a horse doctor, and when he had a case that he was sure was a lost hope, he'd dose them really good with some laudanum. If they didn't live, at least he'd know they didn't suffer toward the end. And more like than not, the deep rest gave their body time to heal that they wouldn't have had if they'd been conscious." She reached over and patted Alex's arm. "You did really good, darlin.' And Kane will be forever grateful."

"I don't really care about that, so long as he's just alive. He's been more than a good friend to me, Pearl. He saved my life, and he's gotten me out of more scrapes than a cat's got lives. I owe him everything."

She moved a chair beside his bed and said, "If you don't mind, I'll sleep in here tonight, so I can hear him if he wakes up."

"Well, this is actually Becca's room, but I'm sure she won't mind if you stay in here. She's going to be sharing my room while Kane is laid up here. And she's going to help you take care of him. Now, hon, he won't be waking up for at least a day or two," Pearl warned. "But you're a big girl. I'm not going to tell you what to do. Sleep wherever you like." She motioned to a chifferobe in the corner. "There's a comforter and some pillows in there, if you want to make a bed on the floor."

Alex smiled. "I've slept on worse beds, Pearl. I'll be fine."

Pearl turned and walked toward the door. "Ellen, if you'll come with me I'll help you make up the bed downstairs in the room beside mine." Ellen nodded and followed her to the door. Suddenly Pearl turned around and said with a sigh. "By the way, from what those men told me, things are getting a little worse than we'd expected. We may have to head out pretty soon."

Alex turned toward her, her face white. "But Kane can't be moved for days, Pearl. Weeks maybe."

Pearl shook her head. "Won't do no good to have saved him if he's here and blue-coats find him."

Alex closed her eyes. "I didn't save him just to hand him over to them again," she said, her voice hard. "Whatever it takes, Kane is going to make it through this. If I have to die trying."

Pearl smiled and walked back toward Alex. She put her hands softly on each side of Alex's face and said softly, "You're a rare person, Alex. If only I'd always had a friend like you in my life."

Alex returned her smile and reached up to squeeze Pearl's hand. "Well, you've got me now, Pearl. For as long as you want."

She went back and sat in the rocker beside Kane's bed. Leaning back, she began to rock gently. "Life's funny, isn't it, Pearl?"

Pearl nodded her head in agreement.

"You know," Alex mused, "six months ago I wouldn't bandage the finger of the person I considered my very best friend when she cut her hand on a broken goblet. I didn't want to get blood on my new dress. So I called for Dessie to come do it for me. Sue Ann just sat there and cried and bled, while I went to find someone else to fix her hand."

She shook her head and mused, "Look at me now. I've seen men's brains and blood and guts spread all over the ground, and I've helped put some of the pieces back together. Hell, I've even spread some of them myself. And now, I'm vowing by all that's holy that Kane is going to pull through this, no matter what I have to do." She gave a short laugh. "Time does change things, doesn't it, Pearl?"

"Yes, honey. It sure does. But I don't think it really changes people. The things you find down deep inside you have always been there. Time just causes circumstances to make you prove it sometimes." She opened the door and stepped out into the hall. "Don't forget I'm just down the hall if you need me during the night."

Alex watched as the door closed behind Pearl and Ellen, then she reached over and took Kane's hand. "Don't you worry, darling," she whispered, patting his hand gently. "You are safe. And I'll make sure you stay that way." A tear rolled down her cheek. She reached up and brushed it away, saying in a voice that was more tears than words, "You're the closest thing to a family I've got now, Kane. You and Pearl." She took a deep breath and put his hand back on the bed beside him. "You get some sleep now. Rest is what you need."

She yawned. "And it's been a long day for me too." She shook her head. "Hard to believe that this time yesterday you were still laying on that cot in that filthy jail."

Her thoughts suddenly flew to the worry-lined face of Captain Sullivan. "You were wrong about one thing though, Kane. There are some good Yankees. And I now have two debts of gratitude to repay one of them." Her voice hardened. "And one debt I still intend to collect from another."

She leaned back in the rocker and began to rock slowly, her mind going back over all the events of the last few months. After a while, her eyes closed, and the rocker slowly rocked to a standstill.

The next days were spent in a flurry of helping Becca change bandages, keeping a damp, cool cloth on Kane's brow, and mixing poultices and potions. She and the quiet young woman became very good friends during their vigil, although Becca told Alex very little about herself. She was a beautiful woman, her olive-colored complexion hinting at a mixed heritage, her beauty marred only by a long, jagged scar that reached from the corner of her eyebrow to her earlobe. Alex resisted the urge to ask her how it happened, realizing that Becca was very self-conscious about it, turning her face slightly away as she talked and pulling tendrils of her long, silky brunette curls across it. Alex asked Pearl about Becca, but Pearl told her it was Becca's story and if she wanted it told, it was hers to tell. So Alex just enjoyed her company and having her help taking care of Kane, and they let the friendship grow on its own.

Each night Alex fell asleep with her hand in Kane's, repeating the same prayer that tomorrow he'd wake up. She always awoke stiff and sore the next morning, but after feeling Kane's heartbeat strong and hard and finding his brow even cooler than the night before, she would soon forget her own aches and pains.

One morning she went down the stairs and into the kitchen to find Ellen and Pearl in a flurry of flour and cornmeal. "Cooking for an army?" Alex teased.

Pearl turned toward her, her face as white as the flour they were kneading. "Not a whole army, but a part of one." She nodded toward the parlor door. Alex opened it a crack and peered through with one eye. When she saw the blue uniforms she whimpered almost inaudibly. She turned back toward Pearl.

"Who are they?" she whispered, her face white above the pale blue gingham apron.

"Some of Sullivan's outfit," Pearl whispered back, nodding for Alex to follow her outside. Once they had the door closed firmly behind them, Pearl leaned against it and let out a deep sigh. "Lord, this is getting complicated."

"But why are they here?" Alex almost shrieked.

Pearl patted her shoulder. "Settle down, hon. They're not here to cause any trouble. They were on their way to Atlanta to carry a message. Sullivan asked them to drop by and make sure that we were all right."

She looked closer at Alex, her eyes narrowing, one eyebrow raised in a knowing fashion. "Seems you made quite an impression on our Yankee captain, Alex."

Alex shook her head. "No, Pearl. It's not me. It's you."

Pearl's eyes widened. "Me?" she said in amazement. "But I never met the man."

Alex smiled. "Yes, you did, Pearl. In that 'other life' you mentioned. Remember Jacob Sullivan?"

Pearl looked as if her knees might collapse beneath her. Her chin quivered. "Jacob? Here? A 'Yankee captain'?" She shook her head and said firmly, "It can't be the same man. I just can't imagine him in a blue uniform."

"But it is the same man, Pearl. And please don't be mad at him, but he told me about you. And him. And Earl. And the baby, and . . ." Her voice trailed away into silence.

"My, he certainly has become talkative in his older age," Pearl said wryly. "Well, so now you know my story, Alex."

Alex reached out and took her hand. "He loves you, Pearl."

Pearl snorted. "Loves me? No, honey, he loved the idea of me. The me I used to be, anyway. He has no idea who or what I am now. And he most certainly does not love me."

"He said he did," Alex said stubbornly.

"I don't care what he said. To me he'll always be just a brash, young law student who I fed enough to keep alive. And he was grateful. He was someone who liked to talk, and I was someone who liked to listen. That's what made me such a good whore, Alexandria. I listen." She shook her head. "Shoot, there's lots of men don't come here for sex a'tall. They just want someone to listen to them. To listen to them brag, mostly. Sometimes to listen to them cry. To listen to all the things their wives won't listen to. Or sometimes just to be able to say things they could never say to their wives. After they're all talked out, they're ready to go home to their wives." She winked at Alex. "If it keeps me off my back, I'll listen all night."

She laughed at Alex's blush. "Alex, now don't go all virginal on me," she said, with a giggle still in her voice.

The laughter faded from her face and voice when she saw the sadness enter Alex's eyes. "Oh, Gawd, honey, I'm sorry. I didn't mean that. I didn't even think. I just meant that surely after living with a bunch of men for six months, you've heard enough licentious stories to be able to make even me blush."

Alex smiled sadly. "But I'm not virginal anymore, Pearl. No matter where I lived. Or who I lived with. Not after that night." She took a deep breath and said sadly, "Maybe I should just stay here with you and . . . you know . . . help you with . . . the business."

Pearl shook her head. "Now, honey. You don't mean that. You'd make a deplorable whore." She grinned at the exasperated look on Alex's face. "Lord, but you're sensitive this morning." She shook her head. "I just meant that your heart wouldn't ever be in it. And men would know. You weren't cut out to be a whore, darlin'. You're cut out to be just what you are. A sweet Southern belle waiting on her gallant prince to come riding in a white stallion and take her to Paradise."

Alex smiled. "Paradise. Isn't that a town in Texas?" She joined Pearl in a burst of laughter, interrupted by Ellen's flour-streaked face appearing behind them.

"Are you two going to stand out here all morning swapping funny stories, or are you going to help me get some breakfast prepared for our guests?" She put a special emphasis on the word *guests* that made Alex's stomach clench.

"What are we going to do?" she turned and asked Pearl.

"We're going to serve these fine boys some breakfast, then watch them ride off down the road."

"But what if they—"

"What if they what, Maggie? Ask us how our dead boy is this morning? If they do, we'll just shrug and say quite sweetly, 'He's still dead, thank you for asking.' Don't worry about it. We'll be fine." With that Pearl followed Ellen back into the kitchen, Alex following close behind.

"I've got the biscuits in the oven, and the cornbread is in the iron skillet," Ellen said.

"There's some ham and beans from yesterday, and I've got a little jelly put aside," Pearl added. "Let's show these boys some Southern hospitality, shall we?"

"Did you tell Mona to stay upstairs?" Alex asked.

"Good Lord! Thanks." Pearl dashed up the back stairs, and Alex could hear her lightly tapping on a door upstairs. After a few muffled murmurs, her light footsteps brought her back into the kitchen.

"Whew, that was a close one. She was still asleep, but if she'd had a good look at the sergeant in there, she'd have had herself a hissy fit 'til she could get his pants off."

She looked at Alex and nodded. "Now, Alex, there's one girl who was cut out from the get-go to be a whore. And she's a good one, too. Good at what she does. And enjoys it too. Brings a lot of money. Or did before the money ran out around here, along with all the able-bodied men." She shrugged. "I figure she'll be heading out any day now. Headed for greener pastures. Pastures with more men. And more money." She stopped for a moment and shook her head. "Too bad that that probably means a whole lot of us is going to be headed up North. Or farther South. Don't look like there'll be much money around these parts for a long, long time."

She sighed as she quickly filled up a platter with large slabs of ham and mounds of beans and motioned for Alex and Ellen to bring the iced tea pitcher and the platter of bread. Soon the blue-coated men were seated around the huge, round, claw-footed dining table, each with a look of bliss on his face. Alex smiled. Their joy made it worth knowing that the larder was mostly empty now and they would all be eating turnips and broth for the next week.

The youngest one looked up at Pearl and said solemnly, "Would you marry me, ma'am?"

Pearl laughed coquettishly and said teasingly, "Marry you? Son, I'm old enough to be your mother."

They all burst into laughter at the young soldier's reply, "Well, then, ma'am would you consider adopting me?"

As soon as their bellies were full, the men said their goodbyes and mounted up for the long ride to Atlanta. As they were leaving, one of the men said, "Oh, yes, I almost forgot. Miss Maggie, Captain Sullivan sent this to you, said you dropped it in his office." He held out a package wrapped in white paper and tied with a pink bow.

Alex was puzzled. "I don't think I dropped anything." Her fingers fumbled with the wrapping as the men rode away.

Pearl and Ellen looked at her with raised eyebrows. "I didn't notice you dropping anything either," Ellen said.

Alex opened the box and took a deep breath. Nestled in a bed of pristine cotton lay an exquisite cameo brooch with a background of pale pink. She opened the note that accompanied it:

> *I didn't want the men to get the wrong impression from me sending you a package. Please accept my story that this is your property, being returned to you. And please do not take offense at my offering. I simply saw this and I thought of you. Please accept it with my best wishes for continued safety through the harrowing events I'm afraid still lie ahead. Consider it simply a good-luck talisman from a devoted friend.*

"Well, what does it say?" Ellen prodded.

Alex grinned. "He told me I need to be more careful with my belongings. He found this under the couch I fainted on in his office."

Ellen frowned. "You weren't wearing a brooch in his office. I know. I helped you dress."

"Actually, Ellen," Alex said, "This is my lucky brooch. I wear it wherever I go, even when it can't be seen." She proved her point, by fastening the brooch inside her dress collar, hidden from view but warm against her skin.

Ellen looked at her suspiciously for a moment then shrugged. "Oh, well, it's a lovely piece, anyway. Let's see if those Yankees left anything for the rest of us to eat."

Chapter Fifteen

For the next three weeks Alex stayed by Kane's bed, watching his color improve and hearing his breaths become deeper and healthier. She watched anxiously for any sign of awareness, but even though he would occasionally open his eyes and seem to look around the room, she could tell his eyes did not really focus and it was more a reflex than anything else.

During those weeks Becca was at Kane's bedside at every opportunity as well. She bustled around the room, talking to him as if he were awake, straightening his bedclothes and giving him baths. Alex would have done the baths, but Becca very matter-of-factly stated that when you'd seen one man's privates, you'd seen them all, and there was no need for Alex to get any education she didn't need.

One afternoon as the two women sat on the balcony outside Kane's room, their chairs leaned back and their feet resting on the railing, Becca suddenly said, "Have you ever been intimate with Kane?"

Alex's chair legs hit the floor with a loud thump. "What?"

"Laid with him. Have you ever?"

"Good heavens, no, Becca. Why would you ask?"

"I don't know. Seems like you're putting an awful lot of time into a man who you say is just a friend."

"If that were true, why are *you* spending so much time with him?"

Becca shrugged. "He's important to Miss Pearl. And I owe her so much, this is just a little way of repaying her."

"You keep saying that, Becca. Why do you owe Pearl?"

Becca sighed. "It's a very long story, Miss Alex. And it ain't a purty one."

Alex reached over and put her hand on Becca's, marveling again at the differences in the colors. So much alike, and yet so different. "I have plenty of time, Becca. I really do want to hear your story, and don't worry about the ugliness." She sighed. "I've seen a lot more of the ugly side of life than you imagine."

Becca looked out over the yard to the fields and to the mountains beyond. "God gives us a world that has such a good chance at being beautiful." She sighed again and shook her head. "Ain't it a shame that man comes along and brings the ugliness into it?"

Alex remembered the vivid scenes she'd witnessed, one man intent on doing harm to another, and then another, with seemingly no end in sight, and she nodded her head in reply.

"At least my life was beautiful for a while. I was born beautiful." When Alex started to protest that Becca was still beautiful, she smiled a sad smile and waved a hand to dismiss Alex's protests. "I'm not beautiful no more, Miss Alex. Not inside nor out. I never will be again. I seen too much, I felt too much, and now I hate too much to ever be beautiful again. Even if I didn't have this." Her fingers touched her scar lightly, her eyes staring off into space.

Alex felt her stomach tighten at the word *hate,* an image of Rafe Peterson flickering into her mind unbidden. She leaned her chair back against the house and said quietly, "So, tell me about it."

~   ~   ~

"Like I said, I was born beautiful. All the women in my family are. My grandmother said it's our blessing and our curse. My mama's mama was pestered by the white man who owned her nearly from the time she was old enough to bleed, and when she birthed my mama and he saw that there was no question about who the baby's daddy was, he sold the both of 'em upstate to keep the neighbors from talking about him. My mama turned out real pretty, so she was sold off early to be a house woman for a rich man down in N'awlins. He lost her in a card game. And the man that won her sold her into a brothel in Atlanta. After she was used up there she went to be a laundress for the Van Crawlins over at Wild Oaks. You know any of them, by chance?"

Alex remembered her uncle taking her with him years ago to visit Elizabeth and Harlan Van Crawlin. They had ridden the train for the first part of the trip and then rented a buggy for the last half-day's ride. Alex remembered enjoying the scenery but being aware of her uncle's mood darkening as they neared their destination. When she'd asked him what was wrong, he'd said that he was hoping to be able to purchase some of the Wild Oaks horseflesh but did not look forward to dealing with the owners. "Are they bad people?" Alex had queried, with all the innocent knowledge and understanding of a nine-year-old, and was told that no, he guessed they really weren't bad people, they just looked at the world in a different way than a lot of folks did. Than he and Aunt Belle did. And the way he hoped to raise Alexandria, Teddy, and Marcus to see it.

He didn't go into details, but he told Alexandria simply that their treatment of their animals and their people was not always what he considered kind. "Do they beat their animals?" Alex had once seen a horse being beaten outside a livery stable and had proudly watched as her uncle had not only wrestled the whip away from the young stable hand but had turned it toward the lad, managing to get in a few good licks before the screaming boy had scrambled away into an alley. "Some things are much worse than being beaten," her uncle had explained sadly, but he refused to explain any further, saying that unfortunately she would understand when she was older.

"Yes, it is indeed quite a small world. I know of them," Alex responded simply to Becca's question.

"Were you friends?"

"Absolutely not," Alex said firmly. "My uncle had some business dealings with them, and I accompanied him on a couple of his trips to their place, but he didn't like them much, and neither did I." Mr. Van Crawlin had paid her a lot of attention on her first trip, and while she was happy to play with the doll he gave her and enjoyed the candy he pulled from his pocket and offered to her whenever they were alone, some of his attention had made her uncomfortable. When she had voiced her feelings to her uncle, he had made sure that she was never again left alone with the man Mrs. Van Crawlin referred to as "Harl Dear." Alex had mentioned to her uncle that when Aunt Belle called him "dear," she had a different tone in her voice than Mrs. Van C ever did when she was referring to her husband. Her uncle had smiled and told her that someday she'd understand that too. How sometimes words of affection could be aimed to hurt when it was obvious that no affection was actually there.

Alex's thoughts came back to the present abruptly as Becca started talking again, slowly, her voice far away. Alex sensed that her friend was revisiting a vignette of life in a distant past.

"My first memories are of Mister Harl bringing me things. My mama, she washed all the clothes for the house and the field hands, and I worked with her. I loved to see Mister Harl coming down the path to our cabin, because I knew that meant I was going to get to leave my chores for a while and either go for a ride on his horse—he used to set me up in front of him in his saddle, and we'd go for fast gallops across the field—or he'd set a while and just talk to me. Me on his lap, him playing with my braids. I thought he liked me, and I bragged to all the other young'uns, saying, 'Mister Harl, he likes me the best.'"

She sighed. "One day, my mama, she heard me talking about it, and she whooped me. Said to not never say those things again where anyone could hear me. And she started sending me out the back door to go gather stuff whenever she seen Mister Harl come ridin' up to the front. One day after he visited her, I come back in and she was crying. Her face was all swole up, and her lip was busted open. She was just standing there with blood and tears runnin' down her face. And I asked her, 'Mama, who done this? Mama, what's wrong?' When I started crying, she stopped and she said—and I don't think I'd ever heard a voice so sad in all my life—she said, 'Becca, I don't think you're old enough to know all the things you're gonna have to learn, but I want you to always know I love you. And if I coulda' kept you safe, I would have.' Then she started crying again.

"I said, 'Mama, let me go find Mister Harl. He likes me a lot. He'll figure out whoever done this to you, and he'll whup 'em. He'll whup 'em good, Mama.'

"But Mama she just laughed a real sad laugh and said, 'Chile, he sho nuff do like you a lot. But talking to him now wouldn't help a thing. Likely just make things even worsen they is now.' And then she turned back around, and she started a-washin' some of Miz Elizabeth's nightgowns like nothing had happened. That night I heard her talkin' to some of the women as they stirred the big ole pot of lye soap they was makin'. Mama wasn't crying no more, but her voice still sounded real sad. One of the women said 'Is she old enough?' and Mama said, 'She started bleedin' two months ago. I lied as long as I could, but Mister Harl, he found out. And he said he'd be making a room for her.' One of the women sighed and said, 'Well, it could be worse, if he takes her hisself, he won't be sharing her none.'

"I couldn't figure out what they was talking about. I figured out they was talking about me, but nothing they said made any sense. Mister Harl wanted me? He already owned me. Making a room for me? I already had a room.

"But the next day Mama, she sat me down and she said, 'Now Becca, Mister Harl, he's took a liking to you that's real special. He wants you to move up into the big house with him and Miz Elizabeth. You're going to be helping the kitchen help with meals. And sometimes, well, Mister Harl, he's going to come to your bedroom when everyone else is asleep and he's going to ask you to do some things you may not want to do, but don't never say no to him. If you do, he'll sell you and he'll sell me. Or worse.'"

Becca shook her head sadly. "I knew she was tellin' the truth about that, cause he'd done sold my daddy a while back. I never knew why, just knew daddy came and tugged on my pigtails and told me to mind my mama, and someday when he could he'd be back for me. His face was smiling, but his voice, oh, I will never forget the tears in that man's voice. And then Mister Harl, he tied him to the back of the buggy and rode off, Daddy having to run some to keep up with him. I worried about what if Daddy got tired, but Mama said they wasn't going far. She was trying not to cry, but she did a little, and I cried a lot. I missed my daddy. And that was the last time I ever seen him. Tied to the back of Mister Harl's buggy."

Her voice grew even more solemn as she said, "So, I knew that if he'd sold my daddy, he wouldn't make no never mind about selling my mama and me too, and most likely not together, so I hugged my mama and told her that I'd do what I was told and not never say no to Mister Harl. And I put all my clothes, both of my dresses and an old nightgown, in a duanner sack and I walked up the house.

"I knocked on the back door, and a big old, fat nigger woman come to the door and asked what I was a-wanting. I knew she was the main house nigger, but I hadn't never seen her before, except when she'd come running out to yell at us kids to get out of her flower patches. I told her I was Esmy's daughter and that Mister Harl had told me to come to stay in the house. She laughed real mean and said, 'Law sakes, they be getting' younger and younger, before long he'll be pullin' 'em right off the tit.' I pretended I knew what she meant, and I laughed too, and then she hit me across the face and said, 'Don't you be making no fun of me, nigger. Mawreen, she ain't got to take it, you hear me? I may not sleep with Massa Harlan, but I'm more important in this house than any of his little toys will ever be.' I just nodded my head. I was afraid to say or do anything else. She walked across the room and pointed through a door and told me to go on in there and put my things away. I asked her what I was supposed to do when I came back. She gave me this real funny look and said, 'I reckon you might oughta take a bath and get into the dress Mister Harl left for you in there. Be sure you wash your hair and don't put it up in no braids, you hear?' As I walked out of the kitchen, I could hear all the rest of the girls that was shelling beans and peeling potatoes whispering and laughing. I wanted to go talk to them, but I was scared of Mawreen. She'd done hit me for laughing, I wasn't sure what she'd do to me for talking."

Alex was mesmerized by Becca's story. Her uncle had always insisted that the blacks on her family's farm be been treated with respect. More than once he'd trounced Teddy and Marcus good for teasing a black or making fun of them. "They don't know any better," he'd say. "They can't help being ignorant, with nobody to teach them. Be grateful you were born into this world with white skin instead of black. There but for the grace of God go all of us."

Becca started talking again. "So, I went into this little room at the foot of the stairs, and there was this really pretty little bed. The head of it and the foot was made of iron, all in curlicues and little balls. It looked like something out of one of the storybooks one of Mister Harl's kids had left out on the veranda and us kids had pilfered to look through. It looked like someplace a princess would sleep. So I got this big smile on my face. I was gonna be a princess. Just like in the stories my daddy used to tell. Mister Harl, he really liked me. And I reckoned he was going to adopt me and I could be his little girl."

"I carried those fantasies into the warshtub that was sitting by the end of the bed, and I sat there breathing in that sweet smell of lilacs and loving the way the suds felt on my hair. My hair wasn't wooly like a lot of the other young'uns I played with. And they'd teased me about it. I envied them their hair that they could do up in braids and not have to take them down for weeks. My hair tangles and comes out of braids. Always did. Mama used to say it would be easier to keep corn silks braided than my hair. When it wasn't braided though, it was always blowing in my face and causing a passel of trouble."

A smile came to her voice, and she paused before she spoke again. "I remember one time, Mama, she took an old wooden bowl and she put it down over my head, and she took a pair of snips, and she cut off everything that stuck out. The other kids called me Bowlhead for weeks. And Mister Harl, he tole Mama if she done it again, he was gonna have her whupped." Her eyes dropped. "Daddy, he said I looked like a little sunflower."

Her voice changed suddenly. "So I washed my hair and I brushed it, and I put on a dress I found a-layin' on my princess bed. And I sat there on the edge of the bed waiting for someone to come and tell me what to do. There wasn't a window in the room, so I don't know how long I sat there. At first I could hear bustling around in the kitchen, and I could hear voices, and then everything got really quiet. And then just as it was gettin' so dark I couldn't see no more, someone tapped on my door. I was scared. But I said 'Who is it?' and then I heard Mister Harl's voice saying it was him. He come into the room, and he had a doll with him. The purtiest thing I've ever seen in my life. It had a china face with little dimples, and the reddest lips you ever seen. Her eyes was green and her hair, well, her hair looked just like mine. I thanked him, and he said it had come back with him from Saint Looey the last time he'd gone. He'd seen it and he'd thought of me. I knew right then and there that I was the luckiest nigger on earth.

"Mister Harl, he sat down on the bed beside me, and he started petting my hair. Told me he loved my hair and that when he was alone sometimes he'd close his eyes and think about how pretty it was. And that always made him happy in a special way. And then he told me to take off my dress. I was real embarrassed, but I did what he said. I thought maybe he'd brought me back a new dress too that he wanted to see me wear. When I was standing there in just my drawers and petticoat he told me to take them off, too. I didn't want to, but I remembered what Mama had said and so I did. I started to cry a little and he told me not to cry, that me and him, we was going to share something that he didn't do with no other niggers on the whole place. That I was special, and I could do something for him that nobody else, not even Miz Elizabeth could do.

"So when he told me to, I laid back on the bed, and when he did things to me and he'd ask if I liked them, he sounded so much like he wanted me to that I told him that yes, I liked it. Then he took all his clothes off. And I watched him and I thought about how ugly his body was. All I'd ever seen was some of the bucks that'd come in from the fields and they'd take off their clothes for Mama to wash, and they'd walk back to their cabins wearing nothing but some drawers. Mama allus told me not to look, but sometimes I peeked. And some of them were just so beautiful. One time Mister Harl, he brought me some chocolate candy and I thought when I was licking on it, that it looked just like the skin on Big Mule, one of the hands that I'd seen nearly all nekkid. I wondered then if he tasted as good as that chocolate. But I never said that out loud, because it sounded like something Mama would whup me for saying.

"Those men were big and strong, with dark skin that glistened in the sunlight." Her voice was wistful. "You could see their muscles under their skin. And their skin would be drawed so tight across it—" Her voice quivered suddenly. "When Mister Harl started taking off his clothes, I got kind of excited, thinking about those field hands, and hoping now I could see up close what a man looked like, without having to peep out between the boards of the shed to look. But when Mister Harl took off his shirt, he looked like a cookie that mama had took out of the oven before it was done. All white and soft looking, sorta dimpled, and all covered with this wispy, light-colored hair. His skin, it wasn't tight like the field hands. You couldn't see any muscles at all, and when he took my hand and put it on his chest it felt soft, like bread dough that was waiting to rise.

"I started to pull my hand away and he said no, he wanted me to touch him. And so I did. And he started moving my hand around, telling me how he wanted me to touch him. And then he stood up and he took off his breeches. And he had this little bitty old pecker that looked like the part of a sausage we throw away cuz there ain't enough meat there to even taste."

She shuddered. "I just sat there waiting for him to tell me what to do next, and he took the back of my head, and he pushed it down to his parts." She stopped for a moment and looked at Alex and said, "I'm sorry—you probably don't want to hear the whole story. I'll just leave it at saying that he had his way with me, and then he told me to wash the blood off myself and go to sleep, and what we'd done would be our secret, and I was never to talk to no one else about it."

Alex's eyes brimmed with tears. "Oh, Becca, I am so very sorry."

Becca looked down. "It was bad, but what was worse was that it made me not belong anywhere. The other niggers wouldn't talk to me no more, they just laughed when they seen me coming. Called me a conkybine. I didn't know what that meant, but I knew by the way they said it that it had something to do with Mister Harl coming to see me and what we done together. I thought since I was special to him that maybe he'd take me some places and we'd do things together other than just in my bedroom, but he didn't want nobody to see me. So he brought me books and toys and told me to stay in my room as much of the time as I could. So I did. One day I was outside looking at a pitcher book in the garden, and Miz Elizabeth, she come up to me and said hello and asked me if I was enjoying my stay in the house. I told her yes, although I really wasn't. I'd druther be working hard with Mama back at the laundry house, laughing and getting each other all soapy and singing together instead of spending my days reading and daydreaming, dreading nightfall and a visit from Mister Harl." She sighed. "I learned pretty quick-like that things are what they are, and they ain't no use wishing for a rainbow when it ain't raining."

She sat there for a moment, her toe tapping against the porch railing. "You know, Miz Elizabeth, she allus had people coming to call and telling her what a fine Christian woman she was, always willin' to help out the less fortunate, but she never treated me like she was no Christian. She stood there looking at me for a moment, and then she reached out and she took my book away and she said, 'If Harlan brings you any more presents, you are to bring them directly to me, do you hear me? And you are not to tell him that you and I have talked. I will allow some things in my house, but I will not allow a nigger to be educated in it. If he wants one for entertainment, so long as he leaves me alone I will allow it, but I will not allow him to teach you to do anything except satisfy his lusts. Do you understand that?' I really didn't, but again I just nodded and said yes, and she turned around and walked off.

"From that day on, every good thing that Mister Harl gave me, I had to take to Miz Elizabeth. And watch as she destroyed it.

Books. Paper and paints. A scarf. No matter what he gave me, she took away and burned it. He never asked me what went with his gifts, and I worried over what I would tell him if he ever did. But all he seemed to care about was to give me something and take his payment. I will give him that much credit. He never took anything from me that he didn't think he had paid for. He had every right to my body. He owned me. But I don't think he ever meant to treat me like a possession. He liked to believe that I wanted him to do what he did. And that he made me happy by bringing me gifts."

Her fingertips on the arm of the rocking chair suddenly whitened as her hand involuntarily gripped. Her voice sounded like steel as she continued. "Then one day, about two years later, a man came to see Mister Harl. But Mister Harl, he wasn't home and wouldn't be for two days, and I remember wondering what he'd bring me when he come back. Even knowing I'd have to give up the gifts, it was still exciting to receive them. Little bits of a world I'd never know. A newspaper from N'awlins that I'd never be able to read, but I pored over the pitchers until I finally carried it upstairs to Miz Elizabeth's room. Scraps of exotic material and laces from the dresses he brought Miz Elizabeth and her daughters. Dolls, long after I'd past the age of playing with them. Once I kept one of them and didn't give it to Miz Elizabeth, and instead I carried it out to a little girl in one of the cabins who'd been runned over by a horse and was going to die. She held that little doll in her arms and she smiled as she died, and I figured that if Miz Elizabeth was any kind of a Christian woman like she claimed, she'd not begrudge me that one failin' to do what she had ordered."

She relaxed a little and smiled a somewhat wan smile in Alex's direction. "I'm sorry, once my mind starts wandering I think of little things I'd forgotten. Sad, isn't it, that we forget the things we should remember, but can never forget the things we'd be best off letting go?"

Alex nodded silently, her heart aching for the beautiful young woman whose life had been so different from her own, who would never know the blessings of the things that she and her family had taken for granted. She wanted to reach over and take hold of Becca's hand and apologize, but she stayed silent, not wanting to interrupt the flow of Becca's memories. She sat back as Becca began to speak again.

"Anyway, this man who came to see Mister Harl, he decided

to stay over. Miz Elizabeth, she comes down and she says to me that I'm to stay in my room that night. I didn't know why she did that; I never went out of my room at night anyway, and seldom during the day. But I just nodded and said, 'Yes, ma'am.' And she said, 'You just remember that what Harlan owns, I own as well. You will do what I say, do you understand me?' I nodded that I did and she said, 'Excellent. You will do whatever our guests ask of you then as well. Do you understand?' I didn't, but I nodded, and I went and set in my rocking chair thinking up pretty things I'd draw if I hadn't of given my paints and paper to Miz Elizabeth.

"Not long after supper, someone opened the door to my room and that visitor man stepped inside. I stood up and said hello. He walked over to me and told me to turn around. I turned around with my back toward him, and he said, 'No, you ignorant darkie, I meant all the way around.' So I turned all the way around. Which put my back toward him again. I didn't know what he wanted. I didn't like the way he looked at me when I'd seen him in the hallway earlier, and it made me nervous to have him in my room.

"'Face me goddammit, girl!' he said, and he put a hand on my shoulder and turned me around. His hand hurt. He was holding tight, and I could smell brandy on his breath. As I faced him I saw him grinning. A really ugly grin that stopped on his lips. His eyes were still cruel. You know what I mean?"

She turned toward Alex and waited for Alex's nod before she went on. "He said, 'Girl, we are going to have one fine time. I am going to show you what it's like to have a real man between your legs, and not that fancy-pants Harlan. Girl, when I get done with you, you're gonna know you've been screwed. I'm gonna put a real smile on that high-yeller face of yours. My, but you are a light one, ain't ya? Be nearly like screwing a real woman and not just some negra. Now, take off that dress.'

"Well, I just stood there. Mister Harl had always told me not to never let no one else touch me. Told me that if anyone else touched me I wouldn't be special for him no more. I didn't want to be sold, didn't want to never see my mama or daddy again. I hadn't seen daddy since he left, but he knew where we were, and I kept hopin' someday he'd find a way to come back. I didn't get to see Mama much no more but sometimes, if I'd made him real happy the night before, Mister Harl would have her come up to the house, and we'd visit for a while.

"So I just stood there, wondering what I should do. I didn't want this man touching me, but Miz Elizabeth said I had to do what her guests wanted. I just hoped that Mister Harl wasn't going to be mad at me. So I reached up to undo the top button of my dress. And this man, he reached out and said, 'Time's a wastin', girl' and he took hold of the collar of my dress and he just ripped it down.

"It was the prettiest dress I owned, one Mister Harl had given me that Miz Elizabeth said was all right for me to keep. So I pulled away from him and said no. All I meant was 'Don't tear my clothes, I'll take them offen myself.' I wasn't telling him no he couldn't touch me. But he got mad. He grabbed me by the hair of the head and he said, 'Girl I don't know why that pantywaist Harlan hasn't taught you some manners, but you don't never tell a white man no, do you understand me?' I tried to say yes, but he was holding my head so far back I couldn't speak. He grinned again and the look on his face scared me bad. He said, 'You ain't never been had by a real man, have you, girl? Is Harlan the only one who's had you?' I nodded, and he said, 'I'll bet a Nancy-boy like him has got a cock the size of a forty-four cartridge. Hell, girl, you ain't been broke in yet. Could he even reach your cherry?' He started pinching my nipples and I twisted to get away. He was hurting me. He said, 'Good, you like it rough.'

"And then I made a big mistake. I said no. I looked him in the eye and I said no. His eyes narrowed and I saw his hands clench up. He reached into his belt and he pulled out a knife that looked to me to be big enough to cut trees. He said 'Gal, I told you, don't you never say no to a white man, not never.' And he twisted my head around, and he took that knife and he cut my hair. All of it, that hung way down my back, loose the way Mister Harl liked it, and he held it out in front of me like a horse's tail and he said, 'Be grateful it was hair I cut and not your throat.' I stood there, looking at that hair, and I started to cry. The man said, 'Don't start caterwauling now. You learned that lesson, now it's time to get another one,' and he pushed me back toward the bed.

"I thought I was going to miss the bed, and I reached out to grab him to keep me from falling, but I hit him in the arm. He thought I was fighting with him, and he took that knife and he—" Her voice shook as she fingered her scarred face. "He gave me this. I started screaming, blood was streaming into my mouth and I thought I was going to die. Then he climbed on top of me and said, 'Ain't nobody going to come in here girl, you just shut up and quit pretending you don't enjoy it.' And when he was done, he climbed off and wiped hisself off on my dress and told me he'd be back the next night to see me.

"I laid there in bed for a little while, then I pulled on a wrapper and I climbed the stairs to Miz Elizabeth's room. I needed her to see to my face. I wasn't sure that any of the kitchen gals would do anything for me unless she told them to. As I climbed to the top of the stairs, I could hear noises inside her room and I knew that the man had gone up to do her too. I started to go in and try to help her, but I listened for a minute and I could tell she was enjoying it. So I just turned around and went back downstairs.

"I went through the kitchen to go to my room. Mawreen was sleeping in a chair by the stove, making sure it stayed lit all night ready to cook breakfast, and she seen me going through. She helped get me cleaned up and put a poultice on my face and she put me to bed. She gave me a cup of something that tasted terrible but made me sleep.

"When I waked up, Mister Harl, he was standing over me. He reached out and he touched my hair, what was left of it, and he touched the bandage on my face and told me that we'd wait and see how my face healed before we decided my future. I just nodded and went back to sleep.

"Well, you can see how my face healed, and although my hair grew back, my face didn't. So Mister Harl, he told me I wasn't special no more, and he had arranged to place me someplace where I wouldn't never have to do no field work or housework, that he felt like he owed me that much for the pleasure I had given him. I cried and begged him to let me stay and work with my mama. He looked real sad for a minute and he said that he was sorry none of the other girls had told me but that my mama was dead. He didn't tell me what happened then, but before I left, Mawreen, she told me that when Mama'd found out what happened to me, she came up to the house, and she ran outside when they told her the man was leaving and she started yelling at him, shaming him for what he'd done. He'd pulled pistol and shot her in the head. Then he put his gun away and pulled some paper money out of his pocket and tossed it to Miz Elizabeth and told her he was sorry about the mess. Then he tipped his hat to Miz

Elizabeth and rode away. I asked what Miz Elizabeth had said or done, and she said she had rolled her eyes and remarked that she certainly hoped that nigger blood didn't stain the veranda stones or they would have to be replaced. Then she asked one of the girls to go get a field hand to bury my Mama.'"

Alex's mouth was open, her brain almost refusing to accept the words she was hearing. What heartbreak for a young girl to experience—so much in such a short time, and at the hands of one man.

Her blood had run cold as Becca repeated the man's words, the same words Rafe Peterson said before he took her: *show you what a real man . . .*

She shook her head to erase the words from it. "Becca, I am so very sorry. Nothing will ever make up to you what you have lost. I assure you, when all this is over you will always have a home with me if you decide to leave Pearl."

Her eyes widened as a thought dawned on her. "Pearl bought you? So, you didn't choose to be a . . ." Her voice trailed off.

Becca gave a short laugh. "No, miss, I didn't choose to be a whore to begin with, but I do choose to be one now. Miz Pearl, she bought me and she brought me here, and she give me my papers. And she told me to go wherever I wanted, and if I could repay her someday she'd accept, but if I couldn't she'd understand. She'd paid five hundred dollars for me, Miz Maggie. So I told her I'd stay. And she could keep whatever she wanted from my take until she was paid back. I've nearly got her paid back now, and I'm saving up whatever I can come up with to try to buy my son."

Alex gasped. "Your son?"

"Yes, ma'am. Didn't I mention that? Mister Harl and me, we made a baby. Prettiest little thing you ever seen. Had his gold hair and my green eyes. I named him Benjamin, and I call him Benjy. They took him away from me when he was borned and put him with a wet nurse, Mister Harl said so's my body would get back to normal quicker and my breasts wouldn't get saggy." Looking at Becca's trim, lithe body, Alex couldn't see any way that would have happened anyway, but to tear a newborn baby away from his mother seemed barbaric for any reason. She said so, and Becca shrugged.

"I was lucky, Miz Maggie. He didn't sell him. Nigger babies on the tit was bringing good money to folks that wanted to raise somebody up from the get-go instead of buying 'em already growed. I still got to see Benjy a lot and play with him. It gave me something to do while I was waiting on Mister Harl to visit me. Benjy used to be able to come to the house and play with Miz Elizabeth's chillen, but one day a guest made mention to her about her 'prettiest child,' and she meant Benjy, not one of Miz Elizabeth's. So she told Mister Harl that that bastard must be sold immediately. Was one of the few times Mister Harl ever stood up to her, but he said no that Benjy was going to stay but he would make sure that he stayed down at the cabins and not come to the house anymore.

"I went down to see him before I left to come here. I told him I'd be back to get him someday. He wasn't old enough to understand what was going on, but he knew I was sad so he cried too. Pert near broke my heart. So when I can, I'm going back and I'm gonna buy him and me and my daddy and him, we're going to go North and be a family."

She suddenly cocked her head to one side and said, "Did you hear that?"

Alex turned her head too. "Hear what?"

But then she heard it again. Both of their eyes flew open wide, and their chairs hit the planks with a thud as they raced inside to Kane's bedside.

Chapter Sixteen

Kane's eyes opened for a moment then fluttered closed again. In a voice weak and somewhat husky, but definitely Kane's, he said, "Am I dead?"

"Kane, can you hear me?" Alex's voice shook with emotion, tears streaming down her face, because of both Becca's story and the answered prayer that was now speaking.

"Yes, but that doesn't answer my question." He shifted in bed and tried to sit up, immediately collapsing back among the pillows. "Are you an angel?" He smiled. "My very own angel, sent to take care of me. God must love me a lot."

"Don't move. You could still hurt yourself," Alex warned.

"Dammit to hell," Kane swore suddenly, and Alex could see the pain etched across his face. "Now I know I'm not dead. Or at least I ain't in heaven. Sorry about the swearin', miss."

Alex smiled. "I've heard worse. And I have to tell you, I've waited so long to hear you speak again, I don't care what you say."

Kane gingerly touched his still-taped ribs and winced as he tried to move his splinted leg. He frowned and asked, "What happened? How long have I been—?"

"Almost a month. You were thrown from your horse when we were ambushed by a Yankee troop."

"We?" Kane questioned, with a look of not understanding.

"Uh, yeah. We—the Rebel troops. You know." Her mind raced, trying to quickly piece together a plausible story. *Damn,* she said to herself. *I've had all this time to come up with a good story, and here I am hemming and hawing like a kid caught with her hand in the cookie jar.*

"How did I get here? And where is 'here'?" He looked up at her and gently touched her cheek with his fingertips. "And who are you? I must be worse hurt than I think to be able to forget ever knowing you."

"No," Alex said with a smile, her pulse racing at his touch. "You didn't know me before. You're here at Pearl's. Ellen and I brought you here."

"Ellen?"

"A friend." At Kane's questioning look, she said quickly, "No you don't know her, either."

Kane shook his head. "It's all a little too much to comprehend right now, I still feel a little fuzzy."

He raised an eyebrow. "At Pearl's?" He looked at Becca. "And who are you?"

"This is Becca, one of my very best friends in the world, and luckily for you, one of the world's best nurses." She turned to Becca and said, "Stay with him? I'm going to get Pearl."

She raced down the stairs and into the backyard where Pearl was tending her herb garden that was just beginning to show some sprouts of green and grey. Ellen was hanging clothes on the line, aided by the two old colored men.

"He's awake!" Alex shouted. "Kane! He's awake."

Pearl threw down her hoe, and Ellen thrust the remaining clothes into a very startled Lije's arms. "Praise the Lord!" Pearl raised her eyes to heaven, tears running down her cheeks.

They all crashed through the door into Kane's room and stood there for a second, taking in the wonderful sight of Kane's deep, grey eyes wide open and comprehending what was in front of them for the first time in weeks.

"Oh, you dear boy," Pearl said, taking his hand in hers, and pressing it against her chest. "You've given us quite a scare."

"Apparently," Kane said dryly. He looked from face to face. "Now, would some of you like to introduce yourselves to me, since apparently you've become quite closely acquainted with me—" He raised the sheet and winced in embarrassment at the sight of his naked, bandaged body. "—over a period of time that I don't quite remember?"

Pearl grinned at him. "Yep, he's going to be fine, girls. He's already grumpy." She squeezed his hand. "Are you hungry?"

"I could eat a horse," Kane admitted. He suddenly took a deep breath and stiffened, again trying to sit up. "My horse. Patch?"

"Is eating us out of house and home in the stable and wreaking havoc with both my mares," Pearl assured him.

Kane leaned back into his pillows. His eyes closed suddenly, "Oh, Lord. What about Alex? Do either of you know what happened to him?"

"He's fine," Alex said. "He told us to take good care of you and send him a message when you woke up."

"I don't remember much," Kane said. "I saw a flash of something shiny in the sunlight, and I yelled at him to get down. All of a sudden a mortar blast hit right in front of us. I barely knew when Patch went down, but suddenly I was underneath him, and then everything went dark. Next thing I remember was waking up in a strange bedroom with strange women." He winked at Alex as his face split into a wide grin. "And may I say, that that's a fine way to come back among the living."

Alex blushed. "Oh, my. Alex told me you were quite the charmer."

"Oh, did he now?" Kane teased. "And what else did the little rascal tell you about me? And by the way, is anyone going to introduce us?"

"This is my niece Maggie," Pearl said quickly, before Alex could answer. "And her best friend Ellen from Monroeville. And Becca is our friend, she's been helping take care of you for these last weeks."

"Monroeville?"

"That's where they found you, Kane. In the prison in Monroeville. Damn Yankees loaded you up on a wagon and took you there to die, I reckon. Lord knows they hadn't done anything much to keep you alive." She straightened the sheet across Kane's chest and then said briskly, "Now, we'll tell you all about it later. For now just lie back there and shut your eyes. Take a little nap, and we'll go fix you some dinner. How does potato soup and cornbread sound?"

"You sure this isn't heaven?" Kane asked with a weak grin. "That sure sounds like manna to me."

"Good. We'll be right back. Girls, you come with me, and let's get this boy something that'll stick to them busted ribs. Becca, you stay here and keep him company."

Ellen and Alex followed Pearl from the room, all of them wearing smiles wide enough to brighten the darkest room.

Alex practically skipped down the stairs she was so happy. "He sounds good, doesn't he Pearl?"

"Yes, he does," Pearl agreed.

"I think he'll be okay now, don't you?"

"Yes," Pearl said. "I don't have any doubt that he'll make it now. I was getting a mite worried, I have to tell you, when he took so long to wake up. Now the only hurdle to cross is to see if he can ever use that leg again. I splinted it as well as I could, but the bones were crushed pretty badly. It sure was a bad break."

She turned to the two girls. "You know, he's going to want some answers about he came to be here. And if you insist in not telling him the truth about your duplicity, I've been giving this some thought, and I think we'll stick to the story that's worked this far. Alex, you're my niece Maggie. We'll tell Kane that his buddy Alex sent word to me that Kane had been taken to Monroeville to the prison, and that he'd been hurt. I sent Maggie there to see what she could do. Then we'll tell him the truth from there—that y'all drugged him to make them believe he was dead, brought him here by wagon, and the rest is history."

Alex nodded. "I guess that's close enough to the truth that we won't get caught up in it, and far enough from the truth that he won't know . . . that I lied to him." She hung her head. Her thoughts went back to the letter she'd sent Verbena so long ago. Even then she'd known that the men she'd served with would be embarrassed to find out they'd had a woman in their ranks and not realized it. "I just don't think he'd understand, and I don't want him to hate me."

Pearl patted her on the shoulder. "Your secret's safe with us, darlin'," she said quietly, "But don't underestimate Kane. I don't think he could ever hate you, no matter what you did. You saved his life, after all." She squeezed Alex's shoulder and then turned toward the door "Now let's get him some food before we starve him to death and won't have to worry about what we're going to tell him."

Later that night Alex sat beside Kane's bed, looking down at her fingers held tightly within one of his hands. Kane was saying with a note of wonder in his voice, "I still just can't believe you did that for me, Miss Maggie." He shook his head. "You know if they'd have found you out, they'd have hung you for a spy."

Alex shook her head. "That didn't matter, Kane. You didn't deserve to die like a dog penned up in a shed. You're a good man. This war has already taken far too many good men. If even one can be saved, so be it. So I didn't do any more for you than you'd have done for any one of your buddies."

Kane gave a short laugh. "Well, there's a big difference in what you did and what I could—and would—do for my buddies. No matter how badly I wanted to. You must have been scared to death."

"Well, yes. But mostly scared that you'd wake up and they'd hang you."

"But didn't you stop to think of the danger you and Ellen were putting yourselves in?"

She shrugged the thought aside. "Not really. I just knew that Aunt Pearl would never forgive me if I came back without you." She smiled at him conspiratorially. "You've seen Pearl mad, I guess?"

Kane returned the smile. "That would explain your commitment, for sure," he said wryly. "I don't know but what I'd just about walk through fire if she told me to do it, just to avoid getting her riled up."

Alex gently pulled her hands free and said softly, "I'd better get out and let you get some rest. You can call me if you need anything during the night. I'm just next door."

"Have you slept there all along?"

"No—actually, I've stayed here in the chair beside your bed every night, and then while Ellen or Becca was in with you during the day I napped some. I have to admit, it'll be good to get back to a regular schedule again." She yawned. "You sleep well tonight, now. And, Kane . . . I'm so glad you're going to be okay."

He squeezed her hand that he still held. "I have you to thank for that. And I won't ever forget it."

He pulled her closer. "When I can get back on both feet, I'll show you how grateful I am." He grinned mischievously. "Although maybe I could show you a whole lot better right here where I am."

Alex pretended to be shocked. "Well, I never!" she huffed.

"Maybe you should try it," Kane joked. "You just might like it."

Alex laughed. "You are incorrigible! I hope I don't find out I liked you better before you woke up."

Kane laughed, and then winced in pain. "Damnation! I'll be glad when these ribs heal up. I forgot how bad they hurt." He suddenly reached up and lightly touched the almost-faded scar across Alex's temple. "What happened to you?"

For a moment Alex fantasized about what his reaction would be if she told him she'd been shot, then she smiled serenely and said, "I was out riding and got hit by a low branch."

He gently touched her cheek. "Take better of yourself, darlin'. You never know when I'll need an angel around to save my neck again."

Alex stood up, hoping he couldn't see the consternation she was feeling at the touch of his fingers on her skin. She pretended to straighten Kane's bedcovers and then tidied the room quickly and blew out the lamp. At Kane's request she opened the curtains so the moonlight could come into the room.

"Good night," she whispered to him.

"Good night."

The hall seemed extra dark after leaving Kane's moonlit room. Leaning against his closed door, she gave a brief prayer of thanks. *I have to admit, Lord, there were a few times there when I wasn't sure we could pull it off. Thanks for bringing us through it. And thanks for letting Kane be okay.*

She felt her way along the hallway to her door and went inside for the first night's sleep in a bed in over a month.

Chapter Seventeen

The next morning Alex awakened with a smile on her lips and a happy heart. Kane was awake, they were all alive, and life was good. Suddenly, however, Becca's story popped into her mind, putting a damper on her spirits. It didn't seem fair that things should go so well for everyone else around her when such a gentle young woman had had so much heartbreak in her life, so much of it irreparable.

Alex turned over on her side, staring out the window for a few minutes and watching a mockingbird flirt with a prospective mate. Suddenly a smile spread across her face, followed by a look of firm resolve.

She jumped out of bed and hastily dressed. With one slipper still unbuttoned, she went downstairs and found Pearl in the kitchen, yawning as she rolled out the dough for biscuits.

Pearl turned around as she walked in and smiled at her. "I thought I'd fix Kane a big breakfast to welcome him back to the land of the living," she said.

Alex nodded in agreement, picking up a piece of bacon and chewing it. Choosing her words carefully, she said slowly, "Pearl, do you think you could do without me for a day or so, now that Kane is awake?"

Pearl looked puzzled but simply nodded. "I'm sure we can— but you're not planning on doing something stupid, are you? Land sakes, I don't think I can take any more drama for a while, sugar. As much as I adore that man upstairs, one cripple at a time is about a body can watch out for."

Alex shook her head. "I think I can stay out of trouble, Pearl. But there's something I need to do really bad, and I need to do it alone. I will try to get back by nightfall, but I'm not right sure. I'll be back by dark tomorrow at the latest."

Pearl slowly shook her head. "I wish you'd tell me what you're planning," she said with a sigh. "But I reckon you'll tell me in your own good time."

Alex sat in silence for a moment, her mind far away. Then suddenly she looked at Pearl and asked, "Can you keep a secret?"

Pearl smiled. "Honey, that's not a question you have to ever ask a whore. We keep more secrets than a Pinkerton security man. Trust me, if we told everything we know, we'd not only cause half the men in this county to be divorced or killed, but we'd cause more than a few impeachments of some pretty high officials in the state. Can I keep a secret? Hmmph!" She snorted and went back to her biscuit dough.

Alex quickly told Pearl her plan. When she'd finished, Pearl clapped her hands. "Oh, Alex, what a wonderful idea! I'd planned to do something about it soon, but I admit I got so caught up in my own life, I just lost track. You're a fine woman. You'll be making such a difference in a lot of lives."

She walked over to the stove and stood there for a moment, then reached behind the flour-sack curtain and dragged out a pry bar from beneath the sink. Alex watched while she pried up a floorboard and reached into the hollow beneath it. She pulled out a small, red-velvet reticule that she turned and pitched at Alex. "Take what you need out of there, and bring me back the rest."

Alex opened it and gasped when she looked inside. "Good Lord, Pearl! This is far more than enough. I think I have almost as much as I need anyway, but I will take this along just in case of an emergency. And I'll bring back what I don't have to use. I'm hoping to make a good deal, but times are so hard, you just never know. I just hope I'm not too late."

Pearl nodded and laid the floorboard back down and stepped on it until it popped firmly back into place. "Just take care of yourself, and I'll be praying until I hear the wagon wheels turning into the driveway."

Alex gave her a quick hug. "I'm going to have Lije hook up the buggy, if that's okay. It'll be quicker." She turned and in a flurry of gingham was out the door.

~ ~ ~

Four hours later, her sunbonnet limp and her bones aching from bouncing along in the wagon on roads that had seen far too much traffic and much too little upkeep, Alex directed Lije to turn down a long driveway that she hoped was the right one.

The last time she and her uncle had made this trip, they had been met at the road by a group of chattering Negro children who had followed them to the house and then helped them out of the wagon and taken their bags inside for them. This time the trip down the driveway was made in silence, and when she pulled up at the front veranda, there was no sign of life except for a thin, mangy hound who peeked out from beneath a bench in the garden and then crawled back into the shade, as if even barking would have taken too much energy.

Alex walked timidly up to the door and pounded with the huge brass knocker until she heard footsteps inside. She took a step backward, a false smile plastered across her face.

Her smile faltered a bit when the door finally inched open and a gaunt woman with pale skin peeked through the crack. Unkempt hair coiled wildly around the woman's face. "Who's there?" she demanded.

"I'm not sure if you remember me, ma'am, but I'm Alexandria McKinley. My uncle and I used to come and visit you and Mr. Harlan with regard to your horses."

The door opened slightly more, and the woman squinted rheumy eyes at Alex's face. Suddenly she opened the door wide and said, "Oh, my goodness, child, do come on in. I swear, it's been so long since I've seen anyone but niggers and soldiers, I don't hardly know how to act. What on earth brings you so far from home, and through such turmoil, too"?

The woman patted her hair, trying vainly to smooth it to some semblance of order, and pinched her cheeks to put some color in them. "I was just out back overseeing some work, and I must look a fright."

"You look fine," Alex lied. "And I apologize for dropping in without notice, but I didn't know of any way to get a message to you. Certainly the mail lines are all clogged up with all the fighting so close, and I didn't want to risk one of my . . . darkies." She hesitated over the derogatory term but figured it was necessary to establish a rapport with the woman.

The woman sighed. "Ain't it the truth. Just a month ago, Union troops came through here, and they took two of my very best men with them. Didn't pay me anything for them, just told me they were taking them. Lord knows, they were sullen, stubborn things. I couldn't do a thing with them now that Harlan Dear isn't here to whip them into shape. I guess by now they've either shot them, or they've set them free." She snorted. "Free niggers. What must Mr. Lincoln be thinking?"

Alex hoped her smile looked natural despite the clenching of her jaw. "I do declare, but you're right. I don't know what we'd do without our . . . niggers."

She followed Elizabeth through a house that stunned her with the differences between what she was seeing now and what she remembered from visits in the past. Light patches on the wallpaper showed where pieces of fine art had hung. Alex wondered if the artwork had been sold abroad, was looted by Union soldiers, or was hidden in what the Van Crawlins must think was a safe place. She thought of the lovely piece by Raphael that had hung over the mantel in the foyer and had entranced her immediately on their first visit. She had pointed it out to her uncle, who had praised her for realizing its importance. Harlan had entered the room and overheard them discussing it, and he had rolled his eyes, saying he couldn't for the life of him see what his wife wanted to bring that "foreign horseshit" into his home for, but he reckoned it might be worth something someday, if that "Raffy-ell feller" made something of himself.

Alexandria had been horrified at the idea of owning such a wonderful piece of artwork without appreciating its beauty, seeing it only as a potential financial asset, but her uncle had explained that the wonderful thing about art was that two people could look at the same piece of painted canvas and see entirely different things. That while to Alexandria and himself the piece was awe inspiring, to a man without creativity and an ability to step a bit outside reality, it might look like just a lot of scrawling and paint-splotches. Alex was sure now that Mr. Van Crawlin must have wondered why he caught so many pitying glances from his young guest over the length of their visit, and now she wondered again where the lovely painting was hanging and hoped that it was indeed safe, no matter where it was.

She pretended not to notice the absence as well of the silver tea service that had graced the center table in the parlor, and she gratefully accepted the cup of tea offered to her by her hostess. She did her best not to grimace at the bitter taste, knowing that it was likely the very best she had to offer, and that it was certainly no worse than what almost every other lady in the South was being forced to drink and serve in the absence of regular visits by a peddler or regular trips to a well-stocked store in town.

She sighed. How she longed for a nice, tall, frosty glass of Verbena's famous sweet iced tea, or a steaming cup of real coffee, sweetened with real sugar.

She smiled and said, "It's very kind of you to not be upset with me for dropping in on you like this, Elizabeth. And I do hope that you won't think me presumptuous to call you by your given name."

"Heaven's no, child. It's so nice to talk to someone like myself, I don't rightly care what you call me. I hope you have some news from Atlanta? Or New Orleans? Or perhaps a recent copy of *Lady Godey's?*" she added, hopefully.

"Alas," said Alex with a wry smile, "I haven't seen a new magazine in simply ages. And all of the news we've received has been so old by the time we received it that we've started calling it the 'oldspaper' instead of the newspaper."

Her humor was rewarded by tinkling laughter that Alex thought sounded as if it might be bordering on hysteria. She decided she should get to the matter at hand and try to get away from Wild Oaks as soon as possible.

"I actually did have a definite reason for dropping by, Elizabeth," she said. "I am on my way back home after visiting my aunt near Atlanta, and I wanted to take a present back to Aunt Matilda. She's been so brokenhearted since Teddy's death—"

Hearing Elizabeth's gasp, she realized that she did in fact have some news to share with the woman. "It's true. Teddy was killed at the hands of a Union officer, just a stone's throw from Twin Cedars," she said sadly. "It almost broke Aunt Matilda's heart. We had just gotten over the news of his brother's death in battle, and this was just almost too much for her to bear. She needed some time alone, so I left to go visit her sister in Atlanta. There we got word that heavy action was liable to be headed our way, so I had our hand pack up our things, and we're headed back to Twin Cedars just as quickly as we can get there. I realized where we were when we got to the crossroads a few miles back, and that you and Mr. Harlan lived nearby."

She stopped for a moment and looked around. "I'm sorry I didn't think to ask sooner—how is Harlan?"

Elizabeth rolled her eyes. "That damn fool man. At the first word of battle, he booked a ticket to France. Told me was going over there to take care of some business interests. When I hadn't heard from him in three months, I was concerned. When it was six months, I became downright worried. It's been a year now, and I know without a doubt that he left me here to fend for myself while he traipsed off to safety."

She leaned forward and whispered conspiratorially to Alex. "It's a bit of a secret, child, but our marriage was never a happy one. Harlan always preferred a little brown sugar to white, and I never quite saw fit to forgive him for it. Granted, it upped the quality of a lot of our stock, but it made for a few embarrassing moments for me from time to time, when some of the get turned out almost as light as our own children."

Alex had listened in puzzlement when Elizabeth first began speaking, but suddenly she realized what she was referring to. She felt a blush heating her neck as she nodded her head and murmured understanding.

"Actually, Elizabeth, that's why I'm here."

The woman looked surprised and suddenly indignant. "Oh, dear heavens, child. Please don't tell me you're bringing yet another of Harlan's bastards to me, thinking I'll help you support it. My coffers are empty, my dear, and I have very little left to take care of my own children. Harlan took my artwork with him, he cleaned out our bank account, and he left me with only enough money to keep food on the table. I haven't even enough money to put new ribbons on my bonnet, much less buy a new one."

Alex let her face show the shock she felt. She couldn't imagine any man walking away from his responsibilities so lightly, and she knew that Elizabeth must be nearing madness to so openly discuss her private life with her. She murmured another platitude, then began tentatively discussing the reason for her visit.

"Do you by chance have a very light-skinned young lad available whom you might be willing to sell to me, as a gift for Aunt Matilda?" she asked, choosing her words very carefully.

"Dear child, I have a stable full of light-skinned lads and lasses. Harlan made quite sure of that," she snorted, and tossed her head. "Unfortunately, these days the price of even high-quality niggers is rock bottom." Suddenly realizing that she might be talking herself out of a sale with her bitter tirade, she quickly added, "Of course, quality is still quality, and worth every penny it costs."

"I agree totally," said Alex, nodding her head. "I'd be very interested in seeing what you might have available."

"There's one little nigger girl who I think you might be interested in especially," Elizabeth said slyly. "She's already bearing a baby, and she's just turned thirteen. She's got a lot of good years ahead of her, and she comes from excellent stock."

Alex tried not to appear shocked. "My, that seems quite young," she stuttered.

"If they don't start young, they can't bear enough to pay for themselves," Elizabeth explained patiently. "A female can't do as much work as a male, so they have to make up the extra money with the sale of their babies. I'd let this little girl go for three hundred dollars, and she's due to drop in less than two months. Two for your money—a great bargain. You should think about it. I'd make you a really good deal on her. Like I said, two for the price of one."

Alex nodded again. "Well, I'm sure she would be a good bargain, but I think I have my heart set on a young boy. Maybe about four or five years old. Very light-skinned, blonde if possible."

Elizabeth's lips tightened. "I might have just what you want, wait right here." Alex watched as Elizabeth sailed out of the parlor and onto the rear veranda. Her shrill voice split the silence as she screamed for someone named Callie to run to the cabin and bring up young Benjamin.

Alex smiled when she heard the name, but she quickly let her smile fade as Elizabeth walked back into the room. "This boy is a very smart young lad," she was saying. "Almost too smart for his own good. Before Harlan left, he was letting him sit with him in the study from time to time, and he realized that the lad was learning to read by listening to Harlan talk about what he was reading in the newspaper and in magazines. I of course put a stop to it; I will not live in a world where niggers are educated. It's just not right. I can't believe that there are people in this world who cannot see the difference between us and realize that the good Lord put us here to take care of these miserable wretches, not be their equals."

Alex nodded in acquiescence, hoping her face wasn't showing the disgust she felt at the conversation.

Suddenly she heard a door open and close quietly, and then a young face peeped around the edge of the parlor door. "You called for me, Miz Elizabeth?" the boy asked shyly.

Elizabeth turned toward him, and Alex saw her expression curl into an almost-snarl that she must have thought was hidden. "Yes, dear boy, I did indeed. Come in and take off your shirt, please."

Alex stopped her. "That won't be necessary, Elizabeth."

"Don't be silly, child. You would look in a horse's mouth, wouldn't you? Before you paid for it? That reminds me, Benjamin. Open your mouth and show Miss Alexandria your teeth."

The boy immediately obeyed, flashing her a wide, toothy grin that Alex couldn't help returning.

"That will do for now, Benjamin. Please stay in the kitchen until I tell you that you can leave."

The boy nodded. "Yes ma'am." Turning to Alex, he smiled again. "And pleased to make your acquaintance, ma'am."

"That will be enough, Benjamin." Elizabeth aimed an open hand at the boy's face, which he adroitly avoided as he disappeared through the door. "I told you I am having a terrible time with insubordination," the woman complained. "They simply do not respect me, or any other white person. How dare he presume to accept your acquaintance in such a personal manner. I assure you I will have him whipped for his insolence."

"There will be no need, Elizabeth. He will be leaving with me, I believe," Alex said, her voice suddenly sounding a bit harsh to her own ears. "How much do you want for him?"

Elizabeth, who had years of experience watching her husband in his horse-trading, suddenly grew coy. "Well, I'm not rightly sure that I want to part with him, Alexandria. He is, as I said, a bright young thing. I am certain with the right training he could become an excellent butler, or at the very least, he will make an interesting houseboy until he grows up. Don't you agree?"

Alexandria was quickly losing patience, so she simply opened her reticule and let Elizabeth look inside. "There is a little over four hundred dollars in coin in there, Elizabeth. Hard coins are not becoming as worthless as paper money. And we both know that in today's market, that lad wouldn't bring even a portion of that much. I am leaving right now, to make it back to the crossroads before dark. Do I take my money with me? Or the boy?"

Elizabeth reached out and snatched the purse from Alex's hand as she called for Benjamin to come back into the parlor. It was only a moment before the tousled head peeked around the corner again. "Go get in Miss Alexandria's buggy, Benjamin. You will be leaving with her."

The boy's eyes grew wide. "I'm—I'm being sold?" His voice wavered. "I don't want to be sold, Miz Elizabeth. I didn't mean to break the peonies. I was just running after the cat, and—"

The woman slapped him sharply, her face drawing into almost a smile as she watched his cheek grew red. "I don't care about peonies, you young fool. And do not ever speak to me or any other white person in that tone of voice. You will do as you are told, or you will be whipped."

The boy's head hung low. "Yes, ma'am," he said sadly. Stepping backward just out of reach of Elizabeth's arms, he said quietly, "Could I please just go out back and say goodbye to Callie and Reggie, and a couple of the—"

"No, you may not."

"Yes, of course you can," said Alex, speaking at the same time as Elizabeth. The women stopped and looked at each other. "You can have a half-hour," Alex said firmly, with her eyes narrowed, almost daring Elizabeth to challenge her, "while Mrs. Van Crawlin writes me out a bill of sale and transfers her ownership of you to me. Then we will be leaving, and you can tell all your friends that we will try to come back soon to visit them." She watched as the boy raced from the room and ran toward the cabins barely visible through the overgrown privet hedge behind the house.

She followed Elizabeth up the stairs and into the same study where she had sat and watched as Harlan and her uncle haggled over horse prices and after finally coming to terms completed the paperwork necessary to transfer horses from state to state.

She had no idea what sort of paperwork was necessary for owning a slave, but it didn't matter. As soon as she got Benjamin back to Pearl's, he would be freed, and ownership would never again be a question.

Elizabeth scrawled out a hasty bill of sale and greedily began to count the coins from Alex's reticule. "It's nothing personal, I assure you, my dear, but Harlan taught me well, you see. When you're livestock dealing, it doesn't pay to trust anyone."

When the coins were counted and placed neatly in stacks, Elizabeth handed the bill of sale to Alex. Alex looked at it for a moment, then said slowly, "I can remember that when we bought horses from you and Harlan, we were given a few pages of

information with regard to their health care, and suggestions for
future care. Is there nothing for young Benjamin?"

The sound Elizabeth made was between a snort and a laugh.
"My dear, surely you understand," she said with one eyebrow
raised. "Those were horses. Delicate creatures that require proper
attention. Benjamin is—well, he's just a nigger. So long as he is fed
and clothed, he will be fine."

She smiled sweetly at Alex and said, "Now, before you leave,
would you like some cucumber sandwiches and more tea?"

Alex shook her head slowly. "No, Elizabeth, I seem to have
completely lost my appetite."

Elizabeth voiced her concern. "Oh, my, I certainly hope
you're not going to be sick. At least not until you get home. It's so
uncomfortable to travel when you're not feeling well."

Alex said truthfully, "Actually, Elizabeth, I am quite sure that
as soon as I get back in the wagon and on the way home, I will be
fine." She stood up and said, "And now if you don't mind, I believe
I'll collect my property and be on my way."

About that time she heard a door at the back of the house
opening, and soon Benjamin walked into the room, his eyes wide
and sparkling with unshed tears. "Can I take some of my things
along?" he asked tentatively, his eyes warily watching Elizabeth,
obviously having been the target of her blows many times in the
past.

Alex smiled at him. "You certainly may. And did you have
time to say goodbye to your friends?"

Benjamin nodded slowly. "I told them I would try very hard to
come back to visit. Do you think that I might, ma'am?"

Alex hesitated, not wanting to lie to the boy but knowing that
at this point there was no way of knowing what was ahead for any
of them. Finally she decided it would be better to allow the boy the
hope that life as he knew it was not completely over. "If it is all right
with Miss Elizabeth, I will be happy to bring you along when I visit
next time," all the while knowing that the chances of her ever
darkening the halls of Wild Oaks again were extremely slim.

Elizabeth shrugged. "You are welcome any time, Miss
Alexandria, and whatever house niggers you choose to bring along
with you is your choice."

Alex looked at the small sack beside Benjamin and said, "Is
that all you want to take with you? Can you carry it yourself?"

Benjamin assured her he had all he needed and that he could carry it, so they walked together back through the foyer and out into the sunshine.

Lije hurried over from the bench where he had been resting in the shade, and he stood there for a few moments, looking at the boy. Alex wondered at the tears that glistened in his eyes. He said nothing, just asked her if she was ready to leave and if the boy was coming with them. She nodded yes to both questions, and soon they were rolling quickly up the overgrown path to the road.

~   ~   ~

They rode in silence for a while, and suddenly Benjamin said shyly, "Ma'am, please, what am I to call you? Where am I going to live? Are there other childrens there? Will I do field work, or garden?"

Alex smiled. "Why don't you just call me Maggie?" she suggested. "And I'm afraid there aren't any other children where we're going, but I think you'll be happy there." Her smile grew bigger. "Benjamin, do you remember your mother?"

His face grew sad. "They took her away. She was bad. She got hurted and the Massa, he didn't want her no more, so they sent her someplace really bad." His eyes got even bigger. "Oh, ma'am. Is that where I'm going? I promise I'll be good." His voice trembled and his eyes began to fill with tears.

Alex pulled him against her and wrapped her arms around him. "You are not going to a bad place, Benjamin. I promise no one is going to hurt you. And no, your mother didn't get sent to a bad place, and she didn't go away because she was bad. Mister Harl and Miss Elizabeth have done some very mean and very stupid things. One of the worst was sending your mother away to be apart from you. That's why I came to Wild Oaks. To find you and take you to your mother."

Benjamin leaned back and looked up at her, his young face hopeful. "Oh, Miss Maggie, you mean I am going to get to visit with my mother? Today?"

Alex shook her head, "No, not visit, Benjamin."

His face fell. "Oh."

Alex smiled again. "You aren't going for a visit, Benjamin, you're going there to live with her. You will be with her for forever. You will both be free—you can go wherever you want, whenever you want. Together."

If it were possible, his eyes got even bigger. It was apparently more than he could comprehend, because he was completely silent. She felt a shudder go through his body, and she hugged him closer. "I am so sorry, Benjy, I wish I had known sooner, but I promise I came to get you as soon as I could."

He relaxed against her and like a young puppy who finds a trustworthy lap to snuggle into, he soon fell asleep. Alex yawned and leaned against the side of the buggy. "I don't suppose you know a shortcut, do you, Lije?"

The old man turned around and grinned at her, tears glistening on his cheeks. "I am riding home on the wings of happiness, Miz Maggie. I'll try to get you there as quickly as possible."

Alex smiled at him then settled back and closed her eyes, contentedly feeling the warmth of the child asleep on her lap. She thought back over the day, offering up a prayer for the women in the world like Elizabeth Van Crawlin who would never know what it was like to have a heart filled with love, or to have someone truly love her in return.

Her thoughts drifted to Lije, and suddenly pieces of a puzzle fit together. She sat upright. "Lije, I just realized something. You're Becca's father, aren't you?"

Lije turned to look at her, his eyes still wet with tears. "I am, ma'am. And today is probably the happiest day of my life. I was happy the day my Becca was born, but I knowed what kind of life she was headed into, so that makes today happier. Knowing her and my grandboy is going to be like me—free. And it pains me to remember how I hated all white folks back then, just because of the color of their skin. And now my happy today is because of two white women who have hearts bigger than heaven. Thank you, Miss Maggie. I ain't got the right words to say, but my heart is singing."

Alex smiled back at him. "Oh, Lije, this makes today even more wonderful. I'm so sorry I never realized before. I guess everyone just thought I knew. But now I understand why Pearl went and got Becca—you had already come to live with her." Her face fell. "I wish she'd gotten there a little sooner."

Lije shook his head. "Things is as they're supposed to be. She went when she was supposed to go. And you did too." He smiled down with eyes that glowed with pride at the sleeping boy. "And now we really is a family. Only thing I regret is that her mama ain't here." He patted his heart. "But she's in here, though, so she knows every step either one of us takes."

Alex leaned back against the buggy seat and drifted off into a happy sleep. It seemed almost no time before she heard Lije telling old Molly Mule to "whoa back" and then the sound of a door slamming.

"Lord, chile, I've been watching out the window for hours. Did you find him? Did you—" Pearl stopped short when she caught sight of the child still sleeping with his head in Alex's lap. One small thumb had found its way into his mouth. "Aww, isn't he adorable," she sighed. "What a beautiful child."

Alex smiled down at him. "He is a sweetheart," she agreed. "Did you tell Becca where I'd gone?"

"I was too afraid something would go wrong and we'd get her hopes up for nothing," Pearl said. She looked at Lije. "So what do you think, Lije? Think we can find room for one more mouth to feed around here?"

The old black face wrinkled into smiles, and he said, "I think he's a fine, strapping young man, Miz Pearl. I'm pretty sure he can already outwork me and Silas together."

Pearl smiled at him and said, "Well, he can work sometimes, but we're going to see to it that he plays a lot, and"—she turned to Alex for agreement—"he's going to have to spend some time catching up with his reading and ciphering."

Lije's eyes widened. "Oh, Miz Pearl. Do you mean it? You're going to teach him to read and write?"

"Gonna teach him to do anything he wants to learn to do, Lije. If he's as smart as his mother, the sky is going to be the limit for this one."

Benjamin suddenly stirred, then sat up and looked expectantly at Alex. "Are we there yet? Where's my mother?"

Pearl laughed and then asked, "Would you like to go inside and have some blackstrap cookies and a glass of milk, while Alex goes to find your mother?"

Benjamin's smile was his answer, and he quickly transferred his attention from Alex to Pearl, following her into the house. "Where is Becca?" Alex called after them.

"She's out in the garden, picking the last of the butterbeans."

Alex walked around the side of the house, feeling as if her heart would burst from her chest. She paused for a moment, looking at the tangle of herbs that was rapidly covering the freshly tilled soil where Kane had supposedly gone for his final rest. How very quickly life could change, she mused. Some for the best, some for the worst, but always a change just around the bend.

A movement caught the corner of her eye, and she turned her head to see Becca turning the end of the row of butterbeans, her apron folded up into an impromptu basket. She waved, and Becca nodded.

She walked toward her and asked, "Need some help?" Becca grinned. "Good timing—I was just stripping the last bush. I'm afraid if we don't get a little bit of rain, this may be all we get, and some of these have dried so much we can put them right up without having to wait." She gathered her apron up closer and said, "I was just headed back to the house. Glad you got back before nightfall. Pearl said you might be gone overnight, and I was going to be worried about you. She wouldn't tell me where you'd gone." Her voice raised into a question that went unasked.

Alex nodded. "Yes, it was a bit of a secret." She could see Becca's curiosity nearly getting the best of her. Alex grinned again. "If you want to ask me, you can."

Becca burst out laughing. "Was it that obvious?"

Alex smiled. "Only a little."

Becca raised an eyebrow. "Well?" she prodded.

"I had to run an errand and pick up a little something for a friend."

Becca snorted. "Well, that tells me a whole lot of nothing," she complained.

"Come see for yourself. Tell me if you think my friend is going to be pleased with the surprise." She turned toward the house, and Becca fell in step beside her.

"Is it her birthday?"

"No."

"Is it a new dress?"

"No."

"Is it sugar? Or tea?"

"No. Better than any of that."

"Hmmm," Becca frowned. "Better than a new dress, sugar or tea? Must be pretty special."

"I think it's really special," Alex replied honestly.

She stepped up on the porch and opened the door to the kitchen. "You tell me what you think."

Becca stepped inside and let her eyes adjust to the darkness. She saw Pearl sitting at the table, eating a cookie with a child.

A familiar face with a mischievous grin turned to face her, and suddenly butterbeans went flying around the kitchen as Becca went running to gather her son into her arms.

Sobbing into his hair, she turned to face Alex. "But how can this be?" she blurted amid her tears.

"Lije and I drove to Wild Oaks and talked Miss Van Crawlin into letting Benjamin come live with you."

"Talked her into it?" She looked at Alex and frowned. "You bought him?"

"Yes," Alex said simply. "And now I am giving him to you. You are both free." Her eyes filled as she watched the young mother alternate between hugging her son to her breast and pushing him back so she could look at him, unable to believe that he was truly there.

Pearl spoke up. "Becca, this brings up another matter. I have been doing the accounting for what you owe me—"

Becca nodded. "This won't make no difference, Miz Pearl. I still want to work off my debt, and now I want to work off Benjy's, too. I want to know we's free because we earned it, not because someone give it to us."

"Let me finish," Pearl said sternly, and Becca's eyes dropped to the floor.

"Yes, Ma'am," she said flatly.

Pearl smiled. "According to my ciphering, you paid off your debt in full to me with this last month's work."

Becca looked incredulous. "Miz Pearl, are you sure? I had thought it would take a lot longer."

Pearl shook her head. "I keep tight books, girl. One thing I don't fool around about is money. You have repaid me in full, and in fact I owe you three dollars."

Becca's eyes shone with unshed tears. "I must be dreaming," she said, pulling one of the chairs back from the table and sitting down on it in a daze. She looked up at Alexandria and said quietly, "I guess I have three dollars to pay you toward Benjy's debt."

Alex started to protest, but she caught Pearl's eye and stopped.

"Thank you," Pearl said simply. "That combined with what I owe you for the hours you spent nursing Kane will more than cover my expense."

Becca shook her head. "No, ma'am. I won't take no money for nursing Mr. Kane. He's a good man, and he's special to the two of you, and you two are special to me. So that sort of makes us family." Suddenly she realized what she had said, and her face flushed. "I mean, I realize y'all ain't niggers, but . . ."

Alex went over to her and enveloped her in a hug. "I can't think of anyone in the world who I'd rather share a family tie with than you, Becca. You're a real lady, and I am honored to be your friend."

Becca broke down into tears. "This is just all too much," she said between sobs.

Benjy had been listening to the interchange not really realizing what they were talking about, but when his mother burst into tears he quickly joined her. Soon the four of them were wiping their eyes and sniffling and looking for handkerchiefs. After several moments of quiet, all of them stopped and looked at each other and burst out laughing.

When their laughter died, Becca looked pensive for a moment. "Miz Pearl, will you still have a job for me? Now that you've been paid?"

Pearl looked at her solemnly and said, "Becca, you always have a home here. You and Benjy both. And you too, Maggie. There may not be a lot of money, but we'll always have love and laughter. And hopefully enough food on the table. And if you want to keep working, Becca, you can. Or if you'd rather just live here and do your part in taking care of things, we'll just be a sort of a family. It's up to you."

Becca looked down at Benjy for a moment, then ruffled his hair. "Why don't you go out back and ask Lije if he needs you to help him with the horses before it's time to clean up for supper?" She watched with pride in her eyes as Benjy stood up, pushed his chair back under the table, and went out the back door. She turned to Pearl. "I want to set a good example for my son," Becca said quietly. "I can't do that if I'm working upstairs for you, Miz Pearl. If you need me, then I can take care of a customer or two. But I'd rather do regular chores and be a mother to Benjy. If you're sure that's all right with you."

Pearl smiled. "It's more than all right, Becca. It's exactly the decision I would make in your position. And just the one I thought you would make."

Becca sat there for a moment, and another tear rolled down her cheek. "Life is a funny thing. Two years ago, I thought mine was over, that the worst thing in the world had happened to me. I had been used and scarred and then got sold away from my boy. I didn't see no way I could ever find anything to smile about. And look at me now—I'm a free woman. I can hold my boy in my arms anytime I want to. Ain't nobody never going to be able to make me do nothing I don't want to do, nor keep me from doing anything I want. And Benjy will have that same life. I just can't believe it. Right in the middle of all this bloodshed and heartaches and misery, I feel guilty to be given so much."

Pearl wiped a tear and said in a husky voice, "Nobody deserves it more, Becca. You are a good woman. And that's more than I can say for Elizabeth Van Crawlin." She turned to Alex. "So, how was dear Elizabeth?"

Alex described the harridan she had seen, including the story of Harlan's abandonment. Pearl shook her head. "And some people wonder if there is anyone up there watching over us. What goes around, comes around, my grandpa used to say—and far as I can tell, what Elizabeth gave, she's getting back now. And I can't feel sorry for her."

Becca spoke quietly. "I feel sorry for her. She ain't never been happy, not really. And now she ain't got much chance to ever be. Mister Harl never loved her, and he ain't likely to come back for her, and she'll be all alone there forever without anybody to love her or for her to love back. I reckon I may have black skin, but I still d'ruther see me every morning in the mirror than to see her. They's folks that I love, that loves me back. And that's something that makes up for a whole lot of nothing."

Chapter Eighteen

Kane's body healed slowly but surely, and within a month he was hobbling around the house, leaning on a set of crutches Lije had spent over a week whittling to fit Kane's body. His ribs had mended quickly; his leg was taking longer. He had tried putting weight on it for short periods of time, but it was obvious it would take a lengthy recuperation to heal enough to walk without crutches, and Pearl prophesied that he would always need at least a walking stick for long-distance walks. She and Alex joked with him about the "Kane cane" Lije was busy whittling from a branch from the cedar tree that shaded Kane's would-be grave.

Like most male patients, soon he was telling everyone what to do, complaining about how it was done, and generally becoming a nuisance. Even Pearl grumbled behind his back that she "should have left him in that damned box."

One Monday morning in mid-April, Kane was on his way upstairs and met Alex coming downstairs with a basket filled with dirty laundry. After exchanging morning pleasantries, he offered to help her with her load.

"No thanks, this is the last load, and frankly I'm in no hurry to finish this job," she grinned impishly. "Pearl says when the laundry is done we're going to scrub floors." She gave a mock shudder. "Washing and hanging out clothes is a breeze compared to that." She moved to one side to allow him to pass, but instead he reached out to take the basket from her.

"Kane, stop it! I can carry this myself. Go sit on the porch. You can't handle this big, old basket and maneuver yourself up and down the stairs on those accursed crutches."

Alex gave a strong tug on the basket handle. Kane suddenly let go, and Alex tumbled headfirst down the stairs, all tangled amongst crumpled sheets, aprons, and shirts.

Kane grabbed the banister and began the arduous task of getting himself down the stairs without making the same type of painful arrival Alex had made at the bottom. He bellowed for Pearl and Ellen, and they came running in from the parlor where they'd been shelling the few peas Lije had been able to find in the remains of their early spring garden.

"Help me!" Kane ordered, a touch of the army sergeant back in his voice for the first time they could remember. They raced to Alex's side and began to pat her cheeks, calling her name. When Kane reached the bottom of the stairs, he tossed the crutches aside and knelt beside her, his face turning white with a mixture of pain and fear. He reached out and gently touched Alex's face, breathing a deep sigh of relief when her eyelids fluttered. She opened her eyes and quickly closed them. "Ouch," she said. "My head hurts."

"Darlin', I am so sorry—" Kane began.

Pearl hushed him. "Enough time for that later," she scolded. "Right now let's just see if anything's broken."

After tentatively stretching her limbs and flexing her hands, and assuring herself and the others that nothing was misplaced, Alex sat upright. Suddenly she reached up and pushed Kane, who was still kneeling beside her, off balance.

"Now dammit, Kane, next time I tell you to leave me alone, I mean for you to leave me the hell alone!"

Kane sat there, his legs sprawled in front of him, a look of bewilderment crossing his face. Pearl and Ellen quickly turned their heads to hide their grins.

"Maggie?" he said, his forehead furrowed. "Are you okay?"

Alex pulled herself to her feet and stood over him, her hands on her hips. "No thanks to you, sir—yes, I think I'm okay. I'm sure it does a body a lot of good to tumble down a flight of stairs." She reached out her hand to help Kane to his feet. He leaned more of his body weight to her than she had expected, and suddenly she lost her balance, petticoats flying, to land on top of him.

"Goddammit, Kane!" she sputtered.

"But Maggie," he protested, his voice high-pitched with shock, his eyes wide in amazement. "You're swearing."

Pearl and Ellen could almost hear Alex's teeth grinding as she said evenly, "Yes, Kane. I am swearing. I almost always do that when someone is doing their dead-level best to kill me." The last words rose to a shout, and Kane ducked his head, as if expecting her to hit him again.

"I really just wanted to help," he complained.

"Nothing on God's green earth could possibly be of less help than a man just out of a sick bed who wants to make sure he's still useful," Pearl said, shaking her head as she and Ellen helped both Kane and Alex to their feet. "Women get sick or hurt, and they stay in bed till they're better, then they get up and go back to work. Men get hurt or sick, and they moan and complain and groan and try to get up and around too soon, and put themselves back in bed trying to help." She shook her finger at Kane. "You're just lucky it wasn't you who took a tumble down those stairs . . . you bust those ribs or that leg again before they get healed proper, you'll find yourself a permanent partner with them crutches. Or a nice, soft wheelchair."

Kane looked embarrassed. "But I was just trying—"

Ellen, Pearl, and Alex joined in a tired chorus to finish his sentence: ". . . to help."

Alex reached out and patted Kane's shoulder, her voice suddenly gentle. "Kane, can't you just relax and let us take care of you?"

Kane looked pensive. "I just ain't used to it," he said slowly. "It don't seem right somehow, a houseful of women taking care of all the chores, and me not doing a thing.

"But you don't have to do anything," Alex said. The hand on Kane's arm tightened as she said quietly, "All we want you to do is heal, Kane. We all went through way too much to keep you with us to be able to just sit back and watch you undo all our good work." She smiled at him. "You know, at one point I didn't think I'd ever be arguing with you again, Kane."

At his look of bewilderment she realized immediately her faux pas. Before she could cover her mistake, Kane asked, "Again? I thought we hadn't met before. So, when did we argue?"

Alex said quickly, "Oh, you just don't know how many times while you were dead to the world you fought and complained about the things we were all doing to you. Pearl said then that you were stubborn and were just missing arguing with somebody. Then when you'd quieten down again, we'd all miss your grumblings."

Kane looked at Ellen and Pearl. "I didn't mean to be so much trouble."

Pearl shrugged. "It's okay," she said, her gruff voice turning unexpectedly soft. "We happen to think you're worth it." She smiled and swatted him playfully on the shoulder as she shook her head and gave him a sly grin. "Even if you would wear the patience of a saint sometimes."

She turned suddenly and walked toward the kitchen, saying over her shoulder, "If you really want to do something, there's a mountain of potatoes in here that have to be peeled for supper. And somebody's got to go pick up eggs if we're going to have breakfast tomorrow. I'm going over to check on Lily and the baby."

One of their neighbors, Lily Morgan, had given birth to her first child, a healthy baby boy, just hours after receiving word that her husband had not made it from his last battlefield alive. The baby was named Anthony Daniel after his father, Lily had proudly announced through her tears as she held the tightly swaddled baby close to her breast.

Alex had taken a pot of soup and pone of cornbread to the woman for supper the day before, and the mixed emotions in the cabin had almost taken her breath away. She had quickly left, and she took the long way back to Pearl's to give herself time to settle her own emotions down.

As many heartaches as she had suffered herself in her short life, she knew she had gone through nothing as heart-wrenching as what the young widow and new mother was facing. She only hoped the birth of a healthy son would be enough to keep the woman's mind off the loss of her beloved. Lily's mother was on her way from Saint Louis to take care of her new grandson while Lily packed up their meager belongings and prepared to move back to Missouri to be nearer her family.

Alex prayed that the rumors of Yankee troops in the vicinity were unfounded—or, if the rumors were true, that they would be diverted into a different direction, at least until the new mother could be strong enough to withstand the rigors of travel.

She frowned suddenly, realizing that even though Kane was healing rapidly, he would be unable to ride in a saddle for some time, and bouncing in a wagon could do almost as much harm.

Kane had started to follow Pearl from the room, but he stopped and looked at Alex. "Why the frown, Miss Maggie?" he said teasingly. "Do you think I would be exposing my body to the chance of serious harm if I sat at the kitchen table and peeled potatoes? Or would you rather I went back to bed and let you women continue to wait on me hand and foot?"

Alex laughed out loud and playfully slapped his arm. "Oh, go on with you. Go ahead and peel some potatoes. Just don't cut yourself, and don't leave too much good potato on the peeling. They're getting hard to come by."

She watched as he hobbled slowly across the floor, every step clearly sending tremors of pain through his body. Her mind was suddenly flooded with memories of his strong, lithe body, running and rolling, dodging enemy bullets, and leaning low over his horse's neck while the stallion raced the wind. She sighed, knowing that as much as she remembered these things, it had to be doubly hard for Kane to be constantly reminded of what he had lost.

Suddenly Kane tripped slightly at the edge of the frayed carpet, and it took all Alex's willpower to keep from running to his side to help him avoid a fall. She heard him moan softly, but he caught his balance and disappeared from her view through the open door. She could hear Pearl mumbling, likely giving Kane instructions for his job.

Alex smiled. She had truly meant it when she said she'd missed their arguments. Over the last months, many a long, lonely mile had been spent in the saddle, passing time with friendly debates over issues ranging from politics to the weather. Kane had a sharp mind and a good heart, which made him a clever and pleasant adversary. Most times she secretly found they agreed on many subjects, but she would play devil's advocate just to be able to sit back and watch him fret over the problem of how to make her views match his own.

She shook her head: Too much to do today to spend time woolgathering. She hitched up her skirts and began filled the wicker basket with the dirty laundry now strewn on the hall floor. As she bent over to pick up the basket a dull ache in her hip caused first a grimace, then a grin as she pictured herself tumbling ass-over-teakettle down the stairs. She shook her head at the picture and chuckled beneath her breath.

~ ~ ~

The bright sunlight caused her to shut her eyes for a moment when she stepped out onto the veranda, and when she opened them she found her world suddenly enveloped by dark blue. A quiet voice spoke her name, and she felt a tremor run through her body. *Impossible,* she thought. She squeezed her eyes shut for a moment, but when she opened them, the blue cloth now gathered with bright brass buttons was still there. She raised her eyes upward and met the smiling eyes of Captain Sullivan.

"Oh, my God," she breathed slowly, her thoughts immediately racing to the kitchen, where Kane was helping Pearl.

"That's odd. Most people don't get us confused." The corners of the captain's eyes crinkled as he grinned widely. "He is actually much taller."

Alex smiled a weak smile. "I'm sorry. You startled me," she said, a tremor lacing her voice. "What are you doing here?"

"I had an errand in Atlanta, and I thought I might as well take advantage of the chance to stop and see how you were doing."

"We're doing just fine," Alex said. "Thanks so much for stopping by." She edged toward the door, wondering how she could warn Kane and Pearl of the captain's arrival. "I do declare," she said loudly. "Captain Sullivan, I do seem to have forgotten my clothespins. Would you hold this basket while I run inside for a moment?"

She shoved the basket into his arms and disappeared through the door, locking it firmly behind her. She raced through the house, finding Ellen and Kane in the kitchen. They turned when she came in, looking in puzzlement at the panic on her face. "We're in a predicament," Alex said quickly. "I don't have time to explain, but Kane, you have to get up to your room and keep the door locked, and don't make any noise." She looked at Ellen. "Captain Sullivan is on the porch."

Ellen closed the book and gave a smile of genuine pleasure. "Oh, how nice," she said. Then her eyes suddenly widened, and she gasped as she realized the potential seriousness of the situation. "Oh, my—Kane, darlin', you must do as Maggie says. You have to get upstairs and be quiet. We can't have him finding you here."

Amid Kane's low grumblings that he was strong enough to take on a single stupid Yankee captain with one hand tied behind his back, Alex took Ellen aside. "Don't let him come downstairs. If you have to shoot him, that's okay, but do not let him come downstairs. I never, ever want Captain Sullivan know that his good nature was taken advantage of." Ellen nodded and said she would make sure Kane understood that he was alive today because of the generous spirit of this one "stupid Yankee captain," and thus he must stay silent.

Left outdoors on the porch, outside a door practically slammed in his face, the captain frowned when he heard the click of the lock but then shrugged, assuming this was a tactic the ladies had begun to keep away unwanted visitors. A good tactic, he thought to himself. Especially with the traffic that might be coming their way soon.

He sat the basket down on a porch rocker and leaned against the whitewashed railing for a moment. He stood there, letting the silence wash over his body and mix with the sunlight into a powerful drug. He felt lethargy beginning to weight his body, and he lowered himself to the porch floor, his knees against his chest.

This must be what heaven feels like, he thought as he felt the warmth of the sunshine enveloping him, as warming as the heated towel his barber laid on his face. He rubbed his chin slowly. When he got to Atlanta he intended to find a good barber first thing—if any were left, that is. The army barbers left much to be desired. He had taken to shaving himself most mornings and had the scars to prove it.

When he opened his eyes again, a smile tugged at his lips as he saw that Alex had rejoined him. She stood there for a moment looking at him, seeing him for a split second as a man and not a uniform of blue. The world suddenly seemed very small to her, everything focused in this one spot, and his smile vied with the sunshine to warm her.

"Captain, do forgive my bad manners. I swear it's been so long since we've seen anyone around these parts, I just clean forgot my manners. Do sit down and visit for a bit. Perhaps you'd like some fresh lemonade?" She smiled. "If you'd like something a bit stronger, I've seen some pretty suspicious-looking stone jugs in the root cellar. I'm fairly certain the contents could be yours for the asking." Her mind toyed with the idea of getting the captain drunk so they could hustle Kane away, but she had a feeling the captain's mind was not one easily made sluggish by spirits—or anything else.

She sat down beside him, arranging her skirts to cover her tattered slippers. She reached up and felt of her hair, tucking some of the curly tendrils back up into the bun they'd escaped from during her tumble down the stairs.

"Oh, my!" she said. "I must look a fright. I do wish we'd have known you were coming." *And that's an understatement,* she said to herself.

"I didn't know myself that I was coming until late last night. Like I said, I had a message that takes me to Atlanta, and since I am soon to be on leave for a trip north for a couple of weeks, I decided to leave my post early and kill three birds with one stone, so to speak." He smiled at Alex, his white teeth glinting in the warm sunlight. "It had nothing to do with the fact that I wanted to see you again, of course."

Alex looked at him in puzzlement. "Of course not," she said. "I didn't think that it did."

Sullivan smiled. "Actually, Miss Maggie, it did have quite a lot to do with that."

She blushed and dropped her eyes as he reached out and touched the collar of her dress where a cameo nestled in the tatted lace. "I see you got my gift."

"I would have returned it if you'd given it to me in person," Alex said primly. "But under the circumstances, I felt it was given to me in friendship, and that is how it was accepted. I wear it as a good-luck talisman." She smiled, remembering the moment she had realized Kane was still alive. "And so far it's done exactly that. Brought me good luck."

"I'm glad. When I saw it, I thought of you. And I wanted you to have it."

He stood up slowly. "Now, Miss Maggie, I have some distressing news." He reached down and took Alex's hand, pulling her carefully to her feet. "There is news of action just south of here that may escalate and bring the fighting too close for your comfort. I thought I'd help you and Pearl and Miss Ellen pack your things, and I can get some of my men to escort you north to safety."

Alex shook her head. "Thank you very much, sir, for your concern, but we'll stay where we are until we're certain we won't be safe here."

Sullivan's voice grew hard. "I'm telling you that now, Maggie. It's not safe here. And I don't want you in the line of fire if things get heavy. And I don't like to think of you women here alone if some rag-tag bunch of butternuts—" He nodded in concession to her unspoken irritation at his choice of words. "You're right, of course," he said. "There are dishonorable men wearing both colors of uniforms, and I don't want you to come in contact with any of them."

He pushed her toward the doorway. "Now, go get your things, and tell your men to saddle your horses and load your wagon. You're coming with me."

Alex backed away angrily. "How dare you show up on my veranda and order me around like some sort of charwoman? I won't have it, sir. I appreciate your concern, but I'll discuss this with Pearl and Ellen, and if we decide to go, we'll do our own packing, and we'll leave in our own time, whether or not you approve."

Sullivan reached out and grabbed her arm. He dropped it just as quickly, then he groaned and rolled his eyes. "This is supposed to be confidential information," he said quietly. He leaned closer and said, "You don't understand, Maggie. I know that things are going to get rough here. That's the message I'm taking to Atlanta— orders to head in this direction. When those orders reach the right ears, Union troops will be converging here from all points west and east. And it is almost a certainty that they will be met by as many Confederates." Without thinking he reached out and took her arm again, the look in his eyes begging her to listen to his words. "And not if but when they arrive here, Miss Magnolia, they will find an empty house. You will not be here. Do you understand me?" He continued his hold on her arm.

Alex's eyes sparkled with fury. "I understand that you can let me go now, sir." Her voice wavered, and his grip loosened.

His tanned face darkened even further with his embarrassed blush. "I'm so sorry, Miss Magnolia. Truly sorry. I just don't want any of you to be in the way of danger." He turned toward the house. "Perhaps if I spoke to Pearl, I could make her see reason."

"Pearl isn't here," Alex said, knowing that it would take Pearl and Ellen both to get Kane upstairs and tucked away. Knowing that the captain would expect an explanation for Pearl's absence, she continued. "She's gone to a neighbor to take some soup. Lily has a new baby and is all alone, but she won't leave her house yet, although Pearl keeps trying to get her to come here until her mother arrives to help with the baby . . ." Her words trailed, once again imagining the young mother's plight. "But I'm sure Pearl will be back soon."

Captain Sullivan shook his head. "So much suffering. And it seems the innocents suffer more than the guilty." His hands ruffled through his hair, and Alex had a sudden, foolish urge to reach out and run her own fingers through it and smooth it back into place. The feeling startled her, and she stammered, "I do appreciate your concern, Captain. Truly I do. I just can't leave right now. And I can't explain it to you, but I just can't go. At least, we can't all leave right now, and I won't leave without Pearl and Ellen, and . . ." Her eyes dropped, unable to meet his as she evaded mention of Kane. ". . . and the hands."

The captain's brow furrowed in frustration. "All right, Miss Magnolia. You win. I'll do what I can to give you ladies protection, although I must say a more stubborn group of womenfolk I hope to never see."

He returned Alex's shy smile. "I really don't have time to wait for Pearl to return," he said suddenly. "I have to meet a train in Atlanta. And if I miss it there'll be hell to pay in Washington."

"Why are you going to Washington?" Alex asked.

He smiled. "Well, it's sort of a double-barrel event." When Captain Sullivan grinned, Alex's heart raced faster. His worry lines faded away and were replaced by laughter lines, which Alex found much more fitting for him. She imagined that in the life he'd led before wartime he was adept at finding the humor in situations.

"How's that?" she asked.

"Well, the commanding officer at West Point is receiving a commendation from the President. I have been 'requested' to be there . . . requested quite strongly. You might say it's as good as a presidential summons."

"My goodness. You must be quite important," Alex said.

"Not really. I fear that I am being invited mainly so General Stout can prove to me that I was a fool to pass up his offer of an office position instead of in the field." At Alex's questioning look, he went on. "I was engaged to his daughter," he said slowly, his fingers idly creasing and re-creasing the side seam of his trousers. "When I refused to sit behind a desk safely in Washington and chose instead to carry a gun and face battle on Southern soil, she suggested we cancel our engagement. Being a gentleman, I accepted. I did ask her again to marry me before I left, but she quickly refused."

"Three weeks after I arrived at my training camp in Tennessee, I received a telegram from a friend that Malinda was engaged to a man I detest more than any other in the world. I would like to believe she only did it for spite. However, along with my summons to attend this commendation ball, I also received an invitation for their wedding four days later. I have no choice but to attend, although I shall feel the laughingstock of every person there. It was no secret how I felt both about Malinda and about her future husband."

Alex reached out and touched his shoulder. "Believe me, I know exactly how you feel," she said sadly. "It's the ones you love and trust the most who have the most power over you. Sad, isn't it?"

Captain Sullivan put his hand over hers. "Thank you for understanding, Miss Magnolia. Perhaps your words will be a balm of sorts when I arrive in Washington and am forced to appear happy for Malinda's good fortune, when in fact I fear she is slated for certain heartbreak. If she loves this man, she perhaps will get what she deserves. I suppose it is possible that I misjudged her completely. If she is marrying him out of spite to me, as I suspect, perhaps she still will deserve what she gets as well. Marriage is a solemn vow, and one not lightly taken."

"I do wish you all the best, Captain," Alex said sincerely. "If there were some way to make the situation easier for you, I would do all in my power to come to your aid. I told you I owed you a great debt of gratitude for your sympathy and your aid when you helped Ellen and me to bring our friend Kane home to be buried." Her voice broke as she remembered her feeling of helplessness, seeing Kane lying broken in the dirty jail-cell.

"You owe me nothing, Miss Magnolia. It was my duty to aid a lady in distress. And if ever a lady were distressed, I believe you fit the standard exactly. It's not every day I come across fainting Southern belles in my office."

"I certainly hope not," Alex said, returning his open smile. "But I'm sure if you do, you'll offer them the same generosity you offered to me." Hearing a noise from inside and fearing that Kane was protesting being kept out of sight upstairs, she said loudly, "Please, do stop by again, Captain. Perhaps on your way back from Washington? It's a place I've always dreamed of visiting. I'd love to hear all about your ball and the wedding, even though it will no doubt be an unpleasant event for you."

The captain nodded, then his eyes narrowed and his lips pursed. "Miss Magnolia," he said slowly, "were you serious about doing all in your power to aid me during my time of need? That you felt you owed me a debt, as it were?"

"Yes," Alex said slowly, her own eyes narrowing.

"Then, Miss Magnolia, I will take you up on your kind offer."

"My offer of what?" she asked, her face crumpled into a

puzzled frown.

"Why, the offer to join me on my trip to Washington, attend the ball with me, and see for yourself what you just said you had always wished to see."

"Oh, my stars! I never offered anything of the sort." The shrillness of Alex's voice brought Pearl out onto the veranda.

"Good heavens, Maggie, what in the world—" Pearl stopped in mid-sentence as she saw the blue uniform and then the face above it.

"Jacob . . . my darlin' boy! I can't believe we meet again, after all these years." She gave Alex a smile, and a nod that Alex assumed was a code to tell her that she and Ellen had gotten Kane safely ensconced in his room, with the door locked firmly behind him. Alex's heart pounded, and she hoped her anxiety wasn't apparent to the captain.

"Pearl, you're as lovely as you were all those years ago. How can it be that age has not touched you, my dear?"

Pearl rolled her eyes, although a tinge of blush edged her cheeks. "Yes, it certainly is you, Jacob. And you haven't changed a bit. Always with a bit of the Blarney stone in your pocket. And just like always, come on inside and I'll feed you." As she bustled back inside she said over her shoulder to Alex, "This boy could put away more cornbread and pinto beans than the biggest fattening hog you ever saw."

"That's just not true," the captain protested with a wide grin. "Remember at the county fair when I joined the pie-eating contest? And Samson Simpson beat me by two pies?"

"That was only because you'd just left my house before you went to the fair and ate three bowls of beef stew and a half a pone of cornbread. And anyway, poor boy—with a name like Samson Simpson, he deserved a few streaks of good fortune. I heard he opened a fine restaurant in Siler City a few years ago."

"He won't make much money if he eats like he used to," the captain said with a chortle. "An appetite like that would literally eat into the profits pretty quickly, I'd imagine."

Alex stood back, enjoying their friendly banter. She edged through the kitchen door, leaving them to reminisce in private, and ran upstairs to the room, where Ellen was reading to Kane.

After beckoning for Ellen to join her in the hall, Alex whispered quickly, "I don't know what to do, Ellen. The captain needs me, and I did tell him that I would do anything to repay his kindness in allowing us to bring Kane here." She briefly outlined the plan and waited, her lips becoming bright red as she chewed on them in her nervousness. "In the world I left behind I would never consider doing such an improper thing . . ."

Her voice trailed off as she thought of the dozens of things she had done in the months since she last rode between those twin cedars that were so far beyond "improper" that she hardly knew how to label them. "But the captain has been so good to me. He has come to my aid twice now, once literally saving my life, and I do owe him a debt that I could not imagine ever being able to repay. And now he has given me a way to do just that."

Ellen considered the situation. "Well, at the very least, if you do this for the captain and he finds Kane here, he'll be more inclined to forgive us and not turn Kane in." She shrugged. "I don't see as how we can risk making him mad, Maggie." Her eyes were troubled and sad. "You know Kane isn't well enough to move. He can stumble around here all right, but if we put him in a wagon and start bumping over these rocky roads, his stitches'll break loose and his ribs could move around." She shook her head. "Besides that, there's always the chance that we'd come across some blue-bellies who'd take him as a prisoner."

Her curls tumbled as she shook her head again, this time a bit more violently. "We've come too far, Maggie. We can't stop now. If the captain thinks Pearl and I are staying here, maybe he'll send some sort of protection if the fighting does get closer." Her glance fell to the floor. "I am assuming that he asked you only as an innocent companion and not with some other nefarious ideas in mind?" At Alex's startled look she blushed. "You're right, of course; the captain is too much a gentleman to treat either of us as anything but a lady."

Alex looked up at the ceiling, her hands tightening into fists. "Oh, for goodness' sake. This thing just keeps getting more and more out of control. I should have never asked you to come along with me."

"Hmmph," Ellen snorted. "I'd have liked to see you try to make me stay behind. You didn't ask me, young lady—I came because I wanted to. I was bored stiff of living under corporal law and having the neighbors hating us for it anyway. And once I knew that George . . . wasn't going to be coming back, I really didn't have any reason to stay behind."

Ellen's voice broke for a moment. Alex's eyes brimmed over, remembering hearing her friend's sobs after one of the men she was caring for told her he had served with her fiancé George and would not be alive had it not been for George's heroics—heroics that unfortunately cost George his life.

Alex patted her arm. "You're a dear friend, Ellen. When all this is over . . ." She sighed. "If indeed it ever *is* over, I will find a way to repay you for your kindness."

Ellen smiled. "Better be careful about vowing to repay these debts, Maggie. Look where it got you with the captain."

Ellen followed Alex back down the stairs and into the kitchen, where they found Captain Sullivan seated at the kitchen table, a huge bowl of beef stew and cornbread and a tall glass of milk before him. He was leaning back in his chair, watching Pearl scurrying around the kitchen. A huge smile adorned his face, and Alex thought again how it improved his already handsome countenance.

He turned around and saw them in the doorway, and his chair tipped forward with a thump.

"Good afternoon, Miss Ellen. May I say that the sun in Monroeville has not seemed to shine nearly as brightly since you've been gone?" He grinned wickedly, and Ellen blushed.

"Captain Sullivan, have you been drinking?" she asked suspiciously.

"No my dear, it must be the company that is so intoxicating." He winked at Pearl, laughing aloud at her discomfiture.

"Oh, get out, Jacob," Pearl scolded halfheartedly. "How you do go on." She shook her head. "You always could charm the knob off'n a door."

Captain Sullivan smiled again. "And you, my dear, were always very deserving of any compliments I may have paid you."

He looked at Alex and smiled. "I was just about to tell Pearl about our upcoming trip, Miss Magnolia."

Pearl looked at Alex, her eyebrows raised in unspoken questions. "Trip?"

"Pearl, I do believe you would vouch for my honesty and integrity, would you not?" asked Sullivan.

"Without doubt."

"Then you can reassure Miss Magnolia that her safety will be of my utmost concern until she is returned safe and sound to your little fold here?"

"Returned from where?" Pearl was obviously curious. *And rightfully so,* Alex thought.

"Washington."

"Washington?" Pearl could not have sounded more surprised, Alex mused to herself, if she had suddenly heard of Alex's plan to fly in a laundry basket to the moon.

"Yes, Washington," Sullivan said firmly. "I need an escort to a couple of important functions, and Miss Maggie has very sweetly accepted my invitation to join me." He nodded in Alex's direction.

"Is this true, Maggie?" Pearl asked.

Alex nodded. "I think so," she said hesitantly. "Captain, would you excuse Pearl and me for a moment while we discuss this privately?"

"Only so long as you both agree you won't say bad things behind my back, when I'm not there to defend myself," he said teasingly.

Alex rolled her eyes and gave a mock sigh. "Oh, believe me, Captain. If I have bad things to say about you, I won't hesitate to let you know immediately." She smiled at him as she followed Pearl from the room.

"Alexandria! Have you lost your fool mind?" Pearl demanded, her voice low but deadly.

"No, Pearl." She hesitated. "Well, yes, actually I probably have. I just don't see how I can refuse. I do owe him a great debt. And Lord knows, I don't want him staying around here long enough to find out who's stretched out in bed upstairs." Alex raised her eyes and pointed over her head. "I'm doing this for Kane, Pearl. And besides, the captain said if you and Ellen were going to stay here, he'd do all he can to divert troops from where they were supposed to meet practically in our back door here. You know we can't move Kane right now. He's got to stay put at least a few more weeks. And if I refuse to go with the captain to Washington and stay here instead, he's likely to demand that we all move out. He came here in the first place to help us pack up and send men to escort us to Atlanta. The offer to take me with him to Washington was an afterthought. And the only way I could stall him was to agree to go with him if you and Ellen—and of course Kane too, although the captain doesn't know about him—would be safe and sound here until I returned. Maybe in two weeks when we get back, Kane will be healed up enough to stand a trip south, toward the coast. They say the salt water's got healing properties. And there ain't been much fighting down that far yet. We'd probably all be safe there."

Pearl mulled over the facts for a few moments, then shrugged. "Well, I don't like the idea of you traveling across the country with a man, without a chaperone along, but I doubt that any of my girls could be considered trustworthy chaperones, and it'll take me and Ellen both to keep Kane from going after you when he finds out where you've gone." She sighed. "I guess you were right. It's the only thing you can do." She sighed again. "Lord, what will you wear?"

"My dresses are the least of my problems," Alex said dryly. She turned and walked back into the kitchen, just as the captain downed the last of the milk and was spooning up the last drops of soup. He looked up as the entered, and Alex smiled at his milk moustache.

"What's the matter?" Captain Sullivan grumbled. "What are you grinning at?"

"You have a milk moustache, sir," Alex said. "May I say, it's quite becoming. Perhaps you should grow a real one?"

"Too much trouble to shave around," Sullivan grumbled as he wiped his mouth with his handkerchief. "Besides, I caught some shrapnel in my upper lip the first week after I signed up. I probably would have a sketchy if not completely uneven growth."

"Well, your moustache of milk was certainly lush and full."

The captain gave her an appreciative grin. "So may I assume that you and Pearl came to an agreement?"

"Yes. She told me she would trust you with her own life, and that she'd certainly trust you with mine. Although she is concerned about the lack of a chaperone."

Pearl had followed Alex into the room, and now she spoke as she bustled around, putting the dishes in the sink and putting a kettle on to boil for wash-water. "I know this is wartime, Jacob," she said. "But is that an excuse to give up propriety?"

"It is wartime, Pearl my dear," Sullivan said slowly. "That's the only reason I would consider asking Miss Magnolia to do such a daring thing. And I wouldn't have done so even then had I not been truly between a rock and a hard place."

"I'm not worried about your rocks and hard places," Pearl said, her eyebrow raised and a wry grin on her face. "I'm worried about Maggie's." Her grin bubbled over to join Sullivan's as his laughter filled the small kitchen.

"Oh, Pearl, I had forgotten how you could turn a phrase," he said.

Alex spoke up. "I don't understand what you two are talking about, but I'd like to remind you both that this is my decision. I've been in unchaperoned situations before." *Quite the understatement,* she thought to herself, thinking of the hundreds of miles she'd covered on horseback alone with Kane, as well as the hundreds of miles in the company of dozens of soldiers. "And after all, my home is now a brothel. I trust the captain to not allow any situations to become compromising, and it's not like we'll be completely alone. We'll be on a train filled with dozens of other people, and then when we get to Washington, we'll be—"

She abruptly turned toward Sullivan, with a puzzled look on her face. "Um, when we get there, where will we stay, captain?"

"We'll be staying with my sister Cecile. I don't remember if you ever met her, Pearl, but you may trust me when I say that Magnolia could not be better chaperoned if she had a true Southern duenna by her side. Cecile has read every book written on genteel living and does her best to follow every word precisely."

Pearl grudgingly gave her approval, asking again what Maggie would wear.

"I hope you'll allow Cecile and me to provide gowns for the ball and the wedding," the captain said. "It would be our honor as your host and hostess to make certain that you are the best-dressed woman in Washington. After all, I will be your escort, and I'm only invited because there are those who will wish to see me with my heart lying wounded on my sleeve." He sat down on the edge of the table. "I already told Magnolia my story, Pearl, but I want you to know the entire reason this is so important to me."

He leaned over and picked up a piece of pound cake Pearl had just taken out of the oven. After declaring it perfection plus and expressing his awe that Pearl could create such a delicacy on such meager rations, he went on with his story.

"I was engaged to a lovely young woman when the war was declared. When I told her my intentions of joining the troops headed South, she was horrified. She begged her father, a ranking officer, to give me a desk job to keep me safe. When I declined his offer, she broke the engagement. Almost immediately she accepted the marriage proposal of the one man in the world I truly loathe. I don't know if she did it to scorn me, or to prove herself still attractive to other men, although most certainly any mirror would give her that information; she did not need a sapphire and diamond ring to do so. Whatever the reason, I have been invited to the ball that will not only announce their upcoming nuptials, but also will announce the promotion of her fiancé to the position that had been previously offered to me."

He asked Pearl for another glass of milk, which he drained in one long swallow. "I had wondered at her acceptance of the proposal from the man who replaced me in her affections, since the job he has filled during these last months has been much more dangerous and dirty than the positions I have filled. But perhaps he did so to prove a point. And now he is willing to follow her wishes and accept a desk job."

"And you want a beautiful young woman on your arm to prove that you are not pining for your lost love." Pearl nodded her head understandingly. "I do understand your position. And of course, Maggie should have a wonderful time. Something she well deserves. I understand that Washington has remained fairly untouched by the ravages of war at this point."

"Hopefully for good," Captain Sullivan said. "I am very saddened to find you and me on opposing sides of this conflict, Pearl. I would have thought we would have always agreed on almost any subject."

"I'm sure we do agree on some points." Pearl shrugged. "I could accept the fact that our country could split apart on discussion of ideas and ideals. I cannot accept the fact that Lincoln called for seventy-five-thousand men to invade the South. That's when North Carolina seceded, you know. They just could not in good conscience allow those men to cross their soil for the express reason of raining hellfire on the South. My mama and daddy were both from North Carolina, and they're both buried there. When I pictured those men tromping across Mama's grave, I couldn't stand it. I vowed then and there that I'd do anything I could to help the cause. And I still would.

"I haven't been able to do much; I've mended a few Confederate soldiers who crawled in here looking for rest, and I've sent a few dollars to Lee to help buy supplies whenever I got the chance. But I fear all we're doing is too little too late, Jacob. And that saddens me greatly. We had so much in common, the North and South. I don't know why we couldn't have drawn on the sameness and worked through the differences."

"I know," the captain said slowly. "I truly do understand why any Southerner would want to defend their land. I do. But when you face the facts, Pearl, this was one nation, under God. It was supposed to be indivisible. Yet thirteen of its states decided that 'twas better to divide than to be a part. And the Union had to do what it's done to prevent that from becoming fact."

Pearl snorted. "Don't give me that political hogwash. Jacob, the reasons for this war go so much deeper that I reckon neither you nor I will ever know what truly began this horrible mess. I realized that when I found out that one of our former vice presidents of the nation is now serving as a Confederate general— General Breckenridge. He was vice president when all the states were united. And were supposedly indivisible? I'm sure he knew firsthand all the politics behind Lincoln's decision to declare war. But he's still dressed in grey, isn't he? And he's out there in the front lines, knowing how many Union bullets are aimed at his heart. And still he fights and declares his devotion to our cause." She shook her head. "It goes beyond all the facts that you or I are privy to, Jacob. And I do want you to know that before I knew what color uniform you wore, I prayed daily for your safety. And now that I know, I shall continue those prayers. You are a good and sensitive man. And when this war is over, both sides are going to need men like you to heal the wounds. I hope the rift can be sealed in my lifetime, but I doubt it." She took the kettle from the fire and poured the hot water over the dirty dishes in the sink.

Pearl was clearly ready to change the subject. "When are you planning on leaving, Maggie? Hadn't you best be packing?"

Alex had listened to the conversation with great interest. She herself had known little of the reasons behind the declaration of war, and she constantly strove to find rhyme or reason for the terror and havoc she saw around them daily.

She sighed. "You're right, Pearl. I'll go on up and ask Ellen to help me. Although I don't really have much to take with me."

"We'll remedy that when we get there," the captain promised. "I'm sure things aren't as normal as we imagine them to be there, but I feel fairly certain we can still rustle up some cloth and a good dressmaker."

Chapter Nineteen

Alex stood in front of the mirror, her eyes wide as she gazed at the reflection staring back, amazed at the transformation that had taken place with little more than a nod and a click of fingers from Captain Sullivan. One word from him, and suddenly it seemed that all of Washington had been at her beck and call. The last two days had been a whirlwind of shopping for materials and meeting the captain's friends, followed by the exhaustion of being fitted for her ball gown.

She pirouetted in front of the mirror, thinking to herself that each stick of a sharp pin and the hours spent standing ramrod-straight during her fittings had been well worth it. Her hair had grown and now fell to her shoulders, where it rested in carefully placed ringlet curls that were interwoven with ribbons and lace that matched the trim on the dress. Her breasts mounded seductively above a bodice cut just high enough to satisfy the chaperones, and just low enough to—as the dressmaker had said with a wicked grin, in what Alex was sure was a fake French accent—"*Make ze men want you, and ze women want to be you.*"

Alex smiled at the reflection. What was it with accents and these Yankees? Seemed as if all the men fell over backward when a woman spoke even minutely different from their local women. The first time she had smiled and said a simple "thank you" to a nice young man who had helped her down from the train when they had arrived in Washington, you would have thought she had said something wickedly common to him. She had pretended not to notice the way he had blushed and continued to hold her hand long after propriety should have made him release it.

As she gently caressed the folds of her gown, adjusting the shoulders to show just a little less décolletage, she shook her head. The women were just as bad as the men, she told herself. When Sullivan had told his sister that Maggie needed a gown for the ball, Cecile had told them both quickly that there was only one dressmaker in town with the talent and expertise to be trusted with such an important dress for such an important event. When Alex had asked about the woman, the first words from Cecile's mouth were "She's delightfully French, Magnolia. Wait until you hear her speak."

"But can she sew?" Alex had asked again, with a wry smile.

"But of course, silly," she was told. "She's French, I said. And wait until you hear her talk."

Alex turned slowly around again and carefully studied herself in the mirror. And who was she to argue, after all? The dress was absolutely divine. And she had to admit it was absolutely perfect for her. She frowned at the white gloves that covered her hands. She hated wearing gloves, but Cecile had been horrified when she'd seen the reddened skin, callused palms, and torn fingernails. The next morning after her arrival, a delivery boy had left a wrapped parcel on the doorstep. Between layers of see-through tissue paper were tucked several pairs of kid gloves, with stitches so small Alex had said to Cecile with awe that surely the fairies had stayed up all night sewing them just for her.

When she asked Sullivan who was responsible for the gift, he had shrugged and said it was all part and parcel of the trip. He had told her to simply relax and enjoy being showered with the gifts befitting the fiancée of a fine young Army captain. Alex had mockingly rolled her eyes and sighed deeply, then her own soft laughter joined the captain's.

"And I'm doing just that," she murmured to the face in the mirror. Her fingers tenderly folded and refolded the silken tucks at her waistline. It certainly was a far cry from the rough wool pants and sweaty jacket she had become accustomed to wearing.

I'm enjoying this far too much . . . I'm afraid I could get used to this quite quickly, she thought. She raised a hand to her hair. It was so wonderful to have a woman's hair again. And to have someone washing, brushing, drying, and arranging it for her. She smiled into the mirror again and then shook her head as she scolded herself. *Seems all I've been doing since we arrived here is smile. Remember, it's not real. It'll all be over in a week, and then it's back to Pearl's, and back to the real world.*

For a brief moment her mind was flooded with scenes from that "real world" she'd left behind. The battlefield horrors and the fear she'd felt over the past months suddenly held her in their grip. *Can I ever go back to that?* she asked herself quietly, her hand absently rubbing her stomach that suddenly clenched tightly. After meeting so many Yankees during these last few days and realizing that most were really no different from the grey-coated men she'd fought alongside, she murmured to the woman in the mirror, "How can I ever aim a rifle at another man again?"

"Begging your pardon, Mademoiselle?"

Alex jumped and turned to look in the direction of the voice. "My goodness, you startled me," she said, her hand resting on her still-fluttering chest.

"*Pardon.*" Estelle the dressmaker hurriedly closed the door behind herself. "Can't have anyone seeing you before you're completely ready," she said briskly. "Ze picture is not complete without ze frame, however."

"I am ready."

"No, *cherie,* you are not."

"Believe me, Estelle, from the bloomers out, I'm about as ready as I can be."

"Mademoiselle, how you do talk!" Estelle said, hiding a grin. She snapped open a small black box. "But you have no jewels around your neck, nor your wrist nor in your hair. If we have no precious gems nearby, how can ze men compare our eyes to ze sapphires, our lips to ze rubies, and our skin to ze pearls? And how can zey tell you that your eyes sparkle like ze diamonds in ze candlelight?"

"My God, woman! Are you planning to deck me out like a Christmas tree?" Alex grumbled. "Sapphires, pearls, rubies, diamonds—I'm a woman, not a jewelry box."

"But zis is an important occasion for ze captain. And he wishes you to look like ze princess he believes you to be." Estelle pouted.

Alex caught herself just before she let out an unladylike snort. "Princess? Me? Wrong storybook, Madame."

Her eyes widened involuntarily as Estelle turned the small box toward her and she saw the sparkling gems lying against the black velvet. "Oh, but sweet Lord, how gorgeous," she breathed.

"Are zey not?" Estelle said proudly, as if she herself were the owner instead of simply the bearer. "Of course, one cannot wear zem all tonight, but we will see what looks best on Mademoiselle, and on zis lovely gown."

Alex reached gingerly into the little jewelry box, feeling like a pirate captain opening a treasure chest. She held one after another of the lovely pieces against her skin, shaking her head each time.

"They're all beautiful, Estelle," she said finally, "but they're just not me. I wouldn't feel comfortable wearing them. I'd feel like an old yard chicken masquerading as a peacock."

Estelle narrowed her eyes and shook her head, her eyes troubled. "I do not understand, mademoiselle. You are not pleased with ze dress? I work so hard to finish in time. Perhaps zere is time to fix what ze mademoiselle does not like?" She frowned again, pondering Alex's words. "Why do you say, 'chicken'? Zere are no feathers." Her eyes widened. "But there is still time, Cherie. We can perhaps attach a—"

Alex shook her head. "No, no, Estelle. It's not the dress at all. I love the dress. It's the most beautiful thing I've ever seen. Certainly the most beautiful dress I've ever owned. And I've never seen such beautiful beadwork. How you completed it in two days is a complete marvel. I'm just saying I don't want to wear any of these pieces of jewelry. Maybe you could find me a foot of black ribbon, or maybe a scrap of velvet?"

Estelle left the room, shaking her head and murmuring beneath her breath. A few moments later she slipped back into the room, and handed Alex a lovely piece of black-velvet ribbon.

"Perfect!" Alex exclaimed. "Now will you help me, please?"

She took the brooch that Captain Sullivan had given her and fastened it to the center of the ribbon. Pulling her hair carefully off her neck, she motioned for Estelle to tie the ends of the ribbon at the back of her neck.

When she had finished, she let her hair down and turned to the mirror. Her eyes met Estelle's, and the older woman nodded. "It is right. You were correct, Mademoiselle. I was wrong. Zer is no need to gild zis lily."

Alex looked at herself critically for a moment. The pale pink of the dress brought out the rosy tint of the cameo brooch, and the ivory silhouette almost exactly matched the whiteness of her skin. "Thank goodness I got my mother's skin," she said quietly.

"Begging your pardon, Mademoiselle?"

"My mother. Her skin never sunburned or tanned or freckled. No matter how long she stayed in the garden without a hat. I remember Aunt Matilda said it used to drive Verbena crazy when she'd see mother outside without her hat. And she'd always bustle out to carry her one. But before too long, they say mother would be kneeling on the ground, coaxing some little shoot of a plant, her hat lying beside her, forgotten." She smiled. "I hadn't thought of my family in a way to make me smile in a long time," she said, her smile tinged with sadness. "This really is a magical night, isn't it, Estelle?"

A knock at the door broke the moment. "Magnolia, are you ready? The carriage is at the door."

"Coming, Captain." She looked at Estelle, winked, and said quietly with a wide smile, "Or maybe I should call him 'my prince' instead. This dress makes me feel like a princess indeed." She impulsively pulled Estelle into her arms and gave her a quick hug. "Thank you so much, Madame Estelle. It's so beautiful."

A blushing Estelle motioned for Alex to stand behind the screen as she opened the door for Sullivan.

When Alex stepped from behind the wicker piece a few moments later, the look on his face was worth all the diamonds and rubies in the world to Alex. She twirled, loving the feel of the satin billowing against her legs and hearing the swish of her taffeta petticoats. "Did we do all right?" she asked coyly.

Sullivan swallowed deeply, his neck a bright red. He nodded and said slowly, "Yes, my dear. I'd say you did all right. All right indeed." He gave a mock groan. "You do realize of course that this means I will have to be at your side the entire evening."

Alex smiled at him shyly. "And why is that, Captain?"

"Because I'll be afraid if I let you out of my sight, some young whippersnapper will toss you across his shoulder and carry you away into the night."

"Oh, my," Alex said in mock horror. "The stories I've heard have not been exaggerated then. You Yankees must not produce any gentlemen after all."

"Oh, we produce gentlemen," Sullivan said with a wry grin. "But I'm afraid the sight of you in that gown would drive the gentlemanly ideas right out of a saint's mind. Much less the minds of we mortal men."

Alex grinned widely. "Captain Sullivan, I do believe we'd best be getting to the party before you embarrass me, or yourself"—she smiled at him and winked—"or before my head gets too big to go through the door, more likely." She reached for the lacy white shawl lying across the foot of her bed.

"Miss Magnolia," the captain said, as he helped her place the shawl around her bare shoulders. "Do you suppose you could do me a favor?"

"I thought I was," Alex said teasingly.

"You are indeed," he said solemnly. "But I'm afraid I need to ask for another."

"Another?" Alex's eyebrows raised, her mind reeling trying to imagine what else he might ask of her.

"Could you please remember to call me Jacob?" At Alex's frown he added quickly, "That is my name, you know. Or even Jake. That's what many of my friends call me."

"And your mother?" Alex questioned.

"My mother?"

"What does your mother call you?"

The captain smiled gently and said, "My mother was hurt very badly three summers ago. Fell from a horse, and we thought sure she'd die before we could get the doctor to her. She lived, but will never walk again." His voice trailed. "She said the thing she'd miss the most is that she can never again dance with my father." He seemed to give himself a mental shake and went on. "They have moved to France, where the doctors give her more hope of a normal life, and where the climate agrees with her more than our cold winters in Pennsylvania. When I was growing up she always called me . . ." His voice hoarsened, and he cleared his throat. "Well, she always called me Sullivan." He straightened his string tie nervously. "She also loved my father very much, and Sully is what she'd always called him, you see. She never thought of either of us as a Jacob or a Daniel."

"*Sullivan.*" Alex tried out the name. "Yes, if it's all right with you, I'd prefer to call you that. It fits you somehow. More so than Jacob or Jake, I think."

One of the captain's eyebrows raised slightly. "Well, if you prefer. I suppose it's better than Captain." He smiled widely and held out his arm. "Now, my dear, our carriage awaits. We'd best be gone before all the guests decide you've changed your mind and fled back to the Deep South."

Alex blanched. "Please stop making this sound like everyone is coming just to see me," she pleaded. "All I promised to do was to pretend to be your fiancée—I didn't promise to be the belle of a ball."

Sullivan smiled down at her. "Miss Magnolia, I don't think

you have anything to say about the matter. In that dress you would be the belle of any ball you attended. Even if the rest of the guests were royalty, dripping in jewels and finery."

Alex rolled her eyes and gave an unfeminine snort that brought a grin to Sullivan's face. "You don't have to start the sweet talk until we get there. Don't wear it out. Keep kissing that Blarney Stone this early in the evening, and it'll be plumb worn out by the time the music starts playing."

Sullivan stood back and looked at her through narrowed eyes. "Now, what's a dyed-in-the-wool, good little old Southern gal like yourself know about kissing the Blarney stone?"

Alex smiled. "My mother was Irish. Her father stowed away on a ship coming to the States from Ireland about fifty years ago now. He died before I was born, but my mother and then my uncle raised me on stories of their beloved Emerald Isle."

"For goodness' sake," Sullivan said, then lowered his eyes. "Miss Magnolia, it appears you can continue to surprise me."

"And it appears to me that if I don't get to call you Captain anymore," Alex said with a wide smile. "You could certainly drop the 'Miss,' and if you don't mind, just call me Maggie again?"

"Yes, indeed, Miss Maggie, it would be my honor." Sullivan offered her his arm and escorted her down the lovely curved staircase that wound its way down to the ground floor of their home.

They passed several portraits of handsome men and women. Maggie stopped before one and said admiringly, "What a beautiful woman—who is she?"

"She was my grandmother. My father's mother. She died just a few years after my father was born, and my grandfather never remarried. Our family has always been known for their steadfast love for their partners. My own parents married when they were barely seventeen years old, childhood sweethearts from the time they played together as babies. There was never anyone else for either of them. My father finally went to my mother's parents and told them that he loved my mother, had always loved my mother, and knew she felt the same way. He asked for her hand in marriage, explaining that they wanted to fill their home with the sound of children laughing, and unless they wanted to have a houseful of bastard grandchildren visiting them, they had best accept his offer of marriage."

Alex blushed and giggled quietly. "And I assume they complied?"

"After a great deal of bluster, my father said that my grandfather took him out to the veranda and told him that while he appreciated his bravado and was grateful for his honorable intentions, he would run him through with his uncle's saber if he ever dared speak to him so brashly again."

"Have you visited them? Since they've been in France?"

"I had just bought tickets for Cecile and myself on an ocean liner the week that we first heard the threat of war. I couldn't leave at that time and be labeled a traitor or a deserter. So I sold my tickets to a friend who wished to send his own parents to a world that was less likely to be in civil turmoil."

They had walked slowly down the staircase as they talked, and now Alex found herself on the bottom step looking down at Cecile, who was smiling her approval of her dress.

"Estelle did a lovely job, didn't she?" Cecile looked like a proud mama seeing her firstborn daughter off to a ball on the arms of a handsome suitor. Alex looked at the captain, noticing not for the first time how well his uniform molded itself to his muscular shoulders, and how the trim cut of the jacket emphasized his flat stomach.

"She did a lovely job indeed, Cecile," Sullivan said, returning the look of appreciation. "I'm quite sure I shall be the envy of every man there."

"So long as you knock that complacent smile off Malinda's face, as well as her beloved's, it will be worth every moment," Cecile said with a quick nod. "You know I never liked her, Sullivan. And you know Mother would not have approved of her, either. The fact that she let you warm her bed before—"

"I think that's quite enough, Cecile," blustered the captain, his neck glowing beet-red above the pristine white collar.

"Well," Cecile snorted, "Mother would not have liked Malinda for a number of reasons, and you know that's true."

"Perhaps," Sullivan admitted. "What do you think Mother would think of Magnolia?"

Cecile stepped back and narrowed her eyes as she studied Alex for a moment. "I think she'd like Maggie very much," she finally said slowly, "and I think she would approve of her as your fiancée. I know that personally I am going to be very proud to call her my sister."

Alex had wondered if Cecile knew the extent of the captain's subterfuge. Her words proved that Malinda was not the only woman in Washington who believed her engagement to the handsome captain to be real.

"We'd best be running along," Sullivan said smoothly. "Don't wait up for us, Cecile. We'll most likely be very late. It's been a long time since either of us has spent a night dancing. We intend to make the most of it."

Cecile sighed. "Oh, Jake, the only time I ever agreed with Malinda was when she wanted you to accept a safer commission. I do worry so about you down there in that land of godlessness."

Alex bristled. "Excuse me," she began, then stopped at seeing Cecile's eyes fill with tears.

"Oh, Maggie, I'm so sorry. I just have gotten so used to believing that everyone below the Mason-Dixon line has horns and a tail that I forget that the majority are people just like us."

"*All* of them are people just like you," Alex said quietly. "The only difference being that our homeland is invaded and our backyards are filled with soldiers and the sounds of gunshots, instead of birdbaths and the tunes of street minstrels."

Sullivan quickly ushered her out the door, where he expertly seated her in a lovely horse-drawn carriage. "We'll make our entrance in style, my dear," he said with a smile. "It's been a while since I've sat behind a horse instead of atop it."

"Me too," Alex said beneath her breath. She thought of the many miles she had covered on horseback, both alone with Kane and in the midst of a troop of soldiers. She wondered what Sullivan would say if she tried to tell her story. She mentally shook her head. Not yet. She ached to be able to talk with him of the things they had in common. Poor meals. The constant threat of death. The sights and sounds of a battlefield during a battle, and the very different ones when the fighting was over. Her eyes brimmed with tears suddenly, and Sullivan slowed the horses.

"Are you all right?" he said softly. "I hope Cecile didn't upset you with her babbling."

"Oh, no," Alex said quietly. "It's just that I have so much I want to tell you. Need to tell you. And I just don't know what the right time would be."

"You'll know when it's the right time," Sullivan said. "Just so long as you know that I'm always here if you do need to talk. About anything."

Remembering Del promising the same thing and realizing how different the meaning was behind the words coming from two such different men, Alex felt tears threatening again. They were blinked away when she realized the carriage had stopped.

"Well, we're here, darling," Sullivan said. "The show must go on, I suppose. Are you ready?"

Alex took a deep breath. "Stay near me," she begged.

"Just try to keep me away," Sullivan teased as he squeezed her hand. He helped her down from the carriage and gave a coin to the dirty young lad who seemed to be there for the purpose of taking care of the horses.

They entered the brightly lit room, and Alex blinked again. It was a beautiful space, with large windows reaching floor to ceiling along one wall. A stage had been set up at one end, and several well-dressed people milled around the floor below it. The musicians were beginning to warm up their instruments, and Alex found herself swaying in time to the music.

"Oh, Sullivan, it's wonderful. Thank you so much for inviting me," she breathed. "I do feel like a princess who's been invited to a lovely ball, in a world far away from my own."

The next few hours passed in a whirlwind of dancing and dining and meeting myriad friends of the captain. All of them seemed entranced with his new fiancée, and Sullivan beamed proudly at their praises.

Alex struck up a conversation with Katherine, the wife of Sullivan's best friend Franklin, and after a while the two women left their men talking politics and went to find the powder room. In the melee of women milling around the long mirrors, Katherine and Alex became separated. Alex started back toward the ballroom to find Sullivan, and she bumped against one person after another in the crush of people with the same idea as hers.

She was startled to suddenly hear a familiar voice from her past. "Alexandria? Alexandria Latham? That is you, isn't it? I do declare I did not believe my eyes earlier."

Alex's eyes opened wide as she whirled around. "Del?" Her face lost all its color, and the room swayed in her vision for a moment. "What are you doing here?"

"I think the question is more likely what the hell do you think *you're* doing here, Alexandria? You're going to ruin everything. What are you doing rubbing up against that blue-belly all evening, pretending to be engaged to him? And why did Malinda tell me your name was Magnolia?" Del's eyes bugged and the veins in his forehead throbbed ominously as he struggled to regain his composure.

"Pretending?" Alex hissed, the color coming back into her face. "What makes you think I'm pretending, Delwood? Are you so deluded as to think that I would be so totally devastated at not having your lukewarm kisses that I would join a nunnery? Captain Sullivan is twice the man you are. Or can ever hope to be."

She looked across the room and met the captain's eyes. For a moment, his eyes narrowed and his back stiffened as he saw the look in her eyes, but he relaxed at Alex's slight nod and smile.

She turned back to face Del. "Make that three times the man you are, Delwood Lange. If you should live to be a hundred— which I sincerely hope you don't—you could never hope to come even close to being the man he is." She gave Del a coquettish smile. "In *every* sense of the word."

"Good God." Del's lips curled unattractively. "Have you lost your mind, Alexandria? Must you rut with every man you come in contact with who is wearing pants? First the man who broke our engagement, now this strutting rooster."

Rage flowed hotly through Alex's body. She leaned closer to him and spoke quietly, her words laced with such venom that Del took an involuntary step backward.

"Mr. Lange, might I remind you that *you* are the man who broke our engagement. And I use the term 'man' very loosely in your case. And as you very well know, you were never allowed more than a few stolen kisses. Thank heavens. After finding out what a sorry piece of maggoty trash you are, I would have put a bullet through my heart rather than ever let you touch it. Or touch me in any way." She spoke between gritted teeth. "You know I was accosted, you know it was not my choice, but you let them all call me a whore. You let Aunt Matilda believe I chose to lie with some damned Yankee, and you let her believe I was responsible for Teddy's death." Her voice lowered to almost a growl.

Her next words turned Del's knees weak. "I know why that blue-coated bastard was in that grove of trees that night, Del." His sudden look of alarm, not masked quickly enough, told her that her words had struck home. "He was there to see you, wasn't he? To get a message from you? Or to bring one to you?"

Her voice broke suddenly, and her words were deadly quiet. "How could you, Del? How could you betray the men you grew up with? The men who admired you, the men who called you their friend?" Her look of disgust would have melted porcelain. "I hate you, Delwood Lange. And I'll see you pay for what you've done. Even if it means I have to meet you in hell just to watch you burn."

Del sputtered expletives, then his frown relaxed suddenly and his face widened into a sly smile. "You know, you're in no position to warn me, young lady. I'd like to remind you that from what I've heard about Captain Sullivan's fiancée, everyone here thinks you're sweet, virtuous Miss Magnolia McVane, a shy young virgin from Georgia. One who's about to lead one of their heroes to the altar. Wonder how they'll take to the information that you're actually just a simple country whore from Alabama, named Alexandria McKinley? A woman whose own family won't admit to bein' kin to?"

He turned as if to walk away. "I think I'll just go ask your soldier boy how much he really knows about his fiancée. Bet with the proper hints I could make your honorable captain come to believe his lady love had not only used him but was here to spy for her countrymen, instead of to celebrate his good fortunes."

Alex placed a hand on his arm. Del turned to face her, expecting to see fear or pleading on her features. The ice in her eyes and the cold smile on her lips surprised him. "Be my guest, Del. Certainly you have it in your power to ruin this night for me. And for Captain Sullivan as well. And you might even get me arrested and put in jail as a spy. But I assure you, when they hang me I won't be waiting in hell alone for very long."

Del looked at her carefully, from the top of her well-coiffed hair to the toes of her satin slippers. "And exactly how do you propose to do bodily harm to me, my dear?" he asked patronizingly.

"Never doubt that it is within my power and most certainly is my desire," Alex said between clenched teeth. "They might drag me out of here in disgrace, but I have done nothing illegal nor even morally wrong, certainly I have not endangered any lives. However, I know more about you than you might think possible, Delwood, and a few well-placed words in the right ears of people here tonight who have a hidden but very great sympathy for the Southern cause, and I can promise you that you'll be hanged or shot before the sun sets again. You'd best find a reason to leave here, Del. And don't look back." Her eyes narrowed, and her voice was like cold steel. "If you look back, you might not like what you find following you."

Del looked at her in amazement. "Where have you been these months, Alexandria? You've changed."

"You began the change," Alex spat the words at him. "You and that damned Yankee friend of yours. I have a score to settle with that slimy piece of chamber-pot leavings. And he won't get off with a warning to stay out of my sight."

"And what do you plan to do to him, pray tell?" Del said with a sneer. "Slap his face, or go tell his mother that he doesn't play fair?"

"I plan to kill him," Alex said flatly. "I plan to put a bullet in his balls first, then when I tire of watching him writhe in agony, I will put him out of his misery with a second bullet between his eyes."

"Great God," Delwood said, his eyes widening and his knees involuntarily coming closer together. "Where in the bloody hell *have* you been? And who have you been with, and what have you been doing. You talk like a . . . like a . . ."

"Like a man?" Alex smiled, this time with some warmth as her laughter rang. "You would be very surprised where I've been, who I've been and what I've been doing, Del. Very surprised indeed. And perhaps even more surprised to see how very good I've gotten at doing it." She turned to walk away, stopped, and then turned to face him again. The laughter left her voice, and sorrow etched her features.

"You're a sad, pitiful excuse for a man, Del, and I pity you." She shook her head slowly. "Other men marched off to war, to do what they believed in, and many lost their lives. Some lost their souls along the way instead. But you? You I pity more than any of them." She turned as she added quietly, "You lost more than any of them, Del. You lost your honor. And if you ever had a soul, you lost that too."

She motioned for the captain, who immediately was at her side. He smiled at her and said, "Forgive me for leaving you alone so long, my darling. But you appeared to be enjoying your conversation with . . ."

He nodded at Del while he waited for an introduction. Alex

crooked her arm in the captain's, but before she could speak
Delwood held out his hand. "Delwood Lange, Captain, sir. I wish
to congratulate you on your commission, and to congratulate Miss
Magnolia on her catch." His smile held no warmth, a fact that
Sullivan didn't understand but filed carefully away as information
for later contemplation.

"I'm afraid in that case you'll have to congratulate me on both
counts, then," Sullivan said, his own smile matching Del's in
temperature. "I am indeed a lucky, lucky man." He placed his hand
over Alex's and smiled down at her sweetly.

"Be that as it may, sir, I'm sure you know what a jewel our Miss
Magnolia is."

"You didn't tell me how you know Mr. Lange, did you,
sweetheart?" Sully asked.

"No, my dear, I didn't. Mr. Lange lived on the neighboring
property when I was growing up."

"Come, come, my dear. I believe that Mr. Sullivan—er, excuse
me, sir, *Captain* Sullivan, was it?—will find out our history soon
enough, don't you? I think it's best to clear the air from the start,
rather than have rumors start flying about."

"Rumors?" Alex and Sullivan said almost in chorus. Alex's
voice was almost an octave higher than normal, Sullivan's deep
and deadly.

Alex quickly recovered. "Oh, my goodness, Del. Surely you
don't mean that childish infatuation?" She laughed gaily. "I don't
think Sullivan would mind too much to know that you fancied
yourself in love with me at one point."

"And you with me, my dear. Let's be fair."

Alex looked up at Sullivan and smiled, then looked back at
Del and said patronizingly, "However you choose to remember it,
Mr. Lange. Those childhood days are far behind me, I assure you."
She nodded toward Sullivan. "And although the thoughts of the
boys I knew back home are sweet and tender childhood memories,
they certainly hold no threat for a *man* like Captain Sullivan."

Alex watched Del's face redden. Patting Sullivan's hand she
said sweetly, "And now, darlin', I think I'm through reminiscing,
and I must apologize for keeping you, Mr. Lange. You did say you
had to leave the party, didn't you? I am so sorry. It's such lovely
music." Pulling Sullivan toward the dance floor, she said, "I don't
want to waste a moment. It's been a long time since I danced."

She nodded her dismissal at Del, her eyes narrowing as they flashed him a warning. He stood there feeling his blood begin to almost reach the boiling point. "Bitch," he hissed as he watched the captain take Alex into his arms and glide across the floor.

His whisper echoed in his head. "Go ahead and dance tonight, sweetheart. Next time we meet, I'll make sure your little soldier boy isn't playing guard." He motioned for the butler to bring his cloak and took a long, lingering look at Alex and the captain, watching their bodies moving in perfect time to the music, Alexandria's head leaning against the captain's blue-clad shoulder. He swore again silently beneath his breath, and with the flash of a cloak was gone into the night.

Sullivan could feel Alex's rapid pulse as he loosely held her hand. "Are you all right, my dear?" he asked, putting his finger beneath her chin and tilting her head back so he could see her face.

"I'm fine," Alex lied. "To be truthful, I don't like Mr. Lange even a little bit, he reminds me of a time I'd rather leave where it belongs. In the past."

"I wondered if you were just possibly uncomfortable with having to dance with me?"

"Why?"

"I remember that you told me once that you didn't like to be touched."

Alex thought for a moment before answering. "There's a difference in touches," she explained slowly. "Dancing doesn't seem threatening."

"But some touches seem threatening?" Sullivan prodded.

"I don't want to talk about it, please, Sullivan." Alex pleaded. "Not tonight." She put her head back against his shoulder and said quietly, "I just want to forget. I don't want to know there is a world outside those doors. I don't want to know that morning will come and this will all be over. I want to pretend for just a while longer that the entire world is as beautiful as my life is tonight."

~   ~   ~

Alex and Sullivan danced until her feet were screaming in protest. Although her buttocks had become accustomed to riding long hours in the saddle, it had been a long time since her feet had been forced into this much action. She finally put her hand on Sullivan's arm and told him she either had to sit down for a few minutes or he would have to carry her around the dance floor.

After making a few suggestive remarks that brought a blush to her cheeks, he led her to a quiet corner and went in search of refreshments. Alex felt a chill across her shoulders suddenly and looked in the direction of the front door to see whose arrival had brought the cool air inside. Her heart caught in her chest and her hand flew to her mouth.

Sullivan's touch on her shoulder made her jump with such force that she almost knocked the plates from his hand. "Maggie? Are you all right? You look as if you'd seen a ghost."

Alex closed her eyes and forced her breaths to become normal. "I just stood up too fast, I think," she lied, her hand rubbing across her brow. "I just got a bit dizzy for a moment."

"You weren't standing up, Maggie. You were sitting down," Sullivan said quietly. "What's wrong?" He sat down beside her, placing the plates on the floor beneath his chair. Taking one hand in his, he leaned forward, forcing her to look him in the eye. "Now, tell me what is the matter. Do you need to leave?"

Alex looked into his eyes and saw the concern in their depths. "It's really nothing," she said lightly. "For a moment I thought I saw someone else who . . . who . . ."

"Go on," Sullivan urged. "Someone who what?"

"Someone whom I don't like very much," Alex said simply, her tone even, but Sullivan could feel, if not hear, the emotion it carried.

"Do you want to talk about it?" he asked quietly, his hand caressing hers gently.

"No. I don't think I can."

"Not to anyone? Or just not to me?"

"Probably not to anyone," Alex admitted. "But especially not to you. Not yet, anyway. Please."

"Why?"

"Because he wears a blue uniform," Alex said simply.

"And why do you think that would matter to me?"

"Because it would," Alex said sadly. "It's very hard to imagine your countrymen doing bad things to another person."

Thinking of one countryman in particular, Sullivan shook his head. Choosing his words carefully, he answered, "I think you'd be surprised, Maggie." He continued to caress her hand somewhat absentmindedly. "I would never put the color of a man's uniform on the stand at a trial. It is the man inside the uniform who does the deed. Good or bad. Right or wrong."

Maggie looked at him for a moment. She lowered her eyes. "There is one man who wears a blue uniform whom I hate more than is Christian for me to admit. He hurt me, and he hurt my family very badly. And walked away not caring. He took things from me that no one could ever replace. And I fear for my soul if we ever meet again under conditions that I can control."

Sullivan reached for her other hand and held it tightly. "I wish you'd tell me the whole story, Maggie," he said, his voice deep and husky. "If someone has hurt you, I would see him court-martialed at the very least, and I'm afraid I too would have to fear for my soul if we were to meet man-to-man."

"That's why I can't tell you," she said sadly. "This is something I must do myself."

"And he's here tonight," Sullivan said, his voice hard as flint.

Alex nodded.

"Is it the gentleman you introduced me to earlier? Your old friend from home?" his grip on her hand involuntarily tightened.

Alex suddenly smiled. "Wrong on three counts, darlin'. Del is certainly not a gentleman; he's not a friend. And no, he's not the man I fear to meet. I can handle Del without bloodshed. He isn't worth it. "

Sullivan relaxed. "Just know that if the time comes for you to share your secrets with me, or if you decide you need my help in seeking revenge, you have only to ask. I appreciate so much what you've done for me tonight, Magnolia. You've turned an event that I dreaded like mortal sin into a delightful occasion. All the men envy me . . ."

Mocking Estelle's accent, Alex interrupted him with a wide grin. ". . . and all ze women, zey vish to be me."

Their combined laughter echoed across the room as the music suddenly died. She heard the sound of silver on crystal, and she looked at Sullivan and rolled her eyes. "Is this the big moment, do you suppose?" she said in a low voice.

He grimaced. "This would be it, darling. Remember, you love me, you adore me, you don't know how you'd live without me." Their laughter was more subdued, but it was still audible to the man who stood in the shadows behind the curtains of the stage.

"But I'll have the last laugh, Captain," a rough voice whispered to no one. "Quite the fancy woman you've got on your arm there. Maybe I'll just have her, too." He turned and smiled at the man standing at the podium and walked across the stage to stand at his side.

Sullivan felt Alex's body tighten and heard her breath almost stop. He looked at her from the corner of his eyes, not wanting to embarrass her by letting her know he was aware of her discomfort. What he saw amazed him. Suddenly, the warm, vivacious woman he had held in his arms on the dance floor had vanished, leaving in her place a stranger. A stranger whose face had shifted into a look of such a mixture of hate and terror that he glanced quickly around to see if anyone else had witnessed the transformation. All eyes were on the stage, and he turned to see the attraction. He suddenly stiffened. His head turned quickly, and he was somehow not surprised to see that the woman beside him was staring in the same direction as the rest of the crowd.

He put his hand on her shoulder. "Maggie, do you wish to leave?"

He was transfixed by the suddenness of the change he witnessed. Maggie's face relaxed, her shoulders suddenly lost their stiffness, and a peaceful smile shaped her lips. "Leave? Why should we leave, Sullivan? The night is young, isn't it?"

She stole one last look toward the stage and then leaned against him. "Do you know the man standing up front? And, perhaps know why he's here?" she asked casually.

"I have the answer to both," Sullivan said with a nod.

"Is he a friend?"

"Hardly. Just because a man wears blue doesn't make him my friend, or necessarily even a good man," Sullivan said simply. "I thought I made that clear. And the reason he's here tonight is to announce his engagement to my ex-fiancée. This is the reason I needed to be armed, in every sense of the word," he grinned. "With a lovely young woman to prove that my heart didn't suffer any permanent damage by Malinda's decision.

"I know. I mean I believed what you said earlier about the man behind the uniform. I just wondered if you knew this one. Who is he?"

"His name is Rafael Peterson. His family is in the steel business in Pennsylvania. Lots of old money, which has helped him move up the ranks of the army a bit more rapidly than he would have done otherwise. Especially considering his education, or rather the lack thereof and the rumors about his private life." He shrugged. "Of course, that didn't make him any less attractive to Malinda. She always was fond of adventure." He smiled a sad somewhat wistful half-smile. "I don't wish her any harm, but I must say I find it rather humorous that she became engaged to the one man I truly despise, thinking it would hurt me. Instead, I find the entire situation somewhat fitting, for them both." His smile grew into a deep chuckle as a lovely brunette in a dazzling red ball gown walked onto the stage and put her arm around Sergeant Peterson's waist.

Sullivan leaned closer to Alex and whispered, "I don't know who'll be the more surprised when they wake up one morning realizing who, or what, they've married. As well as I know Malinda, and even as much as I hate Rafe, I have to say, the man almost has my pity on this score at least. If ever two people deserved each other, I believe perhaps it is those two." He reached for his champagne glass and joined the rest of the audience in a toast to the loving couple.

As the music started again, he reached for Alex's hand. "I think we must dance this set," he said quietly. "I would hate for either of them to think I nursed a broken heart."

Alex smiled up at him. "You hate him too," she said suddenly. "Why? Just because of Malinda's defection?"

"Hate him 'too'?" Sullivan's eyebrows rose slightly. "Mine is a very long story, Maggie." His hand tightened in hers. "Someday when we know each other better, maybe you can tell me yours, and I'll tell you mine. For now we can simply relax knowing that whatever we may not have in common, we find common ground in our personal enemies. That fact amazes me, considering the depth and breadth our worlds have been from each other before tonight, but my mother always said that the world was actually very, very small. And to find that someone across the country despises the same man as do I, for probably very different reasons, really shouldn't come as any surprise to me. He is evil enough to be hated around the world. Now, shall we dance?" She nodded, and they leaned together into the music.

Moments later, her head relaxing against the captain's shoulders, her mind a million miles away from the dance floor, she was startled when the captain suddenly stopped moving. He stiffened, and then held her away from him for a moment, saying,

"Darling, I'd like you to meet an old friend of mine. Malinda Stone. Malinda, this is Magnolia McVane. My fiancée."

The brunette who had shared the spotlight with Alex's sworn enemy was even more startlingly beautiful up close than she had been at a distance. Alex was suddenly very aware of the calluses hidden beneath her gloves, and she had to will herself not to touch her own hair nervously. "I'm delighted to meet you," she heard her voice saying. "Sullivan has told me so much about you."

"Sullivan?" The woman's laugh grated on Alex's nerves like the sound of a tack scratching on a new tin roof. "You call him Sullivan?"

"Well, that is his name," Alex said dryly.

"Well, yes, but I can't imagine calling the love of my life by his last name."

Alex shrugged and smiled a dazzling smile up at Sullivan. "Ah well, he hasn't seemed to mind yet, have you, darling?"

Sullivan returned her smile and put her hand to his lips. "I told you to call me what you like, my darling, so long as you continue to call me at all."

Alex turned to the woman's escort, willing her hands to remain unclenched, and forced a smile, hoping it didn't appear on the outside as the feral snarl she felt in her belly. "Sullivan and I were too near the back of the room to hear your speech, sir, but I assume you must be Mr. Peterson."

"Sergeant, my dear." Rafe's voice brought flashes of memory that Alex fought to squelch. "Soon to be Captain, I guess it's safe to say." He reached for Alex's hand. She suddenly wished she had a mirror to look into, to see if her smile was as frozen and her jaws as petrified as they felt. She was amazed to watch her hand being enfolded into one of his large, suntanned hands instead of burning against his cheek with a slap, as she so deeply desired. She looked at his hands, imagining suddenly the horror of feeling them on her body. The hairs on the back of the man's knuckles seemed as thick as a forest, and the thought went through her mind that perhaps he truly was a beast and not a man. Surely no man could submit anyone to the horrors he had brought to her family and still be able to smile and laugh and supposedly, considering the occasion, even love. She removed her hands decorously.

He laughed. "Well, I guess it's true what they say about you Southern belles," he said, his words echoing in Alex's ears.

"And what's that, sir?" she asked, amazed again at her body's calm exterior response, while her brain was racing so wildly and her pulse was sending blood through her heart like a swollen river in the spring's first thaw. "I assume you've been told we're all alike?" She ached to add the words he'd spoken to her those months ago. *And that you know what we want? That we all want one thing? And I'll bet you'd like to show me what it's like to have a real man . . .*

Her waking nightmare was shattered abruptly with the pressure in the middle of her back from Sullivan's hand.

"Darling, aren't you going to answer Rafe?"

"I'm sorry," Alex apologized. "I'm afraid my mind wandered."

"From the look on your face, it wasn't to someplace very pleasant," Malinda offered.

"No. It wasn't," Alex declined to explain, but she smiled and asked, "What did I miss while I was wool-gathering?"

"You asked me what I had heard about you Southern belles. I asked you if what you were learning on your visit here about what you people call 'Yankees' matched what you had heard about us."

Alex smiled again, fearing her cheeks were going to shatter from her face, leaving her skull gleaming with a bright white smile exposed to the world, teeth gritted firmly together.

She took a deep breath. "From the moment I met Sullivan," she said honestly, "I knew that not all I had heard was true. There were indeed gentlemen in the Union army ranks. And those blue uniforms on occasion cover true men, true gentlemen, in every sense of the word." She smiled up at the man in question. Her voice hardened somewhat, although she tried to mask it, as her eyes then locked for a moment with Rafe's. "I'm sadly afraid, however, that not all men wearing a blue uniform are hiding hearts of gold. I'm afraid there are those whose moral fiber is even far weaker than any tales I might have heard behind opened fans at the ladies' quilting bees back home."

Malinda spoke up suddenly. "Oh, for heaven's sake. Enough of this talk. I want to hear about you, Miss McVane." She batted her lashes seductively as she glanced at the two men. "I know all about both of these blue-clad gentlemen. But how did you and Jacob meet?" She gathered her skirt as she walked toward the row of chairs where Sullivan and Alex had sat earlier. "I just know you have a story to tell me that will rival the stories I read in *Miss*

Prickett's Romance Reader for Young Women." She smiled at Alex, who didn't miss the fact that this was a gauntlet being tossed, and she also couldn't miss the fact that the smile on the lady's lips stopped before it reached her eyes.

"Well," Alex began, wondering if she should fabricate a romantic story or simply tell the truth. The truth won—or at least a partial truth. After a while lies just became too hard to keep untangled. Although the young lad Alex McKinley had met Sullivan months earlier, she told Malinda honestly where he had met Magnolia McVane. "We met in prison," she said simply. She was rewarded with a look of amazement on her adversary's face.

"Prison? Who was in prison?"

Alex giggled. "We both were." She held her hand up to ward off Malinda's questions. "All right, I'll tell the whole story. We were both in prison, but on the same side of the bars. The outside. Thank goodness."

Her voice grew soft with the memory. "My very dear friend was a regular visitor to the Confederate prison in Monroeville where Captain Sullivan is stationed as the officer in charge. She made daily trips to the prison, and carried books, food, and medicine whenever possible to the men who were incarcerated there. She also wrote letters home for many boys who couldn't read or write." She pretended to not hear the comment from Malinda to her fiancé, whispered not quite quietly enough, "Are they indeed all illiterate plowboys?" With an even look at Malinda, she added, "Many of these boys were young enough to still be in school but unfortunately were taken away from their books for a rather extensive field trip. Some of them learned lessons they will never forget. And many learned a final lesson that took all memories of the past as well as dreams of a future away from them."

She licked her lips before going on, her bottom lip caught for a moment between her teeth. "I visited the prison with my friend one afternoon and was horrified to find one of my very dear friends on his deathbed in a far corner of the building. Sullivan had been away from his post for days, or I'm certain he would have issued orders for medical care sooner. Not that it would have mattered. My friend died in my arms." Her voice wavered and then cracked at the memory of her terror during those moments of watching Kane swallow the potion, not knowing what the next few hours would hold for either of them.

She continued. "When Captain Sullivan returned to his post, he allowed me to take my friend's body home to my aunt's place to be buried. I will never forget the compassion he showed to a woman who by birthright was his sworn enemy." Her eyes met his for a moment, and the music faded into the background as they entered a world that seemed to hold only the two of them. "I knew the first time we met that this was a man who didn't hesitate to do what was right. No matter the consequences. No matter the circumstances." Tears welled in her eyes suddenly, remembering the moment that Private McKinley had awakened in Sullivan's camp and then later listened to his declaration of love for Pearl. "I knew he was a man worthy of any woman's love, and the woman he loved would be the luckiest woman in the world, even if she had nothing else to her name, except that love."

Sullivan's eyes grew misty, and he pulled Alex close.

"How very touching," Malinda said, malice brushing the words with acid. "And what do you do in your spare time? Perhaps indeed you do write stories for Miss Prickett?"

Alex laughed suddenly, discreetly wiping away the tear that hovered at the corner of an eye. "No, I don't write stories," she admitted. "I've found that life very rarely imitates the fiction one reads." She smiled up at Sullivan. "And to my great surprise, I have found that life is infinitely better and certainly more exciting than any writer could portray."

She looked at Rafe for a moment, realizing she could meet his eyes without feeling the tremors of revulsion that had rocked her earlier. "For instance, who would have thought when we first met just weeks ago, Mr. Peterson, that we would meet again, in such lovely surroundings?"

"Met—me? Weeks ago?" Rafe looked nervously first at Alex, then at his fiancée, who was watching him intensely, daggers shooting from her eyes. "I'm afraid I have no idea what you're talking about, Miss Magnolia."

Suddenly his eyes widened. "The wagon, in Georgia. Your friend pulled a gun on me." His face reddened, and his shoulders tightened with anger. "I should have remembered you. My apologies, my dear. You certainly look different tonight."

"Yes, my heart was completely broken when you obviously didn't appear to recollect our earlier meeting, Mr. Peterson," Alex drawled, beginning to enjoy the exchange. "Of course, I have to admit, we weren't meeting under particularly friendly circumstances though, were we?" She winked at him coquettishly, rewarded with seeing a dull color creeping from beneath his collar. Uncaring as to whether it was rage or desire that prompted the coloring, she continued her taunt. "Unfortunately I have not since been able to completely recollect the message you told me to convey to Captain Sullivan if or when we met again. Perhaps you recall, sir? Or Sullivan, perhaps one of your men remembered to give you Sergeant Peterson's message when they returned?" Her smile reached her eyes this time, and she enjoyed watching Peterson squirm under Sullivan's warm gaze.

"I'm sorry, Rafe. This is the first I've heard about this meeting." He looked at Alex and nodded. "Do go on darling. I'm afraid you've been a very bad girl to be so remiss in bringing me what could possibly be a very important message."

Alex touched a finger to her cheek, drawing her brow into a pensive frown. "Now, let me see. I seem to recall a threat—"

Peterson's voice stopped her in mid-sentence. "Now, my dear, you know that was indeed a very unusual circumstance, and whatever was said by either of us was most likely said in the heat of the moment, and neither of us should repeat to anyone what was in fact a private moment."

Alex looked puzzled. "Private?" Her eyes widened suddenly. "Good idea, Mr. Peterson. Indeed the private who was escorting me seemed most dependable and could most likely remember the message in its entirety. If indeed he were as addlebrained as I and forgot to give it to you earlier, Sullivan." She touched Sullivan's arm with her gloved fingertip. "Do remember to ask him when you return, won't you darling?"

Malinda had watched with narrowed eyes the exchange between Alex and her own current lover. Not knowing at first exactly what the undercurrent was in their repartee, she was relieved to discover it was not sexual in nature. She could relax for the moment at least. With a randy soldier such as her intended, it wouldn't do to leave him alone for very long. For that very reason, she had instructed her father to offer Rafe an army position here in Washington instead of whatever dull chores he currently did that took him from her bed for too many weeks at a time. She never had to wonder whether other women warmed his bed while he was away, although he was foolish enough to believe her own bed stayed cold until his return. She hid a dark smile. As soon as the wedding certificate was signed, however, his assignations would have to cease. She had the power to give him all he needed, both in his career and in his bed. And she would not hesitate to threaten him with taking either away at the first hint of indiscretion on his part.

She put a hand on his shoulder. "Darling, would you please bring me another glass of champagne?" She looked at Sullivan. "And I'm sure Magnolia is feeling a trifle thirsty after that compelling little story time." The smile she offered Alex made her even more uncomfortable than the earlier hooded ones. This one reached her eyes.

As they watched the men walking toward the refreshment table, Malinda broke the silence. "They certainly cut quite the figure, don't they?" she mused.

Unwilling to pay a compliment to Rafe Peterson, Alex simply smiled. At Malinda's gesture, she followed her to a row of chairs set up near a long row of curtained windows.

"How long will you be in Washington?" Malinda asked.

"We must leave Friday morning. Our train is due to depart at eight o'clock in the morning."

"If it can get through," Malinda said with a grimace. "I'll just be so glad when all this is over and things can get back to normal. I'm so tired of having our train schedules in a snarl, of having to wait for days for shopkeepers to bring our coffee and sugar. And this spring Mother and I were planning a trip to Paris to plan for my trousseau, but now things are in such a mess, I don't know that Father will allow us to go."

"Yes, war certainly can be a hardship," Alex said softly, remembering broken bodies sprawled on the cold dirt and thinking of all the nights she'd gone to sleep on the ground, grateful for the spoonfuls of beans and cold hardtack that would keep the growl of her stomach from awakening her during the night. She wondered what Malinda would say if she described some of the things that she'd witnessed over the past months. For a moment she looked at the beautiful girl and wondered how much differently she herself would have looked at the war had she decided to stay at Twin Cedars that one night so long ago.

The return of the men bringing crystal glasses filled with clear champagne brought an end to her musing. Sullivan handed one of the glasses to Alex and then raised his glass for another toast. "To love," he said carefully, "wherever you find it. And to Malinda and Rafe, who have found in each other what they each so richly deserve. I give my heartfelt congratulations to you both and sincerely wish that life continues to treat you in the manner befitting your contributions to each other and to others."

Malinda's eyes narrowed as she listened, but her smile was warm as she joined the others in raising their glasses. "And to the two of you, Jacob and Magnolia. May life bring you both what you deserve as well."

Alex giggled when the bubbles tickled her nose, eliciting a warm chuckle from Sullivan. "Not used to drinking champagne, I see?" he teased.

"No—only on New Year's Eve," she confessed. "My uncle shocked my Aunt Matilda when I was fifteen years old and he toasted my health with a glass of champagne and then filled my glass so I could return the toast." She smiled. "Teddy and Marcus both tried to be manly when they drank theirs, but I couldn't keep from giggling then either."

"Teddy and Marcus—your brothers?" Sullivan questioned.

"No. They were cousins, but my parents were killed when I was very young, and their parents raised me. They were as close to me as brothers would have been, though. Especially Teddy." Her voice suddenly cracked.

"And where are they now?" Malinda asked.

"Dead." Alex swallowed the lump in her throat, willing the tears that were pressing the back of her eyes to stay back.

"How awful." Malinda seemed genuinely sympathetic. She placed a hand on Alex's shoulder.

"Marcus went down in battle. After only being gone from home for a month. We got the letter, and I thought Aunt Matilda would join him in heaven she was so distraught."

"And Teddy?"

Alex's voice grew hard. "Teddy was also killed at a Yankee's hand. But not in honest battle." Her eyes met Rafe Peterson's and hoped that her words burned his memory. "Teddy died defending me against a Yankee's advances. My last memory of him is washing the blood from the knife wound in his chest. Before we dressed him for the last time." Her voice broke and as hard as she tried, several tears forced their way from behind her eyelids.

"How terrible! How could such a thing happen?" Malinda seemed truly shocked. "Where was your chaperone?"

"War has been more of a hardship to my family than concerns about clothes and coffee and train schedules," Alex said simply, with no malice.

"I am so sorry," Malinda said. Her arms went around Alex's shoulder. "I do wish you were staying longer," she said. "If you will, you can stay with Mother and Daddy and me. You don't have to go back with Sullivan to that awful place."

"It's not an awful place." Alex shook her head until her curls threatened to tumble from their pins. "It's a beautiful place. Full of tall pine trees, and gentle breezes, and bright blue skies and mountains that dip their feet in clear cool rivers and lakes. I wish you could have seen it before . . . before the changes that have been wrought. I fear that nothing will ever be the same again," she said sadly. "Unless blood is a miraculous fertilizer, I doubt that within my lifetime the South will regain all her beauty."

Malinda shivered. "I don't want to think about that."

Alex smiled sadly. "I don't either, Malinda. But I don't have a choice."

"Yes, you do. You can stay here. You'd be safe here."

"But I have friends at home who need me. Who would be worried about me." She smiled, thinking of Kane. "And some who I simply just don't want to be away from unless it's necessary." She shook her head slowly. "No, whenever the whistle blows for the train to Atlanta, I'll be on the station steps."

She sat her glass down beside one of the chairs. "I think it's time we all thought about less maudlin things than war and death, though, don't you? We have a chance to dance and forget. And I for one intend to make the most of it. Thank you so much for inviting us to your party, Malinda. It's a very special night for me."

Sullivan put his arm around her waist, and they glided out across the floor.

"Whew," he breathed against her neck.

Alex giggled and ducked her head. "Stop that! You're doing to my neck what the champagne did to my nose."

"I'm just glad that's over." His arms tightened around her. "I appreciate everything you said and did tonight, Maggie. I realize now that I put you in a dreadful predicament, but you carried through like a real trouper. Please know I had no idea you carried such a scar on your heart, or that tonight could be even more unpleasant for you than I had suspected it would be for myself. I owe you my deepest gratitude and the promise that if you ever need or want anything from me, you have only to ask."

Alex laid her head against his shoulder. "You have already done so much for me," she said quietly, "more than you could ever guess." She added beneath her breath, "or may ever know."

Chapter Twenty

The rhythm of the train rocked Alex to sleep almost as soon as the wheels started to roll. She and Sullivan had spent the last few days in an exciting, memory-making tour of Washington. They had awakened with the sun each day and spent long hours wandering along the Potomac, meeting friends for lunch on the Green, and enjoying the moments stolen from the lives they'd left behind in Georgia.

Alex could certainly see why anyone would enjoy visiting the vibrant city. It seemed there was always something to do and see one day, and plans to make for the next.

She couldn't understand why anyone would want to live there, though. The novelty of all the beautiful, large buildings so close together soon faded, and she began longing for grass and trees and solitude. Besides the lack of natural beauty, as in any other large city there was dirt and noise and the threat of crime. To Alex it seemed as if the personal agenda of everyone she met seemed somehow to focus on how money could be made or spent in a day. Even when the war had been discussed in her presence, the "casualties" had seemed to be lost cargo from plundered ships, misdirected freight, and other losses. Few people openly discussed the loss of lives as anything more than a newsworthy item.

When she spoke her thoughts aloud, Sullivan had shrugged. "There are more differences between the North and South than accents and map lines," he had said. "There's more money in the North, no doubt. Therefore, it has to be of concern. And the people of the South should not think there's a problem with Northern points of view, for certainly much of the cotton and produce grown in Southern fields finds a market in Northern homes."

Alex had not voiced her feelings any further, although to her it seemed that there should have been a way to even things out somewhat. Her family had never had to worry about where their next meal was coming from, since their horses had brought top dollar and had been sought from states across the country, but they had never come near to the lifestyle that the people she had met during the past few days took for granted. So many of her neighbors had lived a very simple lifestyle, eating what they could grow and being grateful for whatever meager coins came their way through honest labor. She had laughed out loud when one person after another had asked her in confidence how many Negroes she had owned, and had she ever had anyone beaten. She thought of Verbena and of the other black people who had lived on their farm, and she told them quite honestly that although she knew there were horrifying situations, even on plantations she had visited with her friends, her family had always considered most of the black people that worked on their farm as they would have a white person they had hired to do a job.

"Sometimes it felt more like Verbena owned me than the other way around," she'd admitted. "She scolded me far worse than Aunt Tilly ever did. And she spanked me a lot more often than anybody else ever did when I'd done something bad."

She could tell that most people didn't believe her, and after reading article after article in the newspaper about the horrifying conditions slaves faced daily, she wondered whether she could really have been that naive, or if perhaps the accounts of a few were being used to blanket the many to sell copies of the paper. As she'd told the people who asked, although she had never witnessed cruelty herself, she had known of circumstances when black people were treated inhumanely. Her uncle had once refused to sell a man a horse that he wanted and could easily afford because it was well known how the man treated his slaves. Her uncle had told him flatly that until he learned how to treat another human, he shouldn't be trusted with good horseflesh. The man had blushed and blustered, but he had left riding the horse he had arrived on.

She couldn't help feeling guilty that they were having such a good time. She was quite certain that the price tag on her ball gown would have fed an entire troop of soldiers for days, if not weeks. And she felt a stab of guilt remembering her pleasure as she stood looking at herself in the mirror on the night of the ball. When she said as much to Sullivan he had just shrugged. "You can't buy apples with oranges, Maggie. If you didn't have a new ball gown, the storekeeper would still have some expensive fabric in stock, unsold. Estelle would have been unemployed the last week and would in turn not have been able to pay her rent, which would have put yet another person's pocket lighter. You didn't help any soldiers, but you did help people who are struggling to keep food on their family's tables. You only saw the upper-class side of Washington. I don't want you to go back home believing that everyone above the Mason-Dixon lives a life of luxury."

Alex thought about what he'd said and then sighed. "I know there's truth in what you say, Sullivan, but I still can't help feeling guilty that I'm here enjoying myself, meeting new people and doing exciting new things. I keep thinking of everyone and feeling that it's just wrong that I'm having such a good time."

Sullivan shook his head. "There'll be time enough to face tomorrow, tomorrow."

"What time does our train leave?"

"Well, it's scheduled to leave at eight o'clock, officially. Unofficially, it's going to leave an hour early. There's been some threats of sabotage, so the train line wants to get an early start and hopefully avert any trouble."

"Is there likely to be any trouble along the way?" Alex asked worriedly.

"Well, we'll hope not. It's likely, though—I won't lie to you. You need to be prepared. But we'll hope for the best, and take whatever comes."

"Whatever comes?"

Sullivan grimaced. "Maggie, we'll be crossing the Mason-Dixon in about four hours after we leave Washington. Beyond that I can't guarantee what will happen. Things have become much more heated in the days since you and I started our journey. I will promise you, however, that I will defend your honor to the death, no matter what happens."

"Oh." Alex fell silent, remembering the many shouts of victory she'd joined in when given news of trains bound for Southern soil carrying Yankee troops and provisions that had been derailed. Many times passengers on those trains were treated as prisoners, along with the Yankee soldiers who were captured alive after the smoke had cleared.

She bit her lip. What would happen to Sullivan if Confederate men seized the train? She did not fear for herself, as she could surely prove her allegiance to the cause. Or could she? Being in the company of a Yankee officer would make her suspect, and rumors of the company they had kept this last week would certainly not help her case. She shivered.

"Don't worry, Maggie. As I said, I'll take care of you." Sullivan looked at her closely. "You can stay here, you know. Where it's safe."

"But what about you?"

"Don't worry about me either, dear. I've traveled back and forth more times than you can count. I don't think it's time for my luck to run out just yet. It does warm my heart, however, to know that you considered my safety along with your own."

"Of course I did," Alex snorted. "You've been very good to me, Captain Sullivan. I do not wish to see you repaid for that kindness by being imprisoned." She shuddered. "Or worse."

Sullivan patted her hand gently. "My dear, you constantly amaze me with your depth of compassion and understanding. I know it must have irked you no end to find yourself in a position of owing anything to a Yankee. And I realize that is the only reason you have been here this past week—to repay what you conceived as a debt. I want you to know that you can go home with a clear conscience. You no longer owe me anything. It is I, now, who finds myself in the unusual position of an army officer owing a debt to a member of the enemy's ranks."

"Do you think of me as an enemy, Captain?" Alex asked, batting her eyelashes flirtatiously.

"I do indeed, Miss Magnolia," he said solemnly. "I fear that you could do me a very great damage."

"Damage, sir? I fail to see that would be possible, considering I am only a woman and you are not only a man, but a well-trained soldier."

"Ah, Miss Magnolia. It is because you indeed are a woman and I am only a man that I am in grave danger."

"And what danger would that be, captain? That I might stamp on your foot in anger? Or possibly slap your hand with my fan?"

"It is more possible that you could steal something I hold very dear," Sullivan said, suddenly very serious.

"Why, captain!" Alex feigned shock. "Surely you must know that I am honest to a fault. To call me a thief is to do me a grave injustice, sir. And what is this dear object I am believed to be in danger of stealing—a pocket watch? Some of the fine jewelry that I was offered the night of the ball? Or perhaps a message of great importance to the Rebel cause, that I shall hide in my skirts until I reach the proper authority?"

"Oh, but Miss Maggie, I only wish it were something so easily replaced or repaired," Sullivan said with a simple smile, and then he quickly changed the subject before Alex could press him further.

Alex puzzled over his words that night as she tossed and turned, unable to sleep. Even the next day, in the flurry of packing the wagon and boarding the train, her mind wasn't fully in the present. After they were seated, Sullivan got her full attention when he made mention of having mixed emotions over his upcoming change of command.

"You aren't going back to Monroeville?" Alex asked.

"No, I requested to be sent back to the front. I found my job far too distasteful for my comfort. I don't enjoy killing, but I'd rather kill in a fair fight than to put men to death whose only crime was their devotion to a cause that differs from my own. I also find myself unable to treat good men with disrespect, and I am told that that habit is considered a weakness."

Alex's lip curled with disdain. "I would imagine there are men such as Mr. Peterson"—her stomach roiled at the sound of his name coming from her lips—"who would find it a great pleasure to be in a position to dominate helpless men in prison, especially those wounded and frightened and unsure of their future.

Sullivan sighed. "It is men like Rafe who will keep this war going for far longer than it by rights should have lasted. Men who profit from other people's misfortune and enjoy seeing their pain." He stared out the window for a few moments, and when he spoke again his voice was low and had a sad note. "Does it bother you that I have killed men, Maggie?"

Alex's gaze followed his out the window, watching the trees flashing by for a moment before she carefully answered. "It bothers me that the man I believe I see behind your eyes has been forced to kill another, but I am proud of that man for doing his job and standing up for what he believes in."

Sullivan turned and looked at her for a moment before answering. "Thank you for those words, Miss Maggie. I have prayed and asked forgiveness from the Lord for my actions, but I do believe that your words give me more peace than I received after my prayers." He looked pensive. "I've sent a lot of good men to heaven, and a lot of bad men to hell. My only sin, I think, is perhaps that I didn't get a chance to ask which were which before I pulled the trigger." He smiled a crooked grin. "Perhaps if I'd taken the time to ask, it would have been me that their bullet sent to one place or the other."

Alex shuddered. "That, Captain Sullivan, would have been a shame indeed. I value our friendship, and I know my life is better because you entered into it."

~ ~ ~

The smile they shared warmed more than Alex's heart, but before she had a chance to examine the feeling she was thrown from her seat as the train stopped abruptly.

"Damn," Sullivan's curse echoed through the car. "I had hoped we were going to be able to get through at least this one last time," he said as he helped Alex back into her seat. "Do as I say, Maggie. Get up and walk to the rear of the train. Do not pay any attention to what goes on in this car. No matter what happens to me, do not let them know that we are together, or you will likely suffer the same fate."

Fear gripped Alex's heart. "Oh, no, Sullivan. Maybe we just . . . . maybe the conductor just . . ." Gunshots echoing across the valley stopped Alex's thoughts and gave proof to Sullivan's fears.

"Go, Maggie, and don't look back! If there is a next time we meet, I will"—he stopped and looked into her eyes for a moment, then leaned forward and lightly brushed her lips with his own—"I will hope to be able to do that again and tell you why." He smiled gently and then pushed her. "Go. Don't look back."

Alex stumbled out of her seat and walked toward the rear of the train. Most of the seats were empty, with most civilians afraid to travel by rail and most soldiers having found other means of travel. Sullivan had explained their choices to Alex, and they had both decided to chance getting through to Atlanta. Yet here they were, just a few hours from their final station, and the trouble they had thought to avoid had found them anyway.

She heard rough voices shouting and a woman's screams. She hurried backward toward the caboose, wondering what she would do when she got there. As she stepped outside the last car, rough hands grabbed her and spun her around. "Be ye friend or foe, little lady?" Alex looked at the man's ragged grey uniform and said very quietly in an exaggerated Southern drawl, "I am not the friend of any man who disrupts my visit to my Auntie Pearl. She is expectin' me, and she is goin' to be most unhappy if I am detained."

The man smiled and said, "You be one of us then, darlin', you'll be okay. Just gonna take care of the Yanks we found in the front cars. I guess you couldn't stand the stink of ridin' with 'em up there?" Alex's eyes flashed, but she kept her lashes lowered so the man could not see.

"My only thought was to get home. When will be allowed to move again?"

"Soon as we round up all the Yanks offen here we'll get her back on track, ma'am, I promise." The man doffed his hat and said, "If you wouldn't mind coming with me though, we will be leaving a few of these cars behind. They make good cabins for some of our wounded."

Alex followed him back through the cars, hoping Sullivan had found a way to escape and would not be at the mercy of the Confederates.

Unfortunately his face was one of the first she saw as she neared the front cars. He was bound to one of the seats alongside many other men dressed in blue, his face bruised and one eye swollen almost shut. Alex swallowed a whimper and forced herself to not appear concerned by his appearance.

He looked up and caught her eye and gave her an almost imperceptible wink. Alex's heart almost broke, but she bravely smiled and nodded at him when she was sure none of their captors were watching.

One of the men waved his gun as he spoke to the man who had escorted her to the front. "I think it's secure—can you handle it alone? We need to get some cargo moved off and onto the wagon, and then we'll be back to help you get these blue-bellies out of here. We'll let the rest of them go on through"—he nodded toward Alex—"being as there's some of our women on board."

Alex smiled an eye-fluttering smile at the man, causing him to blush for moment. "Um, we'll be in the back if you need us," he stammered, and then he followed his comrades through the door.

Alex waited a few minutes, then casually walked over to the man she had followed through the train and asked, "So what will happen to these wretched men, sir?"

The man's smile was calculating and evil. "Well, ma'am, some of them will go with us as bartering tools if we meet up with any more blue-bellies, and I reckon a few will be allowed to try to escape. If you get my meaning."

Alex knew exactly what he meant, which made bile rise in her throat. She had been present when some of her fellow soldiers had used their prisoners as a game, allowing them to think they had a chance of reaching freedom and then using them for target practice as they had raced away from their captors. She shuddered. "That doesn't seem very Christian, sir."

The man laughed, showing rotted teeth and said, "If you want Christian, go to church, little missy. This here is war, and you know what they say about war and love. All things are fair."

Alex stepped away from the man and looked around carefully. "Aren't you a little worried to be all the way up here alone with these men?" she asked.

"Nah. I tied them pretty well, and I've got all the help I need right here," he said as he patted the rifle at his side and pointed to a pistol in its holster. Ain't nobody going to try nothing funny with me."

Alex brought her hand out from the folds of her skirt and pointed her derringer steadily at the man's heart. "Perhaps you should have been a little more worried," she said drily. "Although you're right, there's nothing *funny* about this situation. Now, I think it would be a good idea if you untied at least a couple of these men and let them hold your guns for a while, sir," she added grimly.

The man's eyes widened when he first saw the pistol, and widened further when he realized that the gun was aimed at him instead of their supposed mutual enemy. "What the hell, girlie? You're going to fool around and get us all killed."

Alex shrugged. "Not all of us. Right now you're the only one in any real danger," she said quietly. "Now, pick a man and untie him and give him your guns. And then come back over here and sit down, real calm-like."

The man smiled that same toothless grin at her and started to reach for his pistol. Alex met the action with the sound of her gun cocking. "I don't think I'd do that if I were you," she said calmly, her voice belying the butterflies that were flitting about in her stomach.

"Oh, what are you going to do, sweetheart—shoot me?" the

man leered. "You'll get blood all over that pretty dress, and I won't be responsible for what my buddies will do to you if you happen to actually hit me."

"Untie one of the men and give him your gun," Alex said again sternly. "The only reason I haven't put a bullet in you already is that I don't want to alert the rest of your men. Otherwise you'd already have some new ventilation in a kneecap or a shoulder. Or your balls." She said the last regretting how crude it would sound to Sullivan, but hoping it would add credence to her threats.

The shock factor worked. The man walked slowly over to the first blue-coated man and quickly untied his arms. The man took both guns and then using one hand untied the man sitting next to him, who happened to be Captain Sullivan.

Sullivan immediately went to Alex's side. Alex gave him a warning look to keep him from giving away their relationship. Not knowing what actions lie ahead, she didn't want to give anyone a reason to focus on Sullivan to make a point. He patted her on the shoulder and simply said, "Thank you, Miss." Then he went to the pile of guns behind her and picked out his own. He gathered some of the ropes that had trussed his compatriots and used them to tie their former captor.

After a quick discussion, the men formed ranks, and after assuring Alex that they would be back shortly, they headed to the rear of the train, where they could hear the rest of the men shouting orders, along with an occasional scream or shout from one of the travelers.

Alex stood there for a moment looking at her prisoner, and then she reached down and tore off a piece from her petticoat. After balling it up she stuffed it into the man's mouth. His eyes widened. He tried to talk, but Alex shook her head. "You have nothing to say that I want to hear." The man shook his head wildly. "Don't worry, I'm not going to kill you. I would imagine that you'll simply be taken back to a camp somewhere nearby." The expression in the man's eyes tugged at Alex's heartstrings. For a brief moment, she considered untying the man and allowing him to run, but then she realized that most likely he would simply turn on her and could harm her or someone else.

A few minutes later, Sullivan came back into the car, a wide grin on his face. "Miss Magnolia. You are by far the most amazing woman I have ever met in my life," he said. He pulled her against him and pressed his lips to her forehead. "You not only saved my life, but you saved the life of a lot of other innocent people who could have possibly ended up as victims of crossfire if things had been allowed to progress."

Alex's face burned with the heat of a thousand fire-ant bites. She reached up with her fingertips and was surprised when the heat didn't burn her fingers. Sullivan suddenly blushed. "I'm sorry, my dear. I hope I didn't hurt you. I was just so relieved to find you still here all in one piece. And," he grinned widely, "so incredibly impressed by your actions. You have told me that you could take care of yourself, and I have seen for myself how right you are. As it turns out, you do a fine job of taking care of me, too."

Alex smiled. She leaned over and slipped the derringer back into the holster that she always kept strapped to her ankle. "It was the least I could do, captain," she said teasingly. "After all, you heard what the man said about the possibility of getting my dress soiled if there was action. We couldn't have that. Estelle worked far too hard on it to allow it to be ruined."

Sullivan threw back his head and laughed out loud. "Miss Magnolia. I am once again indebted. Or should I say indebted even further?"

The rest of the men returned to the car and told Sullivan that they had secured the rest of the train and had decided to leave the men tied up in a couple of the rear ones they planned to leave behind instead of attempting to take them with them. To make the ride faster they had decided to move everyone and their cargo into as few cars as possible, abandoning the rest. Sullivan agreed and went to check on the engineers who he was told had not been harmed, simply overtaken and trussed up like Thanksgiving turkeys.

An hour later the train began rocking again as they began moving southward. Sullivan and Alex again sat side by side, and Alex's mind churned. She remembered the searing kiss to her forehead and the look in the captain's eyes when he'd seen her with the gun. She wondered if one would have anything to do with the other.

She turned to him with a question on her lips, but before she could speak she heard him say, "Magnolia, you told me you have secrets, and I would never pressure you to share them, but I am intrigued by your apparent prowess with a gun and your ability to put the fear of God into a battle-weary soldier. I would love to hear your story when you feel comfortable enough to share it with me."

Alex smiled. "I will happily tell you how I came to be so comfortable with firearms," she said. "My uncle and two male cousins used to take me with them to the shooting range they had set up on our farm. Uncle James used to offer little prizes to whoever did the best shooting. At first of course, Teddy and Marcus won everything. But it wasn't long until I was getting my share of the time off from chores and other little presents that Uncle James brought home from his trips. I love to shoot, and I'm pretty good at it."

"I hope you never have to go through with your threat to put a bullet hole in a human," Sullivan said solemnly. "It's a far different feeling than watching a tin can bounce or a glass bottle shatter."

Alex looked at him for a moment, their eyes connecting as she said softly, "Yes. It certainly is."

Sullivan's eyes held hers and he opened his mouth, then closed it slowly. "And as I said, I am here to listen when you want to share your story. Whatever you have to tell me, I am sure will do nothing but make me even more impressed with the woman that you are."

"Thank you," Alex said with a small smile. "I am grateful for your friendship. I hope I never do anything to disappoint you or do anything to change your opinion of me."

Sullivan patted her hand. "I sincerely doubt that there is anything you could tell me that would make me believe that you are anything less than the honorable, talented, beautiful woman whose friendship I so greatly value."

Alex was still smiling when she drifted into sleep, rocked by the rhythm of the train.

Chapter Twenty-One

The weeks that followed Alex's arrival back at Pearl's were spent in a large part describing in great detail to a rapt audience all of the events that had taken place during her trip to Washington. Cecile had insisted on sending Alex home with the clothes that she had worn during her stay. Alex had tried explaining that there would be no fancy functions to give her an opportunity to wear them, but Cecile gave a surprisingly practical argument that even if she couldn't wear them she could use the fabric to make other clothing she could use, and some of the material could be used for bandages, or perhaps she could sell the clothing to buy necessities. Alex had finally agreed, and after seeing the looks on Pearl's, Ellen's, and Rebecca's faces as she had opened the trunk, she was glad she had.

She couldn't wait to tell Sullivan how his gifts had touched so many lives. She sighed. She had hoped to hear from the captain again soon but had heard nothing. In wartime, she supposed that getting no news at all was better than getting bad news, but she was getting nervous as days turned into weeks and she still had had no contact from him.

She gave each of her friends their choice of the clothing, keeping for herself only the dress she had worn to the ball. And the kid gloves, which she sometimes put on before bed, touching them to her cheek and letting the softness remind her of better times in the past and hopefully in her future.

Ellen had chosen a day dress that Cecile had given Alex from her own closet. It had been one of Alex's favorites, and she smiled now to see Ellen's face beaming above the pleated organdy. "It seems so long since I've had anything pretty," Ellen said with a sigh of pleasure at the feeling of the crisp material against her skin. "As much as we worried while you were gone, Alex, I have to admit I'm a little bit selfish. Now, looking at myself in the mirror, I'm quite glad that you went. And knowing you had a wonderful time, of course," she added with a grin. Her face saddened. "I wish George were here to see it." Tears stifled her words. "I'm sorry. I thought I was all cried out, but sometimes . . ."

Pearl reached over and patted her hand. "There ain't a thing wrong with expressing grief," she said firmly. "You suffered a loss. You're one of thousands who share that same grief. Doesn't matter where you're grieving over a son you carried under your heart, or a husband or lover or fiancé you carried in it, the hurt is all the same."

Ellen blushed. "I sort of wish that I'd let George take . . . um . . . more liberties when we were still together," she said shyly. "At least then I'd have memories to keep me warm for the rest of my life."

Becca spoke up. "Shoot, girl. Don't be talking like you ain't never going to find nobody else." Her voice was sharp. "Look at me. Even with this scar on my face and the one on my heart, I still know deep in my soul that someday someone is going to love me and make all the scars fade away. Ain't nothing wrong with you. You're beautiful, you're white, you're young, and your heart may have gotten a little cracked, but believe me, some man is going to fill it up to busting, and everything bad that happened to you ever is going to just slip away like a wisp of fog on a summer morning."

Pearl nodded as she smoothed the silken folds of the dressing gown she had chosen. "You girls know I don't entertain men any more since I got my own place," she said thoughtfully, "but I like to think that someday there may be a special man in my life again, and when there is, I'll feel like I'm giving him a real present when I'm wrapped up in this." The women giggled like schoolgirls for a minute, then turned to see Becca sitting in her rocking chair, rocking slowly as she stared into space, her fingers caressing her new, bright-yellow dress with white organza apron. A tear made a track across her cheek.

Alex ran to her side. "Becca, what's wrong? If you'd rather have one of the other dresses—"

Becca smiled sadly. "That's not it, Miz Alex. I love the dress. And you're so sweet to give it to me. I was just, for a minute, remembering the dresses that Mister Harl used to bring me. And wondering what my life would be like now if that bad man hadn't done to me what he done." She paused. "You never know, Mister Harl, he might have taken me with him to France. He might have started a new life with just me and Benjy." Her voice trailed off. "Or he might have gone off and left me with Miz Elizabeth, and the Lord knows one or the other one of us by now might be dead. I do believe that everything is going to be all right someday for us all. But sometimes it don't seem fair that some of us carry around the burdens we do."

Alex patted her hand. "It doesn't do any good to wonder about what-ifs," she mused. "Heaven knows, I've had my own questions, and wondered if I took the right path when it opened up before me. All we can do is figure that everything happens for a reason and play the cards that's dealt to us."

The sound of hoof-beats in the yard brought the women to the window, where they looked out over the front yard at the group of blue-uniformed soldiers who were tying their horses to the hitching post in the yard.

"Dear Lord," Pearl sighed. "Ellen, go get Kane out of sight. Better take him into the cellar. We certainly can't risk him being seen. Becca, will you go to the front door and invite them into the parlor? See if they're here with a message, or if they're on more personal business. Alex, you come with me, and we'll go make some tea and get some biscuits and jelly ready. No matter what they're here for, you know they'll be hungry."

Alex heard the murmurs of conversation coming from the parlor as she sliced open cold biscuits and put small amounts of the last jar of the apple jelly she and Pearl had canned last fall. She fixed one for Benjy and sent him to the barn to help Lije, hoping to keep him out from underfoot in case the men were making a social call. So far they had been careful to keep the boy from realizing what sort of job all of his new "aunts" had. He had cried when Suze and Collette had left, headed South hoping to find deeper pockets than those in the dirty uniforms that came their way these days.

Alex figured the rest of the girls would be leaving before long, and as soon as Kane had healed adequately, Pearl had already told her that she wanted them to head for New Orleans with him. Ellen was going to go back to her mother's, and Becca and Benjy were going to go North as soon as they decided where they wanted to go and had saved up enough money to get there.

The door opened and Pearl and Becca came into the room, arguing softly. "I don't care, Becca. I won't ask you to go upstairs again. We decided when Benjy came that that life was over for you, and I'm as good as my word."

"But you ain't askin', Miz Pearl," Becca argued. "I am offering. Without Suze and Collette, you ain't got enough girls to go around, and you heard them say that when their captain comes in, he likes a little bit of brown sugar. Please let me do this, Miz Pearl. I don't want to run the risk of one of them having extra time on his hands and deciding to do a little snooping and maybe comin' across Mr. Kane. This don't mean nothin'. Them boys has been on the road a long time, judgin' by the looks of them. It won't take no time at all for them to be done, and then they'll be outa here."

Pearl looked sad. "I suppose you're right, Becca. But whatever the man pays, it's yours. I want no part of it."

Becca nodded. "Thank you, ma'am. Now, I'm going to go up and get Benjy's things put away in my room. It sort of kills the mood for some men to be reminded of their own children."

Pearl turned to Alex and said, "Hand me those biscuits, hon, and I'll take them in to the boys and tell them to head on upstairs when they get done. Although a couple of them may want to wait till after. They were near 'bouts frothing at the mouth when they came in."

Alex watched as Becca started toward the back stairs headed to her room. "Becca, are you sure?" she asked softly.

Becca turned around and smiled. "Sure as can be, Miz Alex. This don't mean nothing. I made the decision on my own. Ain't nobody makin' me. And that makes a ton of difference. Besides, it's the least I can do to help keep trouble from starting. Just hope that their captain ain't some old slobbery fool that ain't had a bath in a month of Sundays." She grinned at Alex and picked up her skirts as she scooted up the staircase.

Alex walked outside, wanting to be sure she didn't overhear any of the sounds that would soon be coming from all the upstairs rooms. Pearl had told her that after a while she wouldn't notice, but she had found that time hadn't made any difference at all. At first, the sounds made her skin crawl and she could feel bile rising in her throat. Occasionally, in the last months the sounds had brought different and equally upsetting sensations that Alex didn't want to spend time deciphering. She decided it was easier to find something to keep herself busy outdoors. In colder weather she usually found a reason to spend time with Lije in the barn, always finding comfort in hearing the snuffles of the satisfied horses bedded down in the stalls and the cackling of the few hens that were left.

Today she decided to hang out the clothes that Ellen had left on the back porch. She picked up the basket and headed for the clothesline. She shook out a sheet and then paused for a moment to admire the flash of vivid blue as a bluebird landed on a limb over her head.

Suddenly the peace of the afternoon was split apart with a woman's screams and a man's curses. Alex quickly stepped into the shadows of the massive magnolia tree that shaded the backyard. She saw Becca come flying out onto the back porch, shaking and crying, wiping blood from her face and screaming for her father. Lije appeared from the barn, carrying Pearl's old double-barrel shotgun that he kept shiny and loaded at all times.

A dark, bare-chested figure opened the door and stepped out onto the porch, one hand gripping his navy-blue pants to keep them from falling around his ankles. "Girl, get your black ass back in here and back up to that bed. I paid good money for this, and Rafe Peterson don't pay for nothing he don't get. Especially nigger tail." He turned toward Lije and said, "Boy, you better be bringing that gun to me. If you have any idea about pointing it toward me, you're going to be eating supper with George Washington tonight. After my boys upstairs have some fun with you."

Becca turned and screamed at him. "I let you hurt me once. I was too little to understand what was happening to me. You ruined my face and my life, and I would rather die than have you touch me again."

Alex understood the terror in Becca's voice, and she saw Lije's face as he recognized it too, and her heart grew cold. She leaned over and drew the derringer from its holster. She stepped out of the shadows and saw Rafe Peterson's leering face grinning at her. She heard the voice that haunted her memories and her dreams, but her hands were steady as she aimed the derringer between his eyes as he said, "Hurt you once? Brown sugar, I don't know what the hell you're talking about, but be damned sure I'm going to hurt you twice to make up for this trouble. And you ain't getting' a nickel out of me for it, either. Now shut up and get your black ass upstairs, or I swear I'll take you right here in front of God and everybody."

"You're not going to be hurting anybody, ever again, Rafe," Alex said quietly. "You didn't remember the first time we met, but I guarantee you will take the memory of the last time we will meet into eternity with you. I hope hell has reserved an especially hot place for you and your kind."

Rafe's eyes had been glazed with lust and anger but now showed brief confusion as they focused on the gun in Alex's hand. "Magnolia?" he asked, a chuckle in his voice. He looked over his shoulder. "Is your fancy captain in one of the rooms upstairs? Or do you entertain him yourself?"

"I don't entertain anyone." Alex's voice had a deadly flatness that even Rafe could decipher. "Thanks to you, I lost my home, my life and what I thought was love. I always felt a kinship with Becca because a man had hurt her so badly too. What a bizarre coincidence that the same man was responsible for the hurt in both of us." Her voice grew steely. "Do you remember a moonlit night when you met with Delwood Lange in Georgia? And under that same moonlit sky you raped a young Southern girl and killed the young man who tried to defend her?"

Rafe's eyes widened. "Now, listen here. That wasn't rape. You wouldn't have been out alone at night if you wasn't prowling like a cat in heat. You got what you asked for, and I admit I was happy to give it to you. As far as the fancy boy that attacked me, he got what he was asking for . . ." His laugh was an evil sound that made the hairs on the back of Alex's neck stand on end. "Even if I reckon it wasn't exactly what he wanted or expected."

Alex's hand tightened on the derringer, and Rafe's back straightened when he heard the deadly click of the hammer sliding into place. "Now listen here, darling. Come on over here and let's us talk about this. No need to do something that you're likely to regret later."

Alex's laugh was short and hard. "Believe me, Mr. Peterson. I will have no regrets. I have dreamed of this moment on more nights than you could imagine. I have seen your bloody face with sightless eyes in my dreams, and I have rejoiced. I promise you that watching you die will be one of the happiest moments of my life."

Rafe's eyes twitched nervously as he made note of the fact that Alex's hands were steady and the barrel of the tiny but deadly gun was aimed straight at his forehead. He reached for his gun, only to remember that it was lying with his shirt and jacket on the board floors of Becca's room. He started to turn and race back inside and yelped when splinters flew from the doorframe beside his hand. "Take another step toward that door, and the next one goes in your heart," Alex promised solemnly.

"My men are right upstairs," Rafe whined, and as if on signal one of the men raised a window and shouted down to ask what the noise had been.

"Lije is splitting firewood," Alex stepped back and shouted up at the men, a pleasant smile on her face. "Sounded like a gunshot didn't it? Just ignore it, he's got a big old pile to take care of."

The man's face relaxed. "Sure glad it wasn't gunshot. I've split a few logs in my day too, I don't grudge him the job. Hey, did Peterson ever show up?"

Alex's laugh sounded relaxed and pleasant, certainly not the laugh of a woman who had a gun targeting a man's forehead. "He did indeed. Decided he'd rather go upstairs than eat a biscuit. Imagine that." The man laughed and pulled down the window.

She turned her head back toward Rafe, who grinned at her. "You ain't fooling me any," he said, his leer growing wider. "You were aiming for me that time, and you missed. I never knew a woman that could shoot worth a damn."

"You do now." Alex turned slightly and aimed at a bottle of vinegar that Pearl had left sitting on the porch railing. Rafe turned white when the bottle shattered into brown shards on the porch, splattering him with vinegar and bits of glass.

He took a step toward the edge of the porch, his voice growing whiny and pleading. "This is all just a big mistake," he began.

Alex nodded. "It sure was. And you made it." Her fingers tightened on the trigger, and she felt her heart racing.

Rafe's eyes grew wide as he realized for the first time that not only was his life in danger, but there wasn't much he could do about it. An obviously experienced shooter had him in her sights, and she had more than ample reason to pull the trigger.

Alex's finger pulled slowly backward, and suddenly the air was filled with sound and blood as Rafe's face exploded and Alex and Becca were showered with a sticky mass of red and white and grey. The sergeant's horse, which had been tied to the hitching post at the side of the house, pulled himself loose and went running across the yard and down the road, trailing his reins and a broken piece of lead rope. Alex looked down at her gun, still cocked, and then looked to her left where Lije stood, holding a smoking shotgun.

"Oh, Lije!" she wailed. "What have you done?"

"I've done what I should have done when he hurt my baby the first time," Lije said firmly. "And when the rope tightens around my neck I still won't have any regrets. I couldn't let you have his blood on your hands for the rest of your life."

They heard the sound of feet hitting the floor as soldiers jumped out of bed and began hurriedly putting on trousers and coats and scrambling for their guns.

"Quick," Alex cried to Becca and Lije. "Pull his body under the porch, and Becca, get that wash-water there and pour it on the steps."

She quickly wiped the gore from her face with a pillowcase, then grabbed Lije's shotgun and raced into the house, meeting the group of startled soldiers, who were still tucking in shirts and pulling on boots as they reached the landing on the first floor.

"Quick!" she cried. "Peterson needs you. Out front. Somebody was trying to break in and I shot at him"—she pointed to the blood on her skirts—"but he ran off. Your sergeant showed up and took off after him. The man went that way"—she gestured toward the road—"and your sergeant went after him. Hurry!" She prodded the men out the front door and watched as they raced down the road.

She ran to the back porch and saw Lije quickly nailing a piece of lattice back in place beneath the porch. Becca had thrown the tub of grey wash-water over the porch and steps, and the blood was mostly washed away. Alex grabbed another sheet from the pile of laundry she had been taking to the clothesline and quickly swabbed the bits of brain and bone and splatters of blood from the door and the railings.

"Lije, you go to the barn and get a horse saddled. Just in case they come back and things go bad, I want you to be able to get away from here."

"But where would I go?" he asked sadly. "This is the only home I've got."

Alex quickly gave him directions and said, "If you do have to leave for good, just go there. When you arrive, ask for Captain Sullivan and tell him that Maggie sent you and said that he would take care of you. He won't let any harm befall you."

"I can't run off and leave you women here alone," Lije said firmly.

"And maybe you won't have to," Alex explained. "But I'd rather have a plan we don't use than to need one and be at a loss. Now go saddle the damned horse." She added, "Go down to the spring and wait for a signal. When it's safe for you to come back, I'll ring the dinner bell. If you haven't heard the bell ring in two hours, you head out to where I told you. That'll give you a head start."

Lije nodded slowly. "Yes ma'am," he said, with one last sad look toward Becca as he shuffled off toward the barn.

Ellen and Pearl had come out onto the porch just in time to see Becca and Lije shoving Peterson's remains under the porch, and they had pitched in without question to cover the signs of bloodshed. Alex and Becca quickly ran upstairs and changed out of their blood-splattered clothing, coming downstairs just in time to see the band of blue-coated soldiers coming back into the yard. One of them was leading the sergeant's horse, still wide-eyed and now flecked with foam from his wild race.

The thought ran through Alex's mind that if his horse had been that skittish, it would have never seen its rider through a battle, and she wondered idly if Rafe had ever actually been part of any fighting, or if his wartime activities had all been of the covert, undercover variety. She knew how many cowards' hearts both blue and grey cloth covered, and she felt no remorse at Rafe's passing. She just felt a little bit cheated that she had had little to do with his step into eternity.

Alex went onto the porch and, wringing her hands the way she'd seen Aunt Matilda do in stressful situations, called out to the men, "Did you catch that horrible man? We would have been happy to have shared anything we had with him, but for him to come in and try to steal from us and from our friends—" She shook her head in imaginary horror. "I hope when you catch him you will shoot him, or hang him. What will we do if he comes back?"

The men shook their heads. "We didn't see hide nor hair of the Sergeant, but we did catch his horse. We searched and searched but couldn't find a sign of him or the man he was after. I am not quite sure what we should do at this point, but we do have orders to deliver, and I don't think even Peterson would think we should ignore them to send out a search party for him."

Alex nodded. "Peterson knows his way around this area, he's been here several times so I'm sure he will eventually find his way back here. Would you like to leave his horse here for him, or take it with you?"

The man pondered, "Well, we didn't hear but the one shot that must have been yours from that shotgun, so I guess he must be okay, since you said he went riding off after the other man." He handed the reins to Maggie. "We'll send someone back for the horse if we haven't heard from Sergeant Peterson in a few days."

"That will be fine. I'll put him out with our horses in the back pasture. There's lots of good fescue coming up out there, and he should stay in good shape."

The young officer smiled and touched his finger to his cap in a courtly salute. "Thanks very much, miss. Sorry we were interrupted. Please tell the ladies we'll be returning soon for— um—second helpings?" He grinned a mischievous grin and, wheeling his horse around, galloped down the drive, followed by the rest of the men.

Alex almost swooned as she let out the breath she'd been holding. Pearl came and stood beside her. "I think maybe I'd like to know what the hell just happened," she said sternly. "Why is there a dead Union officer shoved under my back porch, and how did we end up with a fine Tennessee Walker stud horse like that one?"

Alex smiled and turned to walk toward the house, Pearl at her side. "Sort of a good swap, I guess." She told Pearl the story, from the moment Becca had run out onto the porch until the men had disappeared from their view.

Pearl let out a low whistle. "Damn, that was close." She looked closely at Alex. "Are you all right?"

Alex pondered for a moment. "I really don't know, Pearl. It's funny. Killing Rafe Peterson has been a driving force in my life for so long that I feel kind of empty now. I don't really feel anything, except maybe being a little bit sorry that I didn't pull my trigger a little quicker."

Pearl patted her hand. "But you don't have anything to fear anymore," she said kindly. "You've met your monster and you faced it, and you'll see the sun tomorrow and the monster won't."

Alex shrugged. "I should feel some sort of remorse that a human being is dead, but I've seen so much death, and I've hated him for so long, I really just don't seem to feel anything." She began to cry. "I should feel something. Relief, remorse, anger— something." She wiped her eyes with the edge of her apron. "But I don't feel anything."

Pearl nodded. "I've been there, honey. The night my baby died I couldn't even cry. I just laid there, looking at all the blood, and I looked at Earl, and I wanted so much to wish he was dead. But I didn't. I just wanted to close my eyes and be somewhere else.

Be someone else. And eventually that's what I did. It took me a while, but I've built a new life for myself, and I like who I am now. I never liked me much when I was with Earl. I didn't like the way he treated people, and I sure as hell didn't like the way he treated me. And I didn't like me much for putting up with it." She took one of Alex's hands in her own and squeezed it. "Believe me darlin', before long you'll be feeling again, and you'll be glad that everything that is behind you happened, because it turned you into who you've become. And you'll like you. A whole heckuva lot."

Alex shook her head. "I don't know, Pearl." She looked out across the backyard, where Kane and Ellen were digging a new garden space that she knew would soon hide the grave of her enemy. "I wonder what Kane is thinking. I wonder if any man will ever want me or love me, knowing that I've allowed myself to be taken by another man, and that I've pulled the trigger and ended the life of more men than I can count. Or even know the figures. There have been times when I just closed my eyes and pulled the trigger and just prayed that God would guide my bullets. And I prayed that when I opened my eyes again I'd realize I'd had a nightmare and it was all just a bad dream." She sighed. "And every time when I opened my eyes, the nightmare had just gotten worse instead."

Pearl gave her hand another squeeze. "I don't think you 'allowed' any of the things that have happened to you," she said sagely. "I believe that we make our own destinies, but I also believe that sometimes they are shaped by things that happen to you over which you have no control. I think you've shown exceptional courage and bravery and that you've grown into a hell of a woman. Probably a far better woman than you would have become if you hadn't been touched by the things you've gone through. And some man is going to appreciate all the qualities you can offer that so few others can."

Alex watched as Kane and Ellen laughed together as they worked. "Do you think Kane loves me?" she asked Pearl suddenly, surprising even herself with the words.

"I think he cares about you a great deal," Pearl chose her words carefully. "Whether or not it's the marrying kind of love, I don't know." She stopped for a moment and said, "I don't want to break a confidence, but would you be so disappointed if Ellen and Kane were sweet on each other?"

Alex was stunned. In the back of her mind she'd always harbored a secret fantasy where she and Kane rode off into a sunset that didn't include soldiers or guns or blood or death. She looked down at her hands. "Has he told you that he loves her?"

"No." Pearl said. "But I know that Ellen is falling in love with him. I'm not sure if she even knows it. But she is. One thing I know is people, and I would bet my last gold piece that she can't even remember what George looked like. And in her dreams her kisses come now from a tall, lanky soldier with a limp."

Alex smiled wanly. "I couldn't ask for anyone better for either of them," she said. "I suppose they deserve each other. And I'm not sure exactly what I deserve."

"You deserve the best, darlin'. And that's what you're going to have. You and Kane wouldn't ever be able to live together. You'd have him so whipped that he'd start resenting you, and then you'd resent him for not being someone he can't be. You need a man who's strong enough to stand up to you, and to stand beside you. You need a man who recognizes how special you are, even through dirt and a bad haircut and smelling like the south end of a northbound skunk."

Alex laughed. "I'll let you know when I find him."

"I want to be the first to know. After you tell him, of course." Pearl's laughter joined hers.

They walked toward Kane and Ellen busily digging in the red dirt, musing aloud as to what kind of funeral a man deserved who had brought such pain and heartache into the world.

Chapter Twenty-Two

Alex moped around the next few weeks in a daze. Kane and
Ellen tried to joke with her, Becca fixed her a special pie made with
honey from a hive she'd found in the woods, and Pearl tried to
scold her out of her blues. All to no avail. As she told Pearl, it felt as
if she'd been standing on a rug that had suddenly been pulled out
from beneath her, and she was just falling through air without
knowing into what direction she was aimed.

"I hated him for so long," she explained, eyes welling up with
tears. "And now I can't get out of my head the picture of his face
exploding in front of me. I still can't forgive him for what he did,
and I know if anyone ever deserved to die it was him, but now
there's an emptiness where all that hate was, and I don't have
anything to fill the space with."

Pearl smiled. "Maybe you should think about filling it with
love, hon."

Alex shook her head. "I already love y'all as much as anybody
ever could. You're my family, and that ought to be enough. I feel
guilty to be fretting over this so much and making y'all worry over
me, but I just can't help myself."

Pearl patted her hand. "Darlin', you've had a rough time of it.
You lost your old life, so you made another one all wrapped
around the hate you felt for the sergeant. Rightly so, I admit, but
still hate doesn't ever do a body any good. Now that it's gone, it's
time to work on making a different life around something else."

"But what?"

"I don't for sure know, Alexandria. But when you find it you'll
know it."

~   ~   ~

Alex went for a ride on Birdie in the early hours of the
morning, hoping to enjoy the cool morning air before the hot sun
turned it into a furnace. As she stopped beside a creek to let Birdie
get a drink she heard a man moaning. She pulled a rifle from its

scabbard on her saddle and carefully walked toward the sound. She could see the outline of a man lying beside the creek, trying to pull himself toward the water. She called to him and he raised his head and called for help. She ran to his side and cradled his head in her lap.

"Water, I need water," he moaned.

She helped him to the creekside and held his head as he sipped from the swift-moving stream. "Where are you hurt?" she asked.

"I can't move my left leg, I think it's broke. My horse got shot out from under me, and he rolled onto me. They left me for dead. I've got to get to Sullivan's unit and warn him that his last orders were false. It's a trap. It's going to be a massacre if I can't get to him."

Alex's head spun. "Where is he?" The man gave her directions and watched as she ran back toward Birdie, swinging herself up in the saddle and calling back to him that she would send help. She cursed Sullivan under her breath for still being in action instead of sitting behind the desk as he had promised.

She raced into the yard at Pearl's and went tearing up to Pearl's bedroom. Pearl had come to her door to see what all the racket was about, and Alex pushed her back into the room. "You told me once that you kept all sorts of uniforms here. I need a Union one. And I need it now."

"Land sakes, child. What are you talking about?" Even as she asked the question, Pearl was opening a trunk and pulling out pieces of navy-colored clothing. Alex quickly told her the situation and then handed Pearl a pair of scissors.

"Cut my hair, please, Pearl. Quick. I don't have time to waste, I can't let Sullivan get hurt. Or worse." Her voice broke.

Pearl smiled sadly. "I hate to see that glorious head of hair of yours go, but I'm glad to see you with a purpose again. Just be sure it doesn't get you killed."

"I'll be fine, Pearl. God didn't bring me this far to let me die young. If He was gonna do that, he'd have just let Rafe Peterson kill me while he had me the first time."

As Pearl snipped off her hair, Alex stepped into flannel trousers and buttoned them up. She gave Pearl directions to send Lije for the fallen soldier by the creek. "And you may want to send Becca with him. He's a pretty big guy. May take both of them to put him in the wagon." She ripped a nightgown that was lying on the foot of Pearl's bed, ignoring Pearl's protests. "I'll buy you another one, I promise." She quickly bound her breasts tightly and then rubbed some dirt from a potted plant on Pearl's windowsill onto her cheeks and forehead. She donned a Union cap and asked, "How do I look?"

Pearl shook her head, "I swear, you are a fool for disguise," she said. "I'd have to look twice to know it was you, and I watched the transformation."

Alex hugged Pearl and kissed her on the cheek. "Thanks for everything, Pearl. If something happens—"

Pearl put a finger on Alex's lips. "Stop right there, young lady. I won't even entertain the thought that you might not come back. I'll expect you by supper tomorrow night, and if you're not here by breakfast the next day, I'm coming after you." She gave her a mock swat on the rear end. "Don't make me come after you, Private McKinley."

Alex felt tears burning her eyes. "Pearl, you've been the mother I never had and the big sister I always wanted, all rolled into one. Please know how much I love you."

"Get along with you now, before we both start bubbling like women," Pearl scolded, her voice husky. "And be careful. Keep your head low, and don't let your heart rule when your head ought to." She paused for a moment and said, "And vice versa."

Alex picked up a rucksack that was lying by the door. "I'm going to get some cornbread and ham to take with me. Lord knows when I'll get a good meal again if I'm gone longer than a day or two."

Pearl watched as the lithe, young body rushed down the stairs and toward the back door. "Look over her, Lord," she whispered. "Bring her something good. If ever a body deserved it . . ." She trailed off as she heard the back door slam.

Alex was hoping to be gone before Kane and Ellen got back from their walk, but as she opened the back door she met them coming inside.

Kane's eyes grew wide, "Alex! I didn't think I'd ever get to see you again. Nobody seemed to know where you were or what might have happened to you." His eyes narrowed. "What in the name of the Lord are you doing dressed in blue? Don't tell me you switched sides."

Alex groaned a silent groan. She hadn't planned on having to take time for any explanations. "Kane, Pearl will explain it all to you. I don't care any more. Ellen, y'all tell him everything. Tell him the truth. I'm tired of living lies. I've got to get to Sullivan, he's in trouble and he needs me. Ask Pearl about the wounded soldier by the creek, she'll need help with him when Lije gets him back here."

With that, she pushed past them and ran to the stable, where she found Lije standing with Birdie still saddled and ready to ride. Alex gave him a quick hug and told him to watch over everyone until she got back. Lije could do little more than nod, tears welling in his eyes.

Soon Alex was galloping across fields and through meadows, lying low on Birdie's neck. She found a couple of landmarks the injured soldier had mentioned, and she breathed a sigh of relief. Surely it couldn't be much farther.

A half-hour of hard riding later, she could hear an occasional crack of gunfire and could smell the gunpowder and all the other smells of war that she sometimes thought she would never be able to get out of her memory.

She dismounted and tied Birdie to a sapling, giving her enough rope so she could graze comfortably. She gave her a quick pat and then crept toward the sounds, hoping for the best but fearing the worst.

The worst was what she found. A field and apple orchard, carpeted blue and grey with fallen bodies. Some writhing on the ground, others leaned against whatever tree or rock they could find to support them, still others lying ominously still. The sound of gunshot was fading, so she assumed that the battle was retreating and the threat of being shot or stabbed now was minimal. She stepped from behind a gnarled tree and gasped when a hand grabbed her boot. "Help me," a voice rasped.

"What do you need?" Alex asked, sure that she wouldn't be able to provide it for the poor man.

"I can't see. It turned dark all of a sudden. Do you have a candle? Or a match?"

Alex looked at the man's face, blackened and torn by a cannon blast, both eyes clouded.

Her voice broke as she said gruffly, "Private, we can't risk lighting any fires or candles. It could bring the enemy back to us." She led him to a large rock and told him to lean against it and wait for sunrise. A sunrise he would never see. She was grateful that shock was apparently keeping him from feeling pain, for he had a belly wound that would have kept him from seeing another sunrise even if his eyes were unscathed. The man nodded and said gratefully, "Good thing you came along, sir. I never did have very good night vision. I'm sorry."

"No need to apologize, Private. I'll see that you get a commendation for the way you handled yourself today."

The young man smiled with what was left of his lips. "Why, thank you, sir." He managed a weak salute. "My girl back home will be so proud when she hears. We're getting married in the spring."

Alex swallowed hard, her heart breaking for the young man and his girl. After a moment she collected herself and quietly asked, "Do you happen to know if Captain Sullivan was part of the action?"

"Yes, sir," the young soldier said. "He was front and center when all hell broke loose. His horse went down, and last I saw he was in hand-to-hand combat with a great big fellow over by an old shed of some sort. I think maybe it's a cider press or something."

Alex left the man sitting there alone, staring into the darkness, as she went toward a building she could see through the trees. As she neared it, she heard a familiar voice—familiar, but very weak. "Maggie, what on earth are you doing in that getup? And what are you doing out here? Are you trying to get yourself killed?"

"Oh, Sullivan. You're alive!" Alex ran to him where he lay against a stack of wooden boxes. "Are you hurt badly?"

"I'll be okay. What are you doing here?"

"I came to warn you. But I was too late."

"How did you know where I was?"

"Can I explain later? Right now let's see how badly you're hurt, and let me get you some help." The body of a very large man was partially hiding Sullivan's legs. The man groaned as Alex rolled him off of Sullivan, but having learned the various death sounds human bodies make, Alex knew it was just air escaping from lungs that no longer breathed on their own. She tumbled him aside without remorse and then went to Sullivan's side. "Where does it hurt?" she asked, as she smoothed sweat- and blood-dampened hair from Sullivan's forehead.

Sullivan tried to stand but collapsed. "I believe my leg is probably broken." He grimaced in pain. "And I think I'm shot."

Alex's heart sank. "Where?" She began taking off his coat. His cry of pain stopped her. "Please don't do that. Just let me lie here for a moment until I can get my wind back." He pointed toward the carcass of the lovely bay gelding Alex had admired in the past. "Can you get to my saddlebag? I've got a bit of whiskey in there, and if you won't think badly of me, I believe it would make me feel much better to have just a swallow." He looked out across the field. "Do any of my men need me?"

"You need help as much as any of them," Alex said sternly. "Just be still while I get your whiskey." She ran over to the dead horse and was able to pull the saddle around enough to reach into the saddlebag where she found a small silver flask.

As she turned it over, her heart fluttered when she saw the words engraved on it: *To my Sullivan from Liza, with all my love forever.*

She carried it back to Sullivan, who took a long swallow. He made a face and said, "If it doesn't kill me it should make me strong, correct?" Alex shook her head. "I don't know. I don't like the taste of whiskey, so I don't drink it."

Sullivan closed his eyes. "I think I'm ready to try to stand again," he said weakly. "Although I don't quite know what I'm standing for. I don't have any place to go, and it seems that I'm in no shape to be any help to my men."

Suddenly a group of blue-jacketed men on horseback burst through the trees and came trotting over to Sullivan and Alex. One of the men saluted and said, "I'm sorry, Captain. We got here as soon as we could."

Sullivan's voice was filled with disgust as he said harshly, "Why does it seem as if every person in this godforsaken hellhole knew that I was headed for trouble except me?"

"It was a trap, sir," said the other officer. "We were given misinformation, which sent you and your men straight into the line of fire of the enemy. As soon as we realized what was happening we gathered every man in the area and headed this way. We were able to stop the troops from heading back to their camp for reinforcements, but it looks as if we were too late to be of any help to you."

"Do you have wagons for the wounded?"

"Yes sir, and we've set up a hospital over there. Can my men help you to it?"

Alex spoke up. "Let me take you back to Pearl's, Sullivan. Please."

Sullivan shook his head. "I need to be with my men, not coddled in a soft bed somewhere."

The other officer stepped closer. "Begging your pardon sir, if you have an opportunity to get some real medical help, you'd better take it. The only medical personnel we have with us are some trainees who don't know their ass from a hole in the ground. They'll do okay patching men up until we can get them back to real doctors, but I wouldn't trust a senior officer to their care." He looked at Alex. "Sergeant, if you can get adequate care for Captain Sullivan, please do so. Get him patched up and then send him back to us. We'll need him."

Alex nodded. "Can you help me get him on my horse? I'll lead him back. It took me a half-hour or so to get here, so it'll take us at least an hour with me walking, but I don't know any other way."

One of the other men spoke up. "Will your horse work? To a wagon? I saw one behind this shed. It looks pretty worn out, but maybe it would get you back if you don't have to go too far."

"I've never had Birdie hooked up," Alex said slowly, "but she's always done everything I asked her to do, it can't hurt to try." She ran across the orchard and found Birdie grazing happily in a patch of clover. "Girl, we've been through a lot together," Alex said as she pulled herself into the saddle. "If you'll do this one last thing for me, I promise that I'll give you the best of everything possible for the rest of your life." She patted the horse's neck and was answered with a contented whinny. She smiled. Little had she known the night she helped Uncle James bring Birdie into the world that one day that scrawny little filly would not only carry her into battle but would help her save the life of someone she loved. For just a moment she pondered over that word, then mounted up and rode back toward Sullivan. The men helped rig up a harness of sorts to an old buggy that looked as if it might fall apart at any moment.

Birdie sidestepped a few times and shook her head and stamped her feet, but she soon settled down, listening to Alex's calm voice telling her what was going on. Soon they had Sullivan resting as comfortable as possible in the buggy, and Alex climbed back up on Birdie's back. They had removed her saddle, but Alex had ridden bareback since she was a child so she had no problem staying seated. She gave the men directions to Pearl's, should they need anything or want to check on Kane, and then they were off.

The ride that had taken Alex less than an hour on the way there seemed to take an eternity on the return trip. The groans of pain from the buggy tore at Alex's soul, and it seemed like a lifetime before she saw the red oak and the willow tree that stood in the curve of the road just before reaching Pearl's gate.

Just as they turned the corner, one of the wheels made a loud groaning sound and then popped completely in half. The buggy stayed level for a moment and then began tipping. "Hold on!" she shouted at Sullivan. She jumped off of Birdie and tried to keep the buggy from going over, but it was too heavy. She was able to keep Sullivan from hitting the ground too hard, but his scream of pain almost caused her to cry. Alex was afraid that if Birdie got spooked, she could pull the wrecked buggy over on top of the both of them, so she left Sullivan and went to Birdie's head. She turned her slowly, leading her away from where Sullivan lay on the side of the road.

She looked toward the house, hoping to see someone who would hear her call for help. "I'm going to have to leave you for a minute, darling," she said softly. "I'll be right back."

"How far is it?" Sullivan gasped, his face white with the pain that edged his voice.

"I can see the gate from here—it will take just a minute to get Lije and Kane to come help you."

"Kane?" Sullivan looked puzzled.

"Oh, hell. That's one of the things I really wanted to tell you, but I guess I waited too long. Just lie there, and I'll explain everything later," she promised.

She raced to the house and ran inside shouting, "Help! I need help!"

Everyone came running and followed her back down the road, where Sullivan had pulled himself up into an almost-sitting position, leaning against the wreck of the buggy.

Pearl fussed over him. "Jacob, you dear boy, let's get you inside and get your clothes off."

Sullivan grinned. "Miss Pearl, I spent most of my young life pining to hear you say those words."

She rolled her eyes and looked at Alex. "He's going to be fine," she said drily.

Alex was too worried about him to joke. "Be careful, I think his leg is broken, and he's got a gunshot wound somewhere on his back. He wouldn't let me take his coat off to see, but he's real bloody."

Lije was able to wrestle the floor of the buggy loose, and they used it for an impromptu stretcher carried by Kane, Ellen, Lije, and Alex. Pearl walked beside Sullivan, holding his head and keeping him steady with one hand and leading Birdie with the other.

Alex couldn't help thinking about Sullivan's words all those many months ago when he had confessed his love for Pearl. Could it be possible that the man she believed to be so honorable was indeed a scoundrel? Even while he admitted to still loving Pearl he had become engaged to Malinda, and yet carried a flask engraved with words of love from a woman named Liza. And why should any of those things bother her so? And why did she wish it were her hand that Sullivan was grasping so tightly instead of Pearl's? The sudden thought that this must be what jealousy felt like caused Alex to stumble and almost fall. She recovered quickly, and they got Sullivan into the house and onto the bed in Suze's old room.

She pushed all of the personal thoughts aside as she helped Pearl and Becca clean Sullivan's wounds and set his leg, which appeared to be broken in two places. Kane was full of bluster about a "damned Yankee" being treated under the same roof he slept under, but when Pearl reminded him that it was because of the generosity of this particular damned Yankee that he was still walking and breathing, he lowered his protests to mutters.

After a wearying few hours everyone left the room except Alex, who sat by the bed in the same rocker she had inhabited during Kane's long, grueling recovery. She hoped that Sullivan's injuries would heal faster than Kane's. She wasn't sure she had it in her to go through that again.

She reached over and took Sullivan's hand in hers. It was large and brown and callused, and she remembered it gently touching her face in Washington as he thanked her for being with him. She doubted that she would ever again see kindness on his face once she explained her treachery to him regarding Kane. She sighed. Nobody had said life would be easy, but it seemed that someone should have warned her that it would be this damned hard. She leaned back in the rocker and closed her eyes. As she drifted off into sleep, she smiled at the sound of Sullivan's deep breaths and rumbling snores.

Chapter Twenty-Three

She awakened in the dark, having forgotten to light a lantern before she went to sleep. She fumbled around in the darkness, and finally the glow of the flame brightened the room. She turned around to find Sullivan lying there watching her. "Hi there," she said shyly.

"Hello." Sullivan's voice was thick and quiet; whether from emotion, pain, or the drugs, Alex couldn't be sure. "How long have I been here?"

"This is your first night," Alex explained. "You were hurt this morning."

"And you found me and brought me here?" He shook his head. "Please tell me I was dreaming, and that it was one of my men who came onto the battlefield and dragged me to safety."

Alex shook her head. "I can't do that. I promised myself that the one big lie I already told you would be the only one."

"About that . . ." Sullivan pulled himself farther up on the pillow, wincing at the pain. "Ouch. How badly am I hurt, by the way? It feels as if I've been run over by a buggy instead of just dumped out of one."

"You were shot in the shoulder. But the bullet or whatever it was went clean through. Pearl stitched you up and you're going to have a puckery scar, but it should heal pretty quickly. And your leg was busted pretty badly. They got it set so it should be okay in time, too."

"Thanks. I guess I probably owe you my life, don't I? I keep getting myself indebted to you, with no idea of how I can repay."

"You already have," Alex said simply. "I do have some explaining to do. Are you strong enough to talk now, or later? I told you I would tell you everything when the time was right, and although I didn't think I was ready yet, I really don't have a choice anymore, do I?"

"No, miss, you don't." Alex could hear a touch of anger lacing the captain's voice. "I'm not sure whether I first want to hear the story about the walking-dead Confederate who helped carry me in here, or the story of how you came to be in a Union uniform on a battlefield just when I needed assistance."

"How about I start at the beginning," Alex said with resignation. "It's a long story. Are you sure you're up to it?"

Sullivan shrugged. "It appears that I have nothing but time. I'd imagine at the very least I'll be in this bed a few weeks, and a few more until I can get back on my horse and . . ." His words trailed off. "My horse," he said sadly. "Poor Major."

"I'm sorry," Alex said. "I did bring your saddle with us, and bridle, but your horse was dead by the time I got there."

The pain of the loss showed in Sullivan's face as he pushed his head back into the pillow. "That old man had carried me safely through a lot of skirmishes. I will miss him. We were together when this thing started, and I'd hoped we'd walk away from it together." He sighed deeply. The sound touched Alex's heart. Uncle James had always told her that when the time came to choose her mate, watch how he treated his horse, because a wife usually couldn't expect to be treated any better. She had already known Sullivan was a good man, but it was nice to see it confirmed so proof-positive.

"I'll tell you my whole story," she promised. "But you have to promise to not say anything until I'm done. If you interrupt me I may lose my nerve, and I don't want to have any more secrets from you."

Sullivan promised solemnly, and Alex began her story.

~ ~ ~

She described her home life with her aunt and Teddy and told him about their maid, Verbena. She told him about her love for herbs, and how she helped take care of the sick folks on their farm and for their friends when a real doctor couldn't be found. Her voice wavered a bit when she started the part about leaving home to go tend to a sick neighbor.

"I had never been afraid of the dark," she said. "But after that night, I've hated it. I stepped out of my home into the darkness, and everything changed."

She stopped for a moment, and Sullivan started to speak. She looked at him sharply, and he nodded. "Go on," he said quietly.

"This time there was a man waiting in the shadows—a man I didn't know, a man who didn't know me—who would change my life in so many ways. That man was Rafe Peterson." She ignored Sullivan's sharp intake of breath. "He raped me, and then he killed Teddy when Teddy tried to come to my aid. When I woke up in a pool of my blood, Peterson was gone, and there was nothing left but darkness and blood and tears and death. And it seems that that's all my life has held ever since. Except for the time I've spent with you." She wiped a tear from her cheek. Sullivan reached a hand toward her face, then let it drop back to the bed.

"I was engaged to be married," Alex continued, her voice ragged with unshed tears. "And I went to my fiancé for help that night. But he turned me away—because I was soiled and dirty. He didn't want me anymore." She raised her eyes and looked at Sullivan, surprised at the rage she saw in his eyes. She hoped it was aimed at Delwood and Rafe, and not at her.

"My aunt turned against me. She blamed me for Teddy's death. I couldn't stay there. I knew that I didn't have a chance of seeking revenge against the bastard who had ruined my life. So I became someone else. Being a woman had brought me nothing but heartache, so I cut my hair and dirtied my face, and I became a young man instead of a debutante. I donned a Confederate uniform, and I joined a regiment that was on the move looking for Yankees, because I knew that behind one of those blue uniforms was the man I hated. And so long as nobody figured out what heart beat beneath my grey uniform, there was a good chance I could find him and get my revenge."

She told him about the two Union officers she had killed by that Alabama creek so many months ago, and the talk she had had with the old colonel the night he inducted her into the Confederate Army.

She stood up and began to pace around the room. "I was very lucky. I was put under the watchful eye of a courageous and dependable Confederate officer. He looked out for me, he took care of me, and he saved my life. Physically and emotionally. He had no idea I was a woman. When I brought him here, he met me for the first time as a woman. Until today, he didn't know that that young soldier and the woman who nursed him back to health were the same person."

Another tear rolled down her cheek. "I'm not sure if he will ever forgive me, either. I'm not sure that he can." Her voice broke. "I've told so many lies in these last months that some mornings I wake up and I'm not sure who I'm supposed to be that day. Whether I'm Alexandria McKinley Latham, a pampered socialite from Alabama, or Magnolia McVane, favorite niece of Pearl, or Private First Class Alex McKinley, Confederate States of America. And now"—she looked down at the uniform she still wore—"an unidentified Union soldier caring for his commanding officer."

Sullivan spoke. "So your name is not Magnolia, either?"

She shook her head. "No. When you called me a 'Southern magnolia' in your office, the name just sort of seemed to fit, so I took it. And I like it. I feel more like Maggie than I ever felt like Alexandria. Although," she added, "being Alex wasn't much of a stretch, since that's what my cousins always called me, although Aunt Matilda used to have a hissy fit every time she heard it." She looked sad. "I miss them so much. They were special boys, and I feel cheated that I never got to get to know them as the special men I know they would have grown up to be."

She sat back down in the chair. "The officer who took me under his wing when I showed up in camp that night was Sergeant Kane Stevens. He was with me when we went into battle, he was always at my side, and I always knew he was there, even when I couldn't see him for the smoke. When I woke up after a skirmish"—she touched the scar that still showed against her smooth forehead—"and he was gone, all I could think of was to find him and save him. Like he'd saved me." She told Sullivan about her disguise coming into town, and how she had been taken to Ellen's house to recuperate. And how she had seen Kane in the prison, and was at a loss as to how to save him.

She smiled at Sullivan suddenly. "Do you remember a while back, when a young Southern boy stumbled across your path near Atlanta, with a story about buying horses and a friend who had run away?" At Sullivan's puzzled nod she went on. "Well, Captain Sullivan, that young boy was me, too. And that young boy will never forget your kindness in allowing him to escape. After that night, I never aimed my gun at a Union soldier in battle. I realized then that Rafe Peterson's face wasn't above the collar of every uniform. That his heart didn't beat beneath every blue jacket. That some of those blue jackets covered hearts that were pure and honest and true. And I thank you for that."

Sullivan shook his head in disbelief. "How very small our world is," he mused. "But how could I not have known?" he said slowly. "I recognized you instantly today. I knew it was you. I knew you were a woman. How on earth could your disguise have fooled me so completely back then?"

"Well, it tricked a lot of other people, too," Alex said. "Don't feel foolish, please. This was a secret I had planned to take to my grave. No one but Ellen and Pearl knew my whole story. Until now."

"So what happened after you cajoled me into releasing Sergeant Stevens?"

"I brought him here, we faked a funeral, and we nursed him back to health. He was an old friend of Pearl's, and she was so grateful for what I'd done for him that she offered me a temporary home here."

"What about Peterson? Why didn't you tell me how he had harmed you? You know I would have filed charges against him instantly. He should never have been able to take the commission he accepted. He has no right to wear a Union uniform. He has no right to accept a Union paycheck."

"That isn't a concern anymore." Alex took a breath. "Peterson is dead."

"You killed him?"

"If I told you I had, what would you think of me?" Alex asked.

"I would think justice had been served," was Sullivan's quick reply. "Although I believe I would have preferred it if the bullet had come from my gun, to tell you the honest truth."

"It didn't come from mine, either," Alex admitted. "I'm not sure whether I'm glad or sad about that. I don't have his blood on my hands, but there is so much blood there that sometimes I think perhaps his blood might have washed all the other away if I had been the one to usher his departure from this earth."

"But you'd have been left with his blood, and you might have found it even harder to clean yourself," Sullivan said. "Either way, so long as the man is dead." His eyes lowered. "I am so sorry, Maggie—er, Alexandria."

Alex smiled. "Please call me Maggie. That is who I am. I left Alexandria McKinley back in Alabama with a lot of fancy clothes and ideas. Maggie McVane is someone I like seeing in the mirror."

"I like seeing her, too." Sullivan said simply. "Are you going to tell me how Rafe died?"

"Only if you have time for another story, because I want you to know the whole truth. Not just what it would look like to a jury."

"And what would it look like to a jury?"

"If it ever got that far, and he wasn't hanged first, it would look as if a black man killed a white officer."

"Oh, my. I wasn't expecting that."

"Which is why I want you to hear the whole story. Do you remember Becca, the black woman who helped bandage you?"

"I remember a beautiful woman with an ugly scar."

"Her scar goes as deeply as mine," Alex said. "And by some bizarre twist of the fates that guide us all, the scar on her face came at the hands of the same man that put the scar on my heart."

"Oh, my God." His face looked shocked and sad.

"She was just a child. He cut her, he raped her, and then he shot and killed her mother in cold blood. Pearl bought her and let her work off her debt as she pleased. She chose to entertain men because she felt as if there was no other option for her. She had a son as the result of rape by her previous owner, and I bought him and brought him to her. One last time she was going to entertain a man in her room to keep him from having time to poke around the farm and perhaps find out that Kane was living here. That man turned out to be Rafe Peterson. That old world keeps getting smaller indeed, eh?"

Sullivan's eyes were wide and disbelieving, "This is like a story from a cheap newspaper," he marveled. "Yet I have no doubt that your words are true."

"Every word. I will never again tell you a lie," Alex promised. "I would perhaps lie to save a friend, as I did before, but not to save my honor or my dignity. And never to you. For any reason."

Sullivan nodded. "So he came here and Becca saw him. What happened?"

"She screamed, and he hit her. And broke her nose. She came running out back where I was standing, screaming that the man who had hurt her once had hurt her again. I looked past her and couldn't believe my eyes when they met Rafe Peterson's. His cold, beady eyes had stared out at me from the darkness, from across a ballroom, and now they had invaded my home once again. I pulled out my derringer and I walked toward him. Becca moved out of the way, and just as my finger tightened on the trigger, Rafe's face exploded. Becca's father, Lije, was standing there with a smoking shotgun. We hid the body, sent the men who had arrived with Rafe on a wild goose chase, and Rafe is now buried beneath what will become a lovely rose garden someday." Alex grimaced. "Unless he was indeed so evil that all that can grow from his flesh is a patch of thistles."

She stood up. "I'm fairly sure that after that story you will have no desire for my company, so I'll ask Ellen to come and sit with you tonight. Thank you for listening. I wish I had been able to tell you long ago, but I didn't want to risk losing your friendship." She reached over and took his hand. "Thank you, Sullivan. For bringing light into the darkness for a while."

She felt his hand tighten on hers. "What makes you think I would turn you away? What have you told me that would make me believe you are anything other than courageous, brave, honorable, and faithful?"

Alex looked at him in surprise. "I have admitted to you that I have killed men for no reason other than revenge. I have admitted that I lied to you on more than one occasion. I told you I had been living a lie for so many months that I no longer know exactly how long it has been"—her voice broke—"and I have admitted that I have intimately known another man outside of wedlock."

Sullivan pulled her closer. "What you have told me is that you did what you had to do, in the most dreadful circumstances I can imagine." He shook his head. "No, I must be truthful; they are circumstances I cannot imagine. And I fear that if I had been in your place I would not have managed nearly so cleverly, so gracefully, and so fearlessly. I am proud to be your friend, Private Sergeant Alexandria Magnolia McKinley Latham McVane." He smiled and motioned for her to sit beside him.

Alex began to cry. "I don't deserve—"

He put a finger to her lips. "No, you don't. You don't deserve a single thing that has happened to you. But, if you will let me, I would be honored to stand by your side in the future, and we'll face whatever comes along together. My father assures me that it is much easier to weather storms when you are standing beside a good woman. He used to say, 'Son, without my beloved Liza Jane, I would have floundered against the adversities. But we persevered because we had each other.'"

"Liza? Your mother's name is Liza? . . . and she called your father Sullivan, didn't she?"

Sully looked puzzled. "Yes—and what does that matter?'

Alex smiled at her jealousy of the inscription on his flask. "No matter. Just pondering."

A thought came to her suddenly. "How did you know it was me? Today? In uniform, dirty face, shorn hair, even Kane didn't recognize me as Maggie—he called me Alex. But you knew immediately."

"Why would I not know you? I know and love every freckle on your face, every blond-tipped eyelash, every dimple in your cheek."

"Love?" Alex's heart pounded.

"And the story you have told me has simply made my love grow. Not wither. Now is probably not the time to speak of such things, for I must head back to my men as soon as I am healed. But when this has ended, I will speak of them often. For the rest of my life, if you would do me the honor."

Alex leaned against him and began to cry. "What about Pearl?" she asked suddenly. "You told that young Confederate soldier about your love for Pearl."

Sullivan laughed and held her closer. "My love for Pearl will never die, nor will hers for me. But they are infatuations from different lives, for different people. Deep and honorable, but not passionate."

"I don't want you to go back into battle," Alex said, laying her head against his chest.

"I most assuredly do not wish to. And, to be brutally honest, I am not sure that I can," Sullivan admitted. "Today was a catalyst for me. I realized when those men came dashing out of the woods toward us that there is no way that this can end well for our country as a whole. The original goals of war have been lost along the way, and now it seems to be nothing more than revenge on both sides. And as you have learned, revenge can take your soul if you let it. You were lucky. You kept your soul. Most of the men who fight today will never regain theirs."

"I will continue to love my country, and I would once again take up arms and fight to defend her against an outside enemy, but this war is over for me from this moment on. I will join my men only long enough to place someone else officially in charge. Then I will go to Washington and ask for a desk job. I will lobby our country's leaders to stop this war, no matter the cost. I will not bear arms against my brothers again. The boundaries have gotten too blurred."

He swallowed hard, and a look of sadness cast over his face. "All that's left now is a misbegotten sense of honor and duty. These men fight because their leaders tell them to fight. Leaders who for the most part sit behind a big, oaken desk and make their plans using soldiers made of tin who spill no blood when they die. Their battlefield is of papier maché that does not show the devastating effects of a battle. Bullets fly from guns and balls from cannons only in the leader's mind, not through the air. And when the real bullets have flown, those leaders only help to tally up the numbers of fallen men. They have not seen fields woven with a mixture of red blood, blue flannel, and butternut grey. They have not seen the bark stripped from trees that had stood their ground for hundreds of years, and they have not seen the burned and scarred homes and mutilated bodies. They simply pushed men made of tin through forests made of toothpicks. And they rarely realize the devastation they leave in their wake. I will not be part of it any longer."

He pulled Alex tighter against him, and she sighed a deep sigh of contentment.

"You love me?" she breathed.

"More than life itself. I fell in love with a lovely Southern belle who fainted into my arms, and I love even more the young lady in uniform who scrambled through the smoke and bullets to save my life. And I cannot wait for all of this to be behind us so we can start a new life together. As anybody we want to be, wherever we choose to go. After all, the Chinese say that if you save someone's life you are responsible for it forever. I hope you will not mind being saddled with me for the rest of your life, wherever that life leads us."

"It won't matter where we are, so long as I am with you," Alex said slowly. "I never thought that I would hear those words from a man. And if they were said, I would have thought I would never again believe them. But I believe you. And I love you. More than either of us can imagine."

She raised her head and gently kissed his lips.

~ ~ ~

A few hours later Pearl came in to bring Sullivan's breakfast and found Alex slumbering beside him, his arm around her, and for the first time since Pearl had known Alex, a completely peaceful smile softened the young woman's face. Pearl quietly put down the tray and tiptoed from the room.

The End

Author's Note

I hope you enjoyed reading *Behind the Grey*. More years than I want to remember ago, I sat in front of a little Hewlett-Packard word processor and in the wee hours of a morning when I couldn't sleep, I wrote this sentence:

> *Alexandria stared ahead, forcing herself to listen to the words of the raggedly dressed minister as he raised his voice to compete with the sound of dirt clods echoing off a shabby, hastily built wooden coffin.*

I had no idea then that what I had written was more than just words but was indeed the beginning of a beautiful relationship. Over the next many years, Alex was with me through thick and thin. Sometimes we'd go for months, even a year, without any contact. But as good old friends do, when we met again we always took up right where we left off.

She told me her stories, which I transcribed to my laptop while hooked up to a chemo port, battling breast cancer. She was there when I got a uterine cancer diagnosis. And she was right there with us when I married my husband. I cried when she hurt, and she laughed through her pain when I found joy.

She has been there for me to run to when I wanted to escape from the world, and we've marched into many battles (real and imaginary) together. I have written and deleted a dozen novels based on her tales over that time, and what you are holding is where she has brought me.

I have had chances to introduce Alexandria to the world before, but I've kept our friendship a secret. Until now. I decided others deserved to get to know her too.

I hope you've come to love her as much I do.

Acknowledgements

Writing a book requires a lot of patience, energy, talent, and dedication. Since I was not blessed with any of those things, my list of acknowledgements of those who helped this book come to fruition is fairly lengthy. And I still know I'm going to forget someone. But please know that even if you're not "on the list," you are in my heart.

To Clark Hudspeth, who is always there. And I hope always will be. You have my heart. To Pete Land, who long ago waited patiently while I made rubbings from crumbling tombstones and walked with me across the hallowed ground of Tennessee battlefields and told me that my idea of writing a novel about the women who fought there was a splendid idea. You helped my heart grow big enough to hold everything I needed.

Without Arliss Paddock, my friend and confidante and soul-sister, I would likely still be pecking away writing words that no one would ever see, probably still on an old word processor. She gave me my first computer (her old "toaster" Mac) and worked with me to create my first published book, a cookbook. In the many years since she has read and edited my work, helped me find writing jobs, and always told me I was better than I think I am. My biggest goal with this book is to make her proud.

To Lori Carter, who did absolutely nothing that made this book better. Except making me laugh when I was crying and understanding what I didn't always have the words to say. And to Diane Hutcheson for always listening, and offering advice that I've never regretted taking.

My friend Rick Clark photographed Civil War reenactments with me, which gave me the opportunity to virtually step back into time. He helped me research my nonfiction books and articles and is always armed with an opinion when I ask. Or when I don't.

To my cousin Nancy Hill, who has always been supportive of any wild scheme I hatched, who showed the first chapter of my book to her husband John Hill (Emmy-winning screenwriter, with both *Quigley Down Under* and *L.A. Law* among his credits). Along with his honest, glowing praise he gave me the courage to write chapters two, and three, and . . . finally . . . "The End."

If my book has a heart, it beats because of the people who have read what I have written and urged me to write more and write faster. Mary Land and Michael Patterson, this book is truly for you—because I know you'll read it.

There's no doubt that my love of writing came from my mother. She left a great legacy of written words in the form of short stories on the backs of photographs, in bulging scrapbooks, and in the margins of the books she read. She was the finest historian I have ever known. My dad wasn't a reader or a writer, but he was a storyteller extraordinaire. Whatever talent I have in that area definitely came from him. His imagination was boundless. Neither of them is alive now to share this experience with me, but they made me who I am—the good along with the bad.

The animals in my life are crackers and parsley to my brain. Crackers and parsley clean the palate, and our animals keep my brain from getting cluttered with the emotions and angst that can quickly play havoc with an empath's world. When my mind is blocked, I spend some time sitting in the leaves with Buford, burying my face in Whisper's mane, feeding Jitterbug the baby donkey a carrot, or holding a newborn baby goat, and my brain is refreshed. I could not live without them. I certainly could not write.

Of course without the 400-plus women who battled their way into history, this book would have no reason to be. So to Sarah Seelye, Jennie Hodgers, Frances Clayton, Mary Owens, Mary Jenkins, Satronia Hunt, and all of the rest whose names may now never be known, thank you. For what you did then. And for being my inspiration now. You made a difference.

—B.L.H.

About the Author

Although it would be nice to say that I am fulfilling my childhood dream of being a writer, it wouldn't be the truth. The fact is that when my grandfather Myron sat me down when I was five years old and explained that I was entering a wonderful new time to be alive, that thanks to those who had persevered for the rights of women (and other humans) I could be anything I wanted to be, my first choice was not to be a writer. Or the president. Or a doctor. Or even a ballerina. My heart was broken when I stated my choice and Grandpa explained with a gruff snort that it actually was still impossible to be a horse.

Born on a small family farm in North Alabama as Bobbye Anne Burgess (because of my initials I'm still called "Babs" by my family), I got into a lot of trouble over the years for doing what comes naturally through my family genetics: telling stories. Finally, after a lot of years of failing to color inside the lines and think inside the box, I'm relishing being able to share some of the stories that swarm through my head.

I still live on that same family farm, now whittled down a bit in size to make it easier for my husband Clark, recently retired from teaching at Jacksonville State University, and me to handle. We share the farm with our English coonhound Buford, a family of donkeys (that includes Firefly and Junebug and their son Jitterbug), horses (including my best friend, Whisper the Wonder Horse), fancy chickens, a herd of miniature goats, and four cranky guinea pigs.

Clark and I have always offered our hearts and our homes to animals in need, whenever and however possible. Although I bred and showed English cocker spaniels for 25 years, almost all of the animals on our farm now came to us through a rescue of one kind or another.

A true Gemini, I am happiest when I having several projects going on at one time. The more different the genre or subjects the better, and when I get bored with one topic I can quickly jump to another, or even become a time traveler and immerse myself in an era long past. While Alexandria was battling with the enemy on the pages of *Behind the Grey,* several of my other characters were toodling along and living their lives in present-day Alabama on the pages of another upcoming novel, *Hot Bubbles and Chocolate.*

    It took a wake-up call from breast cancer followed by a bout with uterine cancer to make me decide what I want to be when I grow up. Who knew that it would be a version of what I already was? I decided to break away from doing nonfiction writing and focus on what we Southerners do best: spinning yarns. I hope you enjoy them.

    For more information about women in the Civil War as well as news of my upcoming books and notes about life on the Hudspeth farm, you can visit my website:

www.bobbyehudspeth.com

SEAHORSE PRESS

Quality fiction and nonfiction for adults, children,
and young adults in print and e-book formats

www.seahorsepress.us